ACID

EMMA PASS

EMBER

To Duncan, for everything

Text copyright © 2013 by Emma Pass
Cover art copyright © 2014 by Larry Rostant

All rights reserved. Published in the United States by Ember, an imprint of Random House Children's Books, a division of Random House LLC, a Penguin Random House Company, New York. Originally published in hardcover in the United Kingdom by Corgi Books, an imprint of Random House Children's Publishers UK, a Random House Company, London, in 2013. Subsequently published in hardcover in the United States by Delacorte Press, an imprint of Random House Children's Books, New York, in 2014.

Ember and the E colophon are registered trademarks of Random House LLC.

Visit us on the Web! randomhouseteens.com

Educators and librarians, for a variety of teaching tools, visit us at
RHTeachersLibrarians.com

The Library of Congress has cataloged the hardcover edition of this work as follows:
Pass, Emma.
Acid / Emma Pass. — First edition.
pages cm
Summary: In the year 2113, seventeen-year-old Jenna Strong is helped to escape from Mileway Maximum Security Prison outside London in order to help destroy ACID, the most brutal and controlling police force in history.
ISBN 978-0-385-74387-7 (hc) — ISBN 978-0-385-37241-1 (ebook) —
ISBN 978-0-375-99134-9 (glb) [1. Fugitives from justice—Fiction. 2. Government, Resistance to—Fiction. 3. Police—Fiction. 4. England—Fiction. 5. Science fiction.] I. Title.
PZ7.P269366Aci 2014
[Fic]—dc23
2013002923

ISBN 978-0-385-37242-8 (trade pbk.)

Printed in the United States of America
10 9 8 7 6 5 4 3 2 1
First Ember Edition 2015

MILEWAY

CHAPTER 1

Mileway Maximum Security Prison, Outer London
12 April 2113

The first time I notice the new inmate is when we're all lined up outside our cells for morning head count. He's standing five doors down from me, sneaking glances at the rest of us as the guards wave their wrist-scanners across our hips to read the spytags that are implanted when we first get here.

His blond hair is cropped close and the white T-shirt straining across his gut is crisp and fresh; he must have arrived in the night. When his gaze lands on me, he does a double take, just as I knew he would. Watching him out of the corner of my eye, I can tell what he's thinking as clearly as if he'd said it out loud: *A girl? Here? What the hell?*

And then, so quickly I almost miss it, a smile flickers across his lips, his eyes narrowing as his surprise turns to anticipation. *A girl. Here. What're the chances?*

I curl my lip into a snarl, half tempted to go over there and introduce him to my fists. What a creep. But what did I expect? At Mileway, I stand out like . . . well, like a seventeen-year-old female in a prison full of men.

One of the guards, dressed in a black ACID uniform, reaches me. "Strong, Jenna—Prisoner ID 4347X," he intones. I clasp my hands behind my back, gazing straight ahead, feeling Creep's stare drilling into me. "What's *she* in for?" I hear him ask one of the other guards. The guard doesn't answer, just scans his hip and moves on down the line.

After the count, breakfast is served: cereal and watery substitute milk. A lot of the food we get here is sub–super-cheap, made out of synthetic protein. Real food isn't worth wasting on criminals. As usual, I eat standing up, leaning against a pillar by the catwalk in front of the cells, one foot tucked up behind me. "This crap gets worse every day," one of the guys at a nearby table grumbles, lifting up his spoon and letting the mushy gray cereal plop back into his bowl. Neil Rennick, ex–Anarchy Regiment, who, ten years ago, blew up an ACID van with fifteen agents inside it, before going on the run. ACID finally caught up with him last year, and a month after his arrival he tried to corner me in my cell, which is how he got the scar that runs from his right eyebrow to the corner of his jaw. I got five weeks in solitary, but it was worth it. Now he leaves me alone, just like everyone else.

"They're trying to kill us, is what they're trying to do," Rennick says loudly, looking around, trying to gather an audience. "And you know what? They can go—"

A guard hears him and steps forward. "Watch that mouth of yours, Rennick," he says, jabbing the muzzle of his pulse gun between Rennick's shoulder blades and flipping the charger switch back.

The gun powers up with a whine. Rennick clenches his jaw, and after a few moments the guard steps away. Every so often, the inmates' hatred will spill over, and they'll riot. It's happened four times since I came here—although I'm not stupid or suicidal enough to have been involved—but at this time of day, everyone's still half asleep. Rennick finishes his cereal in silence. I see Creep staring at him and the guard. Rennick sees too, and gives him the finger.

When I've eaten my breakfast, I return to my cell. The other inmates have to share theirs with five, sometimes even six other people, but I have mine to myself—the one and only concession the prison have made to my gender. Peering into the square of polished metal riveted to the wall by my bunk, I run my hand over my scalp. Every other day, I shave it with a razor made out of a sharpened plastic spoon which I keep hidden inside a loose section of my bunk frame. It goes better with the scars on my face and the shadows under my eyes than the waist-length, glossy chestnut hair I had two years ago, when I was a privileged Upper girl with her own en suite bathroom, a chauffeur and unlimited access to her father's bank account who was two years away from being LifePartnered—matched to a partner specially chosen by ACID to be her perfect match, emotionally, intellectually and physically.

I glower at my reflection. Why the hell am I thinking about my parents? I've only been up half an hour, and already I'm feeling depressed. I turn away from the mirror and leave my cell to go down to the gym, a gloomy cave in the incarceration tower basement that smells of mold and drains. No one else is down there yet. After some stretches to warm up, I grab a set of weights and do reps until my arms burn, before moving on to the leg press. After that, I switch to the treadmill. As I lose myself in the rhythmic slap of my feet against the worn rubber belt, the gloomy thoughts that drove me down here fade. I count the miles under my breath, my gaze fixed on the holoscreen display in front of me. "One . . . two . . . three . . ."

I step off eight miles later, drenched in sweat and breathing hard. I'm about to pull up the bottom of my T-shirt to wipe my face when I hear a sound behind me. I turn. Creep's in the doorway, staring. I'm guessing from the way his mouth's hanging open in amazement that he's been watching me work out for a while.

"Take a picture, it'll last longer," I snap, shouldering past him to go back up to my cell. I can feel him still watching me as I go. Hopefully he's got a good view of the tattoo on the back of my neck, the one I did myself, awkwardly, using ink from a pen I found in the laundry and a shard of metal, telling him and anyone else who cares to read it where they can go and what they can do with themselves.

By the time I've showered and changed, the job lists are up on the holoscreens outside the cells, and I see I'm on kitchen detail. I recognize all the other names on the list except one— 6292D Liffey. I feel my heart sink. And when I reach the kitchen, there he is, goggling at me.

Creep.

I ignore him, pulling on an overall and heading over to the other side of the kitchen, where vegetables are piled on one of the battered metal worktops, waiting to be prepared for the evening meal. Creep is sent to operate the dishwashers. I scrub and peel and chop and slice, heaping stuff into the pans on top of the stoves nearby, not letting myself think about anything except the task in front of me. When we get a break for lunch at midday, I line up with the rest, waiting for the guards to hand out the food—dry bread, sub cheese and water, which we eat and drink down in the kitchen to save time.

I'm about to pick up a cup when the guard holding the tray jolts it like he's about to drop it. Instinctively, I reach out to steady it. The guard nods and hands me a cup. The water in it tastes chalky; I gulp it down in three swallows, trying not to make a face. When I put my cup down, I see Creep staring at me again.

6

After that, it's back to food prep: lighting the stoves and fetching trays of gristly meat swimming in brownish, watery blood from one of the vast fridges that line the right-hand side of the kitchen. Usually, I've got a strong stomach, but as I start to saw the pieces of meat up with a blunted knife, the coppery stink of the blood steals into my nostrils and I have to swallow hard against a wave of nausea. What animal did this come from? An elephant? I wouldn't put it past them.

When the meat's ready, I carry it over to one of the stoves so the inmate stirring the stewpots can tip it in. For the first time, I notice how hot it is—much hotter than it usually gets down here. And the stewing meat smells bad—really bad. A headache starts to pulsate deep inside my skull, turning my stomach sour. As I gulp down another surge of nausea, I realize the skin on my forearms feels sore and tight. Great. I must be coming down with something. But what? I felt fine when I got up this morning.

Dammit, I'm not going to the infirmary. I fetch another tray of meat and carry it over to a worktop between the ventilation shafts and the end of the row of fridges, hoping it'll be cooler there. Then I turn back, thinking I'll go and look for a sharper knife and get this stuff cut up a bit faster—although there aren't any sharp knives in this place, not when most of the inmates are blade-happy psychos.

And I almost collide with Creep.

He grins at me, showing yellow, peglike teeth. "Hello."

"Get lost," I tell him. I try to push past him, but he steps in front of me, blocking my way.

"Now, that ain't nice," he says.

"I'm not nice," I say.

"Oh, I think I'll be the judge of that, don't you, darlin'?" His gaze slides from my face to my chest—not that there's much to see—and the tip of his tongue flickers out from between his lips like a snake's.

7

"Don't bother," I say.

"Don't bother with what?" His tone's light, innocent.

"You know what." At my temples, the headache snarls and pounds. *Just deck him!* a little voice in my head says. But I don't want another stretch in solitary. I'll get dragged in front of the governor, lose my gym privileges. It's too much hassle.

"I just want to get acquainted, darlin'," he says. "Must be lonely in here for a young lady like you." His gaze shifts to my legs, then begins to crawl up them.

"Yeah, and you know what?" I say. "I like it that way."

"You don't mean that. Think what a good time we could have, me and you."

"Believe me, it'll be anything but good. For you, that is."

"Really?" he says.

And lunges at me.

I bring my arm up and pivot sideways so that, as Creep tries to grab me, he's thrown off balance and staggers against the worktop. Before he can recover I spin and kick out, planting my left foot squarely in his stomach. He doubles over with a strangled-sounding *oof*. Then, as he tries to straighten up and get hold of the edge of the worktop, I lace my hands together and bring them down hard on the back of his neck. He pitches forward onto the floor, catching the tray with his outstretched fingers and showering himself in watery blood and lumps of meat. As he cracks his chin on the tiles at my feet, he gives a yelp of pain that trails off into a whimper.

"I tried to warn you," I say, my throbbing skin and thumping head momentarily forgotten. "Maybe you'll listen to me next time, huh?"

I push my foot into his neck to emphasize my point. Coughing, he rolls onto his back, trying to twist away from me. Blood is streaming from his mouth; he must have bitten his tongue when he smashed his chin against the floor.

"What're you in here for, anyway?" he mumbles thickly, spitting red froth.

"You really wanna know?" I say.

He nods.

I lean down until our faces are so close we could kiss.

"I killed my parents," I murmur, and watch his eyes go wide.

CHAPTER 2

A guard's shout jolts me back to reality. I straighten up and look around, wincing as fresh pain stabs through my head.

"What happened?" the guard says, disgust flickering across his face at the sight of the meat and blood sprayed everywhere.

"Fat-arse skidded in some water and fell," I say.

"Really." It's a statement, not a question; clearly, he doesn't believe me. But I hold his gaze, and he's the one who looks away first.

"Get up," he tells Creep, curling his upper lip. Creep just lies there, groaning.

"I said get up." The guard slams his boot into Creep's ribs and Creep jackknifes, a sobbing grunt exploding from his lips. I close my eyes, pressing my hand to my forehead, feeling the heat pulsating from beneath my skin. When I open my eyes again, another guard is helping the first drag Creep to his feet so they can haul him to the infirmary. I sag against the worktop, my remaining energy leaving me in a rush.

"Get back to work," the first guard snarls at me over his

shoulder as they leave, but he's not really paying me any attention. Which is just as well, because I'm not sure I can do *anything* right now. My nausea's returned, assaulting me in steady swells. I try to take a deep breath, but the stench from the stewpots coats my tongue and throat. Cold sweat springs out all over my body. My hands are clammy, and even though I still feel hot, I'm racked with shivers. A sharp pain jabs through my stomach. Tearing off my meat- and blood-smeared overall, I run through the kitchen, head down, ignoring the cries of the other inmates and the remaining guards.

But the doors are locked. Of course they're locked. They wouldn't want one of us sneaking out of here with anything sharp, would they? I pound on the doors with the flat of one hand, gripping my stomach with the other. "What the hell are you playing at?" a guard barks at me, grabbing my arm, trying to force me to turn round.

"Open the doors!" I snarl at him. "Now!"

Another cramping pain squeezes through me. Oh God. Oh God oh God oh God.

"Have you gone out of your mind?" the guard snaps. "Get back to work!"

"Seriously," I say through clenched teeth, trying to swallow down the acid rising in my throat. "You need to open these doors."

"Oh. Do I?" The guard folds his arms. His pulse gun dangles from one hand, his finger curled loosely around the trigger. Behind him, the other inmates are watching us with interest. "Why?"

"Because I'm gonna—"

My stomach spasms. I retch. The guard realizes what's wrong and his eyes widen. But it's too late. The acid burns up my throat and I retch again and bend forward, everything I ate for lunch splattering onto the tiles at his feet.

"Oh shit!" I hear him cry as black spots flock across my

11

vision and I collapse to my knees. I feel like someone's trying to crush my skull between two rocks, and there's a high-pitched whining in my ears. I vomit again and again, until there's nothing left to bring up except saliva. Then I feel hands on my arms, lifting me to my feet, but my legs still won't hold me and I stumble and sag forward. I'm lowered, gently, onto something soft.

". . . core temperature dangerously high . . ."

". . . need to get her stabilized . . ."

". . . get a medpatch on her NOW!"

Another tremendous bolt of pain stabs through my stomach, and I scream—it feels like I'm being torn in two. Something's pressed against my neck. There's a sudden spreading coolness.

Everything fades.

CHAPTER 3

I can hear chanting. And shouts. I try to open my eyes, but it's as if they've been glued shut.

The chanting grows louder. With a massive effort, I prise my eyelids apart.

For a moment, everything swims and swirls. Then, slowly, my eyes focus. I'm lying in one of the beds in the infirmary. There's a blanket covering me up to my armpits and a needle, attached to a drip, disappearing under the thin skin on the inside of my elbow.

I turn my head. That's an effort too; it feels as if someone's poured concrete into my skull. When I see that the other ninety-nine beds in the infirmary are empty and that there's no sign of Creep, I feel a stab of disappointment. I was hoping I'd really hurt him.

Standing at one of the tiny, barred windows that run the length of the infirmary is Dr. Alex Fisher, the prison medic, his back to me. When I first came to Mileway—until I learned to punch and bite and kick and snap bones, and the other inmates realized it would mean less trouble for them if they picked on someone else—I was forever being brought here with burns and fractures and concussions and God knows what else, and it was Dr. Fisher who fixed me up every time.

I struggle upright. "Hello?" I call. My throat hurts, and my voice sounds scratchy.

Dr. Fisher turns, and when he sees I'm awake, he hurries over. "Lie down, Jenna," he says. "You're too ill to be sitting up."

Reluctantly, I do as I'm told. "What's wrong with me?" I croak. The pain in my head has dulled to a low throb, but it's still there.

"I'm not sure," Dr. Fisher says. "We're waiting for some test results." His eyes, which are green, the irises flecked with gold, are almost kind—something you don't see very often in this place. He gives me a small smile, something else you never see. "You're doing OK, though. Try and get some rest."

Then the lights flicker and go out. The shouts and chanting—which are coming from outside—rise to a roar. "What's happening?" I say as the emergency lighting kicks in, bathing the room in a weird underwater glow.

"The inmates are rioting," Dr. Fisher says. "The prison staff have shut them out in the yard." His smile has vanished. He runs a hand through his thick, dark blond hair, frowning.

"Why?"

"This time?" Dr. Fisher shrugs. "They didn't like the food, apparently."

I remember the foul smell of the stewing meat. No wonder.

Dr. Fisher walks back over to the window. "This is too much," I hear him mutter during a lull in the noise outside. "ACID will be here too soon."

I stare at his back. What does that mean? ACID always get called in when there's a riot. They're the only ones who can handle it.

14

Closing my eyes, I pray he'll find out what the hell's wrong with me quickly so I can get out of here.

I hear Dr. Fisher walking back across to my bed and open my eyes again. He presses a scanner to my throat, checking my pulse. If it were anyone else, I wouldn't let them within two meters of me. But it was Dr. Fisher who, back in those early days, suggested I start using the gym, arranging to have one of the more sympathetic guards standing watch so that the other inmates wouldn't bother me. It was he who coached me in self-defense and martial arts, telling me it might help if I knew a few moves. Once, when I was in really bad shape after another inmate had pounced on me in the laundry, he even gave me the flask of soup his LifePartner had made him for lunch.

I still wonder, sometimes, why he did those things, whether he ever told his LifePartner he'd given me his soup. Was it because he felt sorry for me? But I've never talked to him about my parents' deaths. By the time I got here, I'd given up trying to tell people that what happened was an accident. No one else believed me, so why would he?

Dr. Fisher tilts his head. His komm must be going off. "Yes?" he says. He listens for a moment to whoever's on the other end. "Where? OK. Thank you."

He turns back to the bed, reaching into his pocket and pulling out a medpatch. "I want to give you another sedative, Jenna," he says. "Things could get very nasty around here once ACID arrive, and I don't want you to get worked up—you're in too fragile a state right now."

I frown, hoping he'll explain what he thinks is going to happen, but all he says is "Please. It really is for the best."

I turn my head to the side so he can place the patch, which is less than half a centimeter square, on my neck, in the hollow just below where my earlobe meets my jaw. As the coolness spreads across my skin and my eyelids grow heavy, Dr. Fisher turns away from me again. In another brief lull in the noise

15

from down in the yard, I hear him say in a quiet but urgent voice, "She's more or less out. We're on our way."

What?

I reach up and, although there's already enough of the sedative in my bloodstream to make my arm feel like it weighs several tons, I manage to tear the patch off my neck, folding it into my palm. When he returns to the bed, I close my eyes so he won't realize I'm still awake. I feel him placing something soft across my face, a cloth or bandage, which he wraps around my head and ties at the base of my neck, leaving my mouth and nostrils free so that I can breathe. I want to reach up and pull it away, but I'm so woozy from the sedative now, I'm struggling to stay conscious.

Dr. Fisher gently tugs the drip out of my arm and lifts me up, tucking the blanket around me. Then he throws me across his shoulders with my head hanging down on one side, my legs on the other. He starts to walk very fast, bouncing me about; I feel the air rushing past me, hear a *clunk* and a *hiss* as the infirmary doors slide back and we pass into the corridor outside.

Fighting panic, I battle to stay alert, yet keep myself floppy so Dr. Fisher will think I'm unconscious. More doors hiss, and although I can't see anything, I can tell by the changing air temperature that we're moving through the prison. When my nostrils fill with the piss-and-mold stink of the cells, I realize we're in one of the incarceration towers. Then I hear something else: a low *thudthudthud*. Rotos.

ACID.

We're heading up the stairs between levels; Dr. Fisher has slowed down, and the back of his shirt is damp with sweat. The sound of the rotos has died away now, and I can hear the clang of heavy boots striking the metal catwalks on one of the floors above us. Dr. Fisher swears, lifting me off his shoulders. As he rolls me onto the floor, the bandage on my face shifts slightly, leaving a gap just big enough for me to see out of one eye.

16

It takes a few seconds to make sense of what I'm looking at. We're hiding behind an overturned table in the middle of one of the recreation areas, the chains that normally secure it to the floor ripped out like plant roots. The rest of the furniture has been tipped up too, the base units for the holopanel news screens smashed, and there's food everywhere, dripping down walls and doors, the rancid stench of the stew almost overpowering. A few meters away from us, an inmate lies facedown, one hand outstretched as if pleading for mercy, his fingers slick with blood.

I can feel Dr. Fisher crouched beside me, shaking. In my medication-fogged brain, the realization forms that he's as scared as I am. But why? Then he reaches across and pulls me farther behind the tables, tucking my legs up; I have to resist the urge to stiffen, to kick out. *What are you doing?* I want to ask him. *What the hell is going on?*

The sound of pounding feet grows louder, and a tide of ACID agents in black jumpsuits and helmets with mirrored visors, which they always wear to hide their faces, pours down the stairs on the opposite side of the recreation area. They're clutching pulse guns and Tasers, and as I watch them, I feel as if I'm locked in a nightmare. I try to scream, to wake myself up, but I can't even force out a whimper. Unconsciousness presses at the edges of my mind like a gray blanket. *Stay awake,* I tell myself fiercely.

Then, as suddenly as they appeared, the ACID agents are gone, heading down to the yard. Dr. Fisher hoists me back onto his shoulders, stands up and runs to the stairs. This time, he pelts up them as if I weigh nothing at all. The effects of the sedative roll over me in waves; it's harder than ever to stay awake. We reach the top of the tower and go out onto the roof.

Outside, the air is cold and sharp. I can hear cries and screams and the crackle of gunfire as ACID and the rioting inmates face each other down in the yard. The roof is bristling with ACID rotos, gleaming black and silver machines almost

17

the size of magtram pods. Dr. Fisher ducks between them, making for a smaller, unmarked roto at the edge of the roof. Both its top and bottom rotor are going full throttle, and a pilot and copilot are seated inside. As Dr. Fisher gets closer, the copilot grins and gives us a thumbs-up. I struggle to stay awake, reminding myself to keep still, stay limp. *Where are we going? What is he up to?*

"Stop right there!" a voice barks behind us.

Dr. Fisher stops. I see the copilot's grin fall away.

"Turn round!"

Slowly, Dr. Fisher turns. There's an ACID agent standing there, his face invisible behind his mirrored visor.

"ID," he says, pointing his pulse gun at us.

Dr. Fisher lets go of my legs to fumble in his pocket for his citizenship card. The agent looks at it for a long time, turning it over and over in one gloved hand, before giving it back. "What about the prisoner?" he asks.

"I . . . I don't have it," Dr. Fisher says. "The inmates' c-cards are kept in the admin block, and I couldn't get there because of the riots."

"What's the prisoner's name?"

"Adam Howell. Another inmate threw chemicals in his face in the prison laundry, and he needs urgent treatment that we're unable to give him here."

What the hell? Who's Adam? I've never heard that name in my life. And why would he pretend I'm a guy?

"It is illegal for a prisoner to be removed from a secure facility without an ACID escort," the agent says robotically.

"I know, but if we don't get him to a medicenter, he'll die!" Dr. Fisher says. "Please, just let us go, will you? He could no more escape in this condition than . . . than fly one of these rotos!"

"Speak to me like that again and I'll arrest you," the agent

18

says. He turns away from us and starts speaking into his komm, requesting backup.

Dr. Fisher turns too, back toward the roto. I watch as the copilot silently slides his door open and holds out his arms. The ACID agent is still speaking into his komm as Dr. Fisher carefully unwinds me from his shoulders and the copilot leans out of the roto, reaching for me.

But my weight throws Dr. Fisher off balance; he stumbles, and the noise of the roto isn't enough to disguise the sound of his feet scuffing against the concrete. The ACID agent whirls. "STOP!" he yells as the copilot drags me into the roto and hauls the door shut. I land on the seat beside him in a heap, my face pressed up against the glass, and somehow I find the strength to reach up and rip the rest of the bandage from my eyes.

So I see everything that happens next.

As the roto starts to lift, the ACID agent aims his gun at us. Dr. Fisher leaps at him and knocks him sideways, sending the shot wide. I see them on the ground below us, struggling. Then the agent's back on his feet, but so is Dr. Fisher, and as the agent tries to fire his gun again Dr. Fisher grabs him from behind, pinning his arms against his sides. He drags him to the edge of the roof and slings him off it, then steps back, his hands pressed to his mouth as the agent plummets down to the yard eight stories below.

I stare at his rapidly dwindling figure, hardly able to breathe.

Then, from out of nowhere, pulses of white light tear through the air behind him and slam into him. He slumps forward, the electric charge crackling around him in a deadly halo before dying away. Seconds later, more ACID agents come running out of the shadows between the rotos: the first agent's backup, arrived too late. They aim at the roto, but we're too high.

The scream that's been trapped inside me finally escapes. "NO!"

"Shit! She's awake!" the copilot says. He turns me over roughly. "Don't! It's OK! It's OK!"

"Oh Christ oh Christ oh Christ oh Christ," I hear the pilot babbling. The horror in her voice is clear. "They killed Fisher, Roy. They *killed* him!"

"Fly, goddammit!" the copilot snarls.

As the roto jerks forward, I start screaming again. Panic is surging through me, my head filled with images of Dr. Fisher toppling over onto the concrete, dead. The copilot pins me against the seat, telling me to calm down. I try to fight him, but there's still too much sedative in my bloodstream.

"I thought she was supposed to be out," he snarls to the pilot. He takes something out of a bag on the floor by his feet and presses it hard against my neck. A medpatch. There's a tingling sensation. I open my mouth to scream again, but my jaw is slack.

My head lolls to the side and darkness rolls over my vision like a wave.

AGENCY FOR CRIME INVESTIGATION AND DEFENSE

Thursday 13 April 2113

Usual Download Charges Apply

The Daily Report

Official News Site for the Agency for Crime Investigation and Defense
All the latest stories, straight to your komm!

Front Page • Crime • Money • Arts/Culture • Sport • Images • Other News

IRB's Most Dangerous Teenager on Run After Mileway Riots

The British public have been advised to be vigilant after the daughter and killer of former ACID lieutenant Marcus Strong and his LifePartner, Reena, escaped during last night's riots at Mileway Maximum Security Prison, having murdered a member of prison staff.

Jenna Strong, 17, was jailed at the age of 15 for shooting her parents dead at the Strongs' family home in London, apparently over a disagreement about their choice of LifePartner for her. After Strong sensationally admitted to the killings, ACID took the unusual step of trying her as an adult, which resulted in her being sentenced to 80 years for the murders and becoming the youngest person ever to be sent to an adult jail since ACID were handed power by the IRB's former British Democratic Alliance government just over half a century ago.

Strong had completed just two years of her sentence when last night's riots broke out. It is thought she managed to get away during a power cut that affected the prison's security systems, meaning they were down for hours. Many inmates, agents and prison staff were injured, some seriously, in attacks and fires.

OTHER HEADLINES

ACID chiefs awarded top accolades by General Harvey

Rumors of food shortages in Outer London "just that," say ministers

Illegal alcohol and cigarette haul seized in Outer London, 100 arrests made

Magtram track upgrade in Middle London to go ahead in 2115

After taking prison doctor Alex Fisher hostage and forcing him up onto the roof of one of the prison's incarceration towers, Strong shot him and an ACID agent with a pulse gun stolen from one of the guards before making her escape. It is believed she may have done this after Dr. Fisher refused to perform surgery on her to alter her appearance, something which, as he was not a surgeon, he would not have been qualified to do.

It is still not clear what sparked the riots at Mileway in the first place. The prison, on the outskirts of London, is one of the Independent Republic of Britain's biggest jails, housing nearly 6,500 inmates. Similar facilities include Salway near Birmingham and Denhall in Cheshire, and it appeared, until last night, at least, that prisons like these were running smoothly.

President of the IRB and ACID chief General Sean Harvey, who has taken personal charge of the investigation, has promised that all departments within ACID will work closely to undertake a full inquiry into the Mileway riots and Strong's escape and to ensure Strong's swift recapture.

"Rest assured, she will be caught," Harvey's spokesperson, Subcommander Anna Healey, said this morning. "Her sentence for the murders of her parents means she has never been Partnered, so as a result she will not be able to find work or a place to live. We expect to pick her up again very quickly, probably within the next few days."

In the meantime, she has asked that the British public remain vigilant. With no recent photographs of Strong yet available, she is described as being around 165 cm tall, with a shaved head and gray eyes. At the time of her escape she would have been wearing the prison uniform of a gray T-shirt, black trousers and black shoes. She also has an obscene tattoo across the back of her neck. ACID strongly suspect that if she has not done so already, she will try to leave London as soon as possible. They have warned that Strong should not be approached under any circumstances. Anyone who sees her, or who wishes to report any suspicious persons or activity, can link ACID on KommWeb9. Any member of the public giving information that leads to Strong's arrest could receive a reward of up to 30,000 kredz, to be used for clothing, food or leisure.

Report by Claire Fellowes
Interviews by Dasha Lowe

For images of the Mileway riots, link **here**
For the story of the Strong murder trial, link **here**
For an interview with General Harvey, link **here**
For an interview with Subcommander Healey, link **here**
To comment on this story, link **here** (will be moderated)

THE FACILITY

CHAPTER 4

13 April 2113
Somewhere in London

"Jenna? Can you hear me? You need to wake up."

The voice belongs to a woman. But there aren't any female guards in our tower. Am I still in the infirmary? Maybe I got worse, and they had to bring another doctor in.

"Jenna."

The voice is kind but firm. Reluctantly, I open my eyes.

I'm not in my cell. I'm not in the infirmary either. I'm lying in a bed in a small, windowless room I've never seen before, wearing a pair of pale blue pajamas, a blanket tucked across my legs and waist. My arm's hooked up to a drip again, and there's a mask across my mouth and nose pushing cool air into my nostrils. The room's lit by harsh strip lights that bleach the walls and ceiling to a glaring white.

I gaze at the drip in my arm and, like a blow, everything

comes back to me: Creep, my collapse, Dr. Fisher trying to sedate me and taking me up onto the roof, the ACID agent appearing out of the shadows behind us . . .

I sit up with a gasp, tearing the mask from my face, and wince as pain stabs through my hip. I'm about to yank the drip out when a hand lands on my arm.

"Jenna, don't panic. You're quite safe."

It's the voice I heard before. I turn my head and see a woman sitting in a chair beside the bed. She's small, plump, the mass of wavy brown hair cascading over her shoulders held away from her face by two silver clips. She pushes her round, gold-framed glasses up her nose and smiles at me. "I'm Mel Morrow."

"Where am I?" I ask.

"I'm afraid I can't tell you. But like I said, you're quite safe. ACID won't find you here." She pats my arm. Then I hear footsteps outside the door. "Ah," Mel says. "Here's Jon."

A few moments later a tall, skinny black man wearing what looks like a doctor's coat comes into the room. He smiles at me too. "Oh, good," he says. "You're back with us. Do you know you've been unconscious for a full day?"

I look at him through narrowed eyes. Who the hell are these people? And why are they being so *nice* to me? "Is this a medi-center?" I say.

"No," Mel says as Jon comes over to the bed. When he tries to check the needle in the crook of my elbow, I jerk my arm away.

"It's all right," he tells me. "I *am* a doctor." I continue to glare at him. "Please. I only want to take a quick look at it."

Grudgingly, I hold out my arm. "Is it OK to check your temperature, blood pressure and heart rate?" he asks, holding up a little scanner. "You had rather a strong reaction to the drugs you were given."

"You mean the sedatives?" I say.

"No, the drugs Alex Fisher bribed one of the guards to give

26

you," Jon replies as he runs the scanner over my throat to measure my pulse, holds it against my inner arm to take my blood pressure and presses a nodule at one end into my ear, which beeps as it reads my temperature.

I stare at him. "Dr. Fisher did what?"

"We had to get you out of there," Jon says, tucking the scanner back into his coat pocket. "Making it seem as if you'd fallen ill meant you could be taken up to the infirmary, ready to leave once the riots were under way."

"Were . . . were they deliberate too?" I say, my voice sounding distant and hollow in my ears.

Mel nods. "Yes. Alex arranged for something to be added to the food."

So that's why the stew smelled so bad.

"But Dr. Fisher . . . ," I say. "He's—"

And for the first time, it really hits me. Dr. Fisher died. For *me*. To save *me*.

Why would he do something like that? Why would *anyone*?

"Yes," Mel says, her face sobering. "ACID weren't supposed to arrive quite so soon."

I stare at my hands, lying on top of the blanket that covers me. They're trembling.

"It's not your fault," Mel continues. "Alex knew the risk he was taking. We all did."

"But why?" I say, looking up at her again. "I'm supposed to be in jail. I killed my—"

"I'm sorry," Jon says, cutting me off. "We can't tell you anything yet."

"You *have* to!" I say. "You can't just tell me something like that and expect me not to want to know—"

This time, it's Mel who cuts me off. "All that matters right now is that you recover," she says, before I can ask any more questions. "You're going to have a lot to take in over the next few days; it's important that you regain your strength. Try to

27

get a little more sleep, and one of us'll be back in an hour or two with some food."

She gets up and she and Jon leave, closing the door softly behind them. I hear the snick of the lock.

I tear the drip out of my arm, barely noticing the sting of the needle as it pulls away from my skin, and with a thin line of blood trickling down my arm I jump out of bed and run to the door, the pain in my hip flaring before subsiding to a low throb. I try the door handle, rattling it, but the door doesn't budge.

I'm locked in.

I pound on it with my fists. "Hey!" I shout. *"Hey!"*

There's no answer. Nobody comes.

I step back to take a flying sideways kick at it, but dizziness rolls over me. Feeling sick and shaky, I stagger back over to the bed and slump back against the pillows, closing my eyes and taking shallow breaths until the room stops spinning. Then I wipe the blood off my arm with a corner of the blanket and stare up at the ceiling tiles, trying to think. It's like I'm trying to swim up from the bottom of a very deep pool and running out of oxygen. My thoughts are sluggish; they refuse to connect.

None of this makes sense.

I remember the pain in my hip. It's still there, a low twinge like toothache. I pull down the waistband of the pajama bottoms and see a neat, centimeter-wide red scar across my left hip bone. The hip bone where my spytag was embedded.

Not anymore, apparently.

And what's on my head? I didn't notice before—I was too busy trying to figure out what was going on—but it feels like I've got hair. I sit back up, tangle my fingers in it and give it a hard yank, hissing as pain shoots through my scalp. It's real. What the—?

I look around the room for a mirror, but there isn't one. Dragging a chunk of hair in front of my face, I see it's a dark red.

It's cut to jaw length in a bob that swishes around my chin when I shake my head. I've even got bangs.

But I've only been unconscious for a day. How did they get my hair to grow back so quickly?

For some reason, the fact that I have hair freaks me out more than anything. I can't stay here. I'm not staying here. I look down at the pajamas. How far will I get in them, and without any shoes? And what if ACID are looking for me? Assuming this lot *aren't* ACID.

I don't spend the next hour sleeping. I spend it planning. And when Mel and Jon return—Mel carrying a tray with a covered bowl, a plate of crackers, a plastic spoon and a cup containing some orange liquid—I'm ready.

"Could I use the bathroom?" I say as Mel sets the tray down on the chair beside the bed.

"Yes, of course," Mel says.

"And could I have something to put on my feet? They're freezing."

"Slippers first or bathroom first?" Jon asks in a brisk tone. He doesn't appear to notice I've taken my drip out yet.

"Slippers, please," I say, tucking my legs up underneath me as if my feet really *are* cold (they're not). He nods and leaves the room. When he returns a few minutes later he's carrying a pair of soft lace-up shoes. "No slippers, I'm afraid," he says. "Will these do?"

Will they do? They're *perfect*. It's all I can do to keep from grinning as I slip them onto my feet and knot the laces as tight as I can.

Then Jon *does* notice the drip. "Oh, Jenna, what have you done?" he says, frowning at my arm, which now has a black-purple bruise where I ripped the needle out.

"It was itching," I say.

"It was only fluids," Mel says. "And they'd nearly all gone. She'll be OK if she eats and drinks something."

29

Jon's still frowning disapprovingly at me, but all he says is "I suppose so."

"Come on, then, I'll take you to the bathroom," Mel says. As I climb off the bed again, she holds out an arm. "Hang on to me if you like. And if you feel dizzy, let me know straight away. The bathroom's not that close, I'm afraid."

I *am* dizzy, although it's not as bad as before. I wonder if I should eat something before I do this. But changing my mind about the bathroom now would make them suspicious for sure. "I'm fine," I say, putting my shoulders back and my head up.

We leave the room and I follow her along a series of corridors that turn at sudden right angles—no windows here either, although there are plenty of doors. I wonder if there are other people like me behind them: people lying in beds and hooked up to drips; people who aren't meant to be here. Eventually, we reach one with a holosign on it that says LADIES.

"There we go," Mel says, pushing the door and holding it open for me. "I'll wait out here. Take as long as you need."

"Thanks," I say. I take a deep breath, close my eyes and stumble against the wall.

"Jenna?" Mel's voice is sharp with alarm. "Are you all right?"

As I feel her move toward me I straighten up, turn and kick out, aiming at the back of her right knee with the side of my foot—not hard enough to injure her, but enough to make her leg give way. She stumbles, flinging her arms out to keep from falling. I don't wait to see if she manages to save herself.

I put my head down and run.

CHAPTER 5

It's not long before I have to slow down. I'm dizzy again for real, my legs shaky and weak, and the pain in my hip has ramped up, making me grind my teeth. I clutch my side. I have no idea where I am; all the corridors in this building look the same, their gray-white walls lined with doors. I feel as if I'm in a gigantic, colorless maze.

Turning a corner, I see a window with a slatted metal blind drawn down over it. I limp over to it and push two of the slats apart so I can see out. It's either just getting light or just getting dark, but I'm not sure which. I'm high up, and all around me a city stretches toward the horizon, its lights glimmering. News screens flicker on the sides of the buildings, showing the square-jawed, heavy-browed face of General Harvey, ACID chief, IRB president and my one-time godfather, as he makes some announcement or other.

Which city?

Then, a mile or two away, I see the black needle of the ACID control tower with its bulbous communications room at the top, ringed with dull blue lights that seem to draw the darkness in rather than keep it at bay. Beyond that, a huge wall stretches from horizon to horizon with more blue lights blinking on and off along the top. The Fence.

I'm still in London, then. And in Middle, by the looks of it. The Fence was built by ACID seven years ago to separate Middle from Outer, a sheer, twelve-meter steel wall that's blistering hot in the summer and frostbite-cold in the winter, and the only way to get past it, unless you go over in a roto, is on the mag. I remember flying to the opening ceremony with my parents and asking my father, "Why are they doing this, Dad? Why do they want to make it more difficult for people to get through?" and my mother shushing me even though, apart from the pilot, we were the only people in the roto that ACID had sent to pick us up.

"But, Mum," I said, glancing at my mother, who had turned to gaze out of the window, her expression thoughtful, "*why?*"

My father rounded on me fiercely, hissed, "Jenna, be *quiet!*" Then he sat back in his seat, his face grim, and during the ceremony he held on to my arm so tightly that the next day I had bruises.

A few months later, we were invited to another opening ceremony, this time for an invisible pulse barrier between Middle and Upper.

Guilt and sadness seep through me as I remember the look on my mother's face. Why does *everything* still remind me of my parents?

I watch a roto lift off from the top of the tower and lumber slowly out toward the edge of the city. It's definitely getting lighter. Maybe I should stay in the building and find somewhere to hide, and wait until night comes before I try to escape. There'll be more people around during the day.

And more ACID agents.

"Jenna!"

I let go of the blind slats. They spring back together with a metallic clatter. Jon is marching down the corridor toward me, his face grim. I step away from the window and turn to start running, but another wave of dizziness assaults me, making the walls and floor seesaw sickeningly.

Jon rushes up to me and catches me by the arm just before I fall.

"What on earth are you thinking?" he says, pulling me upright and putting an arm around my waist to support me. "You're going back to your room now."

Back to my room. Like I'm a naughty kid. But I feel too sick and dizzy to protest. Seething inside, I let him lead me back.

Mel's sitting on the chair by the bed. She doesn't say anything as I lie down and lean against the pillow. I close my eyes and take shallow breaths in and out through my nose. Slowly, the seasick feeling eases, although my hip's still screaming.

"Jenna, you absolutely cannot do things like this, do you understand?" Mel hisses when I open my eyes again. "You're here for your own safety. To protect you from ACID. You do realize General Harvey is leading the investigation to find you?" She sounds almost as angry as Jon.

He's leading the investigation? A shock goes through me, but I quickly regain my composure. "Why should I stay put when you won't tell me anything? You drug me, you spring me from jail, I've got *hair,* for God's sake, and you won't explain any of it!"

"We *can't,*" Mel says. "Don't you see? ACID are out there right now, combing the entire country for you. And they've framed you for Alex's murder—they're saying that you held him hostage and pushed him off the roof."

I stare at her. "What?"

"We're doing everything in our power to keep you safe,"

Mel goes on, "but if—and it's a very big if, I hope—they catch up with you, the first thing they'll do is try to find out who helped you. So if you don't know—"

"I can't tell them," I finish dully.

"Exactly."

"Great." I gaze up at the ceiling, letting out a sigh. "Can I at least have a mirror?"

I see Jon and Mel exchange a glance. Then Jon shrugs. "I'll get one," he says. "In the meantime, will you *please* eat and drink something, Jenna?"

While he's gone, Mel hands me the tray. The covered dish contains vegetable soup, so good that after the first couple of spoonfuls my appetite wakes up and I'm soon scraping the bottom of the empty bowl. I can't remember the last time I had a meal that actually tasted like real food. I eat all the crackers too, then drink the stuff in the cup, which turns out to be orange juice. It's sweet and tangy and cold.

"Better?" Mel asks, smiling as she takes the tray.

"Mmm." *Much* better, actually, but I'd rather shoot myself in my bad hip with a pulse gun than admit that to her right now.

A few minutes later, Jon comes back in with a large hand mirror. I practically snatch it from him, squeezing my eyes shut before holding it up in front of my face.

I open one eye. Then the other.

I forget all about the pain in my hip.

The face that stares back at me has brown eyes instead of gray. The nose is smaller, the chin rounder. The eyebrows under the heavy fringe of chestnut hair are darker and heavier, and the cheekbones are more pronounced. And all my scars, the battle wounds I picked up in prison, are gone. My skin is as smooth as it was when I was a little kid.

I'm almost *pretty*.

I press my chin and cheekbones, turning my head left and

right, looking for evidence of surgery. There's none. I feel numb, emptied out by shock.

"We had one of the best surgeons in the country work on you while you were unconscious," Jon says, pride tinging his voice. "Your hair's real—you were given drugs that made it regenerate in just a few hours. And not only are those implanted irises a different color, but their pattern's been altered too, so you won't be picked up by ACID's iris scanners."

"And you've got nanochips in your palms, fingers, thumbs and toes and in the soles of your feet," Mel adds. "They'll give a false result on even the most advanced print-readers."

I put a hand to the back of my neck. "What about my—"

"That's gone too," Jon says. "Sorry. But it wouldn't have exactly helped you to blend in."

"Blend in *where*?" I say.

They look at each other. Then Jon says, "We'll be back to talk to you later, Jenna, OK? No," he adds firmly when I start to protest. "You need to rest now. We need to get you back to full strength as quickly as possible. You're going to have a lot to take in over the next few days."

Like what? I want to scream at his back as he walks to the door. Mel picks up the tray and follows him.

All I can do is watch as the door closes behind them and they lock me in again.

CHAPTER 6

The pain in my hip has faded to a dull ache, and the food's made me so drowsy that my anger soon subsides. I kick off my shoes and pull the covers over myself. It's warm in here, and the bed is comfortable, which is something, I guess. The bunks at Mileway were as hard as concrete and the cells were either freezing cold or stiflingly hot, depending on the time of year.

But as soon as I close my eyes, questions start to beat around in my head. *What is this place? Why am I here? And why am I still in London? Isn't that the first place ACID would think to look for me? And what about Alex? Why would they say I killed him? He was the only person there who was ever nice to me. I would never have harmed him. Never.*

My stomach twists. It's bad enough that I killed two people for real without being falsely accused of murdering someone else. I try to breathe, to stay calm. But what else is there to think about when you're locked in a tiny room in a strange building and no one will give you a single straight answer about anything?

I go over and over everything until my head aches. And I still can't join up the dots.

Several hours later, Mel and Jon return. The sound of the door clunking open jolts me back to full awareness and I scramble upright.

"How are you feeling?" is the first thing Mel asks.

"Fine," I say, and when Jon takes the scanner out of his coat pocket to take my temperature and pulse rate, I give him such a glare he puts it away.

Mel sits down on the end of the bed, Jon in the chair. "We've come to talk to you about what's going to happen next," Mel says.

My heart skips a beat. Some answers, *finally*.

"Providing you're well enough, you'll leave here next week," she says. "You're going to be living in an apartment in Outer—I know it's not what you're used to, but there are so many people there that it'll be easier for you to stay under ACID's radar."

I shrug. Two years ago, the thought of living somewhere like Outer would have horrified me. But spending twenty-three and a half months in a place like Mileway has a way of altering your perspective. "Sounds fine to me," I say.

"You'll have a job," she goes on, "and we've set you up with a new identity, which someone will start going over with you tomorrow. Jon and I are LifePartners, and live in a part of Middle that's quite close to your part of Outer, so we'll continue to be your contacts after you leave. And we've got you this—although your kommweb access will be rather limited because you're in Outer, I'm afraid."

She holds something out to me. A komm. It's a circular piece of plastic about three centimeters wide that fits into your right ear, black with tiny purple lights pulsating on the touchpad on its outer surface. You control it by moving your head and eyes. As I take it from her, I think about how my mother used to joke about how I was surgically attached to my komm. But I was no different from any of my friends. We all spent hours on them, especially me and my best friend, Nadia, linking each other to chat or play games. For the first time in ages, I find myself wondering where my old friends are and what they're doing. They'll all have LifePartners now, and soon, some of them might even get their notifications from ACID to say they can have a kid. I try to imagine Dylan—Dylan, who turned everything into a joke, even the fact that ACID could arrest both of us just for spending time together because we were unPartnered and underage—helping to change diapers and mop up vomit.

Or did ACID catch him and send him to jail too? He gave me the gun; his prints must have been all over it.

I feel a flash of familiar bitterness. It would serve him right if they did. Even now, I still wonder what came over me, letting him convince me to go along with his crazy plan like that. Love? All I know for sure is that I'd never felt anything like it before, I haven't felt anything like it since, and I don't intend to feel it ever again.

"Jenna?" Mel says.

I realize I've not been paying attention. "What?"

"I *said,* there are a couple of other things you need to know. The first and most important is about the news screen you'll have in your flat."

She's talking about the holoscreens people have in their homes, which show a constant feed of news and stats from ACID. We had a huge one at home, although my father was the only one who used to watch it regularly.

"I know that in Upper, you didn't have to watch the screen unless you wanted to, but Outer citizens are expected to have theirs on for at least five hours every day—preferably more," Mel says. "Obviously, you don't have to sit in front of it the whole time, but whenever you're in, it's best to leave it on.

38

ACID do spot-checks to make sure people are following the rule about the screens by looking at information sent from data chips in active screens to their control center, which tells them how often the screens are used, and for how long, and they arrest anyone they suspect isn't watching theirs enough."

I nod, dismayed at the thought of constantly having to watch news reports about ACID trying to hunt me down.

"The second thing is that in Outer and Middle, there's recently been a curfew placed on all citizens, which begins at twenty hundred hours and lasts until oh-seven hundred. It's absolutely *vital* that you not get caught outside your flat between those times, or you'll be arrested immediately."

I nod again.

"Lastly, we've set you up with a LifePartner—not a real one, of course," she adds quickly when she sees my face fall even further. "He's someone else our people are helping. No, I'm afraid I can't tell you why, but we think you should get along OK together. You'll *need* to get along OK together if you don't want to attract any attention from ACID. You'll meet him in a couple of days. And no, he won't be told who you really are. Have you got any questions?"

"Yes," I say. "I'd love to know why you're setting me up with a new life for apparently no reason whatsoever. I'm guessing there *is* one, but you can't tell me about that either, right?"

She shoots me a warning look.

I sigh and fit the komm into my ear.

I spend the rest of that day browsing the kommweb, checking the news sites on the wraparound, the holoscreen which is projected in front of your eyes and automatically adjusts to the right distance so you can focus on it comfortably. They seem to be about all I can access now I have Outer status. I realize to my horror that not only is what Mel said about me being framed for killing Alex true, but there's a huge reward on my head. *Everyone's* going to be looking for me, not just ACID. Is my new face really going to be enough to keep me safe?

I don't get much sleep that night.

Two days later, I'm feeling much stronger. Mel brings me some clothes, a pair of soft trousers and a white fitted top with lace at the hems and a tie at the waist. Then she leaves the room so I can change. I quickly take off the pajamas and pull the clothes on. The top's the sort of thing I used to wear before I went to jail, but now, after two years in a prison uniform, it feels way too feminine. The tops of my arms are so muscular that the sleeves cut into them, and even in a bra I don't exactly have cleavage anymore.

"You look lovely," Mel says, smiling, when I call her back in. I scowl.

Mel ducks out of the room and comes back with an airchair, which looks like an ordinary soft chair but with hoverpads underneath it. I scowl again, but she insists I use it. As I sit down, a thrum goes through it as the hoverpads power up, adjusting to my weight and keeping the chair a couple of centimeters above the floor. Mel shows me which buttons to press to turn left or right, or to keep the chair moving straight ahead, then tells me to follow her.

The building's much busier now, men and women in white coats like the one Jon wears bustling to and fro. They all seem to know Mel, and they don't seem surprised to see me with her. Through an open door, I catch a glimpse of what looks like a lab: rows of benches with complicated-looking equipment set up on them.

"OK, so if this place isn't a medicenter, what *is* it?" I ask Mel.

"A food research and testing center," she replies.

I see a tall man with rimless glasses and a shaved head walking along the corridor toward us.

"Felix," Mel says as he reaches us.

Felix, who I guess to be in his early fifties, looks at me down the bridge of his nose. "So this is the girl," he says to Mel. His voice is deep, with just a hint of an accent, and even though he's only wearing a shirt and jeans under his lab coat, there's an unmistakable air of authority about him. "How is she doing?"

"She's adjusting as well as can be expected," Mel says. "She only woke up a couple of days ago. We're going to see Steve now about her new identity."

Um, excuse me, I'm right here, I want to say. Felix nods. "Good, good. Well, I won't keep you."

"Who was that?" I say as he walks away.

"The boss," Mel says.

"The boss here, or your boss?"

"Both."

"Is this *really* a research center?" I say.

"Of course," Mel says. But she won't quite look me in the eye. *Aha,* I think. Finally, I have an answer to one of my questions. This place might well be what Mel says it is—the lab I saw looked too elaborate to be a setup—but behind the scenes, it's something else. A place where people like me and this fake LifePartner I'm going to have are given new identities by whoever's in charge—whoever Mel and Jon work for. And whoever they work for uses this place as a front, to hide what's really going on.

Although who *they* are, I still have no clue, of course.

Mel takes me to a little room next to another lab, this one full of people looking into microscopes and dictating data into their komms. "Does everyone here know what's going on?" I ask her. "I mean, with me, and—"

"Yes," she says without looking at me.

She knocks on the door, opens it and motions for me to go in. "Here she is, Steve," she says. A short, potbellied man with long hair tied back in a ponytail, a sandy-colored goatee and glasses, who's sitting behind a little desk with a holocom in front of him, looks up as I maneuver the airchair into the room.

"Ah, Mia," he says as the door clicks shut behind me and I switch the airchair off and get out.

I stare at him. "What?"

"Mia Richardson," he says. "That's what we're going to be calling you from now on." The screen is angled sideways, and I catch a glimpse of the word FREE and a graphic of a butterfly. Steve sees me looking at it and taps the screen so that the image disappears.

"Take a seat, and we can start going over things," he says smoothly, pushing his glasses up his nose.

I do as he says, feeling more bemused than ever.

CHAPTER 7

Going over my new identity takes nearly all morning. Steve lets me read through the details on his holocom, then quizzes me on them over and over. I'm the same age, but with a different birthday; my parents are warehouse workers; I have no siblings; I went to one of the huge city schools in Zone P, from which I graduated without any qualifications, and I'm going to be living in Zone M, in a place called Anderson Court, with a job in a factory in Zone R that makes parts for magtrams. Oh, and I'll have one day, Sunday, off every week.

"We can't link the information to your komm, I'm afraid—ACID might find it—but I'll ask for a holocom to be set up in your room later on so you can look at everything again," Steve says as I rub my temples, where a headache is starting to niggle. "And I've asked people to fire random questions about your identity at you so that you get into the habit of being able to answer them on the spot. I'm sure I don't need to remind you of this, but when you get out of here, it could be ACID asking you those questions."

I nod.

"Another thing to remember is that the arrests system works slightly differently in Outer. People who get into trouble with ACID in Upper are given two warnings before they're arrested—"

"Amber and red," I say, unable to hide the boredom in my tone. I'm hungry again, and my headache's getting worse; I don't mean to sound so grumpy, but I'm starting to feel like crap. "But in Outer, they just swoop in and grab them. I might have grown up in Upper, but I'm not totally naive, you know."

I remember what my father told me when I was thirteen and he caught me reading a hacked link on my komm I'd found by accident when I was looking for some stuff for a homework assignment. It was a page about how the IRB used to be called the United Kingdom, and about how, when it was, people had the right to vote and to travel freely to other places outside the IRB, including Europe and America—places my teachers had told us were evil, full of crime and poverty and hate. As I read it, my heart began to pound. How could any of this be true? And yet, there was something about it that made me think it *was,* and I started to wonder what life would be like if we could choose who was in charge; if there wasn't a Fence; if we could go and see those so-called evil places for ourselves.

I was so engrossed, I didn't hear my father come into my room. "What are you doing?" he said. Guilty and terrified, I tried to cut the link, but he was too quick, ripping my komm out of my ear. He screamed at me for half an hour solid, finishing with "I should report you and get you an amber warning, just to teach you a lesson." Then he took my komm away.

Shortly after that, I met Dylan for the first time, at Nadia's birthday party.

"I'm being serious, Mia." Steve uses my new name without missing a beat, jolting me back to the present. "The one thing we cannot change about you is your DNA. If you get arrested, all ACID have to do is take a blood test, and you'll be back inside before you can even blink."

I look down at the surface of the desk.

"From now on, Jenna Strong no longer exists," Steve says. "Is that clear?"

I nod, still staring at the desk. *Jenna Strong no longer exists.* Wow, that feels weird.

"Well, it must be nearly lunchtime," Steve says more brightly. "Shall I call Mel to take you back to your room, Mia?"

I nod gratefully. Steve speaks into his komm, and a few minutes later Mel appears. Back in my room, lunch is already waiting for both of us—jacket potatoes with chicken salad— and while we eat, Steve comes in and sets up a holocom on a little table in the corner.

"What are your parents called?" he shoots at me over his shoulder as he walks to the door.

I look up at him, startled. "Um . . . Martha and Anthony," I stammer.

Steve shakes his head. "No *um,* Mia. *Um* could get you into a lot of trouble."

I feel a flush rise in my cheeks, and my stomach turns sour. I push the remains of my jacket potato away, my appetite gone.

"Have you finished?" Mel says as Steve leaves. I nod. "Right, then," she says. "Time to meet Cade."

She tries to get me to use the airchair again, but I refuse. I don't want my new pretend LifePartner thinking I'm some frail little thing.

We take a lift to another floor, where Jon's waiting for us. "He's in here," he says, smiling as he holds a door open for me.

We walk into a lounge filled with low, comfortable-looking chairs. It's empty except for a boy sitting in one of the chairs at the far end, a cane beside him.

"Cade," Mel calls. "This is Mia."

The boy turns. He has very short blond hair and a prominent

45

Adam's apple, acne scattered across his cheeks and forehead. As we walk toward him, a nervous frown creases his brow. "Hi," he says. As he gets up, he reaches for the cane, and his shirt rides up and I see he has a scar, identical to mine, on his left hip. So he had a spytag too. I wonder what his real name is and which jail he's been broken out of. Not Mileway, that's for sure; he doesn't look as if he'd have survived two seconds in there.

Mel gives me a nudge. "Um, hi," I say.

Silence.

"So," Mel says after several seconds. "I'll leave you two to get to know each other, shall I?"

"OK," I hear myself say.

"Can I get you anything?" Mel asks. "Tea? Coffee?"

"I'm all right," Cade mutters, scowling at the floor.

"Me too," I say.

"Well, shout if you need me," she says, and beaming at us one last time, she bustles out. *Come back!* I want to shout. Then I realize how ridiculous I'm being. I've just spent the last two years in prison, for God's sake. I can take on men four times my size and reduce them to a bloody, blubbering pulp. And now I'm nervous about being left alone with an ordinary seventeen-year-old guy?

"So I can't tell you anything about me, and you can't tell me anything about you," I say, trying to sound light-hearted. "Lucky we're not really LifePartners, isn't it?"

He gives me a shocked look. "What do you mean?"

I realize I've said the wrong thing. He probably thinks I've guessed who he really is or something. I shake my head. "Never mind. I was only messing about."

"Oh, right," he mumbles.

I decide to try again. "So what d'you reckon this place really is? D'you think they're secret agents? They could be plotting to take over the world, and when we get sent to Outer we'll start

46

receiving envelopes with instructions for secret missions inside them."

He gives me a strange look. Clearly, he thinks I'm absolutely mad.

Trying to ignore the frustration building inside me, I rack my brains to think of something else to say. I can't. Cade fiddles with the hem of his shirt, studiously avoiding my gaze. The silence between us stretches out until it's way past uncomfortable, and I have to resist the urge to bury my head in my hands and groan.

Why have I got a bad feeling about this already?

foundation for
rights, emancipation
and equality
free

FOUNDATION FOR RIGHTS, EMANCIPATION AND EQUALITY
GENERAL COMMUNICATION

Date: 19.04.13

Please note: access to this communication is available only to those entering the correct passcode. The file containing the communication will automatically corrupt five minutes after it is opened and become unreadable/unrecoverable.

Update #1 – Mia Richardson and Cade Johnson

Little to report. MR and CJ left our facility two days ago for their new home in Zone M. So far, one contact has been made between them and MM and JM, who have established that they are settling well. Both started their new jobs yesterday; MR at the Zone R magtram factory and CJ at the Zone Q sub food packaging plant, as planned. No problems reported by either so far. MM and JM intend to make contact once a fortnight from now on, unless any issues arise.

Update #2 – Trial

Progress steady but slow. AH is still in the process of recovering deleted files from ACID databases. Plans are in place for the mission to Innis Ifrinn in a few months' time. If successful, we are confident that this and all the other evidence we will have collected will be sufficient to bring ACID to trial for numerous human rights abuses. Contact has now been made with officials at the European Criminal Justice Bureau, who have agreed to allow their agents to assist us with arrests and to hold the trial for us at their central headquarters in Frankfurt, where those arrested will be taken before it begins.

No other business to report. End of communication.

OUTER

CHAPTER 8

Zone M, Outer London
18 May 2113

As soon as I walk into the flat, I see the dirty clothes still in a heap in front of the washer and the dishes piled in the sink in the alcove that passes for the kitchen. Cade's stretched out on the sofa, surrounded by more mess, to which he seems oblivious as he eats a sandwich and stares at the news screen.

"For God's sake!" I bark, slinging my bag and jacket onto the hook by the door, before stomping into the kitchen to shovel the clothes into the washer.

"What?" Cade says.

"You get back from work half an hour before I do. Couldn't you . . . you know?" I flip out a hand to indicate the mess.

"I'm *tired*," Cade says, not taking his gaze off the news screen. There's an ACID agent on there—Subcommander Healey, she's called—reading a report about crime and LifePartnering in clipped tones. I've never seen her in real life, but she's on the screens practically every day, even more than General Harvey. Her skin is pale and flawless, and her glossy dark hair, cut in a neat, slanting bob, never seems to move. It makes me wonder if she's really a robot or something.

"Statistics show that ACID's LifePartnering program has reduced problems such as littering, vandalism and graffiti to virtually zero. It has been our greatest success," she says now. I roll my eyes. She obviously hasn't been to Outer London in a while.

"Well?" I say to Cade, but he continues to stare at the screen. I don't want to argue with him again, but I'm tired as well, and I've spent all day with my supervisor getting at me for messing up one tiny part of an order. My anger ignites. "You're such a slob!" I snap.

"And you're such an uptight cow!" he snaps back.

Fresh anger boils up inside me. If the walls of this flat weren't so thin, I'd scream insults at him, but because they are, we're forced to argue in whispers. Mrs. Holloway's already reported one couple to ACID for fighting this week, and they came to take them away in the middle of the night. I don't want us to be next.

"All I asked you to do," I say through clenched teeth, "is put some stuff in the washer if you got back from work first, and pick up the crap that's all over the living room. I'm sick of tripping over it, and I don't see why I should have to do all the cleaning by myself! Why is it such a big deal?"

"Because all you ever do is bitch and moan at me," he says. "I've been at work all day as well, y'know?"

He scowls at me. I scowl back. We've been posing as LifePartners for about a month now, and every time I think about how we're going to be stuck together for the next God knows how many years—if that's what whoever Mel and Jon work for has planned for us—I want to wail in despair. I'm sure he feels exactly the same way about me.

I open my mouth to snap at him again. Then I catch myself and take a deep breath. "Screw this," I say. "I'm going for a run."

I go into the bedroom to look for my running shoes, jogging bottoms and sweatshirt, which I begged Mel to get me a few days after Cade and I moved here. There are no gyms in Outer, and the cost of the gyms in Middle are way beyond the reach of my salary, even if I could travel there without the risk of a stop-and-search from ACID. The shoes and clothes are secondhand—new would attract too much attention around here—but they're comfortable, and that's all I care about. Exercise is one habit from prison I have no intention of breaking.

Once I've laced my shoes, I check that my c-card's still in my trouser pocket, pull on my jacket and zip it up and storm out of the flat as quietly as possible.

Outside, it's starting to rain. The dull skies sap my energy almost instantly, so I jog instead, heading down the footpath at the back of Anderson Court that runs alongside the river. There's no one around—most people avoid this footpath even in daylight, as there have been three muggings along here already this month, two of them attacks on people in my building. They happened before curfew too. Not that you'd know about them from looking at the news screens, where Agent Robot and her clones are forever spouting about crime figures being at their lowest ever level and how London is the safest city in the IRB. But then, ACID pretended I killed Alex Fisher, so who knows how much of their other "news" is made up too. Anyway, I'm in the sort of mood where I'd be pleased to bump into a mugger. I could vent my frustration by breaking their legs and chucking them into the river.

As I plod along, grumbling at Cade inside my head, a magtram streaks across the top of the bridge opposite, a blur of lit-up windows, almost silent despite its speed. There's rubbish everywhere, most of it coming from a broken-down vacuubin a few meters away, which, instead of sucking the litter people have stuffed into it down into the underground recycling system, keeps spitting it out like an old man hacking up phlegm. The whole area is overlooked by apartment blocks, their concrete stained and cracked and their grimy windows like half-blind eyes, reflecting the dull iron color of the sky. Even the water in the river looks polluted and sickly, a sheen of oil floating on its surface. It couldn't be more different from my old district in Upper, with its elegant stone buildings and wide, clean streets.

As the path snakes under another bridge, I notice a small lightffiti tag on the brickwork above my head, spiky black and pink letters spelling out three letters: NAR. *Who's that?* I wonder. I look for the projection unit, but it must be hidden in one of the straggly bushes growing up the bank beside the path. Losing interest, I turn up the collar of my jacket, hunching my shoulders. Being down here is doing nothing to improve my mood, and the rain's starting to fall harder now.

Reluctantly, I return to the flat, knocking as I wave my c-card in front of the scanlock to warn Cade I'm back. He doesn't answer, and when I step through the door, I hear him thumping about in the bedroom. He's pulling clothes out of the rickety wardrobe—we both keep our stuff in it, even though he sleeps on the couch—and stuffing them into a bag.

"What are you doing?" I say.

"Packing," he says without looking round at me.

"Why?"

"I'm going."

"Going? Where?"

"To stay with my cousin. He knows about my situation."

"Your situation? You mean me and you?"

"Yeah. He'll keep ACID off my back."

"Does he live in Outer too?"

Cade nods, shoving more clothes into the bag. "We grew up together," he says, his tone curt.

So Cade's from Outer? I wonder what on earth he's told this cousin of his. He must trust him, that's for sure. "How long will you be gone?" I say, thinking of Mrs. Holloway.

"Dunno," he says. "I might ditch London altogether."

"Ditch London?"

"Yeah. There is a whole *country* out there, in case you hadn't noticed."

I know that, I want to snap at him. *And I bet I've seen more of it than you ever will.* I stop myself just in time. Jenna Strong and her family might have taken holidays in luxury countryside villas provided by ACID, in places like the Scottish Highlands and North Wales, but Mia Richardson has never left London. No one from Outer would ever be able to afford to do stuff like that.

"But where will you—" I begin.

Cade cuts me off with a humorless little laugh. "Mia, would you stop with all the questions? I'm leaving. As in, for good."

"But you *can't!*" I say. "You're supposed to be my Life-Partner."

"You're kidding, right?" he says, whirling round to face me. "We're the most unconvincing Partners ever—you won't even hold hands with me in public! I know I'm getting paid for this by whoever Mel and Jon work for, but no one's gonna keep believing we're for real with you acting so spiky all the time."

"So why don't you ask Mel and Jon to find someone else?" I say, thinking, *You're getting paid?* I had no idea. How much? And why aren't *I* getting paid to put up with him?

"That's exactly what I'm going to do, once I get away from here." He turns back to the bag on the bed and yanks the zip closed, and I think about how, before I started to question things, my friends and I used to devour romance eFics on my komm. Then I'd watch the small number of boys who attended my academy and imagine being Partnered to the one who was the most handsome, or the one who had the kindest smile.

I guess the reality is pretty different, especially if your LifePartner is fake.

He hefts the bag onto his shoulder. "I'll see you around," he says, walking past me to the door.

"What about Mrs. Holloway?" I say. My mind's screaming at me to stop him—I know moves that could have him flat on his back before he's taken another step—but then what am I supposed to do? Knock him out? Chain him to the wall?

"You'll think of something," he says as he yanks open the door.

I watch it close behind him. This cannot be happening. If Mrs. Holloway sees him leaving . . .

The news screen, which is flickering like crazy—you have to kick the base just to get the damn thing to come on most days—is still blaring in the corner. I go to turn it down and see Agent Robot's still on.

"Subcommander Healey, do you have an update on the whereabouts of escaped murderer Jenna Strong?" a man in a cheap-looking gray suit with a microphone says, and I realize this isn't the report that was on before, but a live feed.

Subcommander Healey nods. "We believe she is in Edinburgh," she says. "Our tracking system has placed her—"

Snorting, I mute the sound. At least if ACID think I'm in Scotland, they won't be looking for me here. I slump on the sofa and wonder what to do about Cade. Then there's a tap on the front door and a faint call from the other side. "Coo-ee!"

Ugh. But I can't ignore her; she'll just lie in wait for me next time I leave. "Mrs. Holloway," I say, forcing a smile onto my lips as I open the door.

"I've told you a hundred times, dear, call me Lynda!" she trills. She's trimmed her hair since I last saw her, by putting a bowl on her head and cutting around the rim, from the looks of it. And either she's got a wardrobe full of vast belted cardigans made out

56

of lumpy heather-colored wool, or she never takes this one off. Looking at the specks of food clinging to her bosom, I think I can guess which.

"Was that Cade I just saw going into the lift?" she says, peering myopically at me through the thick, smeared lenses of her spectacles.

"He's been called in for an emergency shift at the food plant," I say quickly.

"Oh. I thought he was carrying a bag. . . ."

"Clothes. He hasn't had time to change since his last shift."

"I see." Mrs. Holloway—I refuse to call her Lynda—nods so vigorously her chins wobble. "Anyway, Mia dearie, I came to see if you and Cade would be interested in attending one of my workshops at the end of the month. I've posted the information on the kommweb—you know the ID. . . ."

"Oh right, great," I tell her with forced enthusiasm. Mrs. Holloway, who lives two floors below, nobly agreed to stay on at Anderson Court as LifePartner Ambassador even though she was entitled to move into a house when she had her first child—a brat who thinks the funniest thing in the whole world is to hide in the lobby and jump out, screaming, as you walk past—is head of Anderson Court's Young Partners Committee. Among other things, she runs workshops for them about how to be a good LifePartner. Cade and I went to one not long after we moved in here, and its awfulness was the only thing we've ever agreed on. "We'll try our best to make it," I say, pasting another smile onto my face. I touch my ear, as if I can hear my komm going off. "I'm really sorry, Mrs. Holloway, but someone's linking me. I think it's Cade. You don't mind, do you?"

I close the door and retreat into the flat.

Cade, you cannot do this to me! I think as I stare out the living-room window at the street outside. Without a LifePartner—even a fake one—I'm going to stick out like an Outer at an Upper dinner party. All it'll take is for Mrs. Holloway to realize Cade's not around, and she'll report me to ACID quicker than you can say *You're screwed*.

I turn away from the window and slump onto the sofa with a groan. One thing's for sure: Mel and Jon are going to kill both of us.

CHAPTER 9

I'm itching to link Cade and order him to come back, but I can't. I've been warned against talking on my komm about anything to do with our setup here in case ACID are listening in. Not that I need telling. I remember when I was thirteen and went into my dad's study to ask him something; he wasn't there, but the holocom on his desk was on, and there was a list of transcripts of people's kommweb conversations on the screen. I couldn't help starting to read it; I was fascinated and horrified at the same time.

"What do you think you're doing?" my father shouted when he came in and saw me, lunging across the room and dragging me away from the computer.

"What is that stuff?" I challenged him back. "Why are ACID listening to everyone?"

"That's none of your business," my father snapped. I started to protest—he was still holding on to my arm, his fingers digging into me, hurting me—but he shouted, "You've got a rebellious streak a mile wide, Jenna Strong, and it's getting out of control."

Then he locked me in my room, to think about my behavior.

Bloody ACID, I think now. *They make everything so bloody difficult.*

I wait all evening for Mel and Jon to link me, my stomach churning with anxiety. But I don't hear from them. When they still haven't linked me the next morning, I stop feeling anxious and start feeling puzzled. Hasn't Cade told them he's left me yet? Unless he didn't want to lose the money he was getting to pretend he was my Partner. I wonder if the story he told me about going to his cousin's was true, or if he's just buggered off somewhere, gone underground.

For all of two seconds, I'm annoyed with him. Then I realize that I can use this to my advantage. I did an extra half shift at work last week, so I've got a couple of hours owing to me. If I get off early, I can go to the plant where Cade works and wait outside for him to finish. Then I'll follow him back to wherever he's staying and try to get him to talk to me, to make him see that he's got to come back. If I can do that, Mel and Jon won't even have to know he left.

And if that talk ends with my knee in his throat and his arms up behind his back, well, he's in just as much danger going around without a Partner as I am, and I've got to make him see that.

The mystery is finally solved when I check my kommweb messages on my way to work and find one from Mel, saying her mother's been taken ill unexpectedly and she and Jon have had to go up to Birmingham. *Sorry we didn't link you,* the message says, *but we had to leave in the small hours of the morning and we didn't want to disturb you. Mum's not seriously ill, but there are a couple of things we need to sort out for her. We should be back in a day or two.*

When I get to the factory, everyone's gathered around the news screen that dominates one wall in the foyer, talking in shocked murmurs. Glancing up at it, I see a head-and-shoulders shot of a teenage boy. I can tell from his clothes, casual but smart, and his clear, tanned skin that he's from Middle, not Outer. His mop of dark hair falls in a curtain over his eyes, which are a shade somewhere between green and blue, and his grin, which is endearingly crooked, shows two rows of straight, white teeth. In my old life, he's the sort of boy my friends—especially Nadia—would have looked down their noses at for being from Middle but that I'd have daydreamed about when I was on my own. He's not handsome, exactly, but he looks friendly and normal and nice; the sort of guy, if you were lucky enough to get Partnered to him, you could imagine curling up with and talking to until the small hours of the morning and not even noticing what time it was.

There's also something about him that's maddeningly familiar. Then I see the headline: MURDERED MILEWAY DOCTOR'S SON STILL MISSING. Underneath is a line that reads: *Max Fisher, 16, disappeared shortly after the escape of killer Jenna Strong.*

The screen changes; there's a picture of me now too, which ACID must have found in the prison files, my head shaved, my mouth twisted in a scowl. My fantasy about Max dissolves into a wave of freezing cold that leaves my hands tingling, and I want to charge out of the foyer as if ACID are already on my tail.

The mutters and murmurs around me rise to an almost hysterical pitch. "Just imagine, he could be anywhere. He could be here. . . ." "Look, it says his c-card was traced to a mag stop in Outer!" "What if he's helping her?" "What if they both start killing people?"

The girl who just spoke, Louisa, is someone who works in my department. I wouldn't say she's a friend, exactly—I've kept myself to myself since I started here, too wary of making a

61

slip-up that would reveal my true identity to want to get close to anyone—but we're friend*ly*, I guess. She looks round at me, her eyes wide with fear, and for a moment, I forget how to breathe.

She can't know it's you, I tell myself. *She can't.*

"Oh, Mia," Louisa says. "Did you see that? Maybe we should set up a rota so no one has to go home alone—find out who lives near each other and get them to drop each other off."

"Yeah, definitely," I say, and push through the crowd to go to my station just as our floor manager appears, demanding to know why no one's started work.

To my relief, she grants my request to leave early without asking any awkward questions, and after lunch I take a mag to Zone Q. The food packaging plant where Cade works is nearly a thirty-minute walk from the mag terminal, a squat building opposite a huge statue of General Harvey, which I notice, with some satisfaction, has a huge streak of bird shit across its forehead. I find an empty doorway across the street to wait in, leaning against the boarded-over entrance behind me as I keep watch, not only for Cade but for ACID patrols and spotters—small, crescent-shaped drones that have vidfeeds and link information directly back to ACID—too. In Outer, if you're not careful, just being out on the street is enough to get you stopped and searched. Hell, some days, just existing is enough.

Seventeen hundred hours comes and goes. People start to leave the plant, but there's no sign of Cade. I wait a bit longer, gazing at the giant news screens on the sides of the buildings, displaying ACID public warnings in between news stories that seem mostly to be about me or Max Fisher. Agent Robot's face looms down at me as she appears on the screens at various intervals to read out statements. When I get bored with watching her, I look at the drifts of litter that people have thrown at the vacuubins and missed; the flock of mangy-looking pigeons settled on top of the statue of General Harvey; the bank of ancient-looking PKPs—public kommweb points—under a glass shelter nearby, all but one of them smashed up; at the girls not much older than me struggling past with screaming babies or hyperactive toddlers, their faces prematurely lined with exhaustion and despair.

If I'd been Partnered for real, I think, *I might have had a kid by now.*

The stream of people leaving the plant dwindles to a trickle, and I still haven't seen Cade. I ask a girl coming out if she knows where he is.

"Don't think I know him, sorry," she says.

I think about going inside, trying to find his supervisor, but what if he's gone AWOL for some reason? ACID could be involved already, and if I turn up saying I don't know where he is, they'll want to speak to me about it. And if he is supposed to be somewhere else, shouldn't I, as his Partner, know about it already?

Face it, I tell myself. *He's not here. You'll have to try again tomorrow.* I push myself upright with an angry sigh and start the long walk back to the magtram terminal.

A few hundred meters down the road, I realize I've lost my bearings. I pass an elderly woman carrying an empty shopping bag on her arm. "Excuse me?" I say.

She stops and peers at me. She's so hunched over that the top of her head is only just level with my shoulder. "Do you know how I get back to the Zone Q magtram terminal?" I ask her.

"Head in the direction of the old town hall," she says, and points at a tall brick building some streets away. Even from this distance, it's clearly derelict, with a rust-streaked clock tower rising from its roof, the hands frozen forever at fifteen hundred.

"Thank you," I say. I'm about to start walking when she plucks at my sleeve.

"Did you see if there were lines to get into the shops back there?" she asks me.

I shake my head. "Sorry, no. I didn't come that way."

She sighs. "I expect there will be, but I suppose I'd better go and have a look anyway." Then, all of a sudden, she beckons me to lean closer. "You know, it never used to be like this," she whispers. "You're too young to know any different, dearie, but before the Crash people had a say in who ran this country. You didn't have to line up to get into the shops, and you didn't have ACID agents pointing guns at you to make sure you didn't complain about it."

The Crash. She's talking about fifty-three years ago, when, after a decades-long global recession, the IRB went completely bankrupt and got kicked out of Europe, and the government collapsed. ACID, who were just a police force at the time, seized power and have run the country ever since. I remember learning about it at school. There, we were told how corrupt and lazy the old government had been, how it was their incompetence that allowed the Crash to happen in the first place, and how, if it hadn't been for ACID, the IRB would have tipped over into complete disaster. It wasn't until my conversations with Dylan that I started to wonder what ACID *weren't* telling us about life before they took over, and to see them in a different light—the same light this woman sees them in, apparently.

The woman's eyes burn with anger as I take an involuntary step away from her, automatically looking around for ACID agents.

"Oh, I'm too old to worry about getting into trouble," the woman grumbles. "But I guess it's different for you young folk."

She shuffles away in the direction she came from. *If only you knew the trouble* I've *been in,* I think as I watch her go. Certainly, she's right in thinking I don't want any more.

Keeping the clock tower in my line of sight, I find my way back to the mag terminal. Soon, a mag going to Zone M pulls up, bullet-nosed and incongruously sleek in the midst of the squalor surrounding it. I get on and flash my card at the kredzreader, waiting for the glass doors that lead from the vestibule into the pod to hiss open. As the mag begins to pick up speed, I grab a strap hanging from the ceiling near the doors and wonder, with a growing sense of despair, what I'm going to do if (no, face it, Jenna, *when*) Mrs. Holloway realizes Cade's not around. I guess I could say he's got a family emergency or something, but with her links to ACID, she could check up on things like that.

When I get off, I scan my c-card again to deduct the right number of kredz for my journey. I decide to take the footpath along the river back to Anderson Court. As I'm about to turn onto the footpath, I see something out of the corner of my eye. A flash of bright green. I stop and turn. There's nothing behind me except an empty alleyway.

But as I start walking again, I think I hear footsteps. I whip back round. Nothing. I walk a little farther. Then I turn, and this time, I catch sight of a shadow disappearing down another alleyway.

It could be anything, I tell myself. *A kid, a cat, a feral dog . . .* But unease is pricking at the base of my spine—a sixth sense that, in prison, saved my life a hundred times. Just because I'm not in prison anymore doesn't mean it's a good idea to ignore it.

There's a wall sticking out from the side of a building to my left, concealing a row of recycling hatches. I duck behind it and wait, peering round the corner at the entrance to the alleyway. Several moments pass. Then someone emerges. A boy in a stained green hooded sweatshirt with the hood pulled up and filthy, ripped jeans.

He stands looking up and down the street. Although the top half of his face is hidden by his hood, I can see his mouth, twisted in a frown. Clearly, he's wondering where I've gone.

He starts walking up the street toward where I'm hiding.

My first instinct is to jump out and challenge him, but as he gets nearer I draw back into the shadows so he won't see me. If I cause a scene, someone might link ACID, and once they've arrested me, all they have to do is take a blood sample and I'll be back in jail.

I wait until Hoodie Boy is ten meters or so ahead of me, then slip out and creep after him. He stops, and I draw back into the shadows.

When I emerge again, he's gone.

I walk slowly, trying to figure out where he went. But he's nowhere. I finally reach the footpath and turn onto it; at the mag bridge, NAR has left a new lightffiti tag in glowing orange letters, almost too bright to look at. I frown at it—what *is* that?—but my thoughts soon return to Cade. The sound of my trudging feet echoes off the wall opposite, and I shove my hands in my pockets. Maybe I should go to Zone Q on Sunday and find out if anyone there has seen him. But where would I start? The closer they are to London's periphery, the bigger the Outer zones get.

Then I hear them.

Footsteps.

I stop. So do they. I look behind me, but deep shadows pool across the path and the murky surface of the water, and it's so gloomy that I can't see anything.

"Whoever's there, you don't scare me," I say, whirling round. "Come out and face me if you've got the guts."

I fold my arms, waiting.

"I mean it," I snarl. A familiar sensation is creeping through me, adrenaline distilling into anger, pure and sharp and cold.

Nothing.

Wrapping my arms across myself, I turn back round. I'm thirty seconds from home. Whoever it is can go jump in the river.

I've barely gone two steps when someone runs up behind me. They slam into me with full force, grabbing me around the waist and trying to pin my arms against my sides. "Give me your c-card! And your komm!" a male voice growls, blowing hot, foul-smelling breath into my face. "I've got a knife!"

CHAPTER 10

I jab backward with my elbow and heel, connecting with his groin. As he grunts and staggers back, I twist out of his grip, hook my arm round his neck and spin him forward and over my shoulder, swatting him onto the ground and pinning his neck with my foot.

He stares up at me, gasping.

Hoodie Boy.

"You know, your breath stinks," I say.

His mouth moves, but nothing comes out.

"Why are you following me?" I say.

He makes a wheezing sound. Realizing he can't speak because of the pressure of my foot on his throat, I step on his chest instead.

"I—just—needed—some—stuff," he chokes out.

"So you thought you'd pick on some poor defenseless girl?"

"I'm—sorry—"

"You will be. Where's this knife, then? If you've actually got one."

He shakes something out of his sleeve.

"Give it to me," I say.

When he passes it to me, I laugh. It's a knife, all right—a butter knife, the blade dull, the plastic handle yellowed and chipped. Almost an antique. "Wow, terrifying," I say, tossing it into the river.

"I—I'm sorry," Hoodie Boy says again. His teeth are chattering.

"Who are you?" I say.

"I—"

"No, actually, don't tell me. I don't care. All I'm bothered about is that you made my already crappy day even worse." This time, my anger's hot and spiky. "Who the hell d'you think you are, trying to rob me? No one's got anything around here, or hadn't you noticed?" I know he probably doesn't give a shit, but I need to vent. "And as for trying to nick my c-card, how would I get to work or buy food? You can't use other people's cards anyway."

Hoodie Boy doesn't reply. He just lies there, shaking. I take my foot off his chest, reach down and rip off his hood.

And step back, my eyes widening, one hand plastered against my mouth in shock.

CHAPTER 11

No, I tell myself. *It can't be.* How could that boy I saw this morning on the news screen, the one with the fashionable haircut and teeth so white it almost hurt to look at them, have turned into—

Into this?

But even though I only saw the picture for a few moments, and the boy lying at my feet has lost so much weight that the skin of his face is stretched across the bones like paper, his resemblance to the man who sacrificed his life to get me out of Mileway is unmistakable.

Hoodie Boy is Max Fisher.

Oh God.

"Max," I say softly. "Max."

He looks up at me, his blue-green eyes clouded and unfocused. "How d'you know my name?" he slurs.

I'm about to answer him when, behind us, I hear a call. "Mia! Is that you? Coo-ee!"

No. Please, no.

I leave Max lying on the ground and hurry up the path to Mrs. Holloway before she can get too close.

"Oh, Mia!" she says. Her face is blotched and tear-streaked, her glasses crooked. "It's my Sammie. One of the children took him out a little while ago and he slipped his lead!"

Sammie's her dog, a skinny, shivery little thing that always bark-screams at you like he's wishing he were bigger so he could rip your face off. "I'm sorry, I haven't seen him," I say, desperately resisting the urge to glance behind me at Max.

"Are you sure?" Fresh tears well up in her eyes. "I'm so scared someone's taken him!"

If only, I think. I try to arrange my expression into something suitably sympathetic. "I know," I say. "Why don't you go that way"—I point down the river path in the opposite direction to Max—"and I'll go that way." I jerk my thumb behind me. "If two of us are looking, we're more likely to find him."

"Oh no, I only came down here to wait for Dean. I'm not looking anywhere else until he's home," she says. Dean's her LifePartner, the only person in the building who makes her look intelligent by comparison. "And neither must you! You don't know who could be down here now it's starting to get dark!"

Behind us, Max groans.

"Is that Cade?" Mrs. Holloway says, squinting into the shadows as I try to keep the panic off my face. "I've not seen him today. What's he doing on the ground?"

"He's been teaching me some self-defense," I say quickly. "You know, what with it being such a dodgy area and all. Only it went a bit wrong and he's hurt his back."

Max groans again.

"Oh dear," Mrs. Holloway says. "I do sympathize—I have such trouble with my back. Let me help you get him inside."

"No!" I say. "I mean, it's OK. It's just a spasm—it's

71

happened before. If he lies still for a bit it'll pass, and he'll be fine. Honestly, moving him right now will just make it worse."

Mrs. Holloway frowns, her chins quivering. "Well, if you're sure . . ."

I glance back at Max, relieved it's so gloomy down here that you can't see his face or the state his clothes are in. "I'm sure," I tell her, trying to smile.

"I'd better get back, then," Mrs. Holloway says. "I need to put a page up on the kommweb for Sammie, and organize the search party—you and Cade are welcome to join us!"

"We will if his back's all right!" I promise with as much fake enthusiasm as I can muster. I watch as she trots back up the path, then turn back to Max. His arms are clenched round his body as if he's trying to stop himself breaking into pieces.

"Thanks," I tell him. "Now I'm really in the shit. If I leave you here and someone finds you, Mrs. H'll remember seeing me with you and report me to ACID. They'll find out Cade's gone and I'll probably never see daylight again."

Max moans. His face is so pale that, in the gathering dark, it's almost luminous, and his teeth are rattling together harder than ever. With a wave of pity mixed with disgust, I realize what's wrong. He's a niner—a CloudNine addict. A few of the inmates at Mileway were hooked on the stuff, blue granules you take by dissolving them under your tongue. The first time you try it, apparently, it's awful—a short high followed by such intense sickness and dizziness you think you're going to die. But after that the effects are completely different: it ramps you up, making you feel as if you have superhuman energy. The comedown is brutal, though, and by the looks of it, that's what's happening to Max now.

"H-have you g-got any—" he begins, the rest of the sentence lost to the shudders racking through him.

"Gear?" I say. "No. Do I look like a niner to you?"

I push my hands through my hair. What do I do? I could

72

carry him a bit farther along the path, find somewhere to hide him, but what if someone sees me or a spotter comes along? And even if I manage it and ACID never find him, what will happen to him after that? I might not have actually killed Alex Fisher, but it was because of me that he lost his life. Whenever I close my eyes, I see him lying facedown on the incarceration tower roof, the charge from the ACID agents' pulse guns slowly fizzling out as his life ebbs away with it. I can't let his son die too.

Anyway, if I go back to Anderson Court on my own, Mrs. Holloway's going to want to know where "Cade" got to.

"Get up," I tell Max. When he doesn't move, I lean down, yank his hood back up and scoop him onto his feet so he's propped up against me. "Walk," I hiss, wrinkling my nose at his stale, sour odor.

"I can't," he says.

"You can, or I'm gonna leave you here for ACID."

He starts to move, a jerky shamble, stumbling against me every few steps.

"Walk properly," I say. "Otherwise you're gonna get us both arrested.'

He tries to straighten up. The improvement is negligible.

Slowly, we make our way to Anderson Court. The foyer's empty, so I drag Max into one of the lifts and jab the button for my floor. As soon as the doors close, he starts to sag. "Not in here," I whisper fiercely. "There are cameras!" I haul him upright, one arm clamped around his waist. A little voice in my head keeps asking me what I'm going to do when I get him up to my flat. I have no idea, so I ignore it.

When the lift doors open, I peer out, my heart thudding, but the corridor leading to my flat is empty too. Fumbling my c-card from my pocket, I haul Max down it. He's barely conscious, a dead weight against me. I don't even want to think about what'll happen if someone comes out of one of the other flats and sees us.

I have to pass my card across the scanlock twice before the lights change from red to green, and it makes a horrible grinding sound as it disengages. As soon as I've kicked the door shut behind me, Max slides from my grip, curling up on his side with his arms clutched across his stomach. "Hurts," he groans.

"Yeah, that's what happens when you take CloudNine," I snap. I'm more shaken up by my near miss with Mrs. Holloway than I thought.

"I need some gear!" he says. He looks up at me from beneath the hood, grimacing.

"I told you, I don't have anything like that," I say, thinking with panic of the neighbors beyond the flat's skin-thin walls.

"So find some," he snarls. His mouth twists in anger and he uncurls and hauls himself to his feet. I brace myself to fight, but as he lurches toward me his eyes roll back in his head and his legs fold underneath him like a puppet that has just had its strings cut. He lands facedown. I wait a few seconds, then cautiously approach him.

He's not moving. I roll him over, pushing back his hood, and when I see his gray lips and greenish face, my heart squeezes in panic. Then his eyes fly open and he sits up, coughs, and vomits a stream of bile down his front and onto the floor, missing my feet by inches.

"Great," I say. "Thanks."

By the time I've bunched his hoodie up, wrestled it over his head and thrown it into a corner, I'm close to puking myself. I go into the kitchen, taking deep breaths. Our building's automated recycling system broke down last week, so ACID have given all the residents special boxes to sort our recycling into until the system's fixed, and for some reason, I've ended up with two. I grab the spare one from by the fridge and wedge it between Max's knees, then clear up the mess, dropping the hoodie into the washing machine and pouring in half a box

74

of detergent pods before setting it to the highest temperature it can go.

In the living room, I hear the unmistakable sound of Max throwing up again. When I head back in there to open the window and let in some fresh air, he's curled around the box, his head hanging down. He mumbles something that might be *Sorry* or *Help me,* but his voice is so shaky I can't be sure.

Eventually, he pushes the box away and I help him over to the sofa, where he crunches up, shivering. I throw the box into the incinerator chute, then find a blanket to cover Max. Only as I tuck it around his shoulders does it occur to me to check whether he has a komm. To my immense relief, he hasn't.

By the time he's drifted off into an uneasy sleep, it's completely dark outside. I pace around the room, wondering what the hell I'm gonna do. Max needs medicine, but I have no way of getting hold of the drugs to get him through CloudNine withdrawal safely. I can't even look up any information on the kommweb, because it'd be flagged as a suspicious search and an alert would be sent to ACID. And I can't ask Jon or Mel, because they're away, and linking them on my komm would be way too dangerous.

I don't remember falling asleep, but I must have, because I'm no longer in my flat but in the hallway of a house I haven't seen in two years. Everything's just as I remember: the high ceiling, the gold and white papered walls, the expensive paintings (real, never holocopies), the antique black and white tiles that I creep across in total silence.

I don't know why I'm being so quiet, but a little voice in my head is telling me that something's wrong, that I mustn't let anyone know I'm here. My heart's pounding and my palms are damp, my stomach churning with apprehension.

The living room door is open, and I can hear my parents' voices. They're pleading with someone. *We'll do whatever you want—pay a fine, go to jail, even. But please, not that—we have a daughter!*

I peer round the doorframe. Facing away from me is an ACID agent wearing a helmet, so I can't tell if it's a male or a female. My mother and father—who, when I went upstairs to do my homework an hour ago, were sitting in their armchairs, watching the news screen and relaxing after a long day at work—are backed up against the fireplace, their faces masks of terror.

Then I see the agent has a gun and is pointing it straight at my parents.

The agent eases back the gun's charge switch. It fires up with a faint whine. I open my mouth to scream, but no sound comes out. I can't move. I can't do anything.

I have my orders, the agent says in a gravelly, mechanical-sounding voice—it's been disguised.

The agent pulls the trigger.

Bang!

I jerk awake, gasping, for a moment unable to work out why I'm sitting in a chair instead of lying in my bed or what that thrashing shape on the sofa is. Then I remember. I get up and hurry over to Max. At first, I think he's having a fit, but it's just a nightmare, like mine; the bang I heard was his flailing feet knocking over the table by the sofa. He quickly calms down, turning his face against the sofa back and sighing as he falls more deeply asleep.

I pick up the table, my heart hammering, then sit back down. The dream hangs in the air around me like smoke. What was *that* about? It wasn't an ACID agent who shot my parents. It was me. And it wasn't deliberate. It was an accident. All I meant to do with the gun was frighten Dad. If my mother hadn't thrown herself at me to try to get it off me, it wouldn't have gone off.

And if my father hadn't grabbed her as the charge went through her, and it hadn't arced across to him . . .

I grind my knuckles into my eyes. *Stop thinking about this stuff. Stopstopstop.* I need to decide what I'm going to do with Max, and quickly.

You could take him to Mel and Jon when they get back, I think. *They'd help him, wouldn't they? After all, he is Alex's son.*

I mull it over. It *could* work. . . . In Zone O there's a free medicenter for Outer's poorest residents, where Mel and Jon both volunteer: Jon as a doctor, Mel as a receptionist. We usually meet there once a fortnight so they can check how everything's going, and to explain me going there so regularly, I've got documents on my komm saying I require ongoing treatment for a blood disorder. But of course, I can't do that yet, not while Mel and Jon are away. And in the meantime, somehow, I need to keep Max away from Mrs. Holloway.

Despair crashes over me.

Face it, Jenna, I think. *You're screwed.*

CHAPTER 12

I spend the rest of that night constantly checking on Max to make sure he's breathing. By morning, he's running a temperature. There isn't much I can do except stick a medpatch on his neck and hope it helps. I change his filthy jeans and T-shirt for a sleeveless vest and some slightly-too-large jogging bottoms Cade left behind and take the dirty clothes to the kitchen to chuck them in the washer. Just before I switch it on, I remember to check through the pockets of the jeans. All I find is a battered leather wallet. I'm about to look through it when I glance at the clock and realize, shock penetrating sharply through the thick fog of tiredness wrapped around me, that it's almost time to go to work.

I have to go—I can't call in sick without a doctor's pass. But it means leaving Max here all day on his own. What if he makes a noise? Falls off the sofa and hurts himself? What if he gets worse?

But there's nothing I can do. I stuff the wallet in a drawer to look at later, and, after checking on Max one last time, find some clean clothes for myself. Then I splash water on my face, clean my teeth and leave.

At lunchtime, instead of eating, I catch a mag back home, running all the way to Anderson Court. Max is exactly as I left him, curled in a ball on the sofa. I have just enough time to tip a few drops of water into his mouth before I have to leave again. The only blessing is that both Mrs. Holloway and Dean come down with heavy colds that day. Apart from knocking on the door once in the evening to tell me Sammie's home safely and to ask if I could walk him for her—I lie and tell her I'd love to, but I'm allergic to dogs—she stays in her flat.

By the following evening, Max's temperature has finally dropped, but he only stays awake long enough to drink half a cup of instant soup. I spend most of the night at the window, watching the street below for ACID vans and the sky for rotos.

When it starts to get light, I change into my pajamas, crawl under the bedcovers and close my eyes. I'm sure I won't sleep, but if I don't at least try, I'm going to go crazy. When I open my eyes again it's daylight, sunshine streaming in the window. I check the time on my komm and see I've been asleep for over four hours. I scramble out of bed, my thoughts still muddled with sleep, on the verge of panic until I remember it's Sunday and I don't have to be at work.

Max, I think. I rush into the living room.

The sofa's empty.

Panic jolts through me. He became delirious and tried to escape. Or Mrs. Holloway reported us, and ACID came while I was asleep and took him away. They could still be here, waiting. . . .

I look around the room, the blood pounding in my ears. It looks much tidier than before I went to bed. The blanket I covered Max with has been folded over the sofa back, the windows are open, letting in fresh air, and Max's shoes are lined up neatly by the door.

79

Then I hear a hissing sound coming from the bathroom. My pulse slows. Would ACID really be taking a shower and waiting for me to wake up?

The sound of the water stops and the door opens. "Shit!" Max yelps, stumbling back, making me jump too. He has a towel wrapped around his waist and grabs at it just before it slides off. As we stare at each other, I become uncomfortably aware that I'm still in my pajamas—a pair of shorts and a skimpy cami with a low neck and very thin straps—and he's, well, more or less naked, his wet hair plastered to his head and drops of water beaded on his too-prominent collarbone and ribs.

"S-sorry," he stammers, his face going pink. "I would've asked if it was all right to use the shower, but you were asleep, and—"

"It's fine," I say, clearing my throat and feeling my face warm up too. Now he's clean and smells good, I realize for the first time how cute he is. His eyes, fringed by dark lashes, have flecks of gold in the irises, and there are a few freckles scattered across the bridge of his nose.

And *God,* he looks like Alex. He looks so much like Alex it takes my breath away. I cross my arms over my chest, fighting back guilt and embarrassment. "D'you feel better?"

"Loads," he says, coughing. He looks around and frowns. "Where am I?"

"My flat," I say. *State the obvious, Jenna.*

"Am I still in London?"

"Yeah. Outer. Zone M. I'm Mia." My heart does a quick double thud as the name rolls off my tongue. It still doesn't feel as if it belongs to me, and every time I say it, I'm scared I'll stumble over it, give myself away.

His frown deepens. "How did I get here?"

"You tell me," I say. "You were the one who tried to mug me."

He stares at me. "What?"

Despite my nerves, I smile; I can't help it. "With a butter knife," I add.

"So what am I doing here?" he asks. "Why didn't you report me to ACID?"

"Would you prefer it if I had?" I say in as casual a tone as I can manage.

"No! Of course not! ACID are—"

"Looking for you. I know. You're Max Fisher, aren't you?" I can tell he's a little suspicious, so I act as if I'm unsure, although of course, I'm anything but.

"How did you—"

"How do you think? You're all over the news screens. Don't worry," I add as his eyes widen and he glances at the window as if he expects to see an ACID roto hovering right outside. "No one knows you're here."

I hope, I think, mentally crossing my fingers.

Max looks down at himself. "Um, do you have anything clean I could put on?"

Feeling my face warm up again, I fetch Max his now-clean jeans, T-shirt and green hoodie, plus some underwear left behind by Cade (which I tell him I bought for him), and he retreats into the bathroom to dress. By the time he reemerges I've thrown some clothes on too, and made coffee and toast and jam. As he devours it, I gaze at the floor. Even though I know there's no way on earth he could possibly recognize me, I'm nervous about maintaining eye contact with him for more than a few moments. I'm scared he'll be able to read my thoughts somehow; my thoughts, which are screaming: *This guy's dad died for you. He thinks you killed him! Do you have any idea how much trouble you are in right now if he* does *realize who you are?*

"So I really tried to rob you?" he says through a mouthful of toast.

"You don't remember?"

He shakes his head. As I tell him what happened, the little color that had come back into his face drains away. "You're kidding," he says.

"How the hell did you end up on CloudNine in the first place?" I ask.

"Caz and Tam."

"Who?"

He sighs. "I guess I'd better start from the beginning."

Um, yeah, that'd probably be a good idea, I'm about to say, but the look on his face stops me. I press my lips together. *Go easy on him,* I think. *You need to convince him you're on his side so you can get him to Mel and Jon without any hassle.*

Max frowns into his coffee mug. "It was about three weeks ago, I think. I'd just got to college—I was supposed to be starting my tests to figure out what sort of job I'd have after I got LifePartnered—when Mum linked me from home. She was hysterical, saying someone was trying to break down the front door. I asked if she'd called ACID, and she said it *was* ACID, that a van and a roto were outside. I didn't know what to think. What happened to Dad . . ." He swallows, his throat jerking. "It wrecked her. Really wrecked her. I thought she'd finally cracked, that she was having a nervous breakdown or something."

I think about my own mother. Guilt twists inside me as Max's face pinches into a scowl. "I hope they catch that girl, wherever she's gone," he says, his voice full of venom. "Or that she's living somewhere really shitty, with no food and nowhere to get warm."

I force myself to keep my expression neutral, my breathing steady.

"I kept telling her to calm down," he continues. "But she wouldn't. She kept telling me ACID were coming for me too—that I had to get away. She kept saying, 'You mustn't let them catch you!' again and again and again. I asked her why but

82

she wouldn't tell me. Then my friend Josh burst into the class-room and said that ACID had just arrived and were asking for me. A few moments later I heard someone shout, 'Where is he? Where's Max Fisher?'

"That's when I realized that Mum had been telling the truth. I thought about hiding under a table or in a cupboard—stupid places like that. Josh was staring at me. I tried to explain, but I was so scared I couldn't get the words out. I ran over to the window and opened it. Josh was shouting, saying I was insane, that I'd be in even more trouble if I tried to escape, but I ignored him. Then the door crashed open. ACID had found me."

He pauses for a moment, his gaze becoming troubled and distant. "I just panicked," he says. "I hadn't got a clue what ACID wanted, I just knew I had to do what Mum said—I had this *feeling*, you know? So I ripped my komm out, climbed out the window—the classroom was on the ground floor, thank God—and started running. I jumped on the first mag I found and rode it to Outer, right to the end of the line. I ended up in this park—it was really run-down, and the only place I could find to hide was a shelter by a lake.

"I'd not been there long when this man and woman came in. They were really surprised to see me. When they asked what I was doing there, I didn't want to say anything at first—ever since I was a little kid, I'd always heard how dangerous Outer was—but they were so friendly, I ended up telling them every-thing. It turned out they were looking for somewhere to have a cigarette. The woman, Caz, said if I kept a lookout for ACID for them while they smoked, I could stay with her and Tam—that was the guy's name—that night, and the next morning she'd let me use her komm to get in touch with someone. I was so desperate not to spend the night in that park I said yes."

You idiot, I think. I can almost predict what he's going to say next.

"Their flat was horrible—crap everywhere—but I didn't

83

want to seem rude, so I tried to ignore it. Caz made me a sand-wich. About ten minutes after I'd eaten it I started to feel really sick and dizzy. Then I passed out. Next thing I knew, it was morning, and I wanted to die, I felt so bad. I tried to find the kitchen to get some water and collapsed. When Caz found me she started accusing me of being a niner. I couldn't convince her I'd never been near the stuff, and I was in total agony, pains everywhere. She said she'd got something that'd help, but I had to earn it. She got this little bag out of her pocket, with blue crystals in it. I realized what it was straight away. I didn't want to take it, but . . ."

"You felt so bad, you did," I finish for him. It's how the nin-ers at Mileway got other inmates addicted to the stuff: by telling them it would make them feel better; reassuring them that one more dose wouldn't get them hooked. And that the one after that wouldn't either. Or the one after that.

Max hangs his head, looking ashamed.

"How did you have to 'earn' it?" I ask, although I'm not sure I really want to know.

"They were running this business making fake c-cards," he says. "Me and this other kid, who they'd got hooked on CloudNine too, we had to go out robbing people to fund it because they didn't want to spend the money they were making from the cards." He looks up at me and shrugs. "I don't really remember much after that. Until I woke up here, that is." He gives me a shaky smile. "Thank you for taking me in and not telling ACID about me. You probably saved my life."

My stomach jolts. What would he think if he knew the truth—that I only took him in because I had to, to save my own skin?

I feel a sudden burst of anger at ACID—for killing his dad, for the lies they've spread about Alex's death, for wrecking a family and—although I feel selfish for even thinking this—for making my already difficult situation so much harder.

"Yeah, well, you can't stay here," I say, struggling to decide what to tell him that will sound believable without coming too close to the truth, and that will also explain the very obvious absence of Cade. "I'm hiding from ACID too. I ran away from my LifePartner and some friends of mine got me this flat. If we can get you to them, they can help you. Do you still have your c-card?"

"Not my real one," he says. "Caz and Tam took it away from me. But I had this fake one they made me so I could travel on the mag—it was in a wallet in my jeans."

Suddenly, I remember the wallet I found when I changed his clothes a couple of days ago—things have been so crazy I forgot all about it. I fetch it for him.

"That's it," he says, looking relieved. He pulls out a c-card. I take it and examine it. When you look closely, the holopic's a little blurry—probably deliberately—but apart from that, you'd never know it wasn't genuine. Across the front, in red letters, are the words THIS CARD ENTITLES THE HOLDER TO CITIZENSHIP OF THE INDEPENDENT REPUBLIC OF BRITAIN, just like on mine. The ACID logo is emblazoned across the top, and there's a picture of General Harvey's face beside it. Under the holopic is the name ADAMS, MICHAEL.

"Impressive," I say. "And actually, this is better than you having your real one. ACID will have flagged that already, to try and track you. With this one, we should be able to get you to my friends without anyone realizing."

As I hand the card back to him, I hear my komm pinging softly on my bedside table. *Mel,* I think. I jump up and run to the bedroom, jamming my komm in my ear. When Mel's face comes up on the wraparound, I'm so relieved my legs go wobbly and I have to sit down on the bed.

"Mel!" I say. "How's your mum?"

"Much better, thank you," she replies. There are dark circles under her eyes, though. "Are you OK? You look worried."

85

For a moment, I'm tempted to tell her everything, and to hell with worrying about whether or not ACID are listening. I stop myself just in time. If ACID hear the words *Max Fisher*, they'll be swarming all over this building like termites.

"I think I need an appointment at the clinic," I say. "I'm—I'm not feeling so well."

"Oh," Mel says. "How urgent is it?"

My heart's pounding. "Fairly," I say, unable to keep a note of desperation out of my voice.

Mel's expression stays calm. "Is Wednesday soon enough? That's ceremony day, so you should have the day off work, shouldn't you? We do."

I nod. Ceremony day, when the latest lot of just-turned-sixteens get Partnered, takes place every month, and it's always declared a public holiday.

"Come over to the clinic in the morning, at oh-ten hundred."

"OK," I say. I wish I could get rid of Max sooner, but Wednesday's probably the best day. Mrs. Holloway will be out at the Partnering ceremony at Zone M's ceremony square, and if I'm lucky, I might be able to get Max out of here without her seeing us.

"See you Wednesday, then," she says, and cuts the link. I let out my breath in a shaky sigh. Three days. Seventy-two hours. I can keep Max a secret till then.

Can't I?

**AGENCY FOR CRIME INVESTIGATION AND DEFENSE
ARREST REPORT**

WARNING! This document is to be viewed by permitted persons only. Copying or sharing this document is a criminal offense.

Date of arrest(s): 22.05.13

Time of arrest(s): 0300 hrs

Time of report: 0600 hrs

Agent submitting report: 7865 Johnson

Suspects apprehended:

1) Name: Caroline Jane Nicholls
   Age: 23
   Sex: F
   C-card number: 987523436CJN

2) Name: Tam Nicholls
   Age: 23
   Sex: M
   C-card number: 987523437TN

Circumstances of Arrest: Prisoners suspected of manufacturing and selling counterfeit citizenship cards. Team of agents raided prisoners' address—3 Marks Court, Leopold Road, Zone S, Outer London—following arrest on 19.05.13 of another suspect holding counterfeit card, which was traced back to prisoners **<link to case KN67B>**. Equipment found on premises includes holocameras, holocoms and a 3D printer used to print cards. Agents also found drug apparel, tobacco and alcohol on premises.

Action: Prisoners charged for all offenses and detained for questioning at Upper London Interrogation Center. ACID Counterfeit Goods unit to place tracker alert on link ID used to activate cards so that holders of other cards produced by Mr. and Mrs. Nicholls can be traced and arrested when cards used.

Additional Notes: 1 genuine card found on premises belonging to Maxwell Fisher **<link to case JS45H>**. It is not yet known how Fisher came to be at the premises or where he is now. Prisoners deny all knowledge. Suggest tracking fake cards to be best course of action, as Fisher may be in possession of one.

END REPORT.

CHAPTER 13

"Remember, you talk to no one. And you don't leave my side for a second," I tell Max as he pulls up the hood of his dark blue sweatshirt. I bought it for him secondhand to replace the green one in case Mrs. Holloway *does* see us and remembers Cade was supposed to be wearing it the other day. Max nods, tugging the hood forward as far as it will go so his features are lost in shadow beneath it. The sweatshirt's a little too big because of all the weight he's lost, but if he rolls up the sleeves it's not too bad. "And whatever I say," I add, "you do it and ask questions later, OK? Especially if we bump into Mrs. Holloway."

Max nods again, shifting from one foot to the other. As I grab my jacket, I catch him looking at me. He's been doing it all morning. "What?" I say.

"Um, nothing," he says, but his face goes pink.

"So why do you keep staring at me?"

"I was just—just thinking that it suits you, having your hair like that. That's all."

I reach up and touch the short braid I've plaited my hair

into, my face warming up too, feeling a secret spark of pleasure. Usually, I wear it hanging down, a curtain between me and the world, but today it was annoying me, so I tied it back.

"Let's get this over with," I say, pulling on my jacket. Max nods, then starts coughing. He's been coughing all night. Even though he's recovered from the CloudNine withdrawal, he's clearly run-down.

As I turn to check that I've closed the windows and turned off the news screen, my mouth's dry and my heart's thudding. *In less than an hour,* I remind myself, *Max will be safe. Then you can sort out the situation with Cade and things can go back to normal.*

I let out a slow, shaky breath. "Got your c-card?" I ask Max.

He waggles it at me. I check my pocket for my own, fix my komm a little more firmly into my ear and unlock the front door.

I peer out. The corridor is deserted.

"Keep quiet, OK?" I say as I step through the door and beckon to Max to follow me.

The apartment building is silent. As we creep down the corridor, I realize I'm holding my breath. If we can just make it out of the building without bumping into her again—

"Mia!" a voice says just as we reach the lift and the doors open. I look round to see Mrs. Holloway plodding toward us. "Would you mind awfully if I . . ."

Then she looks past me and sees Max. Her voice trails away.

"This is Mikey," I say hurriedly. "He's Cade's brother. He came to get me so we could find a really good spot for the ceremony."

Three different expressions are jostling for position on Mrs. Holloway's face as she tries to make out Max's face: suspicion, confusion and happiness.

"Oh, how lovely," she says as happiness wins the fight—just.

I shove the side of Max's foot with mine. "Y-yeah, we're really excited," he says, and starts coughing.

"Anyway, Mrs. Holloway," I say, super-bright, "we must go. I'd hate to get stuck at the back and not be able to see anything! See you there!"

I stab the DOWN button with my thumb.

"Shit," I breathe, leaning my forehead against the cold metal wall of the lift as it jolts into motion.

"Who's Cade?" Max says, looking puzzled.

"No one," I say. "Don't worry about it."

Outside, rows of gold and white banners have been strung up between the buildings, flapping and cracking in the breeze. It's cloudy and starting to spit with rain. The pavements are packed with people moving toward the ceremony square in one seemingly solid mass.

"ID, please."

I jump, turning to see an ACID agent standing just outside the entrance to Anderson Court. His visor's pushed up, and as I fumble in my pocket, my heart hammering inside my chest, he watches me coldly. I hand over my c-card, telling myself to stay calm. ACID always do spot checks on ceremony days—with so many people converging on the ceremony squares, I guess they think they can't be too careful.

It's just, with everything else, I'd forgotten all about them.

I hold out my card. The agent scans it with the microreader embedded in the wrist of his glove, waits a few seconds and nods. Then it's Max's turn. My heartbeat climbs another few notches. The agent passes his wrist across the card, eyeing Max as he does so. "I didn't realize it was raining that hard," he says, narrowing his eyes, and I feel my heart skip a beat altogether. "How about taking that hood do—"

Then someone cannons into him from behind. A man, frustrated with the slow-moving crowd, has shoved right into him. *Unlucky for him, lucky for us,* I think as the agent, forgetting all about waiting for the results of Max's c-card check, turns with an angry "Hey!" and grabs the man, pinning his arms behind his back so he can cuff him. I grab Max's arm, muttering, "Come on," and we melt away into the crowd jostling its way along Treynold Road.

On the way to the mag terminal, we pass the square, where the ceremony has already begun. I can't help slowing to look. Like all the squares in Outer, the buildings overlooking it are faced with fake stone to make them look smarter—and they probably did before it started to crack and crumble away, revealing the stained concrete underneath. In the middle is a huge statue of General Harvey, people climbing onto its base for a better view of the stage at the far end, which is decorated with limp swags of gold fabric and hung with ACID logos and gigantic banners reading: CONGRATULATIONS, NEW LIFE-PARTNERS, ON THIS JOYOUS DAY! The ten couples being Partnered today are already lined up on the stage, the girls wearing elaborate dresses that their parents probably had to save for years to buy—lace and beads, foamy chiffon and heavy silk—while the boys are more soberly attired in suits, shirts and ties. The sense of excitement in the air here is palpable. People are chattering, laughing, admiring each other's outfits and proudly pointing out their relatives on the stage, and cheering as the ACID official standing at the front of the stage starts to read out the names of the couples behind him. It's nothing like the ceremonies in Upper. Mine—if I'd had it—would have been a private, elegant affair, with just my family and my Partner's family present. I remember how, when I was a kid, I used to draw pictures of the dress I was going to wear and practice the speech I was going to make when my Partner and I made our vows. I don't know whether to be relieved or sad that it's never going to happen now.

Then I notice the ACID agents standing in front of the stage and at various points around the square, their faces hidden behind their visors, pulse guns held ready. A little shiver goes through me as I remember the agent on the roof at Mileway firing at Alex Fisher; the halo of electricity fizzing around Max's dad as he lay facedown on the concrete. I turn away from the square and walk quicker, head down as I push my way along the busy street with Max following me. "What's wrong?" he says as we leave the square behind.

"Nothing," I tell him, swallowing hard against the guilt rising in my throat.

The rain's spitting harder now. I can feel it against my face. Up ahead, I catch sight of the mag terminal. A mag to Zone X is just pulling up, and we jump on it—we can change onto a mag to the medicenter at the Zone X interchange. The only other passengers are an elderly couple at the far end of the pod, which means, for the first time in as long as I can remember, I've got a seat. "Keep your hood pulled up," I mutter to Max as we sit down. He nods, coughing. I settle back and sigh.

As the doors close, I glance out the window.

And see the agent who checked our c-cards outside Anderson Court striding across the terminal toward us.

ACID

AGENCY FOR CRIME INVESTIGATION AND DEFENSE

Transcripts of KommWeb9 links between ACID Control and Agent 563 Devlin

Date of link: 24.05.13
Time of link: 0900 hrs

\<Agent 563 Devlin\> This is Agent 563 Devlin, requesting backup.

\<Control\> Agent Devlin, this is Control. Please clarify.

\<Agent 563 Devlin\> Suspicious c-card flagged during routine stop check at Anderson Court, 35 Treynold Road, Zone M. It's one of the Nicholls cards. There was a scuffle with another member of the public as I was doing the check and the suspect left the scene before I could apprehend him.

\<Control\> Do you have a visual on the suspect?

\<Agent 563 Devlin\> Not at the present moment. Am attempting to follow but am being hampered by large crowds traveling to the ceremony.

\<Control\> Can you describe the suspect?

\<Agent 563 Devlin\> A young male. The name on the card was Michael Adams. He was wearing a blue top with the hood pulled up and was accompanied by a female of a similar age with dark red hair by the name of Mia Richardson. I stopped them for a routine check as they left Anderson Court.

\<Control\> One moment, please. I'll link to kommsat and try to locate the suspect.

\<Control\> We have a link to Mia Richardson's komm; Adams doesn't appear to be wearing one. Suspects are three hundred meters away from you at the Zone M mag terminal. Can you follow on foot? I will request backup ASAP. Be as covert as possible, we don't want to panic the public.

\<Agent 563 Devlin\> Understood.

Date of link: 24.05.13
Time of link: 0910 hrs

<Agent 563 Devlin> This is Agent 563 Devlin calling Control.
<Control> Agent Devlin, this is Control, have you appre-
hended suspects?
<Agent 563 Devlin> Er . . . no.
<Control> Please clarify, Agent Devlin.
<Agent 563 Devlin> Suspects had already boarded the mag by
the time I reached the terminal. Due to the crowds, I could not
reach them before it left, and could not disperse said crowds
without drawing attention to myself. I need another link to
kommsat to locate them.
<Control> One moment, please.
<Control> I have a location. Suspects are on their way to the
transport interchange at Zone X.
<Agent 563 Devlin> Do you want me to follow?
<Control> No, I will alert agents already out there. Please
return to Treynold Road. We have just received a report from a
bystander about one of the residents at Anderson Court. The
bystander is the building's LifePartner Ambassador and the
resident she reported is Mia Richardson, who she says she saw
leaving this morning with a male who is not her LifePartner.
I am sending a team over to search Richardson's apartment
and reassigning you to them.
<Agent 563 Devlin> Understood. On my way.

CHAPTER 14

Max has seen him too. He whips his head round and under his hood I can see his eyes are open wide. "Is he—"

"Shut up," I murmur through clenched teeth. "Act normal."

For a few awful seconds I think the agent's going to reach the mag before it sets off. He's right outside, and as he reaches a gloved hand toward the button for the doors, he looks through the window. Even though I can't see his face behind his visor, I know he's looking straight at us.

Just before he can press the button, the mag begins to move, quickly picking up speed.

"Was he after us?" Max says. His voice is quiet, controlled, but he's jogging his knee up and down rapidly.

"I don't know," I say.

"It was my card," he mutters, glancing at the elderly couple, who are absorbed in conversation and taking no notice of us whatsoever. "He realized it was a fake, didn't he?"

A coughing fit doubles him over. "I don't *know*," I say when he's recovered, panic making me irritable.

"What are we gonna do?" he asks. "We can't go to your friends now. We could lead ACID straight to them."

Shit. I hadn't thought of that, but he's right. I stare around the pod, as if I'm hoping the answer will be on one of the ACID holoposters above the windows or scratched into one of the walls.

"We'll have to get out of London," I say, being careful to keep my voice down. Max leans closer to me so he can hear. "When we reach the interchange, we'll get on a train."

"Where to?" Max says.

"Anywhere," I reply.

He leans his head back against the window behind him, and I see his throat jerk as he swallows.

Twenty minutes later, we're at the interchange. "Wait," I say quietly to Max as we get off the mag and it slides away behind us. "I need to link my friend and let her know we're not going to be at the clinic."

I try to work out how I'm going to hint to Mel about the trouble we're in without giving anything away. The interchange's concourse is almost as busy as the streets around Anderson Court, so I find a quiet spot by the main tram terminal and speak Mel's kommweb ID, waiting for the link to connect. I feel sick. My stomach's tying itself in knots.

Two words flash up on my wraparound: ACCESS DENIED.

The knots in my stomach tighten. I try again.

ACCESS DENIED.

What the hell? I take my komm out of my ear and give it a little shake, trying to convince myself that the network's jammed up because of everyone being out at the ceremonies. But even after I've switched it off and on, I still can't get through. I take it out of my ear again and look around for a PKP. There's a bank of them about seven meters away.

"Mia," Max murmurs, touching my elbow.

"What?"

97

"I think we're being watched," he says quietly. "Don't turn round." He glances to our left. "Over there. Two ACID agents."

Surreptitiously, I follow his gaze, and a thread of ice worms its way down my spine. Because he's right. There are two ACID agents.

They are watching us.

And across from them, to our right, I can see two more, and another pair standing by a mag terminal a little farther away. They catch sight of us watching them and exchange looks with the other agents. Then all six of them start to walk toward us, casually converging on us like lions stalking their prey.

Mrs. Holloway, I think. She got suspicious and linked ACID, and they've realized who Max and I are and blocked my kommweb access so I can't call anyone for help. Maybe they've even found out about Mel and Jon. For a few seconds, I can't move or breathe. A dull roar starts up in my ears as I imagine them grabbing us and cuffing our arms behind our backs and saying, *Jenna Strong, we're arresting you for the murder of Alex Fisher* right in front of Max.

"Mia, we need to get out of here," Max says, jolting me back to my senses.

I look around and, behind us, see the National Departures terminal, a huge building with a curved glass roof shaped like an upturned watermelon slice. "In there," I say. We turn and begin walking very fast toward it, trying to get swallowed up in the crowds of people heading inside. When I glance behind us, the ACID agents are still following, but the sheer number of people in the way has forced them to fall back. As Max and I duck through the massive glass doors into the terminal, we're almost running.

"Did you call your friends?" he asks, breathing hard, as we jog past the information booths and giant holoboards with train times and destinations scrolling across them, and, of course, the news screens.

"I can't," I say. "ACID've blocked my komm." I realize it's still clenched in my fist and I drop it onto the ground, where it's kicked away by the feet of the hurrying commuters around us. "Watch it!" a man cries as I accidentally shoulder-barge him. I babble an apology but he's already way behind us.

"Where are we going?" Max says. "Mia, they're right *there*—"

I reach out and grab his hand, ducking down a passageway signposted ALL TRAINS NORTH. Our feet slap against the tiled floor, our breath tearing from us in ragged gasps. We burst out of the passageway onto a busy platform just in time to see a train pull up, holosigns announcing NEWCASTLE—DIRECT SERVICE. It looks ancient, like something out of the twenty-first century: boxy carriages covered with many layers of scuffed, peeling paint, and thick, grimy glass in the windows.

"Come on," I say as the doors slide open, letting go of Max's hand and ignoring the stares of the other passengers, who, after our dramatic entrance, are staring at us as if we've just arrived from another planet. We jostle our way onto the train and flash our cards at the kredzreader. Mine's accepted, but when Max scans his the reader bleeps and REJECTED blinks up on the screen.

"Oh crap," he says, coughing, his chest still heaving from our mad flight through the terminal. "I don't have enough kredz."

In my head, I do a quick calculation. My train ticket just cost me two hundred kredz. I've got another two hundred and fifty in my account, but if I buy Max a ticket too, what will we buy food with? Where will we stay?

And hang on, if ACID are on to us, why does my card still work? Shouldn't they have frozen it? Or are they allowing it to work so they can track me? *Shit.*

But we need to get out of London. That's more important than anything.

"Come on, will you?" says a sandy-haired man wearing an oversized leather jacket and way too much aftershave, his podgy face creasing in annoyance. "This train's about to leave."

When I turn to look at him, he eyeballs me. Resisting the urge to tell him where to stick it, I flash my card at the kredzreader again to buy Max a ticket and we hurry into the carriage. "I need to sit down," Max croaks, coughing.

"Not yet," I say. I lead him to the vestibule at the other end of the carriage so I have a clear view of the platform. If ACID turn up now, we'll have to jump off the train and make a run for it. It'll mean all that money I just spent on tickets being wasted, but I'd rather that than go back to Mileway.

I'd rather do *anything* than go back to Mileway.

Move, I will the train. *MOVE.*

Then I see an ACID agent walk out of the tunnel we ran down. I draw back into the vestibule, sucking my breath in sharply.

Max stares at me. *How many?* he mouths.

I hold up a finger.

Is he getting on? Max mouths.

I peer round the door with one eye. The agent's still standing on the platform, close to the train. He's taken his helmet off and is speaking to a woman who's about to get on board. Then he turns, looks back up the tunnel.

I draw back, shake my head. Max's shoulders slump forward.

Another minute passes, feeling like a year. Then the doors slide shut and the train jolts into motion.

Max and I sink into seats by the doors, and I wonder how long it'll be before reports appear on the kommweb about us, feeding directly into the komms of all the people on this train.

We're not safe, I think. *We're not safe anywhere. Especially not together.*

So leave him. Go off on your own, a little voice in my head says. It's so persuasive that I feel an almost overwhelming sense of relief as I imagine how I'd do it: us arriving in Newcastle, me telling Max I'm going to use the toilet and, instead, walking out of the train terminal and leaving him behind.

I glance round at him. What am I thinking? He's ill again. And his dad died for me.

Died.

Max is my responsibility now, and I owe it to Alex Fisher to keep his son safe.

NAR

Black lightffiti on a wall next to magtrain track,
Newcastle–London line

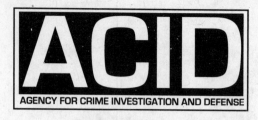

AGENCY FOR CRIME INVESTIGATION AND DEFENSE

Transcripts of KommWeb9 links between ACID Control and Agents 954 Betts and 487 Bryce

Date of link: 24.05.13
Time of link: 1100 hrs

<Control> This is ACID Control calling Agent 954 Betts. Can you confirm your location, please?

<Agent 954 Betts> This is Agent Betts. We are still at Anderson Court.

<Control> What is your situation?

<Agent 954 Betts> We have performed a thorough search of the apartment but did not find any suspicious items. We're waiting for DNA spot-check results on hair samples found in the apartment's bathroom by Agent 563 Devlin to come through before we leave. What is the current situation with the suspects?

<Control> Richardson's c-card was used to purchase two tickets on a train bound for Newcastle. One of the agents following them at the Zone X transport interchange has reported that he was able to board the train, although he has been told to stay out of sight to avoid creating panic. We have a team waiting at Newcastle who will arrest them on arrival.

<Agent 954 Betts> Understood. I'll . . . Wait, the DNA results are coming through.

<Control> Do they match the suspects?

<Control> Agent Betts, can you confirm results, please?

<Control> Agent Betts, do you read me?

<Agent 954 Betts> I'm here, Control. I . . . Holy shit. It's Strong and Fisher.

<Control> Please repeat, Agent. I don't follow you.

<Agent 954 Betts> Richardson and Adams . . . they're Jenna Strong and Max Fisher. Hang on, I'm linking you the results now.

<Control> Good God.

<Agent 954 Betts> They were here. All this time. Under our noses.

<Control> I'll alert Agent Bryce. Please return to base and file your report immediately.

<Agent 954 Betts> Understood.

Date of link: 24.05.13
Time of link: 1103 hrs

<Control> This is ACID Control calling Agent 487 Bryce. Can you confirm that you are on board the Newcastle train, please?

<Agent 487 Bryce> This is Agent 487 Bryce. Yes, I am on board the train.

<Control> We have DNA results for Mia Richardson and Michael Adams. They are Jenna Strong and Max Fisher.

<Agent 487 Bryce> Sorry, Control, could you repeat that, please? It sounded as if you said Richardson and Adams were Jenna Strong and Max Fisher.

<Control> That is correct.

<Agent 487 Bryce> Jesus Christ. What do you want me to do? Should I apprehend them?

<Control> Not there. It's too busy and there are too many other trains they could escape onto. We're going to wait until we're at one of the provincial stations where there's no one around, and stop the train—it'll be harder for them to get away. And in the very unlikely event that they give us the slip then, both their c-cards are flagged, so the minute they try to use them anywhere, we'll have their location.

<Agent 487 Bryce> Understood.

CHAPTER 15

The lightffiti flashes past so quickly that by the time my brain has registered what my eyes have just seen, it's gone. So NAR has made it all the way out here too? Whoever they are, they must be good at evading ACID to have tags all over the place like that. I sit back in my seat, feeling a sudden, unexpected pang of nostalgia. Anderson Court was a dump, but now that I'm leaving it behind, I realize how much my apartment had come to feel like home.

Where will we stay now? And how the *hell* will we stay hidden from ACID?

I glance at Max. We've been on this train for a couple of hours now. After it left the outskirts of London, we managed to find seats in a corner of one of the carriages, and he's asleep with his hood still pulled up to hide his face, his head against the window beside him, his breathing slightly wheezy. I feel a sudden rush of empathy and protectiveness toward him, so strong it threatens to overwhelm me. He's lost everything because of me, and now here I am, leading him into even more uncertainty and danger. *I'm sorry,* I tell him inside my head. *If I can ever make this up to you, I will, I promise.*

Beyond him, through the rain-speckled glass, the landscape whips past: fields edged by hedges and trees, the hills behind them almost lost in low cloud. Everything looks silver and green. The view reminds me of the holidays we had when I was a kid at the luxury countryside villas provided by ACID. I loved them. I could spend all day by myself, roaming around fields and through the woods nearby, and for a few blissful hours, the feeling I always had—that every little thing I did or said was being watched and analyzed by my father—would leave me. In fact, we were supposed to be going on holiday the day after I—

I shut that thought out of my head. Instead, I consider the possibility of living rough in the countryside: camping out, lighting fires, catching rabbits and birds for food. ACID would never think to look for us out here.

But I don't know how to light fires or trap animals, and I doubt Max does either. Country holidays or not, I'm a city girl, and I always will be.

I sigh. At least that ACID agent didn't board the train. Getting rid of my komm should have bought us a bit of time; if we don't use our cards again, we might be able to disappear off ACID's radar completely.

At that moment, we start to slow down. My heart jumps into my throat. Have ACID stopped us? I tense, ready to shake Max awake, wondering how I can force the doors open and just how dangerous it would be to jump from a moving train.

The train's komm system gives a soft *bing!* "Due to a broken-down train ahead of us, this service will be making an unscheduled stop at the next station to allow the track to be cleared," a robotic-sounding female voice says. "IRB RailNet apologize for any inconvenience this may cause and would like to reassure passengers that this incident will be dealt with as quickly as possible. I repeat, due to a broken-down train . . ."

I sag back against the seat. For a moment, I feel relieved; then I think, *But what if it is ACID? What if they've just made that announcement to try to trick us?* and my heartbeat speeds up again.

Roused by the announcement, Max sits up. "What's happening?" he says, his voice blurred with sleep. He reaches up to pull his hood back. I yank his hands away. "Don't!" I whisper fiercely.

Around us, the other passengers are grumbling, but quietly, as if they're afraid the wrong person might hear them. "It's about time ACID opened up their damn wallets and spent some money on these junkheaps," I hear a woman behind us complain to her companion. "But will they? Oh no. They spend all their funds turning London into some sort of show city while the rest of the country goes to hell."

Her companion hisses, "Be *quiet*, Ally. *Please*. You don't know that's even true."

"Really?" Ally says. "Why don't you look out the window, then?"

The landscape around us has changed from rolling countryside to the outskirts of a large town: rows of concrete houses with boxy backyards, then apartment blocks. They're just like the buildings in Outer, except the whole town looks like this.

She's right, you know, I want to lean over the seat and tell Ally's companion. I remember visiting another town like this when I was eleven, accompanying my parents on a business trip because they couldn't get a babysitter. We flew up there in a roto and were taken by electro car to the offices where my father was having his meeting. As we traveled through the streets, I was shocked at how run-down everything was, and at the lines outside all the shops. I didn't know at the time that it was the same in Outer London too—back then, Outer was a place I knew only from rumors and nightmares. When we returned home that night, looking around our luxurious home, I asked Dad why we in Upper had so much and people in that town had so little. Why wasn't the wealth

110

more evenly distributed? "Because we deserve it," Dad told me. "The people who've earned the right to live in Upper work hard to keep this country running. Go and take off your shoes, Jenna, and stop pestering."

Was that when I first started to question things more? When the beginnings of my rebellion against ACID and my parents quietly ignited in my soul?

Five minutes later, the train pulls into a little station with tubs of withered-looking, rain-drenched flowers and flickering holo-signs saying WELCOME TO CLEARFORD STATION along the edges of the platforms. We come to a grinding, squealing halt, and the komm system *bings!* again. "Any passengers wishing to use toilet facilities or buy refreshments may alight at this station," the robot voice says. "There are vending machines at the edge of this plat-form. Please listen carefully for announcements about the train's departure. I repeat . . ."

Several of the passengers stand up and start to move down the carriage to the doors.

"We need to get off too," I mutter to Max when the seats around us have emptied.

"What?" he says.

"We used our c-cards when we got on. If ACID find out we're on this train, they'll be waiting for us in Newcastle."

"Shit, I never thought," he says, coughing.

I nod. "It was the only way we could get tickets, and we were in such a hurry to get on the train . . ." I look up and down the carriage. It's nearly empty now. "Come on."

Outside, it's raining hard, the drops of water bouncing off my head with so much force it hurts, and as we stand on the platform and I look for the exit, I hear a low rumble of thunder overhead.

"There," I say, spotting a set of white-painted wooden gates in front of an underpass to one side of a little waiting room. They're padlocked but unattended; if we wait until no one's looking, we can climb over them.

111

I look around for the attendant. He's making for the waiting room, not paying us any attention in his hurry to get out of the rain. I jerk my head at Max and we cross the platform, heading for the gates.

"Hey!"

I whirl round.

The ACID agent I saw on the platform back at the transport interchange is running toward us.

CHAPTER 16

"Stop right there!" he shouts as he comes toward us, fumbling his gun from his belt. His helmet's strapped to a loop beside it, bouncing against his thigh.

"Run!" I snap at Max, never taking my eyes off the agent. "I can keep him here!"

"No, I'm not leaving you!" he says.

"For God's sake, Max!"

He starts to say something else but starts coughing and can't speak.

The agent reaches us, breathing hard. He points the gun at me, its muzzle only centimeters from my chest. "You're coming with me," he says.

You've done this before, Jenna, remember? I think as the memory of being cornered in my cell at Mileway by Neil Rennick comes back to me. He had a shank made out of a piece of sharpened plastic, which he held up to my throat. He said, "When I'm done with you, I'm going to cut you." But thanks to the moves

I'd learned from Dr. Fisher, Rennick was the one who ended up getting cut.

Only that was a shank. This is a *gun*.

"Why?" I say. I'm stalling, playing for time. If there's even the tiniest hope of this working, I need to catch the agent off guard.

And I need to do it before he tells Max my name.

"I think you know why," the agent says. "Put your hands up. And you," he tells Max. "Take down that hood."

Max slowly reaches up and pushes his hood back. His eyes are wide, his face pale.

The agent smiles and, with his free hand, reaches for one of the sets of cuffs that are hanging from his belt.

Now, I think.

I start to raise my hands, then quickly step sideways so the gun is no longer pointing directly at me. I use my right hand to slap the agent's wrist down and my left to grab the barrel of the gun, twisting the weapon up and out of his grasp. I point it at him. "Don't you *dare,*" I snarl as he reaches up to activate his komm and call for backup, the color draining from his face. "Keep your hands down by your sides and don't speak."

He lets his arms drop. I glance around to see if any of the other passengers are watching us, but we're out of sight of the waiting room and there doesn't seem to be anyone left on the train. Of course, there are probably spotters everywhere, but right now, that's the least of my worries.

The agent's face is chalk white. For the first time, I notice how young he is—only a few years older than me and Max. I guess when he was shaving the fluff off his chin back in London this morning, he wasn't expecting his day to turn out like this.

Max looks pretty shocked too. "Mia . . . ," he says.

"Go," I tell him, jerking my head toward the gates. "*Go.* I'll be there in a second."

He takes a step back, then stops. "Wait," he says. He pulls

the agent's komm out of his ear, dropping it on the ground and grinding it into pieces under his heel. Then he nods at me, turns and runs for the gates, vaulting them and landing with a thump on the other side.

"You're gonna stay right here," I tell the agent. The rain's streaming down my face, plastering my hair against my head. Above us, there's a flash of lightning and, immediately, a ground-shaking clap of thunder. The storm's right overhead. "If you move, I'll shoot you, get it?"

He nods, swallowing.

I start to walk backward toward the gates, keeping the gun trained on him the whole time. He stands there with his jaw clenched, staring at me. I reach the gates and climb over them, still pointing the gun at the agent. I glance behind me. Max is waiting in the shadows. I take another step back, jamming the gun into the waistband of my jeans without even thinking about it, and hiss at Max, *"Run!"*

We sprint through the underpass, emerging onto a narrow street. To my relief, it's deserted; the storm's keeping everyone inside.

Clearford's streets aren't laid out in a grid like Outer London's. They're a sprawling maze, crowded in by jumbled buildings that might be apartments or warehouses or something else entirely. As we race along them, I see battered-looking news screens looming down at us, plastered with warnings from ACID about Clearford's twenty-hundred-hours curfew and what will happen to you if you're caught not carrying your c-card. Soon, I hear the thin wail of an ACID siren heading in the direction we've just come from.

"Mia," Max gasps. "I need to stop. I can't breathe!"

He stops, bent double with his hands on his knees, his body jerking with hacking coughs. *Damn.*

"Down here," I say, pulling him down a narrow paved alleyway on our left. He slumps onto a step next to some bins, his chest heaving as he tries to catch his breath. His face is pale, two hectic spots of color high up on his cheeks, and for a moment I'm worried he's going to pass out on me or puke.

"Are you OK?" I say.

He nods. Finally, he manages to stop coughing. While he rests, I keep my gaze trained on the entrance to the alleyway, watching for ACID. *God, we're in a real mess now,* I think, blinking rainwater out of my eyes. *Why did you get me out of Mileway, Alex? WHY?*

If I ever see them again, I'm going to make Mel and Jon tell me everything.

Then I feel something digging into my side, and I remember the gun. I take it out. It's heavy and cold, its silver casing gleaming dully. The charge light on top of the barrel is green, indicating it's ready to fire. Just looking at it sends a cold, sick feeling through me. When I glance at Max, he's staring at it too.

"Who taught you those moves?" he asks me hoarsely. He's coughed so much he's almost lost his voice. "I mean, to get the gun off him like that?"

I swallow. *Your dad,* I think. But of course, there's no way I can tell him that. "It was those friends I was going to take you to," I lie.

"Huh," he says. "It was really something."

"Um, thanks." I give him a quick smile, which he returns, and I feel a flash of warmth go through me.

Then Max's expression becomes serious. "What are you going to do with it?"

I look at the gun again. "Get rid of it," I say as the warmth inside me turns to a chill. "I don't want it."

"But what if we run into ACID?" Max asks. He coughs. "We might need it."

"I don't want it," I repeat. It's identical to the one I shot my parents with. *Identical.*

116

"Give it to me," Max says. "I'll look after it."

I switch it off, hand it over to him, and he stands up and shoves it into his waistband, pulling the oversized blue hoodie down to hide it. I wonder if his dad ever showed him how to use one. I wouldn't be surprised.

We go back out onto the street. It's still raining, there's still no one about, and because of Max's cough we walk instead of run, keeping a lookout for ACID patrols the whole time. We're in some sort of commercial district, flickering holosigns above the buildings advertising services and goods. We can't stay in Clearford long—it'll be crawling with ACID agents looking for us—but I wonder if there's an empty warehouse or depot where we can take cover until nightfall so we've got more chance of getting out of the town without being seen.

Then, glancing back up at the sky to check for rotos or spotters, I see something that turns my blood to liquid nitrogen.

My face—my *new* face—staring down at me from a gigantic news screen, next to a picture of Max. DNA EVIDENCE REVEALS STRONG AND FISHER WERE LIVING IN OUTER LONDON FLAT, the headline screams, above the line: *Fugitives now on run, reports coming in that ACID agent has been attacked with own gun by Strong at provincial railway station.*

I have to read it twice before it makes sense. *The one thing we cannot change about you is your DNA,* I remember Steve telling me back at the labs just after I was broken out of Mileway. I hear a rushing sound inside my head, and realize I've stopped walking. So has Max. He's frowning at me.

In a few seconds, he'll look up and see the news screen too and my cover will be totally blown.

"Shit!" I say, ducking my head.

"What?" Max croaks.

"A spotter! It was right on us! Come *on!*"

I break into a jog again. Max swears and runs after me. "Where?" he says. "I didn't see—"

"Shut up and move!" I tell him.

We keep running until we reach a street without any news screens. By then, Max is coughing his lungs up again. Even I'm starting to feel tired. I'm starving and thirsty too. I wonder where we are—near the center of Clearford or its edge? The buildings in front of us are identical: gray concrete with rows of small, grimy windows. There's nothing I can use to get my bearings.

Max leans forward with his hands on his knees. I'm convinced his coughing fit's never going to end, but at last it eases. He straightens up. Then he looks behind us and says, "Huh. Creepy."

I turn and see a street that looks as if it was abandoned years ago. There's sodden rubbish strewn across the pavements, and all the holosigns have been vandalized. Halfway down the street is a large building, sticking out from the flat-fronted buildings on either side of it in a kind of hexagon shape, four stories high, with most of its long windows boarded up. Old-fashioned spray-painted graffiti is looped and scrawled across the brickwork and wood, so many layers it's impossible to make most of it out, although I can see a couple of NAR tags, their paint looking a little fresher than the rest. A flight of crumbling steps leads up to the entrance, which is set back under a triangular canopy of thin metal girders that look like they once had glass in between them. Above it, the remains of a sign—a printed one, not a holo—clings to the brickwork: WELC ME TO CLEA ORD UBLI IB RY.

"What does that say?" Max asks.

"Welcome to Clearford . . . something something?" I say. "No idea."

Then I hear it, coming from somewhere to our right. The deep bass thud of a roto. Max hears it too; his head jerks up.

"In there," I say, pointing up the steps at the entrance to the abandoned whatever-it-used-to-be. We run up the steps and,

118

as the roto draws closer, start tugging frantically at the boards across the doors, trying to find a gap or a loose edge. There's nothing. I get a jagged splinter in my palm, which I yank out with a hiss, pressing my hand to my mouth to stop the bleeding.

"Mia!"

I turn. Max is over by one of the windows. "This one's loose," he says. He pulls up the board to show me; beyond it is an empty black square. "And there's no glass on the other side." He pulls it up farther until there's a gap big enough for me to squeeze through. With the sound of the roto throbbing in my ears, I clamber through and drop as quietly as I can onto the floor. Max follows, the board thudding back into place behind him, and we crouch side by side, listening to the roto fly overhead.

When it's gone, we stand up, brushing dust off our hands and knees. It's dark, but not as dark as I thought it would be; light steals through gaps and knotholes in the boards across the windows, bathing everything in a dull, grayish twilight. We're in a long, low-ceilinged foyer. Ahead of us are two wide counters, backed by rows of empty shelves. On the counters themselves are big, flat, upright objects that, when I look closer, I realize are solid-state computer screens, the sort people used to use before holocoms came along, with little scanners in holders beside them. There's a strong smell of damp and everything is centimeters deep in dust, making my nose tickle. I have to pinch my nostrils to make the itch in them disappear.

Max sniffs, rubbing his nose too. I nudge him to make him shut up, then listen. I hear nothing. Whatever this place was, it's been empty for a very long time.

We pass the counters and walk to the end of the foyer. It turns a sharp corner, then opens out into a wider space, also lit by chinks of daylight. The room is full of shelves, fixed to the walls or shorter, free-standing ones in the center, filled with what, in the gloom, looks like hundreds of small, flat boxes standing on their ends. I step closer to look. Maybe this place used to be a shop?

I take one of the boxes from the nearest shelf, brushing away dust and cobwebs, and realize it isn't a box at all. It's a book—a real book, made of board and paper and glue, like the ones my father used to have locked away in a glass cabinet in his study, which were far too old and valuable even to touch, never mind read. This book isn't anywhere near as old as the ones in my father's study were, but it's definitely seen better days. I take it over to one of the windows where there's some light coming through. The cover is so damaged by damp I can't read the title, or who the author was, and the pages are brittle and yellow, spotted at the edges with mold. I thumb through them, wrinkling my nose at their musty odor, then turn back to the first page. There's a label with dates from over a hundred years ago stamped one under the other in crooked columns. The lines THANK YOU FOR USING CLEARFORD PUBLIC LIBRARY. BOOKS RETURNED AFTER THE DUE DATE WILL BE CHARGED AT THE CURRENT OVERDUE RATE are printed at the bottom.

"What's a public library?" asks Max, reading it over my shoulder. He presses the inside of his elbow against his face to muffle a cough. I shrug and slide the book back onto the shelf, wiping my hands on my jacket.

We walk farther into the library. The shelves of books seem to go on forever, stretching away into dark corners. We come to a flight of wide, shallow stairs, curving round and up. I look at Max. He looks at me and shrugs, and we go up them.

The boards across the windows on the first floor are more solid, so it's darker than the ground floor, and more shelves loom around us; I keep having to put out my hands so I don't collide with anything. There doesn't seem to be as much dust up here, for some reason, although the smell of damp paper is just as strong.

Max clutches my arm. At first I think he's tripped and

grabbed me to stop himself falling over. I start to ask him if he's OK.

"Shh!" he hisses.

I turn to look at him. His eyes are wide, the whites shining in the gloom.

What? I mouth.

He points. I look, and at first I can't see anything.

Then I do.

A pale glow, coming from between the shelves over to our right, that flickers and jumps and moves.

CHAPTER 17

As we tiptoe closer, I see that the shelves have been pulled round to form a rough rectangle. From within them, I hear a murmured voice, a soft laugh. Max and I stare at each other. Who's here? And what are they doing here?

Max steps forward again. I put a hand on his arm, shaking my head. I see him swallow. *Please don't start coughing,* I think as I tiptoe to the edge of the bookshelf walls and peer round them.

In the center of the rectangle, two girls are sitting back to back on a heap of blankets and cushions. They've both got books open on their laps, with more piled around them, and on the shelves are several glolamps—the source of the flickering light.

The girls, one petite and sharp-boned with short, dark hair, the other plumper with reddish hair falling in thick waves past her shoulders, don't look much older than fourteen or fifteen, and there's an easy intimacy to the way they're leaning against one another, the dark-haired girl with her head on the other's

122

shoulder, twirling a strand of her hair lazily around one finger, that makes me think they're more than just friends.

I remember a conversation I had with Dylan once, about how his father, a prominent ACID agent who worked for my father, had arrested two men who'd been having a relationship with each other behind their LifePartners' backs. "Can you imagine it?" Dylan said to me. We were sitting on his sofa after school, and his parents were still at work. "Being a girl who gets Partnered to a guy when you don't even find guys attractive, or a guy Partnered to a girl? It must be awful."

I frowned. Up until then, I'd never given it any consideration; I'd just accepted it was wrong, like everyone else seemed to. As the warnings on the news screens and news sites said, *It is illegal for any person of any age, LifePartnered or otherwise, to engage in any sort of Partnership with a member of the same sex. Any person found guilty of this offense will be imprisoned immediately without trial.*

But Dylan's question made me think. I started to wonder just exactly what *was* so wrong about it. Why *couldn't* people choose who they were Partnered with, whether it was someone of the opposite sex or the same? Who would it hurt, exactly?

I sense movement beside me. Max. He looks shocked. I give him a frown, shake my head. I'm afraid even to breathe in case the girls realize we're here. I take a step back.

And collide with a bookshelf, the corner catching me in the small of my back. Without thinking, I swear loudly.

The girls jump up, dropping their books, the one with the dark hair letting out a little scream. "Who—who was that?" the red-haired girl says. "Paul?"

Crap. My heart thudding, I step into the rectangle of shelves, Max behind me.

The girls clutch at each other. "Who are you?" the red-haired one says.

"It's OK," I say, holding my hands up, palms out. "We're not going to hurt you. We thought the place was empty."

The girls stare at us. I can see they're wondering whether to believe me.

"I'm Sarah," I say. "And this is, um, Declan."

The girls exchange glances. "I'm Neela," the dark-haired one says. "And this is—"

"Don't!" the red-haired girl hisses at her.

"What?" Neela asks her.

"How did you get in here?" the red-headed girl demands.

"We—climbed in the window downstairs," Max says.

"Why?" Her eyes are narrowed; suspicion is coming off her in waves.

"It's OK," I say again. "We'll go somewhere else. I'm sorry for disturbing you." I take a step back, taking care to avoid the bookcase this time, cursing myself for being so clumsy before. What if ACID come here? Will these girls tell them they saw us?

Overhead, the roto does another flyover, low enough to make the whole building shake. And over the roar of the rain, I hear more sirens, frighteningly close.

"Shit!" Neela says. "Is that ACID?" She goes over to the nearest window and peers through a knothole.

The red-haired girl looks at me and Max again. "Are they after you?" she says.

I glance at Max. The girl frowns, pressing her lips together, and I become aware of how shabby we are, our clothes soaking wet and smeared with grime from climbing in through the window. We might as well have a big flashing holosign saying FUGITIVES over our heads.

"You'd better come with us, then." She crouches down and shakes all but one of the glolamps to extinguish them, plunging us back into gloom. "I'm Shaan, by the way."

Max coughs. I look at him again and see, in the half-light, that he's looking back at me. I'm almost certain we're thinking the same thing: *Who are these people? Why are they here? Can we trust them?* But what choice do we have? We can't go back outside—not with ACID hunting for us.

"What is this place?" Max asks in the hoarse half-whisper his voice has been reduced to as, holding the remaining lamp, Shaan leads us and Neela through the maze of shelves, the lamp's glow bouncing off the rows of books. "It said in one of those books it was a public library or something."

"Yeah," Neela says, and laughs at his puzzled expression. "I'd never heard of one either. Apparently people used to borrow these books"—she sweeps her arm out, indicating the shelves—"and then they'd bring them back and swap them for new ones. For nothing."

"But you can get books now," Max says. "On your komm. OK, you have to pay, but—"

Shaan snorts. "Yeah, if you can call eFics books. Crap that's been censored to within an inch of its life, just in case there's something in it that might make people realize that LifePartnering and ACID aren't the best things that ever happened to them."

The venom in her voice takes me aback. Outside of Mileway, I don't think I've ever heard anyone talk about ACID with such open dislike before. What would she say if she knew who I was? Would it make me her enemy or her hero? A shudder wrenches its way up my spine.

"Jacob says this was the last public library in the country," Neela says. "They used to be everywhere, apparently, but ACID shut them all down because it was easier for them to control what people were reading if the only place you could get books was on the kommweb. He says this place was meant to be knocked down ages ago, only the town buildings bureau ran out of money, so it got left behind."

Who's Jacob? I think as we reach a narrow, windowless stairwell and begin to climb it.

"Most of us live down in the old children's library, but Jacob's got one of the offices upstairs," Neela continues over her shoulder, the glolamp casting strange, leaping shadows on the walls and ceiling. "He likes a bit of privacy. He'll help you with anything you ask for, though. He'll help anyone. That's what he does."

Max and I exchange glances but say nothing.

Shaan and Neela take us to a room at the far end of the top floor. Through a window in the door, I can see lights burning— more glolamps.

Shaan knocks, rapping her knuckles against the wood. There's no answer. I can hear my pulse thumping in my ears, not because I'm scared, but because this is all so strange. I keep thinking that at any moment, I'm going to wake up and find myself back in my flat in Outer, with Cade slobbing out on the sofa, old pairs of socks and underpants balled up in random corners of the living room, and the milk left out on the kitchen worktop to go sour with dirty dishes heaped up beside it.

Then, from the other side of the door, a male voice calls, "Come in!"

CHAPTER 18

Shaan twists the handle, pushing the door inward, then steps back and motions for me and Max to go through. She and Neela stay outside.

We're in a small square room lit by glolamps hung from metal brackets. They turn it into a flickering cave. It's colder in here than the rest of the library; cobwebs of mildew spread across the ceiling. Pushed against the far wall is a metal-framed camp bed heaped with pillows, and beside that, on the floor, some grubby blankets. Piles of books line the corners of the room, most of them battered-looking and coverless. On a small wooden table nearby are more books, paper, mugs and a metal dish full of what, after squinting at them for a moment, I realize are cigarette ends. But it's the walls I'm staring at: they're covered in pictures—jagged cityscapes and screaming faces, blending into one continuous mural. At first, I think they've been stuck up there by someone. Then I realize they've been drawn straight onto the paintwork in thick black and red pen.

"Well," a voice says. "Who do we have here?"

I jump. Standing behind us in the rectangle of light cast by the open door is a man I guess to be in his late twenties. As soon as I notice him, the rest of the room suddenly feels very small indeed. He's nearly two meters tall, broad-chested, with a square jaw and shoulder-length, wavy, dark-blond hair. The sleeves of his striped shirt are rolled back to show muscular forearms, which are criss-crossed with marks and scars, and when he moves I catch a glimpse of a tattoo on his left bicep, a red circle with something black inside it.

Shaan sticks her head round the door. "Jacob, this is Sarah and . . ." She glances at Max and frowns.

"Declan," Max says quickly.

"Have you got komms?" Jacob says.

"No," I say.

Jacob narrows his eyes. "Show me."

I lift my hair to show him my ear. So does Max.

"What about your pockets?"

"We don't have komms, OK?" I say, keeping my gaze steady.

He looks us up and down. "Why are you here?" he asks.

I sigh. "We needed somewhere to hide from ACID, that's all. If we'd known there were people already here, we'd have found somewhere else."

"Hiding from ACID? Why?"

I look at Max. He looks back at me, wearing an expression like that of a trapped animal. *Think of something,* his gaze pleads with me.

"We're . . . not LifePartners," I say. Heat steals up my neck and into my face as I realize what I've just implied about us.

Jacob nods slowly. "I see. Shaan!"

She steps into the room.

"Search her. I'll do the boy."

Shaan nods and walks over to me. "Put your arms up," she orders.

I look over at Max. He's frowning.

"What the hell?" I say.

"You can't go back outside," Jacob says. "The town's crawling with ACID agents—they'll pick you up straight away. But if you're going to stay, I need to make absolutely sure you don't have any komms on you—or anything else."

I remember the gun. *Crap.*

"Put your arms up," Shaan repeats. I think about how easy it would be to fold her in two with a punch to the gut or by kicking her legs out from under her. Jacob would be more of a fight, but . . .

No. I can't, no matter how badly I want to, because Max and I really *do* need somewhere to hide out. Like Jacob says, going back out there is not an option right now. If I fight him and Shaan, I might as well be signing our arrest warrants.

I sigh, very quietly, and lift my arms up. First, they find our c-cards; Shaan hands them both to Jacob without looking at them, but Jacob studies them carefully. *Now he knows we're not Sarah and Declan,* I think. *To him, we're Mia and Michael.* Then he finds the gun. "What are you doing with this?" he asks Max, holding it up.

"Sarah took it off an ACID agent," Max says.

Jacob gives an incredulous little laugh. "What?"

"It's true," I say. "He cornered us. He would have shot us if I hadn't got it off him."

Jacob shakes his head slowly, looking down at the gun. "And there I was, thinking you were just a couple of runaway lovebirds."

I've had enough of this. "Look, as soon as it gets dark, we'll leave, OK? You won't even know we've been here."

Jacob doesn't say anything, just turns and reaches under the camp bed, pulling out a large metal strongbox. He lifts a silver chain from around his neck. Dangling from it is a small key, which he uses to unlock the box. He puts the gun and our c-cards inside, then locks the box and nods at Shaan. "Take Declan and *Sarah* downstairs," he tells them, putting another slight emphasis on my fake name.

My *fake* fake name.

"What about our stuff?" I say, turning back to look at the strongbox, which he's still holding.

"I'll let you have everything back when you leave," Jacob tells me, sliding the box back under the bed and putting the chain around his neck again.

"What?" I say. "No way! You can't just—"

Then I hear footsteps running along the corridor outside. A boy bursts into the room, his eyes wide.

"An ACID van's just pulled up at the end of the road!" he gasps.

CHAPTER 19

Jacob reaches under the bed and grabs the box, which he hands to Shaan. "Basement," he says. Then he heaves the bed onto its side and starts to kick over the piles of books. In less than thirty seconds the room looks like nothing more than a junk store where someone might have squatted once, many years before.

Neela and Shaan hustle us down to the ground floor, then down again. I get a brief glimpse of a wide, low-ceilinged room where the bookshelves have been pulled into squares to make little dens, with blankets and sheets draped over them for privacy, glolamps flickering inside. "ACID!" Shaan calls. The glolamps start to go out. I hear people stirring, muttering; the sound of the sheets being torn down and a thudding that I realize is the bookshelves being tilted and laid flat on the floor.

"This way," Neela tells me. She sounds frightened. She leads us to another door and thrusts her glolamp into my hands. "When you get down there, go right to the back and climb the shelves. Lie on top of them as flat as you can. And put the light out!"

131

Other people are coming up behind us. I shove the door open, making the hinges squeal loudly, and an almost overwhelming smell of damp and mold hits me in the face. I'm at the top of a flight of stairs. When I reach the bottom, in the pale light thrown out by my glolamp, I can just make out rows of shelves that reach almost to the ceiling, stretching away on either side of me. They're unevenly spaced, and they have spoked wheels on their sides. We thread through yet more piles of paper and books that have spilled from them—or perhaps been pulled, to make it harder for anyone to get through here— and head for the back of the room.

Max climbs the shelves first. I hand the glolamp up and scramble after him. The top is easily wide enough for us both to lie facedown and side by side. I can hear the clang of feet against metal as other people climb the shelves around us. Max shakes the glolamp to extinguish it. Then he starts coughing again.

"Shut up!" someone hisses.

Somehow, Max gets his coughing fit under control. The basement goes quiet. All I can hear is the blood roaring in my ears. I wonder how many other people are down here. And why *are* they here? What *is* this place? I curse myself for not finding somewhere else, somewhere empty where we could have hidden out by ourselves before trying to slip out of Clearford unnoticed.

"Are ACID really—" someone starts to whisper to my left.

Then, overhead, we hear a thud.

And footsteps, moving slowly across the floor.

"Everyone *shut up*," says another voice, unmistakably Jacob's. Even though he's whispering too, it carries right across the room. "Don't even *breathe*."

I inhale and exhale as quietly as I possibly can through my nose. I'm aware of the heat of Max's body pressed against mine. We're shoulder to shoulder, thigh to thigh, ankle to ankle. He smells like dust and rain.

At the top of the stairs, the door to the basement squeals open.

Two pairs of feet walk slowly down them, their tread heavy and deliberate.

"Look at this place," says a man's voice, filled with disgust. "If they're in here, we'll never find them."

Please don't say my name, I think, closing my eyes. *PLEASE.*

I hear a click, and when I open my eyes, I see the blaze of two flashlight beams at the other end of the room. The agents walk slowly across the basement. The flashlights are fixed to their gun sights. As they direct them between the shelves, I'm convinced that at any moment, they'll point them up and see a foot, a hand, a pair of eyes shining in the dark. . . .

Beside me, Max has started to shiver. I concentrate on my slow and silent breathing, praying that he won't start coughing; praying for this to be over.

There's a crash, heart-stoppingly close, as one of the agents collides with something and knocks it over. "Ouch!" she cries. "For God's sake, it's a death trap down here."

They're right below us. Her colleague points his gun upward; my heart lurches as the flashlight beam glances off a tangle of pipes and ventilation shafts on the ceiling just centimeters from the shelves Max and I are lying on.

Then he points it back at the floor. "There's nothing down here except junk," he says, sounding as grumpy as the first agent. "Why would they stick around here, anyway? They know it's the first place we'd look. I bet they're miles away from Clearford by now."

They leave, tramping back up the stairs, and I hear the door squeal again as they go through.

CHAPTER 20

"Wait," Jacob whispers. "Nobody move."

I can still hear footsteps over our heads. Max is shivering harder than ever, his teeth chattering together. "Are you OK?" I murmur in his ear, but he doesn't respond. It must be a reaction to ACID's raid and everything else we've been through today.

The footsteps upstairs fade away. We wait another ten minutes; then Jacob says, "I'll see if the coast's clear."

I hear him climb down off the shelves somewhere in front of us, and the door scrape open as he leaves.

A few moments later, he's back. "They're gone," he says. "It's safe."

I scramble to my knees, wincing at the stiffness in my arms and legs from lying still for so long, and climb down from the bookshelf, reaching up to give Max a hand down. As soon as his feet hit the floor, he starts coughing again. The skin on the back of my hands is prickling at our near escape.

Glolamps flicker into life as Max and I follow the others out of the basement. "Are you sure you're OK?" I murmur, noticing that he's still shivering. He nods. Then, just as we're about to go up the stairs after everyone else, he grabs my arm, stopping me. "Are we pretending we're a couple, then?" he whispers, barely loud enough for me to hear.

"Yes," I whisper back. "We'd better, if Jacob thinks we are. Sorry. I couldn't think of what else to say."

"It's fine," he answers.

Back on the floor above, everyone, including Jacob, sets about righting the bookshelves, picking up sheets and putting the dens back together. I stand with Max, watching and trying to ignore the suspicious looks people are shooting at us. I'm startled at how young most of them are. There's a boy and a girl who are about my age, but the rest, three boys and another girl, can only be fourteen or fifteen at the most, including the boy who ran into Jacob's room to warn him ACID were here.

It doesn't take long to make the dens. When they're done, Jacob claps his hands.

"As you might have guessed," he says, "ACID were here looking for our new arrivals, Sarah and Declan."

Several of the suspicious looks become openly hostile. *Thanks a lot,* I think. I scowl, stick my chin out and square my shoulders, shaking my still-damp hair out of my face. Max shuffles his feet.

"I've agreed that they can stay here until tonight, which is when they want to leave," Jacob continues. "That offer still stands. It's not the first raid we've had and it won't be the last, and if ACID weren't looking for Sarah and Declan, they'd have come here for something else."

He looks over at me and, to my surprise, he smiles. I don't smile back. I'm thinking of the gun in the box under Shaan's arm. Don't ask me why, but I have a feeling getting it back isn't going to be as easy as just asking for it.

Jacob takes the box from Shaan and goes back upstairs.

I remember that Max and I are supposed to be a couple.

Feeling horribly self-conscious, I reach for his hand. His fingers twitch in surprise, but then he realizes what I'm doing and threads them through mine. He gives my hand a little squeeze, as if to say, *We'll be OK,* and I find myself squeezing his fingers back. I'm glad he's here with me.

The girl who's the same age as me steps forward. She's pretty, almost doll-like, with feathered blond hair and blue eyes and porcelain skin, wearing a loose dress sewn from a patchwork of fabric scraps and a flowery scarf tied round her slender waist as a belt. "I'm Elyn," she says, then indicates the boy behind her. "This is Rory."

Rory nods at us.

"And this is Jack, Lukas, Paul and Amy," she continues, pointing at the younger teenagers.

"I'd better get back upstairs," Jack says. "I've still got half an hour of watch duty left. Then it's your turn, yeah?" he adds, looking at Rory. Rory nods.

Max starts coughing again. It sounds much worse than before: a harsh barking sound from deep inside his chest. He lets go of my fingers and plasters both hands across his mouth, his shoulders shuddering. "You're not all right, are you?" I say.

He shakes his head.

"What's up?"

"I can't get warm," he says.

I touch the back of my hand to his cheek and feel a sinking sensation in my stomach. He's fever-hot. Crap. Maybe he *hasn't* just got a cold. And if it is something more serious, getting soaked and running away from ACID won't have helped at all.

"We've got some medpatches. D'you want one?" Elyn asks him.

Max nods. She ducks into one of the dens and reemerges with a blister pack, which she hands to him. Max takes one of the medpatches out and sticks it on his neck, just under his jaw.

"I can get you some blankets if you're cold," Elyn adds as

some of the others start to drift back to their bookshelf-dens. "We've got a few spare."

Max nods again. "If I can sleep for a couple of hours, I'll probably feel better," he says.

Elyn leaves the room, returning a few minutes later with an armful of blankets. We take them to an empty corner of the room and I help Max spread two of them out on the floor. It's less dusty down here than in the rest of the library; I wonder why they haven't cleaned anywhere else, then realize it's probably deliberate, to make it look uninhabited.

Max stretches out on the blankets, and I crouch down beside him to wrap the other blanket around him. "I'm sorry," he croaks.

"Don't worry about it. You can't help being ill," I say. His hair is hanging in his eyes. Without thinking I reach out to brush it to one side, then realize what I'm about to do and pull my hand back.

"I'm sure I'll be all right in a bit," he croaks. His eyes are too bright, shining with fever.

"Don't talk, sleep," I say gently. "D'you want some water?"

He closes his eyes again and nods gratefully. I get up and go to find Elyn.

CHAPTER 21

For hours, I sit cross-legged next to Max, watching him drift in and out of sleep. Despite the medpatch and the blankets, whenever he wakes up he complains that he's cold, and his face is damp with sweat, even though I keep wiping it with my sleeve. Elyn comes over a few times to see if we're OK. "D'you think you'll still be leaving tonight?" she asks after bringing us another bottle of water and some more medpatches.

I look at Max, who's dozing again. "I'm not sure."

She frowns sympathetically. "Well, if you need anything, let me know."

"Thanks," I say, giving her a small smile.

The rest of the afternoon passes slowly. I watch as, across the room, the others duck in and out of their dens. Where are they from? And what do they do here? Do they just sit in here all day, hiding from ACID?

Come on, I plead with Max silently. *Get better. I don't want to stay here.* Elyn seems nice enough, but the instincts I developed in prison are in overdrive, whispering warnings in my ear. I've no interest in actually working out what they're trying to tell me. I want to get out of here *before* I find out what's not right.

I lean forward, burying my head in my hands, wondering what the hell we're going to do. Then I hear feet scuffing against the carpet. I look up and see Jacob, gazing down at Max with a grave expression on his face.

"He's going to need to stay put for a few days," he says.

I scowl. "We need to leave tonight."

"If you do, he'll end up with pneumonia."

I don't answer him, just gaze at Max's flushed face, listening to his noisy breathing. Does it sound worse than it did earlier or better?

"Where are you going to go, anyway?" Jacob asks.

"I've got some friends who can help us," I say. I'm not about to tell him that those friends are back in London and that I have no way of contacting them, so actually, they're not going to be any help at all.

"We're about to have a meal. Will you join us?" he says.

I look up at him in surprise.

"You'd be most welcome," he adds, then turns and leaves us.

At first, I stay put, determined that I'm not going to take anything from these people, that I won't owe them anything. But then the smell of food starts to drift across the room, making my stomach growl, and I remember that the last time I ate anything was this morning, back at the flat.

"Sarah!" I hear Elyn call.

I rub a hand across my face. My stomach growls again. It feels as if it's trying to turn itself inside out.

"Sarah?" Elyn says.

I sigh, and get to my feet.

The others are sitting in a rough circle on the carpet in the middle of the dens. Elyn's spooning something that looks like noodles and smells like chicken into bowls from a big pot. She smiles and moves over so I can sit down next to her.

For a little while, the only sound is the clinking of spoons against china. The noodles and vegetables are rehydrated, the meat sub, but I'm so hungry I could eat the carpet. "We'll make some more for Declan when he wakes up," Elyn tells me as I eat and wonder how the group manage to get all this food. Do they steal it? Does Jacob have money from somewhere to buy it? I want to ask, but it seems rude, so I don't.

"So," Jacob says, when everyone's finished. "You never told us why you were on the run from ACID, Sarah. Must have been something fairly serious for them to come after you like that."

Is it me, or is he trying not to smile?

I glance over my shoulder, in Max's direction. "I *did* tell you," I say. "We're not LifePartners. ACID found out and came after us."

"Of course you did. My apologies." Jacob puts his bowl down on the floor.

I decide to challenge him back. "So what about you? What are you doing here?"

"Oh." Jacob stretches, lacing his hands together and cracking his knuckles. "The same as you, I suppose. Keeping out of the way of ACID." He gets up. "There's something I need to do," he tells the others. "I'll see you all later, OK?"

He leaves the room. An uncomfortable silence falls, and I see Elyn and Shaan exchange glances, giving me the feeling I've asked something I wasn't supposed to.

"We were the same as you," Elyn says, gathering up the empty bowls. "Me and Rory, I mean. We met each other last September, a few months before our LifePartnering ceremonies. I knew Rory was the one I really wanted to be with—I didn't get on with the guy my parents and ACID had chosen for me—so we ran away."

Memories of Dylan flicker through my head. I push them

away irritably. The guy ruined my life. Why can't I just forget him?

"Our dad got sent to prison," Amy says, indicating herself and Jack, and for the first time I notice how alike they look. So alike that I'm almost certain they're twins. "Our mum was re-Partnered and the new guy was awful; he wanted to split us up and send us away to this military camp run by ACID. 'So you don't turn out like your father,' he said."

"Really, I think he just wanted us out of the way," Jack adds.

Paul and Lukas tell me that they're runaways too, both from unhappy, violent families. And Neela and Shaan, as I suspected, ran away together because their feelings for each other were simply too powerful for them to ignore. Not for the first time, I wonder why I didn't just run away. Why I let Dylan talk me into taking the gun and threatening my father with it. Surely, if we'd tried, we could have found another way to get me out of there? And yet I felt so strongly about him back then that I went along with his crazy plan without even questioning it. Sometimes, I hardly recognize the girl I used to be before I went to Mileway.

"So how did you all end up here?" I ask, frowning. It seems a bit of a coincidence that they all just found this place some-how.

"I met Jacob in Manchester when I was squatting in an abandoned apartment block," Paul says. "He was recr— Ow! What was that for?" He glares at Elyn, who's given him a sudden, sharp nudge with her elbow.

"We're from all over," Elyn says smoothly. "Jacob travels around a lot, and we all happened to cross paths with him one way or another."

"So he offered you somewhere safe to stay in return for nothing?" I say. "That's very . . ."

"Very what?" Elyn narrows her eyes.

Selfless, I want to say. *Weird.* But I don't. With that suspicious look on her face, she isn't so sweet or pretty anymore; it's like there's something dark shifting under the surface. "Nothing," I say. "Don't worry about it."

The conversation seems to dry up after that, so I go and check on Max. To my relief, his breathing sounds a little easier, although he still feels hot.

"Do you want to make a den?" a voice says behind me. I jump and turn to see Elyn standing there. She's come up behind me almost silently. "It'll be more private for you."

"Um, OK," I say.

"There are some spare bookshelves over there," she says, pointing to the other end of the room. "I'll get Rory to come and help you move them. They're heavy."

"I'll be all right," I say. I cross the room to where the spare shelves are. One still has a dusty, damp-speckled poster pinned to the side of it, announcing STORYTIME EVERY FRIDAY AFTER-NOON 2–3:30 P.M., with a picture of a smiling teddy bear. God, this place *must* be old if they were still using the twelve-hour clock. I drag the shelves across to where Max is lying, then go back for another set. When I've pulled the third shelf across, Elyn has returned with an armful of sheets and blankets. "Wow," she says. "I can't move those by myself."

I shrug, arranging the shelves in a three-sided square, and she helps me drape the sheets over the tops of them and spread the blankets on the floor inside. "I got you these too," she says, handing me a couple of glolamps. I shake them to light them, placing them on the shelves. Then I gently shake Max awake and help him inside.

"If you need a toilet, there's one through there," she says, pointing to a door nearby. "It's chemical, so it's pretty horrible, but it's better than nothing."

I nod again, and with a small smile, she drifts away. I watch

142

her go. She looks so delicate. It's amazing to think she's managed to evade ACID for so long. But then, isn't it always the innocent-looking ones who surprise you? There were plenty of people at Mileway who assumed I was weak and fragile. And who found out, to their cost, that I wasn't.

I crawl into the den. "Mia?" Max croaks. "Are we staying?" he asks.

"Until you're better, yes," I say.

He gives me a weak smile. "I guess it's better than nothing, huh? I thought we'd be spending tonight in an ACID cell." He coughs, then swallows, wincing.

"How d'you feel?" I say.

"OK," he says.

He doesn't *look* it, though. I sigh inwardly. We'll probably be here for two or three days at least. But he's right—it is better than an ACID cell.

I wait until he closes his eyes again, then lie down on the blankets beside him. It feels strange being in here with him like this. I've never even shared a room with anyone, never mind a space this intimate. It's even smaller than my prison cell was; there's about thirty centimeters of space between us. The floor beneath me is hard and uncomfortable, but I don't want to move around too much in case I bump against him and wake him. For some reason I keep remembering how it felt to be pressed against him on top of the bookshelves when we were hiding from ACID; it sends little waves of hot and cold through me. To distract myself, I stare up at the sheet draped over our heads and think about how Jacob evaded my question earlier about what he was doing here. Why would he do that unless he had something to hide? After all, haven't Max and I done the same thing? And what was that nudge Shaan gave Paul all about? What had he been going to say?

It doesn't matter, I think. *As soon as Max is better, you'll be out of here. Who cares who they are or why they're here?*

143

Except Jacob has the gun, and our c-cards, which I want back, even though they're useless. The thought of him hanging on to them makes me nervous. Will he give them back? Why did he even take them in the first place?

Maybe he knows who we really are, I think. *He said no one had komms here, but what if he was lying?*

Right now, this is the safest place you could possibly be, I tell myself. *Go to sleep and worry about this stuff tomorrow.*

But that's easier said than done, and I lie awake for hours, my mind buzzing with questions.

25 May 2113

Dear Jenna,

I've written so many of these letters to you since you were born. Even though I've never sent them, I've always imagined you reading them and replying. Almost as if we were having a real conversation with each other. It seems silly, really. But until your father and adoptive mother's deaths, and then FREE agreeing to get you out of jail in return for my help with collecting evidence against ACID for the trial, I thought I'd never be able to see you or talk to you in person, and that thought was so painful that I had to find a way to make it less so. So I wrote you letters.

And now here I am, writing you another.

I have so many questions. Where on earth did you find Max Fisher, and how? And where have you both gone? As soon as I heard about the incident at Clearford station yesterday, I wanted to rush up there. But I couldn't, because I knew if I found you I would have had to let ACID take you, and I couldn't have done that. I just couldn't.

And FREE can't go up there yet either. Now ACID have found out where you were, and because they were already looking so closely into Alex Fisher's affairs, we need to keep as low a profile as possible – at least for the next few weeks. As a precaution, Mel, Jon and other members of FREE who were based in London have been moved to another location. We have also managed to get Max's mother out of custody and taken her to a safe house.

We have other resources we can use to track you down, though, and believe me, we are using them. And we don't think this will affect the trial. We have gathered over half of the evidence we need to bring our case against ACID so far, and hope to have the rest by the end of the summer, no matter what. The key will be finding out what's really going on at a place called Innis Ifrinn – Hell Island – on what used to be the Orkney Isles. It's not even supposed to exist, and we've already seen documents and images that make us think they're treating the prisoners there very badly – we suspect as many as twenty people have died there already since the beginning of the year. Getting evidence of this would strengthen our case against them greatly.

It gives me shivers to think that we might – just might – have the key to bringing ACID's half-century-long stranglehold on this country to an end. Bit by bit, they've cut the IRB off from the world, controlling its people with intimidation, and it's just not right. Your father would have wanted to see them gone too – not the father you remember now, but the father you really had. The one who was as passionate about fighting ACID as me and the rest of FREE.

Jenna, wherever you are, please look after yourself. Please stay safe. I've already lost my daughter once. I don't think I could bear for it to happen again.

All my love,
Your mother xx

CHAPTER 22

"D'you think you'll feel up to leaving tomorrow?" I ask Max quietly. We've been here three days. Although it's early, and everyone else is still asleep, we've both been awake for a while. I've made some coffee using the bottled water and the little stove that's kept in a room next door, and we're clutching half-full mugs.

Max nods. "We can go today if you want," he says, keeping his voice low too. "I'm OK now, really. You don't need to worry about me."

I shake my head. "Tomorrow's fine," I insist. "You only just started feeling like yourself yesterday afternoon. And I need to get our c-cards back."

"Where are we going to go?"

"I don't know. Another big city, maybe. Not Newcastle, though—ACID might still be expecting us to turn up there."

"*Do* we need our c-cards back? We can't use them."

I chew my lower lip, considering. "I don't like the idea of

Jacob hanging on to them. What if he tries to use them for something?"

Max frowns. "Like what?"

"I don't know. But I don't trust him."

"Me neither," Max says.

"You don't?"

He shakes his head. "Dunno. The others seem OK—Elyn's nice, isn't she? But Jacob—there's something . . . not right about him."

"I know what you mean," I say. For the last three days, while Max has been recovering from his illness, I've been observing Jacob, trying to figure him out. Except for reading and exercising, there's not much else to do. The others seem to have some sort of rota drawn up for watch duty, cleaning, preparing food and so on, but they haven't asked me to join in, and I haven't volunteered to.

"It's the way he looks at you when he talks to you," Max says. "Like he's trying to hypnotize you or something. And he's so *intense*. I feel like I have to watch what I say around him all the time; otherwise I'll end up telling him too much."

"Yeah, that's exactly it," I say. Jacob usually only appears at meal times, but he seems to know just which questions to ask, which compliments to drop into the conversation, to make whoever he's talking to feel like they're the absolute focus of his attention. I remember people—inmates *and* guards—like that in Mileway; they were always the ones you had to watch, because they were the ones with darkness bubbling underneath their easy smiles and jovial laughter like lava, ready to erupt at any minute.

I glance at Max and, just like when we first got here, feel a little burst of gratitude that he's here with me.

"So how will we get out of Clearford if we can't use our cards?" he asks.

"We'll have to walk, I guess," I say. "If we leave tomorrow night, we should be out of town before there's anyone about."

"We need to get the gun back too. Just in case."

I nod.

"D'you think he'll let us have it?"

"I don't know." I'm not sure I even *want* it, but Max is right—we need the gun. It'll give us some protection against ACID. "I'll go up there in a bit. You can come with me, if you want." I gather up the mugs. "I'll take these back."

I duck out of the den and pad silently across the floor. There's still no sign of life in the other dens. My internal clock is telling me it's about oh-six-thirty, which means no one else will be up for another hour or so. I go back to the storeroom, where all the supplies are kept in a big locker behind a pile of junk, to hide it from ACID when they raid the place, and rinse the mugs out in a bucket with the last of the water I boiled on the stove. Thinking about how I'm going to get our c-cards and the gun back has made me feel too antsy to sleep, though, so instead of going back to the den, I do a few stretches to warm up my muscles, then drop to the carpet and start doing push-ups. The repetitive movement calms me, focuses my mind.

"Impressive," a voice murmurs above me, just as I hit the two hundred mark.

I jump and look up to see Jacob standing there. Hurriedly, I get to my feet, brushing dust off my hands and blowing my fringe out of my eyes.

"Look at you," he says. "You're hardly even out of breath."

"Yeah, well," I say, shrugging. "I like to keep in shape."

"I can tell." Jacob gives my biceps an appraising look that sets my teeth on edge. I fold my arms across my chest, wishing I were wearing longer sleeves.

Behind us, the door squeaks open and Elyn, who's been on watch duty, comes in, rubbing her eyes.

"Good morning," Jacob says, smiling broadly at her. "Any problems?"

"Nothing. Everything's quiet," Elyn says. "Sarah! How's Declan?"

"He's OK," I say.

"Oh *good*. I've been really worried about him, you know."

"Well, you've done a great job of helping him to get better, haven't you?" Jacob says smoothly. And I can only nod in agreement, because she has—she's been super-attentive, making sure he has medpatches and water and that our den's comfortable and warm enough. Every time I turn round, she's there.

"Who's on duty next?" Jacob asks her.

"Lukas," Elyn says. "I'll go and wake him up." She crosses to his den and hisses his name through the sheet hanging over the entrance.

Jacob turns back to me. "Sarah, once everyone's had breakfast, would you be kind enough to take over from Lukas?"

"Um, I guess," I say, narrowing my eyes.

"We're having a meeting—just a regular thing we do, to check there aren't any issues or problems. If you could take over Lukas's watch, just for half an hour or so, then he can be there."

"No worries," I say. I duck into my den, eager to get away from Jacob. Even standing next to him makes the hairs on the back of my neck stand up.

"Want me to come up there with you?" Max says. He's still awake.

"Yeah," I say. "That'd be good."

About forty minutes later, everyone starts getting up. I wait until I hear Elyn call, "Come and get it, guys!" and Max and

I join the others. We sit close together, our legs crossed and our knees touching, trying to look as much like a couple as Rory and Elyn, or Neela and Shaan. I can feel my skin tingling where his knee is resting against mine, like there's an electric charge between us. It's the same when we're in the den at night; I'm still not used to being in such a small space with him. Every time I accidentally brush against him, or he turns over in his sleep and flings a hand out and it bumps against me, I go hot and cold all over.

Then, without warning, Max puts his arm around me. It's the first time either of us have ever taken our charade that far—up to now we've limited it to hand-holding and sitting close to each other—and I'm not expecting it at all. I get a jolt, a rush of heat going through my body, and stiffen for a moment. *For God's sake,* I scold myself. *Why can't you just act cool?*

I close my eyes briefly. *You are not going to fall for him, Jenna,* I tell myself. *Our situation is complicated enough as it is. And look how things turned out with Dylan. You decided you'd never fall for anyone again, remember?*

But Max isn't Dylan. The feelings I have for him are nothing like that . . . obsession. Instead, I have a sense of rightness, of something fitting into place without anything having to be given up to make room for it.

When breakfast is over and it's time for everyone to go up to the second floor, and he takes his arm away and gets to his feet, I feel a fleeting sense of loss.

"This is where you keep watch," Elyn says once we're upstairs, leading us along a corridor to a couple of dusty chairs beneath one of the windows. She points out the knotholes in the boards nailed across it. "Keep looking through them, and if you see anything, come and knock," she says, before following the others into what looks like an old meeting room nearby. "Thanks!" she calls over her shoulder, and, with a smile, she

151

pulls the door to after her; it doesn't actually shut because the frame is warped with damp.

When she's gone, Max turns to me and says, "Was that OK earlier—me putting my arm around you, I mean?"

"Oh, yeah, fine," I say, a little too quickly. "Why?"

"I didn't know if it was going too far."

I shake my head.

"Only I heard Jack and Amy talking outside our den last night and they were saying we didn't seem very couple-y," he says. "So I thought . . ."

"It's fine," I say. "Great idea." I'm both relieved and disappointed—relieved because it means my tangled feelings about him, all the guilt about his dad and me lying to him, don't have to get any more complicated. And disappointed because, well . . .

I decide not to go there.

He kneels in one of the chairs and peers through a knothole. "Nothing out there," he says. I look too and see a view of the empty street below. Was it really only three days ago that we were running down it, pursued by ACID? It feels like much longer.

On a run-down-looking building opposite, I see a news screen. My stomach lurches, then settles again as I realize it's broken, flickering uselessly. Then I see yet another NAR lightffiti tag, shining on the wall beside it. Who on earth *is* that? I'm starting to feel as if they're following me.

I turn round and drop into the chair. We sit for a while in companionable silence. It's something I'm really starting to appreciate about Max: not having to talk constantly just to keep from feeling awkward.

"What d'you reckon they're doing?" Max says eventually, glancing at the room the others have disappeared into.

"Dunno," I say. "Wanna find out?"

"What if they catch you?" he says, looking apprehensive

as I get to my feet again and creep down the corridor to the meeting-room door. I flap a hand at him—*They won't*—and press my eye to the gap between the door and the frame.

I frown.

What the hell *are* they doing?

CHAPTER 23

I glance round. Max is looking through one of the knotholes. *"Max,"* I hiss, frantically beckoning him over.

He gets up and hurries along the corridor to where I'm standing. *Look,* I mouth, indicating the gap.

He looks. When he steps back, I'm pretty sure the expression he's wearing is identical to mine. *What are they up to?* he mouths. I shake my head.

Jacob's standing in the middle of the room, which is lit, as always, by glolamps. There's a table beside him with a box, a bit like the one he put the gun and our c-cards in, but bigger and painted green, on it. The others are sitting around him on chairs that have been arranged in a rough semicircle, looking at something he's taken out of the box—a metal disc with a slightly domed top, about half the size of my palm. "This isn't live," he's saying. "But the ones you'll have with you on the day will be. You need to be very, *very* careful not to drop them or jog them. Otherwise—*boom!*" He throws his arms out.

Elyn, Rory, Jack, Paul, Amy, Lukas, Neela and Shaan all

nod. Their faces are sober masks of concentration, especially Elyn's.

"You need to locate your target, attach them and pull this pin out to activate them," Jacob says, pointing at something on the side of the disc. "Then you'll have thirty minutes to get clear."

The others all nod again.

"This is a plan of the square." Jacob puts the disc back in the box and lifts out something else—a square of paper, which he unfolds into a large sheet and smoothes out on the table beside the box. "I've marked the targets with a red cross, and next to each one are the initials of the person whose target it is. Is it clear enough?"

The others get up and gather around him to look at it. I squint, trying to make out what's on it, but it's too far away, and the light in there is too dim.

"It's estimated that there will be about two thousand ACID agents attending this rally," Jacob continues. "There are going to be a lot of people watching too. And our esteemed president, of course. It'll be carnage." He grins. So do the others, and Elyn's eyes shine as she gazes at Jacob with that unsettling look of rapture I've seen her and the others wear around him so often.

I stare at them through the narrow gap, Jacob's words replaying in my head. *Be very careful. Otherwise—boom! Targets . . . two thousand ACID agents . . . rally . . . carnage . . .*

Everything clicks into place like the pieces of a puzzle.

I realize what he's talking about.

I realize what that metal disc is, and what these people are going to do.

"What's wrong?" Max says when we're back over by the window. "You look pale."

I motion frantically for him to keep his voice down, glancing at the door. "What is it?" he mutters.

155

I beckon for him to lean close to me and, in whispers, I tell him what I saw. The color slowly drains from his face too.

"What do they mean, a rally?" he says.

"I'm not sure," I say. Without access to a komm or a news screen, I have no way of finding out. "It sounds like an ACID thing. I don't know if it's in this town or somewhere else."

"We have to leave tonight," he whispers.

I nod. "I'll go and ask for the gun and our c-cards as soon as Lukas comes back."

"But what if he won't let you have them?"

"I'll get them," I say. "It'll be all right." But I don't feel nearly as confident as I'm trying to sound.

"God, Mia," Max whispers. "They're terr—"

"*Shhh.*" I can hear voices; the door to the meeting room's opening. "Act normal. They mustn't suspect we know anything."

Max turns and kneels and looks through one of the knotholes. I sit, my hands resting lightly on the chair arms, and somehow manage to return the pleasant smile Elyn gives me as she walks up to us. "Thanks *so* much, guys," she says, tucking a lock of her feathery blond hair behind her ear. She's wearing another homemade patchwork dress over a pair of jeans, and there's a purple crystal on a leather thong round her neck. I try to imagine her planting one of those devices, pulling out the pin, walking away to safety and calmly waiting for it to detonate. I remember the way she was looking at Jacob, as if she'd let him have her soul if he asked for it.

A chill goes right through me.

"No worries," I say.

"Lukas can take over again now," she says, turning to glance at him over her shoulder.

Max and I get up.

"So, was it a good meeting?" I say as we go back downstairs. "Did you sort everything out?"

"Oh yes," she says airily. "We were just discussing the watch rotas and what sort of things we wanted Jacob to get next time he goes out to buy food, boring stuff like that."

I nod, my heart sinking. But what did I expect? That she'd tell me, *Yes, we were planning where to plant explosive devices so that we can kill hundreds of ACID agents and innocent members of the public?*

You have to stop them, a little voice inside my head says. But *how?* The only way I have of contacting ACID right now is to walk up to an agent and do it in person. Not an option. And I don't even know when this rally is. Maybe if Max and I can get away and find a PKP . . .

"Oh!" I say when we get back down to the children's library. "I forgot—there's something I need to ask Jacob."

"I'll go if you want," Elyn says. "What did you want to ask him?"

"Don't worry, I'll do it," I tell her, giving her another fake smile.

"OK. I'm going to make some coffee. D'you want a cup?"

"That'd be lovely, thanks," I say. I glance at Max, who's standing behind the others.

Be careful, he mouths at me.

CHAPTER 24

I think about going up to the meeting room first, to see if the box containing the device and the plan is still there, or if I can find any other evidence of what Jacob and the others are planning to do. Then I remember Lukas is on watch just meters away. *The best thing is to act like you were planning to leave tonight all along,* I think as I head up to the top floor. *Be casual about it. Jacob knows you don't want to stay anyway, so what's the problem?*

The corridor leading to his room is even darker than I remember. I feel as if the walls are leaning toward me as I walk down it and knock on his door.

There's no answer. I peer through the little window in the top, but the glass is too grimy for me to see anything through it except for the flicker of glolamps.

I knock again and try the handle.

It's open.

I push the door with my fingertips. It swings inward silently. "Hello?" I say quietly, but I can already see that the room's empty. The strange drawings on the walls leer at me as I step inside, looking around. It looks just as it did on the day Max and I arrived, with blankets in a crumpled heap on the bed and piles of books everywhere.

I glance back at the open door behind me. Where is Jacob? Perhaps he's gone out to buy food already. Crossing to the bed, I crouch down and look underneath it for the strongbox. Jacob has the key, of course, but I might be able to force it with something. I *have* to get the gun and our cards back.

But the box isn't there. I straighten up, looking around the room. Then I begin to search the desk, carefully lifting up piles of paper and placing them back down in what I hope is their original position. I slide drawers open and shut. The box is nowhere. *Shit.*

I turn my attention to the piles of books along the back wall, moving them a few at a time. Jacob's obviously hidden the box, but where? Christ, I hope he hasn't got it with him.

I reach the bottom of one book pile and am about to start on the next when, suddenly, I get a prickling feeling across the back of my neck, like I'm being watched. My heart hammering, I turn, expecting to see Jacob standing in the open doorway, but there's no one there.

Chill out, I think, letting out a slow, shaky breath. I shake my head and carry on searching through the books.

Nearby, I hear a soft click.

I jerk my head up, my heart hammering again. The noise came from my right, near the end of the bed, but at first, I can't see anything. Then part of the wall begins to move outward. It's a door, I realize, camouflaged by those weird drawings.

"Looking for something, *Sarah?*" a voice says as it opens.

Jacob's standing on the other side, smiling at me.

CHAPTER 25

He's holding the strongbox in his hands. I stare at him, my heart beating unpleasantly fast. He stares back.

I give myself a mental shake. "Mikey and I want to leave tonight," I say, squaring my shoulders. "We'd like the gun and our c-cards back."

"Would you," Jacob says. It's a statement, not a question.

I curl my hands, which are down by my sides, into fists. "Yes," I tell him.

"Why the hurry, *Sarah?*" he says. "ACID don't know you're here. You're as safe at the library as you are anywhere."

In what universe? I think. "We want to leave," I repeat, trying to keep my voice steady. "Like I told you, we need to get to our friends. And you know my name's Mia, so why don't you just call me that?" I'm sick of him sneering *Sarah* at me.

Jacob steps through the doorway. Behind him I see a little sink and a chemical toilet like the one downstairs. "Very protective of Mikey, aren't you?" he says, putting the box down on the end of the bed.

"He's my"—I swallow—"boyfriend."

Jacob nods slowly. "Have you heard of the NAR?" he asks.

I blink.

"The NAR, Mia. Have you heard of it?"

"Um, no," I say, and then I realize I *have.* That lightffiti I saw in Outer, and on the wall when we were on the train here, and on the building across from the library, which had been cleaned away now—it must have been new when I saw it, and ACID hadn't had a chance to remove it. "You mean Nar?"

Jacob gives a little laugh, as if I've just said something amusing. "That's another name for us, I suppose."

I frown. "For *us?*"

"For the New Anarchy Regiment," Jacob says. He rolls up his right sleeve, twisting his arm toward me so I can see the tattoo I caught a glimpse of on our first day here. It's an "A" and an "R," black letters in a red circle—a heavily stylized version of the logo of the Anarchy Regiment. I used to see it all the time at Mileway. Forty years ago, when the Anarchy Regiment were at their peak, they carried out dozens of bomb attacks and shootings every year, usually targeting ACID but inevitably killing innocent civilians as well. ACID clamped down, and they went quiet, but never really disappeared completely. Then, in 2085, they carried out a series of bomb attacks on schools. Hundreds of people, most of them children, died. After that, ACID launched a massive two-year-long operation to round them up. About half of Mileway's population was made up of ex-AR members.

But it looks like ACID didn't get everyone.

The scene I witnessed in the meeting room takes on a new, even more sinister significance. Jacob and the others aren't just some random group of bomb-happy ACID haters; they're the AR reborn: the NAR, who are obviously in London too, who could be *everywhere* for all I know, quietly growing like fungus in

161

dark city backstreets and run-down buildings. Just the thought of it sends chills down my spine.

I remember what Paul said that first night we were here, when Shaan nudged him to shut him up. *I met Jacob in Manchester when I was squatting in an abandoned apartment block. He was recr—*

Recruiting. He'd been going to say recruiting.

Another chill threads down my spine.

"So you have heard of us?" Jacob says, and I realize I must be wearing my shock and dismay all over my face.

"Kind of," I say, trying to compose myself. *God, most of them are so young,* I think, picturing innocent-looking Amy and Jack, bubbly Neela and thoughtful Shaan. And fragile, pretty Elyn.

"There are groups of us all over the country," he says. "ACID have no idea we exist. We're going to rise up, and this time, we're going to take them down."

I stare at him again. I have no idea what to say.

"Just think, Mia," he says. "We could go back to what this country was like before ACID."

"You weren't around then," I say numbly. "None of you were. How do you even *know* what it was like?"

"I know, all right," Jacob says. "People could choose who was in power. They didn't have to watch the damn news screens all day. Food wasn't rationed. The IRB wasn't isolated from other countries. Do you know they even had something called the Internet, where you could exchange information and connect with people all over the *world*? It's still out there, but we don't have it. And if ACID stay in power, we never will."

I frown. I found out about a lot of stuff that ACID had got rid of or changed from Dylan, but he'd never told me about that.

"So you think that's going to work?" I say. "Taking the country back to how it was before ACID by bombing the hell out of—"

Too late, I realize what I've said. I clap a hand over my mouth. Another smile spreads across Jacob's face, slow and reptilian. "Quite the little eavesdropper, aren't you?" he says.

I glance at the door, wondering if I can run fast enough to get back downstairs to Max and get us the hell out of here without Jacob catching us. But Jacob sees me looking. In two steps, he crosses the room, blocking my escape route.

"It's OK," he says. "I expected you'd spy on us. I *wanted* you to. That's why we chose a room with a door that didn't fit properly. Usually, we meet down in the children's library."

Despite the voice in my head that's screaming at me to duck round him, wrestle him away from the door and get out of here *now,* I hesitate. "You what?"

"I wanted you to know what was going on here," he says. "About what we're going to do."

My mouth tastes bitter. "What exactly *are* you going to do?" I say. "Apart from murder people, that is?"

"There's an ACID rally in Manchester in two weeks' time," Jacob says. "Two thousand agents— Oh, wait." He smiles again. "You heard that bit, didn't you?"

He yawns, rolling his shoulders, before he continues, "They're holding it in the central ceremony square. General Harvey's going to be there. We plan to plant explosives at strategic points around its edge so that when the rally's at its height, they'll go off." He digs in his pocket and brings out a piece of paper. When he unfolds it and hands it to me, I realize it's the plan he was showing the others earlier. It's a map of the city, with a zoomed-in plan of the square and the surrounding streets at the top. Unlike London, there only seems to be one square. The rest of the city is divided into roughly rectangular zones marked RESIDENTIAL, COMMERCIAL & BUSINESS and EDUCATION, CULTURE & LEISURE.

I look at the plan of the square. As I heard Jacob tell the

163

others earlier, there are red crosses marked on it with their names beside them.

And in the bottom left-hand corner of the square, I see he's written *Declan and Sarah*.

I go cold all over.

"No," I say. "No way. We're not getting involved with this."

"Really," Jacob says, plucking the sheet of paper out of my fingers. "That's funny."

"What is?" I say.

"That you should have developed morals all of a sudden."

"Why?" I say, narrowing my eyes.

"Because I'd have thought if anyone was up for a killing spree," he says, "it'd be you, Jenna Strong."

CHAPTER 26

Jenna Strong.

My real name echoes in my ears.

He knows who I am.

For once, I can't be cool or tough. I can't even pretend. I gaze at Jacob. "How did you—"

"I see the news screens when I go out to pick up food." He shrugs. "ACID are going crazy looking for you and Max Fisher, you know. They've put the reward for finding you up to seventy-five thousand kredz."

My legs feel like they might be about to give way beneath me. Slowly, I sit down on the chair beside the desk.

"Jenna, Jenna, Jenna," he says. "The most-wanted girl in the IRB, and she's right here in front of me."

"Don't tell Max," I say. "He doesn't know."

"Of course," Jacob says. "You killed his dad as well, didn't you?"

"No," I tell him. "It was ACID—his dad was the one who got me out of jail and an agent shot him."

"So why don't you just tell him that?"

Because he's convinced that Jenna Strong did do it. Because I've lied to him so much already that there's no way he'll believe me. Because I still don't know why his dad helped me. There are so many reasons, I can't pick one.

"Why do you want us to get involved with your bomb plot?" I say. "You could give us up, claim the reward. Seventy-five thousand kredz is a fortune."

Jacob sits down on the bed, regarding me coolly. "Like I said, our movement is growing. We have cells all over the country, planning action on many levels, whether it be vandalism, graffiti, inciting riots or what we're planning to do next month. Anything to stir up discontent and make the public question ACID's authority. But we lack a figurehead—someone who will inspire people to join us and take up our cause."

"So . . . what, *I'm* that person?" I say.

He shakes his hair out of his face. "You're notorious, Jenna. You killed one of the most senior ACID agents in the country—and he was your own father. Think what it would mean if someone like you was helping to coordinate our attacks and train up new followers, for example. People would look up to you. The NAR would be unstoppable."

A cold, sick sensation is stealing through me. "For your information, my parents' deaths were an accident," I tell him. "I'm not a murderer. And I certainly don't want to be your *figurehead*." I spit the last word at him like a poison dart.

"Are you sure? You'll be paid. I'll even see what I can do about moving you and Max into more private living quarters while you're here at the library, if you like. And of course, you'll have protection from ACID—I'll make absolutely sure of that. What do you say? Help us with the Manchester rally, and I'll take you to meet some of my associates and we can work out exactly what your role should be and where you and Max should stay."

"Are they paying *you*?" I say. "These *associates* of yours? Have they offered you money to bring me to them?"

"That's not important," Jacob says, but I can tell from the way his gaze momentarily flicks away from mine that I'm right.

"You're insane," I snarl at him, getting to my feet. "Let me out of here."

I try to shove past him to the door, but he blocks my way again. "Aren't you even going to consider my offer? Think about it, Jenna. Money, safety, the chance to be a hero—you'll have none of those things if you walk out of here now."

"I don't give a shit about those things," I say. "There's nothing heroic about murdering people, even if they are ACID. Let me past."

But he doesn't move.

I relax my body, looking away from him, trying to make myself appear submissive. Then I lash out, aiming for his groin and his eyes. Just as quick, he whips his hand out and grabs my wrist, clamping his fingers around it in a steel-hard grip. He twists my arm behind my back and slams me face-first against the wall, pressing his knee into the backs of mine so I can't wriggle free.

"Nice try," he says in my ear. "Who taught you that move, I wonder?"

I try to strike out with my other hand but he grabs that and holds it against the wall too, pinning me there like an insect on a piece of card.

His strength is frightening. He's more powerful than any of the guys who tried to corner me in prison, even though some of them were bigger. For the first time ever, I've met my match.

"You were right, Jenna," he hisses at me, and now all the

charm has gone from his voice. "There has been money offered to anyone in the NAR who found you. A *lot* of money. As much as ACID's reward, if not more. You're valuable to me, Jenna, so don't think I'm just going to let you leave."

After remaining still for a few more moments, I buck violently, hoping to catch him off guard. It doesn't work. He wrenches my arm farther up behind my back and I go still, stifling a cry of pain. *Stop trying to fight him,* I think. *Otherwise he's gonna break your arm.* I relax as much as I can, trying to hold myself in a position that will lessen the pressure on my shoulder joint.

"If you don't do what I want," he says, his voice still soft, "I'll tell Max who you are, and I'll shop you both to ACID. Understand?"

I close my eyes. I don't answer.

"Understand?" He bends my arm up even farther, until it starts to feel as if he's ripping it from the socket.

Clenching my teeth against a moan, I nod. He lets me go. I keep my face pressed to the wall and my eyes closed, gasping at the pain in my shoulder.

"Go," Jacob says. He sounds bored now. "Go back down there and tell your boyfriend you've decided to stay."

"What am I supposed to say to him?" I say, not turning round.

"You're good at lying, I'm sure you'll think of something," Jacob says. He reaches past me and opens the door. I stumble through it. My ears are ringing, and pain pulses through my shoulder in sickening waves.

"And, Jenna?"

I turn back. The glolamps behind Jacob create a halo effect around his hair, making him look like some sort of terrible angel. "Don't even think about trying to escape. The others don't know who you really are yet, but they know I want to keep you here. They'll be watching you very closely from now on, especially Elyn. She has that gun you brought with you."

I want to spit in his face, but the ache in my shoulder is a reminder of what might happen if I do. In a haze of horror and rage, I turn and head back along the corridor.

CHAPTER 27

Back down in the children's library, the others are sitting in a little group outside the dens. As I walk past them, Elyn locks gazes with me, and I wonder if Jacob was being truthful when he said he hadn't told the others who Max and I really were. No wonder she's been so attentive, so *kind*. She's been keeping an eye on us for Jacob.

I duck into our den with a shudder, glad I can talk to Max in relative privacy. But what am I going to tell him?

The truth, I think. *You're going to tell him the truth.*

He's sitting at the back of the den, legs crossed, reading a book without any covers. "You OK?" he says, seeing my face as I sit down too.

I shake my head.

He puts the book facedown on the floor, its pages splayed so he doesn't lose his place. Then he scoots closer to me. "What's up?" he says. When I don't answer, he lays a hand gently on my arm. "Mia? What's happened?"

I motion for him to keep his voice down. His eyes are full

of concern, and I feel my stomach turn sour. First, I get his dad killed; then he nearly gets arrested and ends up on CloudNine. And now I've delivered him straight into the hands of a group of terrorist lunatics who think that, somehow, we're going to help them topple ACID.

I'm the worst thing that ever happened to him, and yet here he is *again,* worrying about me. Shame pours hotly over me, and for a moment I'm tempted to *really* tell him the truth—about who I am; about everything. I don't want to keep lying to him. It's too hard.

"I saw Jacob," I say quietly. "He isn't going to let us leave."

Max frowns. "What? *Why?*"

As I tell him, his eyes get rounder and rounder. "And if we don't do it, he'll hand us over to ACID," I finish, not quite able to meet his gaze as I think about the bit I'm leaving out: *And he'll tell you who I really am.*

Max snorts. "Not if we leave now," he says. "We can be well away from here before he even realizes we're gone."

I shake my head. "The others know all about it. They've been told to keep us here."

"*Them?*" Max says.

"Jacob says Elyn has the gun," I say.

"He could just be saying that," Max says. "I mean, c'mon. *Elyn?* She doesn't look as if she could even lift the thing."

"I wouldn't be so sure," I say. "She—"

Without any warning, the sheet at the entrance to our den is pulled back, making us both jump. "Hi, Sarah!" Elyn says, sticking her head inside. Although she's smiling sweetly, her eyes are hard. "You've talked to Jacob?"

I return her gaze, determined to show her I'm not scared of her. "Yes."

"So what are you going to do?" She's wearing her dress over a pair of jeans today, and as she waits for my reply I see her casually but deliberately move her hand to her waist. Following

171

her gesture with my gaze, I see a shape through the thin fabric: the gun, tucked into a holster on her belt.

"We're in," I say. She narrows her eyes slightly to check I've understood, and I give her a small nod.

"Oh, *fab.*" Her smile widens into a grin. She takes her hand away from her waist. "If you guys want tea or coffee, I'm about to make drinks for everyone."

"We'll be out in a minute," I say, finally managing to give her a sickly smile.

As soon as the sheet's dropped down across the entrance, Max grabs my arm. "Are you *crazy?*" he hisses. "I'm not *bombing* people!"

"I never said we were going to," I hiss back. "But you saw the gun, didn't you?"

"Yes, but—"

"Listen," I whisper. "*This* is what we're gonna do." I try to sound confident, like this isn't just something I'm thinking up as I go along. "We go along with it, pretend we're part of the gang and travel with them to Manchester. OK?"

"But—" Max is still looking at me like I'm insane.

"*Think* about it," I whisper. "If we try and escape from here, even if Elyn doesn't shoot us, we've got to get out of Clearford somehow—then what? If we're in a big city, it'll be easier to give them the slip. We might even be able to find somewhere decent to hide out. And we can warn someone about the bombs."

"How?" Max says. "And who? You tell ACID, they'll arrest us on the spot."

"I'll think of something," I say. I let out my breath in a sharp, unhappy sigh, closing my eyes.

After a pause, Max lays a hand on my arm again. "This isn't your fault," he says. I open my eyes, look up at him. *But it IS,* I want to tell him, only, of course, I can't.

"Let's get that coffee," I say, gently moving my arm out

from under his hand, then crawling past him. I look at him over my shoulder. "I think we should act like we really want to do this, OK?" I add quietly. "The less suspicious they are, the better."

Max nods. His face is white and unhappy, but he follows me out of the den and we go and sit with the others. They all grin at us, so I'm guessing Elyn's told them that we know about them and that we're joining their cause. I smile back and, after a surreptitious nudge with my foot, so does Max.

"So what did Jacob tell you?" Amy says, passing us each a mug of coffee. We both set them down on the floor.

"Oh, pretty much everything," I say. "About Manchester and the rally and all that."

"And you're really OK with it?" Shaan says. Her eyes are narrowed with the same suspicion she regarded us with when we first arrived.

"Of course," I say, forcing myself to put some passion into my voice and plaster another grin onto my face. "I hate ACID as much as you guys do. It'd be great to teach them a lesson."

Obviously, I've said the right thing, because the suspicion fades from Shaan's face and she smiles.

"We should have a toast," Elyn says, holding up her mug. "To the NAR!"

"To freedom!" Jack chimes in.

Max and I pick up our mugs and clink them against everyone else's without looking at each other. I'm afraid that if I do catch his eye, I'll see my own horror at what we're getting ourselves into reflected there, and that the smile on my face will drop off and shatter like glass.

CHAPTER 28

The next day, Jacob calls another meeting to "welcome" me and Max into the group, this time down in the children's library. He's holding the deactivated bomb in his hand, moving it from palm to palm as if it's nothing more than a beach pebble. I stare at it. In the flickering light from the glolamps on the tables around us, its silver casing gleams dully. Elyn's already explained to me how the devices work: there's a pad on the back that allows them to be stuck to any surface—metal, plastic, even stone—and they have a blast radius of almost twelve meters, sending out a deadly cloud of superheated shrapnel as they explode.

Even the thought of it makes me feel sick.

Jacob looks straight at me. "So," he says. "Jen—"

My heart stops beating. My chest constricts, and I forget how to breathe.

He clears his throat. "Sorry. *Generally* speaking, I think we're ready. But we'll keep going over the details right up until the day. It's important we don't leave anything to chance, especially now we have some additions to the group."

My heart starts to thud, and I'm able to draw air back into my lungs. But as the others murmur their agreement he catches my eye again and winks, and I know that he just did what he did on purpose, and I hate him for it.

"I'm sure you're all as thrilled as I am that Declan and Sarah have decided to join us," he goes on. "It's very *gen*erous of them to accept our offer to continue sheltering and feeding them in exchange for their help. I'm sure they'll be a *gen*uine asset to the group. They will help us achieve *gen*esis into something truly great as, together, our actions *gen*erate renewed interest in removing ACID from power."

My heart stop-starts, stop-starts. I want to get up and punch him in the face.

"So, I think that for their benefit, we should go over the plans from start to finish, in case there's anything we haven't told them. Is that OK?"

The others nod.

"Elyn," Jacob says. "Would you do the honors?"

She nods enthusiastically. "The rally starts at oh eight hundred," she tells us. "Jacob's arranged for us to hide away in a van that's taking a delivery into Manchester that morning. There'll be some empty crates in the back, which we'll get inside, and if everything goes to plan, we'll be taken straight into the city center without being stopped at any checkpoints. Once we're there, we'll wait until oh-eight-thirty to let the rally get going. Then we'll plant and arm the bombs. There's a thirty-minute delay on them, which will let us get back to the van. After that, in all the chaos, it should be easy to slip away."

Everyone nods.

"What if we get caught?" Max says. I glance at him. His mouth is set in a thin, flat line.

175

"Set off your device," Elyn says immediately.

"What?" Max says. "But that'll—"

"So you'd rather get arrested and thrown in jail?" Elyn says. She sounds shocked. "How will that change anything? If ACID lock you up, they've won."

I see Max opening his mouth to protest further and nudge him to stop him saying anything more. But inside, I feel sicker than ever. So Jacob expects us either to kill hundreds of people, or, if we get intercepted, kill ourselves.

What a lunatic.

By the time the meeting finishes, I realize I've been clenching my hands into such tight fists my fingers have gone numb. "Does anyone want a drink?" Amy asks when Jacob's gone.

"I'll make it," I say, getting up. I need a few minutes away from them to compose myself, otherwise I'm going to scream, and now that Max and I are supposed to be part of the group— and willingly—I can't just hide away in our den anymore.

"Want a hand?" Max says.

"I'm OK. But thanks." I try to smile at him, searching his face for signs that he might have picked up on the hints Jacob was dropping like hand grenades into his little speech at the start of the meeting. To my relief, I don't see any.

"What does everyone want?" I say with a brightness I couldn't be further from actually feeling. Once they've told me, I go into the storeroom, where, out of sight of the others and Max, I lean my head against the wall and close my eyes. I feel like I'm at the start of a tightrope that has a thirty-meter chasm underneath it, and no safety net. Somehow, I've got to get myself and Max across.

And I have no idea if I'm going to be able to do it.

Over the next two weeks, as the group prepares for the attack on the rally, there's a sense of purpose about them that wasn't there before. We have meetings every day, during which Jacob keeps using words beginning with "gen" and winking at me whenever no one else is looking. In between the meetings, the others no longer spend most of the day reading or lounging about in their dens, with short breaks for watch duty or to clean up; instead, they practice pulling out the pin on the deactivated bomb, or pore over Jacob's plan of the square where the rally will take place, making sure they know where they're supposed to be. Max and I pore over them too, but for a different reason: we're trying to memorize the layout of the streets around the square and work out the easiest route for us to make our escape. The best way looks like one of the side streets on the eastern side of the square. There's a commercial district nearby, which will mean—if it's anything like London—PKPs. If we can find one that works, we're going to use it to send an anonymous warning about the attack.

And then we need to find some way to get hold of Mel.

The night before the rally, everyone goes to bed early, but I've never felt less like sleeping in my life. "What if we don't manage to warn anyone in time?" Max whispers as we lie side by side. "What if the bombs go off and people get killed?"

I stare up into the darkness. I'm thinking the same thing. I've been thinking it every day. Along with: *What if we don't manage to escape?* and *What if we get killed too?*

I hear his blankets rustle as he moves and, suddenly, I feel his fingers thread through mine. I clutch his hand tight, as if somehow this will make everything turn out all right.

"I'm scared," Max whispers.

"Me too," I whisper back, because I am—I really am. It's the first time I've felt this frightened in a long, long time. And I hate it. "But we can do this. We *have* to."

I turn my head, and it's only then that I realize he's moved closer. I can feel his breath tickling my face. He's so close we could . . .

I shut my eyes and, for a few dizzying seconds, let myself

imagine what it would be like to kiss him. I've never kissed anyone, not even Dylan. After he told me how he felt about me, I wanted to, but he said we should *wait until the time is right,* whatever that meant. Now, I find it harder than ever to believe I threw everything away to try to be with him. He never made me feel like this.

And what would it be like, as Max kissed me, to touch the soft hair at the nape of his neck or stroke the stubble shadowing his jaw?

Get a grip, Jenna, I tell myself furiously. *People's lives depend on you tomorrow, and all you can think about is snogging Max.*

I let go of his hand. "We should get some sleep," I say.

Max is silent for a moment, long enough for me to wonder if he was thinking the same thing as me just now. Then he murmurs, "Yeah," and I hear his blankets rustle as he turns back over.

I continue to stare into the darkness, wishing that tomorrow were over and that we were already far away from here.

CHAPTER 29

The next morning, after a hurried, silent breakfast, we all head down to the covered car park connected to the library basement, a concrete cavern with water plopping down from the roof. Outside, the sun's up—I can see fingers of gray light coming down the ramp at the far end of the car park—but in here it's gloomy and dank. Jacob, a pack slung over one shoulder, watches the ramp with a pensive expression while the others cough and shuffle their feet. All of us, including Elyn, are wearing clothes Jacob's given us: jeans and sweatshirts and hooded jackets in dark, nondescript colors; clothes that will let us blend in with the crowd and make it easy for us to get away. The mood is nervous, charged with tension. I rub my eyes. In the end, I got about an hour's sleep last night, and everything feels brittle and surreal.

A few minutes later, I hear the burr of tires, and a large, boxy white van comes bumping down the ramp, its electric motor humming. It pulls up nearby, and the driver, a middle-aged guy with stubble on his face and a protruding belly, gets out. He and Jacob have a discussion in lowered voices, the driver glancing over at us every now and then.

The driver goes round the back and pulls up the door. Inside are stacks of plastic crates with numbers stamped across them. Jacob jerks his head at them. "Get in the crates near the back. I'll put the lids on."

Max and I go first. The empty crate Jacob directs us to is just big enough for both of us to fit inside if we sit with our spines curved over and our arms hugged around our knees. I'm relieved to see there are small holes along the sides of the crate. At least we'll be able to breathe.

I don't know how long it takes us to get to Manchester—I have no way of telling how much time has passed—but it feels like hours. The van speeds up, slows down. A couple of times, it stops altogether and I think, *We're at a checkpoint. ACID are going to search the van and find us.*

But it doesn't happen. Eventually, the van stops again and I hear the door rattle open. A few minutes later, the lid is lifted off our crate.

"Get out," Jacob says above us.

I climb out, my muscles twinging in protest after being crunched up for so long, and turn to help Max. I realize we're in some sort of gigantic warehouse, the van parked in front of stacks of wooden pallets that reach almost up to the roof. A couple of flickering strip lights above them cast a small patch of watery light down onto the area directly in front of the van; the rest of the warehouse is lost in darkness, the air filled with the smell of dust and chemicals.

The others are already out of the van. As I jump down onto the stained concrete floor of the warehouse, I see Jacob and the driver standing at the front of the van, discussing something in quiet, urgent tones. When they've finished talking, he comes back over to us, lifting the pack off his shoulder and unzipping it.

"Strap these round your middles, underneath your clothes,"

he says, reaching inside and lifting out a bundle of small fabric wallets on clip-clasp belts. "And remember: be careful. They should be perfectly safe until you remove the pins, but they *are* live."

When he passes mine to me, he holds my gaze for a few seconds. "Don't forget to be *gen*tle with it," he says. I keep my expression neutral, not wanting to give him the pleasure of knowing how much he gets to me, and pull up my sweatshirt. Through the wallet's lightly padded fabric, I can feel the shape of the explosive device. My mouth is dry as I clip it round my waist. With my sweatshirt pulled down again, you'd never know it was there.

"What about metal detectors?" Paul says.

"The wallets are lined with a substance that blocks whatever's inside from metal detector signals," Jacob explains. "ACID could scan you from head to toe while you're wearing those things, and they wouldn't get a single bleep."

He puts one on too. Then he says, "OK. It's oh-seven-forty. We're pretty near the ceremony square, and there are already a lot of people about, so you'd better head over there. There's a door on the far side of the warehouse that opens out into an alley between here and the next building. Slip into the crowd in ones and twos without drawing any attention to yourselves and get to your positions. And you two, wait," he adds as Max and I start to follow the others to the exit. "Elyn!"

Elyn stops, looks back.

"Slight change of plan. I want you to stay with Sarah and Declan."

"OK," she says, flashing him one of those sweet smiles. *Damn,* I think.

"Everyone be back here by oh-nine-hundred," Jacob calls after us.

The alley running alongside the warehouse is narrow and choked with rubbish, and it's raining. As we make our way to the alley entrance, everyone, including me and Max, pulls up their hoods. Rory slips out first, then Neela and Shaan, then Jack, then Paul and Amy, then Lukas.

"Follow me," Elyn says after a few moments.

The street in front of the warehouse is as busy as any of Outer London's on ceremony day. The difference is that there are no banners, no girls in fancy dresses or guys in smart suits, and there isn't the same buzz of excitement in the air. People look tense, and they're moving along almost in silence. As the three of us slink in amongst them, I notice the ACID agents standing on either side of the road, guns held ready as they watch everyone through their mirrored visors. I pull my hood down farther over my face, more relieved than ever that it's raining.

Walking behind Elyn, Max looks over at me. He doesn't need to speak for me to know what he's thinking. *How are we going to get away from her?*

I lift one shoulder in a tiny shrug. *Don't know. I'll think of something,* I telegraph back.

The buildings in Manchester seem to be mostly concrete tower blocks, laid out in a grid pattern—another thing that reminds me of Outer London. The streets between them are confusingly similar, and I wonder if it will be as easy to find our way to the commercial district as it looked on the plan.

When we reach one of the entrances to the square, I see a huge metal detector arching across it, and ACID agents carrying out random c-card checks. As we pass under the detector, I hold my breath, but it doesn't go off, and Elyn deftly avoids the agents by leading us through the middle of a throng of people. "Stay at the back of everyone," she murmurs as we make our way to the spot where Jacob marked our names on the plan, which is near the entrance to another apartment block.

I can't actually see the square—there are too many people in front of us—but the news screens around us are showing its vast, empty center and the crowd surrounding it, held back by rope barriers. In the corners of the screens, I see the clock displays: 0757. My stomach clenches.

Elyn is standing almost directly in front of Max, her hands jammed in her pockets. I look at the people around us. They're all watching the news screens; no one's paying us any attention. Maybe I could grab her, pin her arms against her sides and— No. She'd struggle. Make a noise. And then people *would* notice us, and someone might link ACID.

The clock displays on the screens flick over to 0800. All of a sudden a roar goes up from the crowd, the people around us throwing their arms up in the air and cheering. On the screens, I see a column of ACID agents marching into the square through the steadily falling rain, a vast black caterpillar that seems to go on and on. They move like robots, their arms and legs swinging in perfect synchronization. Another column marches in, and another. Music, a harsh brass band tune, starts playing from hidden speakers somewhere, and as the square continues to fill with ACID agents, those who are already there begin a slow parade around it. I don't think I've ever seen so many agents in one place before.

Then one breaks away from the end of the first line to stand in front of them all and shouts something I can't make out, because his voice is too distorted by the amplifier he's using. When the cameras zoom in on his face, which you can see because he's pushed the visor of his helmet up, the roars of the crowd intensify, and I gasp. It's General Harvey. With his face on the screens in close-up, it's as if he's staring straight at me. I stare back, mesmerized, until the clock on the screen flicks over to 0810, jolting me back to reality. In front of Max, Elyn is cheering along with everyone else, pumping a fist in the air in time to the music. I nudge Max and mouth, *Shift over*. There's just enough space for him to take a couple of steps to his left. It's all I need.

Moving behind Elyn, I check no one's watching us and I

take a deep breath. This move is something I've never tried before, only been told about by Dr. Fisher, and if I don't get it right it'll either do nothing at all or kill her.

But I have to try it. It's our only chance to stop this.

Standing slightly to her left, I put out my arm, ready to catch her when—*if*—she falls back. Then I bring the side of my right hand into her neck in a hard chop and use my right leg to sweep *her* right leg out from under her.

Immediately, she sags back against me. I lower her gently to the ground, saying, "Elyn? Elyn! Are you OK?" while I reach under her hood to place two fingers against her neck, checking frantically for a heartbeat. When I feel the steady thud of her pulse, my legs go weak with relief. She's just unconscious. It worked.

"Is she OK?" a woman standing next to Max says, seeing me holding Elyn up.

"Yes, I think she's fainted—she doesn't do very well in crowds," I say. Glancing around, I see an alleyway. "We'd better give her a bit of space."

With the woman's help, Max and I push through everyone, carrying Elyn between us to the alleyway, which is blocked off at the other end by a brick wall. "Will you be OK?" the woman says, glancing behind her. I nod, smiling at her, and she heads back into the crowd to reclaim her spot.

"We need to get rid of our belts," I mutter to Max as we lay Elyn down on the ground. He nods and moves to block me from the view of the people behind us while I reach under my sweatshirt and unclip the wallet, placing it next to Elyn. Then he does the same.

"Go," I mutter to Max. We push back out into the crowd and inch along the edge of it. I'm looking for a way out of the square that isn't manned by ACID, and trying to keep my bearings and remember where the others are stationed. If any of them catches sight of us, especially Jacob, we're dead.

184

Then I see it—another narrow gap between two buildings, but this time it isn't blocked off. After one last glance at the crowd to make sure we're not being watched, Max and I dart down it. The street on the other side is empty now; everyone must be at the rally, even the ACID agents who were out here before. I look around for a news screen to check the time: 0815. Fifteen minutes until the bombs are armed. *Shit.*

"Which way?" Max says, his face white and strained under his hood. "I can't remember."

I try to picture the map. "Down there," I say, pointing to our left.

"You sure?"

I nod, even though I'm not. I just hope we're not too late.

CHAPTER 30

We can't run in case anyone sees us and wonders what we're doing, but we walk as fast as we can. Although the streets are completely empty, I keep getting the feeling we're being watched, my scalp and the skin on the backs of my hands prickling. If we had more time, I'd check it out, make sure, but we don't have any time at all. So I tell myself I'm being paranoid. Who'd be following us anyway, except for ACID? And they wouldn't sneak up on us, they'd point their guns at us and shout at us to stop.

The streets begin to widen, the tower blocks giving way to shops and offices. Everything's shuttered, with holosigns in the windows saying CLOSED FOR RALLY DAY, and there's still no one about. It's kind of unnerving, actually—like everyone's been beamed up and Max and I are the only people left on earth.

"Look for a PKP," I tell Max as we reach a junction with a network of mag tracks running across it, although I can't see any mags anywhere. Being out in the open like this is making me nervous. I scan the area, but there don't seem to be any

PKPs either. Perhaps Manchester's already ripped its PKP network out. After all, who uses it these days when everyone has komms?

With the rain spattering down on my head, I weigh up our options. If we can't find a PKP, I'll have to convince someone to let me borrow their komm. Or knock them out and steal it.

If I can find anyone.

"There!" Max cries. I look in the direction he's pointing and see, near a dilapidated foodmart, a single PKP in a scuffed perspex booth, graffiti (nothing from NAR, thank goodness) etched deep into the plastic. *Please let it work please let it work please let it work,* I pray inside my head as we run across to it.

There's no holodisplay, just an old-fashioned printed sign next to it, barely readable. ALL LINKS EXCEPT THOSE TO ACID ARE CHARGEABLE AT THE USUAL RATES—PLEASE INSERT A VALID CITIZENSHIP CARD WITH ENOUGH KREDZ TO MAKE YOUR LINK.

"But you should be able to get through to ACID without one if it's free to link them, right?" Max says.

"I don't know," I say. I'm trying to remember how these things work. There are two buttons on the top, one green and one red, and a keypad underneath them with numbers on it. I hit the green button.

Nothing happens.

I press it again, jamming my thumb down on it. Suddenly, a holoscreen crackles into life at the back of the booth, the words PLEASE INSERT C-CARD jumping about on it. I remember that whoever picks up the link at the other end will be able to see me, so I pull my hood down farther over my face and tug the neck of my sweatshirt up to cover my chin and mouth. Then I stab the 9 key on the keypad.

For a moment, I think it's not going to work; that even to link ACID, you need a c-card, so they can check out who's linking them. Then the words disappear and the color of the screen changes from silver to green as the link goes through.

I look around for a news screen so I can check the time: 0829. Staring at the screen again, I shift from one foot to the other. *C'mon . . . c'mon . . .*

A woman's face appears; not a real woman but a static image—neat blond hair, saccharine smile. I wonder if it's supposed to be reassuring. "You are through to the ACID Crime Report Hotlink," a robotic voice says. "Everything you say will be recorded. Please state your name and c-card ID number."

"Listen," I say from behind the neck of my sweatshirt, desperately hoping there's a real person on the other end somewhere. "I'm in Manchester where the rally's taking place. You have to clear the square. There are explosive devices stuck to the buildings around the edge, and they're going to go off in thirty minutes." When there's no response, I say it again. "Clear the square. There are bombs. You have thirty minutes."

The woman's face disappears. She's replaced by an ACID agent, his expression shocked and angry. "What?" he says. "Who are you? Take your hood down and identify yourself."

"You have thirty minutes," I repeat, and hit the red button to cut the link.

Max and I walk away quickly, heading for a little side street beyond the shops. I still can't shake the feeling that someone's watching us, but every time I turn round, there's nothing there. No footsteps, no figure slipping into a doorway. I *must* be imagining it.

Then we hear sirens, and the thud of a roto—two rotos—approaching rapidly. Max grabs my hand and pulls me into the entranceway of the foodmart. Moments later, three electro vans with blacked-out windows and the ACID logo on the side go flying past, sirens screaming. The two rotos lumber overhead. Max and I press ourselves against the foodmart's shuttered doors, trying to melt into the shadows and become invisible.

"We did it," Max whispers when they've gone as, from a

distance, the wind blows the sound of the sirens and amplified voices back toward us.

"I hope so," I say. I don't feel so sure, but when I look at him, he's grinning, and there's something about it that's infectious. I feel a smile spread slowly across my face too, starting to feel almost hysterical with relief.

I shake my head. "We should get out of here."

Max's smile falters. "What if more vans come? We'll be right out in the open—they might recognize you from the PKP screen."

Shit. I hadn't thought of that. Only seconds after the words have left his mouth, I hear another siren approaching, and moments later a fourth van speeds past.

"Wait a bit, then," I say. "People will start coming back this way soon—if we're part of a crowd, we'll be less easy to spot."

We both pull back our hoods and crouch on the damp concrete in the entrance to the foodmart—it's too wet to sit—huddling side by side to wait.

"Mia?" Max says after a few moments.

I look round at him again.

"D'you think we'll ever make it back to London?"

"I don't know," I say. "D'you want to go back?"

"I'd like to know what's happened to Mum," he says, his forehead creasing with worry, and I feel guilt tug at my insides.

"What about your parents?" he says suddenly. "They must be worried about you."

I swallow hard. "I . . . don't have any parents," I say. "They died when I was little. Accident."

Max's expression changes to concern. "I'm so sorry."

"It's OK," I say, hating myself for lying to him; for all the lies I've ever told him, layer upon layer upon layer of them. "I don't really remember them."

"It still sucks, though," he says quietly.

189

I don't say anything. I can't look at him. But I know he's looking at me, and in the end I can't help it: I have to drag my gaze up to meet his. And when I see the concern still plainly visible in his eyes, mingled with sympathy and sorrow, I hate myself more than ever. I should get up. I should walk away from him. He'd be better off without me, even if he doesn't know it.

But I can't. I *can't*.

And I can't tear my gaze away from his. The air between us feels as if it's suddenly become charged with electricity. I remember last night, when he held on to my hand and we were so close I could feel his breath against my face.

I don't need to wonder if he was thinking the same as me anymore. I can see it in his eyes, as plainly as if he'd said the words out loud.

There's a pause, several heartbeats long. Then, still holding my gaze, he dips his head toward mine.

I come to my senses with a bump. "Max, *no!*" I gasp, pushing him away. "I can't—we mustn't—it's too dangerous—we have to get out of here and—"

"I thought we were waiting for there to be more people around?" he says, sounding puzzled and hurt.

"No. Actually, I think we should go," I say. "ACID will be looking for the people who sent the warning—they'll have figured out which PKP it came from—we have to leave *now*."

I scramble to my feet, brushing dirt off my back where I had it pressed against the shutters. Whichever way I turn, I seem to hurt him. But I *can't* let anything happen between us. Apart from anything else, it's too risky; he could find out who I am.

Max gets up too. "So, which way?" he says. His voice sounds cool, emotionless, and when I sneak a glance at him, I see his jaw is clenched. I open my mouth to speak, realize I have no idea what I want to say to him, and close it again.

"Mia. *Which way?*"

190

I blink, trying to regain my focus. "Um, down there," I say, pointing to the side street we were heading for before the vans went past. "We should keep off the main roads, I think."

"Fine." He pulls his hood back up and walks out onto the street, his arms wrapped around his middle. I hurry after him.

"Going somewhere?" asks a voice behind us.

We both turn to see Jacob step out of a shop doorway a few meters from where we were hiding, a smile on his face, his pack over his shoulder and a gun in his hand.

CHAPTER 31

"Walk," he says, pointing up the street with the gun. "And don't try any of that kung fu shit," he tells me. "If you so much as *twitch* in the wrong direction, I'll put a bullet through your boyfriend's head."

Max's eyes go wide.

We walk.

"Where are you taking us?" I say.

"The church," he says, pointing again, and I see a spire looming above the roofs to our left.

"Did you follow us?" I say, remembering the prickling sensation in my scalp and across the back of my hands as we made our way down here and wishing desperately that I'd paid it more attention.

"I certainly did." He sounds so smug that I want to take a swing at him, gun or no gun. "I had a feeling you were going to try to mess things up."

"You're too late, anyhow," I say. "I linked ACID. They know."

Jacob laughs. "Do you have any idea how long it's going to take to get everyone out of that square? They're panicking. It's chaos. And anyway, I might not have been quite accurate about the timers on the bombs."

I whirl round. *"What?"*

"Keep moving," he says, sliding his thumb across to the gun's charge switch.

I start to walk again, shaking. He's lying. He *has* to be. If the bombs go off while everyone's still trying to get out of the square . . .

We reach the church, which has boarded-over windows and a huge FOR SALE holosign outside. The doors have chains looped through the handles, but the padlock's missing. Jacob unwinds the chains and nudges one of the doors open with his foot. "In," he says.

Max hesitates.

"GO." Jacob jabs him in the back with the muzzle of the gun. Max stumbles forward into the church, and I follow.

Inside, it's so dark I can't see anything. There's a strong smell of damp and piss and mice. I hear Jacob take something out of his pack and shake it. A few seconds later, a glolamp flares dully into life.

In its weak glow, I can see we're near the altar. There's a vandalized holoscreen projector on the wall behind it. In front of us, rows of pews disappear into the shadows at the back of the church, and to our left is the pulpit, decorated with a massive, peeling gilt eagle with outstretched wings. Near the altar are some lightweight wooden chairs, piled one on top of another, most of them smashed to pieces. Jacob grabs a couple that are still in one piece, keeping the gun trained on me and Max the whole time, and places one at the base of the pulpit and one beside the front row of pews. "Sit down," he tells Max, taking some lengths of rope out of the bag.

Max sits, and, keeping the gun pointed at my head, Jacob

makes me tie him up, binding his wrists and legs and tying him and the chair to the pulpit rail. Then I sit down and, tucking the gun into his belt, Jacob binds my arms and legs so fast I don't even have a chance to *think* about fighting him off.

"Let us *go!*" I snap at him. "You can't do this!"

"I believe I just did," Jacob says, standing back and folding his arms, the gun hanging loosely from his right hand.

I strain against the ropes, but they're so tight, all that happens is I start to feel like I can't breathe. I relax, gasping again. "So what are you going to do?" I say when I've got my breath back. "Just leave us here?"

"Oh, don't you worry, I've got something special planned for you two," Jacob says, and I feel fear clench inside me.

"But all those people, they're going to die," Max says. His voice sounds hoarse and desperate.

"And?" Jacob says.

"They've done *nothing!*"

"It's a necessary sacrifice," he says, his voice as empty of emotion as his flat, unwavering gaze. "Their deaths will be a tragedy, but you need to look at the bigger picture here. ACID need to pay."

"You're crazy," Max says.

One corner of Jacob's mouth curves up in a smile. "How kind of you to say so."

"You're *sick,*" I say.

"Sick?" Jacob's smile broadens. "Really? If so, I'm in good company."

And in an instant, I know exactly what the next words out of his mouth are going to be.

"Don't," I say, hearing the pleading whine in my voice but too desperate to care. "Do anything you like to me, but not that."

Jacob's smile disappears and his face snaps back into a chilly, expressionless mask. "I warned you, didn't I?" he says.

194

"Mia?" Max says. "What's he on about?"

"She's not called Mia," Jacob says. "She's called Jenna Strong."

Then he turns and walks out of the church without another word.

CHAPTER 32

"Max . . . ," I say.

His face is white.

"You," he says. "*You.*"

"Max, I—"

"You lying bitch." His voice echoes around the empty church.

"Max—"

"You lying, murdering *bitch.*" His eyes are shining with fury and hate. "All this time, I thought you were helping me. I thought you *cared.* And it was all *lies.*"

"No," I say. "It wasn't. I *do* care!"

"You killed my dad," he says.

"No, I didn't! It was ACID!"

"*Liar.*"

Outside, I can still hear the cries of the crowd, ACID shouting orders through their komms to try and get everyone under control. A roto thuds overhead. Something hits the church doors with a crash, making me jump.

"Max, it was ACID," I say. "Your dad was the one who got me out of jail. An ACID agent caught him when he was up on the roof and tried to shoot him. He got away by throwing the guy off the roof. But then more agents turned up and . . ." I close my eyes and swallow, seeing Dr. Fisher lying facedown on the tarmac.

"That's crazy. Why would my dad do something like that?"

"And why do *you* think your mum told you to get away when ACID came to arrest you?" I say, opening my eyes again. "Whoever your dad was working for, she must have been in on it too. She must have known—and ACID thought *you* did as well."

Max shakes his head. "No. That's not possible. My parents weren't like that."

"How do you know?"

"How do *you*? You're a murderer. You're evil!"

"Max, I'm not." My voice catches. I take a ragged breath. "What happened to my parents—that was an accident too."

"Oh, yeah, of *course* it was." His voice is full of bruising sarcasm.

So I tell him the whole sorry story. About Dylan; about our plan to run away together; about my dad finding out I'd been seeing him and putting me under house arrest. About Dylan appearing like a ghost at my bedroom window one night—how he got past my dad's state-of-the-art security system, I'll never know—and, clinging to the drainpipe he'd climbed, leaning in through the window to pass me the pulse gun. "Use this," he said. "Make him let you go."

I stared at him. "Where did you get this from?" I asked him.

"It's my dad's."

"But what am I supposed to do with it?" I said. "You don't want me to shoot him, do you?"

Dylan laughed. "Of course not. Just threaten him with it. Do it tomorrow evening, after dinner. I'll be waiting for you in the park at the end of the road. I've got enough money to get us out of London. Please, Jenna."

And because I thought I loved him, because I thought this was what I really wanted, I took it. I hoped that he might kiss me for the first time—I felt like I'd been waiting forever—but he just left.

I hid the gun under my mattress until the next evening, when I excused myself from the dinner table to make a start on my homework, like I always did. But instead of calling up my schoolwork on my komm, I took the gun out and went back downstairs with it.

"I only meant to scare him," I said, hanging my head and closing my eyes, my voice barely louder than a whisper. "But my mum panicked. She tried to grab it, and it went off. Dad tried to pull her away while the charge was going through her and it arced across to him and got him too."

"BULLSHIT!" Max screams at me. He's struggling against the ropes around his arms and legs, his face flushed with anger, a vein standing out on his forehead.

"It's not," I whisper.

"Shut up," he says.

"Max—"

"Shut UP!"

I shut up.

Then, from outside, in the direction of the square, there's a dull, concussive *BOOM*.

And another.

And another.

I pull frantically, uselessly against the ropes, throwing my head back and shrieking. The sound echoes back at me from the vaulted roof, over and over and over.

Max watches me.

"I bet you wish you were out there, don't you?" he says. "Watching them go off. Watching people die."

His words are like a punch to the gut. "No!" I say.

He laughs, a bitter, sarcastic sound, then falls silent.

I hear more sirens coming up the street outside. I hold my breath, waiting for them to go past.

Instead, they stop, right outside the church.

I remember what Jacob said just after he'd tied us up. *Oh, don't you worry, I've got something special planned for you two.*

And I remember the seventy-five-thousand-kredz reward on my head.

But that doesn't make sense, I think. *He said he'd get more if he kept me in the NAR. Why would he—*

Because he can make it look as if *I* were behind the bomb attack, I realize. Then he and the others can get away and he can claim the reward somehow. Perhaps that was really his plan all along.

Six ACID agents burst into the church, bringing with them a rush of noise and the bitter smell of smoke. They spread out, five of them shining the flashlights mounted on their guns between the pews, while one walks straight up the aisle. Her flashlight beam gets me right in the face, and with my arms tied behind me, I can't even raise my hands to shade my eyes. I squint and blink, twisting my head to avoid the glare.

"What . . . ?" The agent swings her gun to the right and sees Max. She turns it back to me. Back to Max. Back to me.

"Oh my God," she says. "It *is* you."

I start to thrash and twist again, straining uselessly against the ropes. So does Max. "You don't want me!" he yells. "You want her! She's a murderer!"

"Max, I'm *not*!" I shout.

"Stay still, both of you, or I'll shoot!" the agent yells.

Max and I both sag back in our chairs. The other agents come rushing up the aisle. I close my eyes so I don't have to watch them running toward us, but I can't block out the sound of their boots thundering against the stone floor.

It's a sound like the end of the world.

AGENCY FOR CRIME INVESTIGATION AND DEFENSE

Sunday 11 June 2113   Usual Download Charges Apply

The Daily Report

Official News Site for the Agency for Crime Investigation and Defense
All the latest stories, straight to your komm!

Front Page • Crime • Money • Arts/Culture • Sport • Images • Other News

Jenna Strong Recaptured After Manchester Bomb Blast Kills 10, Injures 120

Teenage murderer Jenna Strong, who has been on the run since she escaped from Mileway Prison in April, was recaptured by ACID last night in Manchester. Her dramatic rearrest took place after an anonymous tipoff led ACID agents to a church near the city center, where she was found with Max Fisher, the son of Mileway doctor Alex Fisher, whom Strong shot and killed when she broke out of jail.

It is thought Strong played a crucial part in the bomb plot, which took place during an ACID rally in the city's ceremony square attended by ACID chief and IRB president General Harvey. The bombs were planted at various points in the crowd gathered to watch the rally and were timed to go off close together, but all but one of the devices failed to detonate and were later destroyed by ACID under controlled conditions.

OTHER HEADLINES

ACID promise swift repairs to infrastructure damaged by Manchester blast

Helplink and shelters set up for victims' families and those left homeless

Reports of riots in York and Cardiff after Manchester tragedy "nothing but rumors," ACID chiefs assure public

"Although today's events are an absolute tragedy, this could have been so much worse,'" ACID spokesperson and subcommander Anna Healey told reporters earlier. "ACID will be investigating Strong's link to the bomb plot as a matter of the highest importance, and aim to bring her and any other perpetrators to justice as quickly as possible." ACID are still investigating how Max Fisher came to be with Strong but have released a statement saying that they suspect she kidnapped him, possibly with the intention of blackmailing his mother.

Report by Claire Fellowes
Interviews by Dasha Lowe

For images of the Mileway riots, link **here**
For the story of the Strong murder trial, link **here**
For an interview with Myra Hogg, link **here**
For an interview with Lukas Jennings, link **here**
To comment on this story, link **here** (will be moderated)

AGENCY FOR CRIME INVESTIGATION AND DEFENSE

PUBLIC WARNING

Remember – it is an offense to display public affection with anyone other than your LifePartner. This includes hugging and hand-holding.

Anyone caught engaging in such activities faces an unlimited fine and up to 10 years in prison.

To report offenders, link KommWeb9

11 June 2113

Dear Jenna,

I don't know what to do. I don't know what to say. This is going to be the hardest thing I've ever done — watching you suffer and knowing there's nothing I can do to stop it. That I'll have to encourage it, even.

All I can do is pray that you'll stay strong. That somehow, you'll know someone's looking out for you, even though you won't know who it is, and I won't be able to tell you.

I promise you this, though: as soon as I can, I'll get you away from what they've got planned for you.

xx

INTERROGATION

CHAPTER 33

ACID Interrogation Center, Upper London
13 June 2113

I hate you. I HATE YOU!

Every time I close my eyes, I hear Max's words, see his face as it looked when they led him away from me, twisted in anger and fury. I try to conjure up other, happier memories, like when we were pretending to be a couple at Clearford Library, and how after a while it didn't feel so much like pretending anymore, or the moment he let slip how he really felt about me and the joy that blossomed inside me, despite my almost instantaneous realization that I had to keep pretending I just wanted us to be friends.

I wish I hadn't done that, I think bitterly. *I wish I'd told him how I really felt too.*

But would it have made any difference, in the end?

The clunk of a lock being drawn back jolts me away from

my thoughts about Max and back to reality: the tiny, window-less cell at ACID's interrogation center in Upper, with a sleeping mat, a lumpy pillow and a thin, scratchy blanket in one corner, and a stinking toilet with no seat or lid in the other.

I've been locked up in here for three days, ever since I arrived. Too wired to sleep for more than a couple of hours at a time, I've spent most of it pacing the floor or doing squats and push-ups. I haven't been allowed to have a shower yet; I haven't even been given a change of clothes. My hair's tangled and greasy, my skin itches and there's a rancid taste in my mouth. It's just like two years ago when I was arrested after my parents' deaths. I had to stay in my blood-soaked school uniform for almost two weeks, until it was time for me to be sentenced. Then I cried and pleaded with them every day to let me have some new clothes. This time, I haven't said or done anything. If they think they can break me, they're in for a shock.

Two ACID agents enter the cell. The first trains her gun on me while the second unclips a set of wrist and leg restraints from her belt. I stand in silence while she cuffs me, smiling inwardly at her sour expression. I know I must smell as bad as I look.

"Walk," she says, giving me a push between the shoulders with her gloved fingertips.

They lead me out of the cell and along a corridor outside. We pass a few other ACID agents, who stare at me. Then we reach the interrogation rooms, a line of doors with little holo-signs on them. The agent with the gun taps a button beside one marked VACANT and, as it hisses open, gestures for me to go inside. It looks just like I remember: a thick Plexiglas screen divides the room in half, and on my side there's nothing but a chair with metal loops so my restraints can be fixed to it, and a microphone for me to speak into. On the other side is another door, a desk, potted plants and a jug of ice water, frosted with condensation, that I'd sell my soul for right now.

I lick my dry lips and sit down on the chair. The second agent attaches my restraints to the loops. Then they both leave.

I gaze through the Plexiglas, my heart thudding, the thick silence in the room roaring in my ears. So they're going to interview me. *At last.* But do they really believe I'm going to tell them anything?

God, I hope Mel and Jon are OK, I think, feeling a chill in the pit of my stomach. *I hope ACID haven't caught up with them.*

And what about Max? Is he somewhere in the building too? Ever since ACID found us, he's almost all I've thought about. The knowledge that he could be just a few doors away from me—in the next cell, even—has tortured me in a way my filthy clothes and cramped cell and the terrible food can't even come close to.

On the other side of the screen, the door slides back, and two more agents enter the room. One of them is a guy: squat as a bullfrog, shaven-headed, with a face like a lump of badly kneaded dough. The other . . .

I stare.

It's Subcommander Healey. Agent Robot. She looks even more plastic in real life than she does on the screens. As she and Bullfrog sit down at the table, she regards me coolly. I shake my tangled hair out of my face and gaze back at her.

She touches her komm—to film the interrogation, I presume—then taps the holocom base on the table to turn it on.

"Please state your name," she says, her voice coming through a speaker above me somewhere.

I lean forward as much as my restraints will let me and say into the microphone, "You know my name."

"Please state your name," she says.

I say nothing.

"What were you doing in Manchester?" she asks me.

"I tried to tell the agents who found us," I say. "No one gave a shit then. Why are you so interested now?"

She taps the holocom base and the side of the screen facing me suddenly flickers on, showing footage from an agent's vid-feed. Me and Max, tied to the chairs. Me squinting in the glare from the ACID agent's flashlight. Me screaming as I'm untied and cuffed, "You have to find a guy called Jacob! He did this to us! There are more bombs out there! THERE ARE MORE BOMBS OUT THERE!"

One of the ACID agents strikes me across the face to silence me; the bruise on my cheekbone is spectacular now. "We know about the bombs," he says. "The guy who linked us to report that he'd apprehended you told us all about them. We're working to defuse them right now."

"But that guy was Jacob!" I cry. "He's the one you want! He made us do this—there are others too—"

"Shut up," the agent says. He hauls me to my feet. I see myself looking at Max, whose face, in the flashlight, is pale and frozen with anger. "Max," I hear myself say.

"Shut up," he says. "I hate you. I HATE YOU!"

Then the agents holding him manhandle him out of the church at gunpoint.

That was the last time I saw him.

"You knew about the other bombs," Subcommander Healey says. "How?"

"No comment," I say. "Where's Max? What have you done with him?"

"We're asking the questions, not you," Bullfrog says. "How did you know about the bombs?"

"No comment," I say again.

The interview goes on like this for what feels like hours, with Bullfrog and Subcommander Healey shooting questions at me about Manchester and Mileway, about Dr. Fisher, about how I met Max and where I was living after I escaped.

I answer *No comment* to every single one.

"So you say you knew nothing about the plan to get you out

of Mileway? That it came as a complete surprise?" Bullfrog says for about the twentieth time. He looks bored as hell.

I yawn. "No comment."

As I wait for the next question, Subcommander Healey stands up and nods at the securikomm mounted on the wall in the corner. Clearly, this session's over. A few seconds later, the door behind me slides open and the two ACID agents come back in. I'm unshackled from the chair, then marched back to my cell.

Inside, with my restraints removed, I slump on my mat with my back to the wall. My stomach rumbles and I try desperately not to think about food. There's no way of knowing when my next meal might be; I don't even know when I'll be dragged back to the interrogation room. It could be twenty minutes before they come to get me again, or it could be twenty hours.

I think about Max again, sick to my stomach that I couldn't make him believe what I told him about my parents or his dad. He'll never know, now, how much I care about him. I want to be back in our little den in the library with him. I want that moment back when he tried to kiss me. And this time, I want to let him, and I want to kiss him back.

And knowing I'll never have that again makes me want to curl into a ball and howl.

Four days pass. In between interrogation sessions, I eat every bit of food they bring me and exercise and sleep as much as I can, determined to keep my strength up. My clothes and hair are disgusting now, but I try not to care, and take pleasure in the fact that most of the agents who come into my cell have started wearing face masks.

I've just got back from an interrogation session and have started doing squat thrusts in the middle of my cell when the door suddenly clunks open again. It's an ACID agent. Sighing inwardly, I straighten up and wait for him to cuff me. Five minutes since the last session? This has to be a record. But instead of going back up to the interrogation room, we take the lift down a couple of floors. Two more agents are waiting for us: a woman with a short, squareish haircut and a skinny guy with a face like a rodent's. Square Hair takes my arm and propels me down the corridor to a little room with a window in the door, which she opens before removing my cuffs and pushing me inside.

"You've got five minutes," she says as she closes the door behind me again. "Leave your clothes by the door."

Puzzled, I look around me. The walls, floor and ceiling are covered in dark green tiles and there's a smell of damp in the air. Over in the corner, I see pipes. A tap coming out of the wall beside them. A thin, ragged towel hanging on a hook nearby.

Oh my God. A shower. They're letting me have a shower. Despite my determination not to let anything get to me, I feel an overwhelming rush of relief, and have to swallow hard against the lump that rises in my throat.

I strip my filthy clothes off as fast as I can, and run across to the shower with my arms crossed over my chest, ignoring Square Hair watching me through the window in the door. The water's cold, but I don't care about that either. Grabbing the bar of bitter-smelling soap from the floor by the shower drain, I scrub myself all over with it, rubbing it through my hair and using my fingers to rake out the worst of the knots. Before I turn the water off I scoop some of it into my mouth and sigh in relief as I feel it flow down my parched throat. Then I wrap myself in the towel, trying not to shiver.

Square Hair opens the door. "Here." She hands me a bundle which, when I unwrap it, I discover contains a pair of trousers with an elasticated waist, a shapeless shirt, some underwear and a thin pair of slip-on shoes. Nothing fits properly—the clothes are too big and the shoes too small—but they're clean. The other agent, Rodent Face, pulls on plastic gloves and piles my old clothes into a bag marked BIOHAZARD—FOR INCINERATION.

It's only when we're in the lift again that I start to wonder what the hell's going on. Am I being moved? As Square Hair jabs the button to take us up, my stomach starts twisting with nerves.

But when the doors open and I see we're on the interrogation-room floor, I relax again. It's just another session with Subcommander Healey and her pet troll. They probably got fed up of me stinking the room out every time I was in there.

Square Hair takes me to an interrogation room—not the one I was in previously, but a larger room with no Plexiglas screen. Apart from the table in the middle, which has two ordinary chairs on one side and one with restraints on the other, it's empty. I sit down in the one with restraints, and Square Hair shackles me to it, then leaves.

I crane my neck, looking round the room. For some reason, I feel nervous again, apprehension fluttering inside me like moth wings. Behind me, the door hisses open. Two ACID agents walk around me and sit down at the table. One is Subcommander Healey, her face as smooth and emotionless as if it's carved from stone.

And the other . . .

He smiles at me, and my heart lurches up into my throat.

"Hello, Jenna," General Harvey says. "What a long time it's been."

CHAPTER 34

General Harvey. The chief of ACID. The IRB president.

My one-time godfather.

The general and my father trained together, were rookie agents together, even headed a department together. But then the general started to rise through the ranks, leaving my father behind. He was elected ACID chief—which meant he automatically attained the status of IRB president—just after my ninth birthday. He and my father kept in touch, though. Sometimes, he'd come over for Sunday lunch with his son, Greg, whose favorite pastime when we were kids was picking his nose, and when we both hit puberty, staring at my chest. The older I became, the more I used to dread being left alone with him. Remembering the way he'd breathe noisily through his mouth as he looked at me makes me shudder even now.

"I must say, Jenna, whoever altered your face was very skilled. Have they been treating you well here?" the general says with a small smile that tells me he knows damn well they haven't, and it's probably been on his orders.

214

I shrug.

"You're not being very cooperative, are you, Jenna?" he says.

I raise an eyebrow. "What's the point? You're going to put me back in jail no matter what I say."

The general raises an eyebrow. I glance at Subcommander Healey. She's fiddling with her komm, not looking at me. "We know Dr. Fisher got you out of jail," the general says.

"Really? I thought *I* held him hostage and made him smuggle me out," I say sarcastically.

"We both know what really happened," the general parries. "What *I* want to know is who he was working for. And I would like *you* to tell me."

"Can't," I say. "Because they wouldn't tell *me*."

"Who are *they*?"

"The three little pigs."

"Jenna . . ." He smiles again, but it's a tight, humorless smile. I can see I'm getting to him. Good.

"I've got a question for *you*," I say. "Why did you say I'd killed Dr. Fisher?"

"Never you mind about that." The general flicks an invisible piece of dirt off his sleeve. "Who got you out, Jenna? What are their names?"

"Eeny, Meeny, Miney and Mo," I say.

A flush is starting to steal up the general's neck. I watch as he clenches and unclenches his fists. Subcommander Healey is still looking at something on her komm, obviously happy to let him do all the questioning. Then he puts a hand to his ear. "Excuse me," he says to Subcommander Healey, frowning. "I must take this link."

He leaves the room, saying, "What? Be quick—I'm in the middle of interrogating the Strong girl!"

As soon as the door hisses shut behind him, Subcommander Healey snaps off her komm and leans forward. "It's all right," she says. "You can tell him Mel and Jon's names. He won't find them. They're safe."

I stare at her. What? How the hell does she know about Mel and Jon? What if ACID have got them and she's taunting me, trying to make me confess to knowing them? I start to ask her, but General Harvey returns. He sits down and sighs.

"I was hoping it wouldn't come to this," he says as I stare at the tabletop, my mind racing as I try to make sense of what Subcommander Healey just said. "But you've left me no option." I look up at him again and he leans his elbows on the table, steepling his fingers. "I'm going to offer you a choice," he says. "And I want you to think very carefully about it before you make your decision."

"What?" I say. For once, I can't come up with a smart answer. My palms are damp with sweat.

"If you tell us the names of the people who helped you," he says, "we will allow you to be LifePartnered. You'll be given accommodation—in Upper, mind—and a job."

"LifePartnered?"

"Yes. Wouldn't that be nice?"

I stare at him. "But why would you do that?" I say. "I'm supposed to be a murderer."

"We will, of course, take steps to ensure your identity is kept secret," the general says smoothly, as if I hadn't even spoken. "You'll undergo a process called cognitive realignment, which will make you, and those around you, believe you are someone else. It's harmless but necessary if you are to make a smooth transition into your new life."

"You'll do what?" I say. Now I don't just feel confused—I feel like none of this is real. I'll wake up in my cell in a minute, still in my old, filthy clothes, and realize that all this is just a dream. "Cognitive *what*?"

"Cognitive realignment. We use a combination of hypnotherapy and drugs to make subtle alterations to your prefrontal cortex. It doesn't hurt, and you won't remember anything about your old life afterward."

I stare at him. I've never heard of it, but it sounds . . . *awful*.

"The other option," the general says, "is rather more drastic. At this very moment, ACID are bringing in a new law. One that will allow us to deal with this country's most troublesome criminals—of which you are certainly one—in, shall we say, a rather more effective manner than we've been doing up to now."

He presses his fingers together again and looks straight at me.

"We are bringing back the death penalty, Jenna," he says. "If you don't sign a confession and agree to be LifePartnered, you will be publicly hanged in one of the city's ceremony squares in three weeks' time."

CHAPTER 35

A wave of freezing cold goes through me, pins and needles scattering all over my body as, in my mind, I see the Zone M ceremony square with a gibbet at one end instead of a stage.

"Why is that the other option?" I say, hearing my voice as if it's coming from a long way away. "Why don't you just send me back to prison? I don't understand."

"I'm not asking you to understand," the general says, standing up. "I'm asking you to choose. You have until the next interrogation session."

It's only after he's gone that I realize he hasn't said when that will be.

Back in my cell—which, in my absence, has been swabbed down with a disinfectant strong enough to make my eyes sting, and the blanket on my sleeping mat exchanged for a clean one—I sit down on the floor with my legs crossed, trying to figure it out. Why has he offered me this choice? Why is the other option being given a new identity and a new life, and not just going back to prison?

It doesn't take me long to figure it out. If I go to jail as Jenna Strong, I'm still me, with my own thoughts, my own identity. Prison didn't break me before and it won't this time either. And because I have associations with the NAR now, there might even be people in jail who view me as some kind of hero. It would be better—*much* better—for ACID to turn me into someone else, someone who'll quietly and willingly become just another cog in the machine of IRB society.

No! I think, despair ballooning inside me. *I won't do it!*

But I don't want to die either. Could I find some way to fight the cognitive realignment—resist the hypnotherapy or stop the drugs from taking effect? I pound a fist against the floor. What the hell sort of choice *is* this?

A short while later, an ACID agent comes to fetch me. General Harvey and Subcommander Healey are waiting for me in the same interrogation room.

"Well?" General Harvey says.

I glance at Subcommander Healey and she gives me an almost imperceptible nod.

I stare at the table.

"Well?" General Harvey says again.

I look up at him and tell him my decision.

JESSICA

CONGRATULATIONS, JESSICA!

You have been assigned your LifePartner!

As you know, LifePartnering is one of the most important—and exciting!—events in any young person's life. It means your life companion has been chosen for you, in a painstaking, individually tailored process that ensures your LifePartner's intellect, values and personality are equal to your own. Once you and your LifePartner have taken part in your LifePartnering ceremony and made your LifePartnering vows, you will both be considered adult citizens, and will be entitled to the many bonuses LifePartnering brings, such as accommodation, a car and employment. You will also be able to start a family!

You will be required to visit your local LifePartner Bureau offices on **24 June 2113** for your LifePartnership Ceremony. Please bring your parents or other responsible adult members of your family as witnesses, and your citizenship-card.

May I once again take the opportunity to congratulate you, and wish you all the best for the future.

Yours truly,

G Holt

Gavin Holt
LifePartner Officer

Reply   Forward   Delete   Store

CHAPTER 36

LifePartner ceremony rooms, Upper London
24 June 2113

Although the dose of medication I took just before lunch is making me feel floaty and surreal, I can't suppress a flutter of excitement as the official from ACID's LifePartnering department enters the room.

Evan's standing beside me, gazing straight ahead. He looks even more handsome than usual, his honey-blond hair combed back, and the purple silk of his tie—which matches the color of my silk sheath dress exactly—bringing out the blue in his eyes. As the LifePartnering official greets his parents and fourteen-year-old sister, Suki, who are sitting on plush chairs behind us, I sneak glances at him. The air is filled with the scent of the flowers that stand in vases on plinths around us, and soft classical music drifts from hidden speakers. Everything is perfect.

A lump rises in my throat. If only *my* mother and father were here to see this. But when the roto my parents, my brother and

I were taking up to Scotland for our summer holiday last year crashed, I was the only one to survive. I was in hospital for three months, and a rehabilitation unit, receiving physiotherapy and counseling, for another two. Then, as neither of my parents had siblings and both sets of my grandparents died when I was very young, I moved into a supervised living facility. It's OK, but it looks and smells just like the rehab unit, and I'm glad that this morning was the last time I'll ever see it.

The medication I take, administered three times a day by a microneedle concealed in the pretty silver bracelet I wear at all times on my right wrist, even at night, is to stop the nightmares and flashbacks that were making it impossible for me to move on, even after my physical injuries had finally healed. I've been on it since March, and although my doctors have had to adjust the dose several times to get it right, it's finally starting to work. Which means I've been able to be LifePartnered and that, very soon, I'll be starting a new job. Everything's back to normal—almost.

I swallow the lump in my throat back down, blink away the tears that have sprung up in my eyes and try to smile at the LifePartnering official as he takes his place in front of me and Evan. He smiles back, distantly. Evan's expression doesn't change. I wonder if he's nervous. He's never *seemed* nervous before now; in fact, this last month, during our chaperoned twice-weekly meetings at his house, he's come across as being quite the opposite—impatient to get the ceremony over with so we can move into our apartment and away from his parents, who, he confided in me once when they were briefly out of earshot, drive him crazy with their constant fussing. Privately, I think he's lucky; I'd give anything to have my parents back to fuss over me. But I didn't say that to him, of course.

The LifePartnering official clears his throat and begins reading out the LifePartnering vows for me to say after him.

"I, Jessica Stone . . ."

"I, Jessica Stone . . . ," I repeat.

"Take Evan Denbrough . . ."

"Take Evan Denbrough . . ."

"As my LifePartner, to whom I agree to be joined for the rest of my natural life."

I repeat the sentence, relieved at getting through it without stumbling or forgetting any of the words. Then it's Evan's turn.

"I, Evan Denbrough . . ."

"I, Evan Denbrough . . . ," Evan intones.

"Take Jessica Stone . . ."

When it's over, Evan turns to kiss me, his lips brushing against mine so briefly I wonder if I imagined it. The LifePartnering official gives us another, warmer smile. "Congratulations," he says. "If you'd like to say goodbye to everyone, a car is waiting for you outside to take you to your apartment."

Evan takes my hand, his strong grip crushing my fingers, and leads me over to his mum, dad and Suki, who are getting up from their chairs. While his mum and his sister are both petite with curly, light brown hair, Evan looks just like his dad—although his dad's hair is speckled with gray and there are faint lines at the corners of his eyes. "Good luck, darling," his mother says, sniffling. "I do hope your apartment's nice. Don't hesitate to link us if you need anything, and don't forget to bring Jess over for lunch tomorrow. I need to go over the plans for your Partnering party with you, and—"

"We'll be there, Mum," Evan says, a barely disguised note of irritation tinging his voice. He moves on to shake his father's hand while his mum hugs me and dabs at her eyes again. I feel another twinge of sorrow, remembering my own mum hugging me, and I'm suddenly very glad of the medication bubbling through my bloodstream. If I wasn't on it, I'd be a sobbing wreck right now.

The LifePartnering official is holding the door open for us, the music that played throughout the ceremony fading. It's time

226

for us to go. As I follow Evan out into the foyer, I can't resist a glance at the next couple who are waiting to be called in. The girl is red-haired and slim, the boy dark and athletic-looking. Their outfits, like mine and Evan's, are understatedly expensive, although, secretly, I think my dress fits me better than the girl's does her. She catches my eye and gives me an appraising stare; for a moment, I think she can tell—about my accident, about the meds—but I remind myself that this isn't possible. The surgeons performed intricate surgery on my face, erasing every last mark from the wounds I suffered when I went through the roto windshield. To look at me, you wouldn't think anything had ever happened. The only scars I have left are inside.

And with the meds, they're getting wiped away too.

Holding my head high, I let Evan lead me through the foyer and down the steps outside, to where a silver car is waiting by the curb. From now on, we'll be able to link for a car whenever we want to go anywhere, even if it's just down the road. The driver's standing next to it and opens the back door as we approach. The sun pours down from a cloudless blue sky.

"Thank God that's over," Evan grumbles, getting in after me and slumping into the seat. He yanks his tie loose and tosses it in my direction. "Get that for me, would you, babe?"

The medication slows my reactions a little, and I fumble and drop it. As I lean down to pick it up, the car starts to move, its electric motor whirring softly. I buckle my seat belt and look out of the window, watching the streets slide past outside. We're in Upper London's business and commerce district, but you'd hardly know it. The shops look like houses and offices that just happen to have goods tastefully displayed in their large front windows. I remember visiting some of them with Lucy and Eri, my best friends, before the accident, when we used to come up here at weekends. We'd head straight for the most expensive clothes boutiques and put whatever we wanted onto our parents' accounts, staggering out with our arms full of bags and boxes, laughing and chatting as we headed somewhere for a coffee.

They came to see me a few times in the hospital, but their visits got further and further apart, and I haven't seen them at all since I got out of the rehabilitation unit. I've thought about linking them a couple of times, but the last time I saw them they were both about to be LifePartnered and kept going on about how busy they were. I kept telling myself I *would* get in touch with them anyway, but every time I decided to do it, something stopped me, and now it's got to the point where it's easier not to bother.

It doesn't matter, anyway. I'm moving on. It's healthier for me to cut the ties to my old life.

I continue to gaze out the window, at the larger buildings soaring skyward behind the shops, graceful constructions of glass and silvery steel that gleam in the sun. Beyond them, because this district is at Upper's edge, I can see the tall screen of poplars that marks the boundary between Upper and Middle. People walk along the wide, clean pavements with the careless air of those who have nothing to worry about, taking their time, stopping to talk with friends. I suddenly feel very lucky to be part of all this, and even luckier that when we have children, Evan and I will be bringing them up to have all this too. My Upper London childhood was idyllic, and I want theirs to be the same.

Then my mood changes. At first, I think I'm about to have a flashback, and I feel my palms turn clammy and my heartbeat speed up. But it's something else; a deeper memory. Disjointed images I can't make sense of flood into my mind: crowded streets hemmed in by concrete apartment blocks that are halfway to being derelict; litter, graffiti, misery. Where is this place? I've never been anywhere like that, have I?

It's too early to take another dose of my meds. I breathe in and out, telling myself, *I am Jessica Denbrough. I am in a car with my new LifePartner on the way to my new apartment.* Identifying who I am and where I am, like they taught me at the rehab center. Slowly, the thoughts fade.

"Are you OK?" Evan says. I look round and see he's watching me.

"I'm fine," I say. "I'm just tired. It's been a—a big day for me."

Evan nods. We haven't talked about my problems much, but he seems pretty accepting, which I'm grateful for.

I sit back in my seat, feeling myself relax. Soon, we've left the commercial district behind and are driving through one of the residential areas. Everywhere I look, summer flowers foam from the window boxes planted by Upper's maintenance crews, who buzz about discreetly early in the mornings and last thing at night, keeping our city looking perfect. At last, the driver pulls into a cul-de-sac and we stop outside an elegant apartment building five stories high.

The driver gets out and opens my door. As I clamber out of the car, I gaze at the building that is now my home. I feel that flutter of excitement inside me again. Even from the outside, it looks beautiful, built from pinkish stone with cream trim and arched windows. Wide steps lead up to the front door, which is flanked by cream-colored columns and a tree in a pot on each side. An engraved sign next to the door says LABURNUM HOUSE, 5–10 ITALY CRESCENT, and a small holoscreen shows a list of names: ours and our neighbors'. We're in Apartment 10, on the top floor.

"Your c-cards work the door to the building and give you exclusive access to your apartment," the driver says as Evan gets out of the car too. "You should receive all the information about your new jobs over the kommweb tonight."

Then, with a slight bow of his head, he ducks back into the car and drives away.

"D'you want to go first?" Evan says.

"Um, yes, thank you," I say. I climb the steps to the front door with him right behind me.

"Here." He reaches past me to wave his c-card across the scanlock, then pushes the door open with his fingertips so I can go through. I step into a hallway with a real wooden floor and cream walls. It's spotless, and the air smells of lemons. We walk down to the lift, which has more wooden paneling inside, and gleaming gold-trimmed touchpads.

"Well, here we are," Evan says as we reach our apartment. He waves his c-card at the scanlock and holds the door open for me again, and I step through and into the huge, open-plan living room of my new apartment. I feel like I'm stepping into the beginning of a whole new life.

Evan slings his jacket on a hook near the door, removes his komm and shoves it in his pocket, then slumps onto one of the sofas (there are two, made from soft brown leather, smelling brand-new but with a finish that makes them look like well-cared-for antiques). He switches on the news screen that takes up almost all the wall opposite where he's sitting. I leave him watching it and start exploring.

Above a long dining table, a window looks out across Upper. I can see the city glittering in the sun, and the trees at the Upper boundary, with the jumble of buildings that make up Middle just visible beyond. Outer is no more than a smudge on the horizon, and I'm glad. I've never been there, but I heard plenty of horror stories about what it's like from my parents when I was younger, and at school—tiny, overcrowded flats, drug addicts and criminals everywhere, despite ACID's attempts to keep them in check. It sounds like a dreadful place.

Just off the living room is an equally large kitchen, all steel and glass, so well stocked it would put any restaurant to shame. Jars filled with pasta and rice and lentils and all sorts of other things line a set of shelves beside the refrigerator. Fresh fruit spills from a gigantic wire basket on the counter next to the stove, and there are ropes of garlic and onions, bunches of dried herbs and chilies and gleaming copper pans hanging from a rack above a long island in the middle of the room, which has a fancy-looking oven and stove built into it. A holoscreen memo panel on the wall near the door has a message informing me that a cleaning service will visit every other day while Evan and I are at work.

And then there are the bedrooms—two, each with a king-sized bed in it, and in the master, a wardrobe full of new clothes and shoes for me and Evan. Both bedrooms have their own en suite bathroom with a shower and a Jacuzzi, baskets of soaps and bottles of bath oil and shampoo on shelves above the tubs. As I go back into the living room, I notice the sensor panels tracking the air temperature and our body temperatures, readings scrolling across little holoscreens on the walls as the heating and air-conditioning adjust automatically to keep the apartment at an optimum temperature.

"It's lovely, isn't it?" I say, dropping onto the second sofa, which has been arranged at a right angle to the other one.

Evan glances round at me before returning his gaze to the news screen, which is showing a report about ACID finding an illegal cigarette and whisky haul in Outer. "Yeah, 's OK," he says.

My eyes sting briefly with tears as I think about how my parents and my brother will never come to visit me here, will never see how well I'm doing for myself.

To distract myself, I get up again. The display at the top of the news screen says it's almost eighteen hundred hours. "Are you hungry?" I ask Evan. "Do you want me to cook something?" I'm determined to be a good LifePartner to him, to take care of him and make sure he doesn't want for anything.

"Hmm? Oh, no, it's all right. I'm going to the gym in a bit, and then I've got to call on a friend. I'll eat there, probably."

"Oh," I say.

He raises his eyebrows. "That OK?"

"Um, of course," I reply. *Except I thought we might spend the evening together, eat a meal, talk . . . ,* I add silently in my head. It's the first time we've ever been properly alone together, and I can't help feeling disappointed that Evan doesn't want to make the most of it.

I remember what my teachers used to say in our Preparing for LifePartnering classes at school. *Your relationship with your Partner will take time to grow. You'll need to be patient with each other and give each other space to get to know each other. Don't feel as if you have to do everything together, or find out everything about each other straight away. Let your relationship develop naturally.*

Of course. We've only known each other a month, after all, and we've never been alone together before. This probably feels as strange for Evan as it does for me.

I take a deep breath. "Sure," I say again, trying to make my feelings match the brightness of my tone. "Will you be back late?"

"Not sure. Don't bother waiting up if I am," he says, getting up and stretching. As he passes me he gives me a quick peck on the lips. "See you later."

I gaze at the door as it closes, fighting a sudden rush of loneliness.

Don't be stupid, Jess, I tell myself as I walk back through to the kitchen with my arms hugged around my middle. *You don't own him.*

And besides, I'm lucky to be *alive,* never mind have a LifePartner.

Reminding myself sternly not to forget that, I pull open the fridge to look inside.

CHAPTER 37

After I've eaten—a small bowl of chicken stir-fry—I run the Jacuzzi, pouring a capful of scented bath oil into the water. Then I soak for almost an hour, surrounded by clouds of foam.

When I get out and I've wrapped myself in one of the fluffy towels from the heated rail near the door, I go over to the mirror and rub away some of the condensation. My reflection gazes back at me, and for a moment, it's as if I'm looking at a stranger's face. This has happened a lot since the accident. It no longer frightens me, though; it's just annoying. To shake my sense of disorientation, I go through the steps I worked out with my counselor back at the rehab unit. *I am Jess Stone,* I think, looking at the mousy brown hair that hangs in tendrils around my face, already starting to take on its usual slight wave even though it's still wet; then at my eyes, which are a nondescript color that's somewhere between gray and green. My face is thinner since the accident and there are shadows under my eyes that weren't there before, but they're the only things noticeably changed. I still have a straight, narrow nose, and my left ear still

233

sticks out slightly more than my right. When I feel like myself again, I turn away from the mirror and grab another towel to wrap around my head.

I spend the rest of the evening in bed, rereading one of my favorite eFics on my komm. It's a romance called *Hidden Hero* where the young heroine, Kelsie, is LifePartnered to an undercover ACID agent, Brad. He can't reveal his true identity to Kelsie in case it blows his cover, as she works with people he's investigating, so all sorts of misunderstandings occur as he's called away for his work, and can't tell her where he's going or why. In the end, though, the people Brad is watching realize Kelsie is linked to ACID. They kidnap her and demand a ransom, and when Brad finally rescues her, she finds out who he really is. I reread the last line three times: *LifePartnering had found Kelsie not only her true love, but her very own hero too.* Then I switch off my komm with a happy sigh.

Please let me and Evan feel like that about each other, I think. I close my eyes, trying to relax, but I can't fall asleep. I'm thinking about when Evan gets home, about when he gets into bed with me. Will he want to have sex? I know what I'm supposed to do, I think. Lucy and Eri and I used to talk about it when we were sleeping over at each other's houses. But what if we were wrong? There's never anything about it in eFics, and the only stuff they ever taught us at school were the biological bits and about our contracep implants, which stop us getting pregnant before we receive our notifications. Mine was put in just before I met Evan for the first time.

Evan gets home about midnight; I can see the time on the little holoscreen on the wall. I watch him undress in the semi-dark, my heart racing. Then he goes into the bathroom and shuts the door. I see a line of light appear underneath it, and hear the shower running. When he comes back out, I close my eyes, pretending to be asleep, feeling the mattress dip as he climbs in beside me. I lie there with my arms rigid against my sides as I wait to feel his hands on my body, his lips against mine. Will it hurt?

But all he does is roll onto his side, taking most of the duvet with him, and a few minutes later he's snoring softly. I gaze up at the ceiling, filled with a mixture of disappointment and relief.

CHAPTER 38

The next morning, I get up early and prepare breakfast in bed for Evan: scrambled eggs on toast, a pot of coffee and a glass of juice, which I take to him on a tray. He sits up, blinking, as I set it down on his bedside table.

"Wow, did you make all this for me?" he says.

I nod.

"Oh, man." He rubs his hands through his hair. "This looks great, Jess, but we're going to Mum and Dad's in a few hours. If I eat all this I won't be able to manage lunch."

Damn. Sunday lunch. I forgot all about it.

"I—I'm sorry," I stammer. "I—"

"It's fine. I'll eat half." Evan flashes me a smile.

Afterward, I take the tray back into the kitchen and scrape the uneaten food into the waste disposal unit, disappointed and annoyed at myself. Surely a good LifePartner would remember important things like going to her in-laws for lunch? They only told us about it yesterday, after all.

"I'm going for a run," Evan says, sticking his head round the door. He's changed into tracksuit bottoms and a T-shirt. "I'll be back in time to shower and change before we leave, OK?"

I nod. *It's no big deal, see?* I tell myself. *He's obviously not bothered about it.*

But it feels like a big deal to me.

When he's gone, I dress, then clear up the last of the breakfast things and turn on the dishwasher. After that, I wander back out into the living room. There's nothing to do, and the apartment feels too big with just me in it. I try to read an eFic on my komm, but I can't concentrate, so I turn on the news screen.

As usual, it's showing a mix of reports and statistics from ACID. "Crime in Outer has dropped to its lowest ever levels, thanks to increased stop-and-search checks by ACID," an agent is saying to the camera. She has shiny, bobbed dark hair and flawless, pale skin. The caption underneath her says *Subcommander Healey.* As I read her name, I feel a momentary flash of something—déjà vu?—that passes as quickly as it arrived. "This last month alone, arrests increased tenfold, with defendants being moved through the courts faster than ever thanks to new legislation brought in by ACID to cut red tape and get criminals off the streets as quickly as possible. A huge number of forged c-cards are being seized every week, and . . . ."

I let her words wash over me, watching the pictures behind her, which show ranks of ACID agents marching through the streets; agents handcuffing scruffy, undernourished-looking people outside grim concrete apartment blocks; agents leading those same people to ACID vans. It makes me feel safe to know that these people are being dealt with so efficiently, yet alarmed to know that they're there in the first place. Why do they break laws and fight against the system like that? Can't they see that those laws are there to make our lives better? It's crazy.

"And now we have an interview with ACID's chief and the president of the IRB, General Harvey, about the recent recapture of escaped murderer Jenna Strong," Subcommander Healey says as the picture behind her changes to show a burly man in his fifties with a neatly clipped mustache. I get another sudden wave of familiarity just like the one I had a few moments ago. It's almost as if I've met them both somewhere. I shake my head. Ridiculous. Why would *I* know an ACID subcommander, never mind the president? It must be because I've seen them on the news screens so many times.

And Jenna Strong. Why is that name so familiar? Then I remember. She's that girl who killed her parents a few years ago and recently escaped from jail. A little shudder works its way up my spine.

"General, where is Strong now?" Subcommander Healey asks.

"She is in a specialist high-security prison," General Harvey replies. "The public have nothing to fear from her anymore. She will remain locked up for—"

Then the sound cuts out and the picture begins to distort, Subcommander Healey's and General Harvey's heads stretching sideways and jagged white lines cutting across the top half of the screen. I frown, wondering if there's a problem with the connection. But as suddenly as it started to flicker and jump, the picture stabilizes.

It's not showing Subcommander Healey or General Harvey anymore. There's a head-and-shoulders shot of a person wearing some sort of mask, so that it's impossible to tell whether they're a man or a woman, or how old they are. They look to one side, then lean forward toward the camera. Their eyes seem to lock onto mine—but that's not possible, is it? "Jess," they say. Even their voice is disguised, sounding gravelly and electronic.

I stare at the screen.

"Don't believe any of it. None of it's true," the masked person says. "You need to remember who you are."

My heart starts to pound. Who *is* this person? Why are they talking to me?

"Jess," they say. "Try to remember. You *have* to remember."

I stand up on shaking legs, feeling a scream building in my throat. Can they see me?

"Jess, you're not really—" the person in the mask begins. In two steps, I cross over to the news screen and tap the base to turn it off. The picture vanishes, taking that sinister, distorted voice with it, and I collapse back onto the sofa, trembling.

I'm still there when Evan gets back forty minutes later, staring at the empty space where the news screen picture was.

"Are you OK?" he says when he sees my expression.

I shake my head. I'm desperate to take another dose of my meds to calm myself down, but my mediband won't let me; it's too soon after the last one.

"What's wrong?" Evan sits down beside me, frowning. He smells sweaty.

"There—there was a—a—*someone* on the news screen," I say. "They kept saying my name and telling me I needed to remember who I really was."

Evan's frown turns into an expression of shock. "What?"

"They were wearing a mask, and their voice was disguised—you couldn't even tell if it was a man or a woman—"

Evan gets up. "Did you link ACID?"

"Not yet," I say. "I—I was waiting for you to get back."

Evan turns on the news screen. It shimmers into life, and a second or two later, I see . . .

Subcommander Healey, calmly reading out her reports, just like she was before.

Evan and I watch the screen for a few minutes in silence. Then he switches it off again. "Looks OK to me," he says, coming back over to where I'm sitting. "Jess, is your . . ."

He trails off. I see him swallow.

239

"What?" I say.

"Is your—you know—working?" He nods at my mediband.

"Yes!" I say. "Of course it is!"

Evan scrubs a hand through his hair. "Well, maybe it was just a—a glitch, or something." He gets up again. "I'd better get changed."

He goes into the bedroom, and I hear the shower running in the en suite.

"Ready?" he says when he emerges again, wearing a shirt and jeans.

I nod, smoothing my dress and trying to ignore the way my hands are still shaking. I can't have imagined that person on the news screen—surely I can't have. I'm not crazy.

Am I?

CHAPTER 39

As Evan and I travel across Upper—his parents live in another residential district on the other side of the zone—neither of us mention what I saw on the news screen again. Or what I didn't see.

"Darling!" Evan's mum says as she opens the door to us, hugging him as if it's been a year since she last saw him, not less than a day. He extricates himself as quickly as possible, but when his mum goes to hug me, I'm happy to let her. His dad emerges from down the hall and greets us both with firm handshakes. Suki hangs back behind him and returns the smile I give her shyly. In her everyday clothes, she looks much younger than fourteen.

"Our chef has made roast beef with all the trimmings," Evan's dad tells me with a jovial smile while Evan answers his mum's questions about our apartment. "I hope you're hungry!"

I nod, trying to return his smile, and still unable to get what happened this morning out of my head. If that person I saw on the screen was real—and I still think they were, despite Evan's doubts—then how did they know who I am? Do they know where I live? The thought sends terror knifing through me.

A bell tinkles somewhere, telling us it's time for lunch. The meal is served by a maid who places the dishes on the table and serves the food without saying a word. Evan, Suki and their parents act as if she isn't there, but I can't help watching her out of the corner of my eye. I wonder if she's from Outer. My parents' staff were. I try to remember what Evan said his dad did; he's the managing director of a sub food supply company run by ACID, I think. Everyone ACID employs at that level is always paid well.

After the maid leaves, I pick at my food, trying to ignore the anxiety that's still fluttering inside me. Evan's mum talks about the caterers she's hired for our Partnering party, which Evan and I will be throwing at our apartment next Saturday, and the people she's booked to put decorations up for us. "They're very good," she says. "Very tasteful. I hope you don't mind me booking them for you, Jess, but, well, you were in your facility . . ." She says the word delicately. "That center, I mean—and I wasn't sure you'd want to be bothered with things like that."

I nod and try to look enthusiastic, but the conversation is piling new worries on top of the ones I'm already having about the person on the news screen. Who am I going to invite?

Halfway through the meal, I feel a sting on my wrist as my mediband administers my meds. The anxiety recedes, although I can't quite stop worrying about not having anyone to invite to the party, and I still can't convince myself that I imagined that person on the news screen.

After the meal, we go back into the living room, where the maid serves coffee. At her father's request, Suki switches on the news screen—which is twice the size of the one back at our new apartment—and we watch an ACID report about how the pulse barrier being built around the IRB's coastline to keep illegal immigrants out and people from trying to leave is entering the final phase of its construction, and is scheduled to be switched on in less than four weeks.

"Damn good job too." Evan's dad grunts at the screen. "It should have been put up a hundred years ago, but of course the government we had back then dragged their heels over it, never got anything bloody done."

I remember learning about the old government at school—about how they almost ruined the country because they were so incompetent—and murmur in agreement. Evan's dad doesn't seem to notice.

Then Evan's mum touches a finger to her ear. "Do forgive me," she says to all of us. "It's the caterers for the party—I'll have to take it." She leaves the room, already starting to talk to whoever's linking her.

"That reminds me, I want your opinion on something, Evan," Evan's father says, getting up too. He turns and smiles at me, and I'm struck again by how alike he and Evan are. "Will you excuse us for a moment, Jess?"

I nod. "Yes, of course."

They go out of the room, leaving me with Suki, who, now that she has the sofa to herself, stretches out with a cushion in her lap, her gaze still fixed on the screen.

"Um, Suki?" I say, after glancing behind me at the door to check Evan's mum isn't coming back yet.

She looks round at me. "Yes?"

"Have you ever, um, seen anything, um, weird on the news screen?" I say, not quite believing I'm even asking her. What if she tells her parents, and they get angry with me? But I have to know if what happened to me this morning has ever happened to anyone else. And right now, there's no one else I can ask.

"Weird like what?" she says.

I swallow. "I, um, saw this person on my news screen earlier. They interrupted the broadcast. They were wearing a mask,

243

like they didn't want me to know who they were." I swallow again, deciding not to tell her that the person spoke to me, said my name. "They were saying all this . . . stuff," I finish.

"Oh my God," she says, her eyes widening. "You mean your screen was hacked? You linked ACID, right?"

"Not yet," I said. "I wasn't sure what it was. Has anything like that ever happened to you?"

She frowns and shakes her head. "I don't think anyone's ever tried to hack our screen." She looks uneasy now, and I'm already starting to regret saying anything to her. If anything, it's made me even more doubtful.

"Don't worry about it," I say. "I'm sure it was nothing. Sorry if I scared you."

She gives me a small smile with one side of her mouth. "It's fine," she says. Then she goes back to watching the screen. We don't exchange another word.

CHAPTER 40

To my relief, Suki doesn't say anything to anyone, and back home that evening, Evan and I sit in the living room on separate sofas, looking through the information about our new jobs that's been linked to us on our komms. We've both got positions at a branch of the ACID Statistics Bureau, checking reports before they go up on the news screens. They're pretty menial, but the job you get when you finish school and get Partnered always is at first. Ours were chosen for us based on the results of our exams and aptitude tests and, despite their ordinariness, have great career prospects. I remember thinking those exams, which I sat back in May last year, were the hardest thing I'd ever had to do in my entire life. I couldn't wait for them to be over. I had no idea that just three months later, I'd give anything to have that time back.

By twenty-two-thirty, I'm so tired I can't keep my eyes open. "I think I'll go to bed," I tell Evan, switching off my wraparound and getting up.

He stretches and yawns. "I should get some sleep too, I

guess," he says. As we get ready for bed, I wonder if tonight will be The Night. But once again, Evan just gets into bed, gives me a chaste kiss on the cheek, rolls over and goes to sleep. I gaze up into the semidark and sigh quietly. Doesn't he find me attractive? I so badly want there to be chemistry between us. I turn over too so I'm facing his back, and tentatively lay my hand on his shoulder. He mutters something and wriggles out from underneath my touch. I sigh again, turn onto my other side and close my eyes.

The next day, we're both up early. I pick out a cream-colored shirt and navy skirt and jacket, which I team up with tights and flat black shoes. Then I make us some toast.

"Aren't you hungry?" Evan asks as I nibble listlessly at a corner, then pass the rest to him. I shake my head. Even the thought of food turns my stomach. I'm so nervous, I feel sick.

"You need to eat something," he says. "Otherwise you'll get light-headed. That might have been why you thought you saw the—you know—on the news screen yesterday."

"I'm fine, really," I say, wishing he hadn't reminded me about the news screen. I've been trying to forget about it.

Evan raises his eyebrows but says nothing.

When we get outside, our car is already waiting, the driver holding the back door open for us. As we get in, I grip my bag so tightly my knuckles go white. What will the people at our new job be like? Will they be friendly? Do any of them know what happened to me? And what about my meds? I glance at Evan, but he's looking out the window, not paying me any attention.

The journey to work takes just ten minutes. "This is it, Mr. and Mrs. Denbrough," the driver says as we pull up outside a towering office block with huge, silvered windows.

"Thank you," I say. My voice doesn't sound quite steady, and my palms are clammy. I wipe them on my skirt. The driver gets out and holds the door open for me. I get out of the car, and, taking a deep breath, follow Evan to the entrance.

"M-my name's Jessica St— *Denbrough*," I say to the holoscreen by the door, after I've waved my c-card at it to confirm my identity and a voice has asked me why I'm here. "I'm starting a job here today."

Evan shows his own card, and the door hisses open, admitting us into the building.

We find ourselves in a wide foyer decorated with lush-looking potted plants. The air is cool and music is playing softly.

"Please take a seat," a woman's voice says from somewhere up near the ceiling. "Someone will be with you shortly."

We sit down, me holding my bag on my lap. A few moments later, one of the lifts opens and a tall woman with red hair strides out, the heels of her shoes clicking sharply against the floor. "Jessica Denbrough?" she says. I get to my feet and try to speak, but no words come out.

"I'm your boss, Kerri Gough," she says. "This way, please." She nods at Evan. "Your manager is on his way down, Mr. Denbrough." She turns and walks back to the lift. I hurry after her.

We ride the lift up a few floors in complete silence. Kerri looks as if she's in her midforties, with a square, hard face, her forehead permanently creased into a frown. When the lift stops, she marches out without waiting for me, calling, "This way, please."

I scurry after her down a narrow corridor. She takes me to a large room with rows of workstations stretching from one end to the other. At each, someone sits in front of a holoscreen. When we enter the room, there's a buzz of chatter in the air, which dies the moment everyone realizes Kerri is there. She leads me across the room to an empty workstation. I can feel everyone's eyes on me as I pull out the chair and sit down.

"You know what you have to do?" Kerri says as I press the power switch.

I nod. "Read the data as it scrolls past, and check for any mistakes or inconsistencies."

"And if you find any?"

"Mark them up and link them through to the Corrections department."

Kerri nods, apparently satisfied, although the frown lines on her forehead never quite disappear.

"I'll put Cara with you for the first hour or so to help you get the hang of things," she says, looking around and beckoning. Immediately, a tall girl my own age, her dark hair tied back in a ponytail, gets up from her own workstation and comes over. "Lunch is at thirteen hundred, but I'd like you to come up to my office ten minutes before for a review of your morning. I'm on the seventh floor, room nine."

Then she turns and says sharply to the people in the room—mostly women, but a few guys too, who have all stopped work to watch me—"Eyes on screens, please!"

She strides out of the room, the door sliding shut behind her.

There are a few moments of silence, and then the low buzz of chatter starts up again. Cara grabs a spare chair and sits down next to me. "Don't worry about Gargoyle Gough," she says. "She hardly ever comes down here."

She gives me a grin. Suddenly, I don't feel so nervous, and smile back.

"So, we'd better get you started," Cara says, leaning across me to adjust the screen. She shows me how to sign in, and brings up a list of options on the screen. "Choose *Start datascroll,*" she says. I touch my index finger to the screen, and a slowly scrolling list of place names and figures appears, all to do with the city's sub food supply. Most of the place names have an "O" next to them for Outer.

"ACID have to keep an eye on things in Outer because of

the population being so big," Cara explains. "Otherwise, the people there'd take everything and we'd be left to starve—after all, there are ten people in Outer for every one of us in Upper. Can you imagine if *we* had to eat sub?"

"I've never tried it," I say.

She makes a face. "God, you don't want to. It's awful. I don't know how anyone can call it food." Then she says, "Ah!" making me jump. She leans across me and jabs a finger at the screen. The scrolling list stops moving. "There," she says. "You see?"

I look.

"There's an extra 'S' on the end of that word," she says, tapping the screen to highlight the mistake in yellow. "It's because the data's input remotely by the people at the distribution depots as they send the deliveries out. They're always making mistakes. The yellow means I've flagged it for Corrections." She starts the datascroll moving again.

An hour later, with Cara watching me, I feel like I'm starting to get the hang of it.

"I need to go back to my own desk," she says, getting up. "But yell if you get stuck, OK?"

The morning passes quickly. The girls on either side of me, Meredith and Hailey, are also my age, and apart from the fact that Meredith's hair is dark and Hailey's blond, they could almost be twins, with identical chin-length bobs, blue eyes and wide grins. They chat to me whenever I pause the screen to give my eyes a rest. "So, you just got LifePartnered, didn't you?" Hailey asks me. "I heard Kerri telling one of the other managers last week, when they were getting ready for you to start work here."

I nod.

"Have you had your Partnering party yet?" Meredith asks.

"It's on Saturday," I say.

"How many people have you got coming?" Hailey says.

"Um, I didn't invite anyone yet," I say.

"You're kidding!" Hailey's eyes widen.

"I haven't had time," I tell her. "I—I've been ill. My Partner has a few friends coming, though. . . ."

I trail off, realizing how lame it sounds—a Partnering party with hardly any people?

Hailey grins. "Can we come? I haven't been to a decent party in *ages*."

Meredith snorts. "Since *my* Partnering party last month, you mean."

"Oh, yeah, that was pretty good." Hailey waves a hand vaguely. "But I bet Jess's will be amazing too, right?" She looks around at the people near us, who all nod in agreement.

"Sure," I say, feeling a little flustered. "You should definitely come."

Before I know it, it's twelve-forty, and Cara's calling across the room, "Jess, you'd better go up to Kerri's office. She'll eat you alive if you're late."

I nod, log my screen out and push back my chair.

"If you don't make it down before lunch, we'll save you a seat in the restaurant," Meredith promises as I bend down to pick up my bag.

"Thanks!" I say.

"The restaurant's on the bottom floor, through the door after the lifts and on your right—follow the signs!" Hailey calls after me as I hurry to the door, trying to remember where Kerri said her office was.

CHAPTER 41

I find it with a couple of minutes to spare. The door is open, but there's no one there. I check the holoscreen next to the door. It's definitely Kerri's office, so I go in and sit down on a chair beside her desk to wait.

There's a holoscreen on the desk just like mine downstairs, with the datascroll paused on it and a word highlighted in yellow. I glance at it, wondering what sort of statistics someone higher up like Kerri deals with. Something more interesting than food supply stats, I should think.

CONFIDENTIAL INFORMATION—NOT FOR NEWS SCREEN BROADCAST. TO BE VIEWED BY AUTHORIZED PERSONS ONLY.

Case Ref: RQ675
Name of prisoner: Maxwell Alexander Fisher
Age: 16
Citizenship-card ID number: 996437865MAF

Charge #1: Evading arrest

Charge #2: Suspected involvement in escape of category A prisoner

Charge #3: Helping a felon evade arrest

Senttence: Life, Innis Ifrinn Prison, former Orkney Isles

My heart skips a beat, then starts thudding at twice its normal speed as I realize what I'm looking at. These must be crime stats, straight from ACID. I'm glad I'm not working with those. They'd give me nightmares. Frowning, I try to work out why the word *senttence* is marked up. Then I realize: the extra "t."

At that moment, I hear the sharp click of Kerri's heels outside in the corridor. I push my chair back a little and turn to face the door.

"Ah, there you are," she says as she comes in. "I got called away, sorry." She sits down behind the desk and taps the screen to turn it off. "So, are you finding you can keep up with the work?"

I nod. "Yes."

"And what about that little . . . problem of yours? It isn't interfering with anything?"

She means my meds. "No," I say, glancing at my mediband and remembering that it's nearly time for my next dose.

Kerri sniffs. "Very well. You may go. We'll have a proper performance review at the end of the week."

I stand up. "Thank you," I say, then hurry out of the office, relieved; I thought she was going to give me a real grilling.

There's still five minutes to go until lunch, so the corridor outside is empty, everyone shut away in their offices. I'm almost at the lifts when I start to get that weird slipping sensation inside my head again, like I did after my LifePartnering ceremony. I stop, frightened I'm going to fall over. Suddenly, I'm not in the corridor at all but a narrow, closed-in space lined with shelves. There's sheeting draped overhead, the light's dim and flickering, and there's someone in here with me—a boy. I can't make out his face but I feel an inexplicable pull toward him, a rush of intense love mixed with sadness and guilt.

I put my hand out, and when I feel the wall beside me, it breaks me out of my trance. My heart's hammering, my breathing rapid. What *is* this? Where are these memories coming from? They're much stronger than last time, when I was in the car with Evan after the ceremony.

My komm *ping*s, and I feel the sting of my mediband's needle sliding into my wrist. I wait, breathing rapidly, as the memory or hallucination or whatever it was is washed away by the chemicals flowing into my bloodstream. Then I stand there holding on to the wall for a few moments, composing myself. A quick glance up and down the corridor reassures me that no one saw me.

Relieved, I walk down to the lifts as fast as I can.

CHAPTER 42

"Oh, that is *perfect*," Meredith says as I step out into the living room to give her and Hailey a slightly embarrassed twirl. The dress I'm trying on was at the back of my wardrobe, wrapped in plastic. It's strapless, dark green silk with a full skirt, trimmed all over with tiny crystals that make it seem to shimmer as I move. The boned bodice hugs my ribs so tightly I can hardly breathe. But it's beautiful. And perhaps, when Evan sees me wearing it, he'll think *I'm* beautiful too.

"Have you got any shoes to go with it?" Hailey says. She and Meredith push past me into the bedroom and make a bee-line for the wardrobe. They argue over which shoes I should wear, until Hailey triumphantly holds up a pair of silver sandals with a dark green crystal flower on the toe. "These!" she says. She thrusts them at me. "Try them on."

I sit down on the bed, feeling slightly bemused but pleased. Tonight, Evan and I are throwing our Partnering party. Even though I've worked at the Stats Bureau for just a week, almost everyone from my office has said they'll come. It's all thanks to Meredith and Hailey; they encouraged me to get the invites linked out. And this morning, just as Evan was getting ready to go out for a run, they linked me to say they were on their way over to help me pick out an outfit. In a way, it feels like having Lucy and Eri back.

"Yep, that's it," Meredith says, standing back with her hands on her hips. "We'd better watch Olly and Tim around her, eh, Hales?" she adds, winking at Hailey.

Olly and Tim are their LifePartners. I blush.

"Are we done? I need *food*," Hailey says dramatically, flinging herself across the bed. "And aren't there people coming in a bit to clean and put up decorations? We want to be out of here before they arrive."

As I change back into my everyday clothes, she links for a car, and after Meredith's helped me wrap the dress up again and I've placed it carefully back in the wardrobe, we head outside.

"There's a *gorgeous* little brasserie we always go to—you'll love it, Jess," Hailey says as we wait outside the apartment for the car. "They do the most *divine* cinnamon lattes."

As we're driven to the commercial district, sun streams through the windows. I lean back in my seat, basking in it. Ever since my LifePartnering ceremony, the weather has been perfect, which I'm trying to take as a good sign. It's been a much better week; I haven't had any more of those funny turns, and my meds aren't making me feel as foggy anymore.

The brasserie is tiny and old-fashioned, with real live waitresses dressed in black and white uniforms bringing the food to the tables, wood everywhere and the rich scent of coffee filling the air. We sit down by the window so we can people-watch. "Isn't that Connolly Tayler?" Hailey says, squinting through the glass as one of the waitresses hands us menus, which are old-fashioned too—actual printed, folded cards. Talk about quaint.

Meredith and I both look. Connolly Tayler is the daughter of an ACID chief. A few years ago, she survived a kidnap attempt by a group of anti-ACID rebels. She's since written an eFic based on her ordeal and it's become a bestseller. I read it last year, before the accident. It terrified me.

"I don't think so," Meredith says, frowning. "Her hair's darker, isn't it?"

I can only see the back of the girl's head, and from here, she could be anybody—although there is an ACID agent walking a few steps behind her.

"I wouldn't like to be her at the moment," Hailey says in a lower voice. "Not when there's been all that trouble with the Strong girl."

"You mean the murderer?" I say, feeling a little shiver go up my spine like it did when I saw the report about her on the news screen the other day. "I thought she was back in prison? A high-security prison?"

"Well, yes, but *Mileway* was supposed to be high-security, wasn't it?" Hailey says. "And she escaped from there. I wouldn't be surprised if she got out again pretty soon."

Meredith makes a face. "Ugh, don't say that, Hales."

Hailey shrugs. "Just telling it like it is." Then she frowns. "Hey, Mer, didn't your cousin go to school with her or something?"

"Oh, Toria, yes. She was in her class."

"Was she friends with her?"

"I don't know. She won't talk about her. And my mum's said I'm not allowed to ask her about her."

"She *must* have been friends with her then," Hailey says, nodding. "Can you imagine, hanging out with someone who was planning to do something like that?" She gives a little shudder, glances around the café, takes a sip of water, then leans forward. "Anyway, girls," she says in a low voice. "You'll never guess what."

"What?" Meredith says, her eyes widening like they always do when she's anticipating a juicy piece of gossip.

"Tim and I have had our notification. It came last night."

"Already?" Meredith squeals, so loudly everyone else in the brasserie looks round at us. "Sorry," she says at a more normal volume. "But ohhh, I'm so jealous! You've only been Partnered four months!"

Hailey shrugs. "I guess they thought we were ready. We're having our implants deactivated next Tuesday evening, and after that, we can start trying."

I don't need to ask who *they* are, or what she's going to start trying for. *They* are ACID, and getting their notification means Hailey and her LifePartner, Tim, have been given permission to have a baby.

I try to imagine what will happen when Evan and I get our notification. It could be soon—as soon as Hailey and Tim—or it could be years from now. But if it *is* soon . . .

Panic catches slightly at my throat. Although he sometimes puts his arm around me when we're watching the news screen now, Evan and I are still sleeping on opposite edges of the bed every night. And I'm still waiting for that feeling, that *Oh! I love you* moment to punch me in the gut.

It's only been a week, I keep reminding myself. But I can't help worrying that things aren't going to change. What if we get our notification in a few months' time and we still haven't slept together? I really don't want our first time to be because we have to.

Then, as I half listen to Hailey and Meredith talking excitedly about whether Hailey will be given permission to have a boy or a girl—as, although most people conceive naturally, they're given hormone injections that determine the baby's gender—a thought comes to me. What if Evan's waiting for *me* to make the first move? What if he hasn't done anything yet because he doesn't want to rush me? All at once, my anxiety vanishes, and I nearly laugh out loud. Of course. That has to be it. How can I have been so stupid?

I think again about the green dress, the way it hugs my hips and the curve of my breasts, and a smile curves my lips. Could tonight be the night?

Meredith, glancing at me, frowns. "What's so funny?" she asks.

"Nothing," I say quickly. "I was just thinking about tonight."

I try to make my expression sober again. But inside, I'm still smiling.

CHAPTER 43

I go to Meredith's after lunch, not wanting to get in the way of the party preparations. Hailey and I help her pick out a dress, and then, on the way back to my apartment that evening, call in at Hailey's so she can collect her outfit.

By the time we get back to my place, it's been transformed. Tiny lights have been strung up across the ceiling and around the window in the living room, and there are vases of white roses everywhere, filling the air with scent. On the table are covered dishes and bowls of brightly colored punch. I can hear people moving about in the kitchen, and when I look round the door, I see two guys and two women, dressed in neat white uniforms, preparing more food on the kitchen worktops. They don't look round at me, just carry on working as if I weren't even there.

"This looks *incredible*," Hailey says. "What time is everyone arriving?"

"I told them any time after nineteen hundred," I say.

259

"It's eighteen-fifteen already!" Meredith says. "We'd better get ready!"

Hailey insists on doing my makeup for me and won't let me look in the mirror until she's finished. "Stand *still*," she says as she strokes a mascara brush through my eyelashes. "Otherwise I'm going to end up stabbing you in the eye."

"Sorry," I say. I'm not used to having this much stuff on my face—all I wore for my ceremony was a slick of colored lip gloss and a touch of pale purple eye shadow.

"There," she says after she's lightly dusted my shoulders, collarbone and cleavage with some sort of sparkling powder. She turns me round so that I can see my reflection in the mirror behind me.

I gasp. Because the girl in the mirror isn't me. Her normally pale skin has a rosy glow, accentuated by the sparkle on her chest and the blusher that's been subtly applied to her cheeks. Her eyes, ringed with black kohl and smoky silver-gray eye shadow, look almost the same shade of green as her dress. Her hair is swept back elegantly, a few softly curling tendrils teased out and tumbling around her face.

Hailey—who's wearing a deep rose-pink dress, her hair held back on one side with a gold clip studded with diamonds—hands me my silver shawl. "You are going to knock. Him. Out," she says.

"Too right," adds Meredith, who's wearing a simple midnight-blue dress with a pencil skirt and ruffles down the front. Then she touches her ear; her komm's going off. "Hi, Olly! Yes, we're already at Jess's. Are you guys on your way? Cool! See you in ten!"

She turns back to me and Hailey. "Olly and Tim are nearly here. Come on, let's go and pick some music. I bet everyone else will arrive soon too!"

She's right: as soon as we go back into the living room, the

260

door buzzer sounds. Over the next hour or so, the apartment begins to fill up. People I only know from seeing them in the restaurant at work compliment me on my dress until I start to feel dizzy with all the praise, and gifts begin to pile up at one end of the dining table—envelopes, mostly, wrapped in fancy paper and ribbon.

The only thing that keeps me from feeling completely happy is the fact that Evan's still not here.

As it gets to twenty-fifteen, then twenty-thirty, I start to feel more and more anxious. Meredith notices me looking flustered and tries to reassure me. "I'm sure he's on his way," she says. "Guys are *always* late for stuff like this." But her words don't comfort me. I want to link him, but I'm scared to. What if something's happened to him?

At twenty-forty-five, just as I've decided I *will* link him, the apartment door opens and Evan steps through. He's wearing a shirt and dark jeans, his hair carefully gelled and mussed up. There are a lot of people here from his office too. They greet him as he comes in with cries of "Evan!" and "Hey, where have you been?"

I stand near the table, waiting for him to notice me. But he takes a glass of punch from one of the white-clad waitresses, then starts talking to a guy with short red hair.

"What are you waiting for?" Hailey says, elbowing me in the ribs. She waves and, pitching her voice over the sound of the music and chatter, calls, "Evan! Over here!"

Evan turns, and I see him do a double take.

He comes over. "Jess," he says. "You—you look amazing!"

He looks me up and down, his usual indifferent expression replaced by something keener, almost hungry, as he takes in my dress, my hair, my makeup, the glitter dusted across my chest.

"Wow," he says again. I feel a blush spread up my neck and

into my cheeks. I suddenly feel very warm, even though it isn't particularly hot.

He leans down and kisses me—a *real* kiss, hard and passionate. I close my eyes, breathing in the scent of his aftershave as I'm overtaken by a giddy, weightless joy. This is the moment I've been waiting for; longing for. It doesn't matter that the stubble on his cheeks is scraping the corners of my mouth. It doesn't matter that he's kissing me so hard he's crushing my lips against my teeth. It doesn't matter that he's probably smudging my makeup, or even that the kiss is kind of . . . wet. What matters is that he is kissing me.

When we break apart, there's a scattering of applause. Shocked, I turn to see that everyone has gathered around us. Hailey's grinning like a lunatic.

The rest of the evening seems to pass in a whirl. Evan doesn't leave my side, and with his arm round me and people I don't even know congratulating me on our LifePartnering, I feel as if my dream of a perfect, happy life is coming true at last.

I need to use the bathroom. "I'll be back in a minute," I tell Evan, reluctantly extricating myself from his grasp. I slip into our bedroom, where everyone's jackets and bags are piled onto our bed, but there's already someone in our bathroom, so I go out again and head for the en suite in the spare bedroom. It isn't until I've used the toilet and I'm washing my hands that I notice the little package propped up on the shelf above the sink.

It's something wrapped in plain white paper, about ten centimeters tall and five centimeters wide. My name has been written on the front in black ink.

I frown. Is it a LifePartnering gift that someone's left in here by accident? If so, why does it only have my name on it? I pick up the package and open it, dropping the paper into the sink.

It's some sort of device, about half a centimeter thick, made from black plastic and metal. There's a little screen and, on the front of it, a round wheel with a button in the middle. Wrapped around it is what appears to be a pair of small earplugs on wires that taper down to a single thin cable plugged into the top of the device. When I turn it over I see a little symbol engraved on the back—an apple with a bite taken out of it—and a word that makes no sense to me at all: iPod. The device is battered and scratched; it looks very old.

There's a note with it:

Put headphones in your ears. Follow instructions to listen to message. Memorize and throw this and iPod into incinerator. VERY IMPORTANT that you listen!! From—a friend.

There are some pictures underneath, showing me how to use the device. I stare at it, my hands starting to tremble. I know, just *know*, that this is connected to the news screen being hacked. But who put it here? *How did they get into my apartment?*

There's a tap at the door, and then Meredith sticks her head round it. "Jess, are you OK?" she says. "You've been gone ages."

Trying to put on a calm expression, I slide the device behind my back, hoping she hasn't already seen it. "I'm fine," I say. "Could you ask Evan to come in here? I—I need to ask him something."

Meredith frowns. "Um, OK." She goes back out into the apartment again. A few moments later, Evan appears.

"Shut the door!" I hiss at him.

Looking puzzled, he does as I ask. "Look," I say, holding out the device. "I found this in here just now, with this note."

Evan takes the device and the note, which he reads, his puzzled expression deepening.

"Who's this from?" he says.

"I don't know. I think it's something to do with the news screen being hacked." My voice is shaky and shrill.

"What do you—" Evan begins, looking more confused than

263

ever. Then he must remember, because his face clears. "Oh, that."

"Evan, someone put this here. Someone's been in our apartment!"

"There are lots of people in this apartment right now," he says. He looks half amused, half annoyed. "Jess, it's probably someone playing a joke on you. Have you even listened to what's on there? I bet it's someone just saying Happy LifePartnering or something."

He unwinds the headphones from around the device.

"No!" I shriek. "Don't do that!" My heart is pounding like crazy. All I can think of is the horrible, gravelly voice that came out of the news screen.

"Jess, stop freaking out," Evan says. He's starting to look annoyed now.

"Please don't listen to it," I say. "Get rid of it." My eyes are filled with tears.

"God," Evan says. "OK. I'll throw it down the incinerator chute in the kitchen. Will that make you feel better?"

"I'm coming with you," I say. I can't bear the thought that, once I'm not looking, he might listen to the device after all, just to see what's on there.

Everyone stares at us as I scuttle after Evan into the kitchen. A few people follow us, Meredith and Hailey among them. "What's happening?" I hear a guy saying. "What's he got there?" Hailey asks, "Jess, is everything OK?"

I ignore her. I ignore all of them. All I care about is seeing that device gone. Evan shoves past one of the hired maids and opens the incinerator hatch, which is next to the cooker. He drops the device inside and I watch it spiral down into the darkness. Then he slams the hatch again. Now I never have to know what was on there.

"Happy now?" he says, brushing his hands off.

"I—I think we should link ACID," I say. I still feel sick with panic.

"What, and have everyone get sent home, and spend hours answering questions? You're kidding, right?"

"But someone was here," I say.

"For God's sake, Jess. Stop being so paranoid!" Evan says. "Did you take your meds tonight? Because you're acting totally weird."

"Meds?" Hailey says behind me, and I remember I haven't said anything to her about them. I've told her and Meredith that my bracelet's an heirloom, passed down from my grandmother, which is why I never take it off.

It isn't time for my meds yet, so I try to take deep breaths like they told me at the rehab unit, but the panic keeps on building. Pins and needles prickle up and down my arms. Sweat has broken out on my forehead, and I feel giddy and faint. I press a hand against my mouth, my chest hitching, my shoulders heaving.

"Jess." Evan's voice is no more than a low growl, but there's no mistaking the anger in it. "Calm. Down." He grabs me by my upper arms, turning me to face him. His eyes glitter angrily as he gives me a little shake, his fingers digging into my arms, hurting me. I've never seen him look so furious, and suddenly, I remember those feelings I had outside Kerri's office on my first day at work—those feelings of love that weren't for him—and wonder if, somehow, he knows. "You're embarrassing me," he says quietly. "Stop acting like such a freak."

I can't explain what I do next. It's as if my brain sits back to watch from a safe distance while my body does all the work. I bring my knee up and drive it into Evan's groin, and, with a strength I had no idea I possessed, throw him away from me. He crashes against the island in the middle of the kitchen, sending the dishes piled up there smashing to the floor, and collapses

265

onto the tiles beside it with his hands jammed between his legs, whimpering.

Everything goes quiet. Even the music stops.

"What the hell?" Hailey says at last, her voice no more than a shocked whisper.

A guy pushes past me and crouches down beside Evan. "Hey, are you OK?" he asks. "Evan?"

Evan groans. His eyes are closed, his face deathly pale.

"I'm linking for a medic," the guy says, standing up again. He touches a finger to his ear, then starts speaking rapidly into his komm, telling whoever's on the other end what happened.

I finally find my voice. "I'm sorry!" I cry. "I didn't mean to do that! I didn't!"

I whirl round. Everyone backs away from me like they're worried I might attack them next. The panic is the worst it's ever been, singing through my veins like fire. Black spots start to appear at the edges of my vision. "Look at her!" I hear someone mutter to my left. "She's completely flipped!"

"Let's get out of here," someone else adds. People start to leave, all of them still staring at me as if I've sprouted horns and a tail and wings.

Escape, I think. I dart forward, but the guy who linked the medic snatches a gigantic rolling pin off the counter and steps into my path, brandishing it. "Oh no you don't," he says as I freeze.

"Oh, Geoff, be careful!" a girl says behind me.

By the time the medics arrive five minutes later, almost everyone except Geoff and the hired staff has left. Geoff explains what happened while one of the medics checks Evan over.

I stare at my LifePartner's prone form, lying in the middle of a spray of cutlery and smashed china.

"Has this ever happened before?" the medic asks as he grabs a medpatch from a holder on his belt and places it on Evan's neck.

"I have no idea!" Geoff says. "I don't even know her. Just him."

The medic looks at me, but I can't answer him. My words are locked in my throat. I need to breathe and I can't. The black spots at the edges of my vision grow and a ringing sound starts up in my ears.

"Better give her a patch too, if it's safe," the medic who's tending to Evan says to his colleague. Before I can react, the medic has pressed a medpatch against the side of my neck. There's a faint prickling sensation and a spreading coolness. The effect is almost instantaneous, as if someone has doused my jangling nerve endings with ice water. I sag against him, and he lowers me to the floor.

"Let's get them both out of here," the first medic says. "We can link ACID on the way."

CHAPTER 44

Apparently, I've cracked two of Evan's ribs and caused severe bruising to his groin. At the medicenter, as the ACID agent who's checking my medical records and questioning me about what happened tells me this, I stare at him, too doped up to feel anything.

Several hours later, when ACID and the doctors are satisfied my outburst was a one-off, exacerbated by stress and a severe panic attack, I'm released from the medicenter with an amber warning and a car takes me home.

When I walk into the apartment, still feeling woozy from the aftereffects of the medpatch and because my mediband kicked in a little while ago, the living room is empty. So is the bedroom. Evan isn't back yet. As I go into the bedroom, I remember how he looked at me tonight, how I thought that *finally,* we had a connection; that he might have real feelings for me.

I sit down on the edge of the bed and burst into tears.

When I finally manage to stop crying, my face feels swollen and my head aches. I can't override the mediband, but there's a small packet of medpatches in the bathroom cabinet. I stick one on my neck, thinking about using the rest as well, but there are only five more. It wouldn't work. And anyway, ACID can send you to jail for trying to kill yourself. I'm in enough trouble as it is.

I lie down, gazing up at the ceiling. All I can think about is what everyone will be saying about me. About how I lost it and attacked my LifePartner at our own Partnering party.

Maybe it won't be so bad, I try to tell myself. *Maybe he'll let you explain.*

But what *is* there to explain? I have no idea why I went for him like that. It was like . . .

It was like I was someone else.

Feeling sick, I turn over, balling the edge of the duvet in my hands. I lie there for hours, gripped by paranoia, until I hear Evan come home and head straight into the spare room, thumping the door shut behind him. Then I remember that I'm still wearing my dress and I still have my hair up and a face covered in makeup. I get up and head into the bathroom to change and wash, deliberately avoiding looking at my reflection in the mirror and leaving my dress in a heap on the floor. I'm sure I won't sleep, but I'm so exhausted that, only moments after I close my eyes, I'm gone.

I'm woken several hours later by a crash, and Evan's screams.

CHAPTER 45

I sit bolt upright in bed, still more asleep than awake, my heart pounding as I call out to activate the light. In the spare room, Evan's still screaming, and I can hear other voices too. Someone's asking, "Where is she?!" Then, "Shut up, or I'll arrest you too!"

Evan's screams cut off abruptly.

She?

Suddenly, my head clears.

They mean me.

I look wildly around the room for somewhere to hide. Not under the bed—it's too low to crawl under, and it's the first place anyone would think to look. What about the wardrobe? No—they'll look in there too. Maybe I should lock myself in the bathroom? Oh God—

I hear footsteps on the other side of the bedroom door. I jump out of bed and leap for the wardrobe to yank it open, but just as my outstretched fingers brush the handle, the bedroom door flies inward. Two ACID agents in jumpsuits and helmets burst into the room. "Don't move," one says, pointing his pulse gun at my head.

I stare at him, my insides turning to water. "But I have an amber warning," I say in a shaky voice. "What happened with Evan was an accident—I explained—"

"Shut up and sit down," the second agent says. He has a gun too, his fingers curled loosely around its grip. I walk backward until I hit the bed, and sit. The second agent takes a set of restraints off his belt. Removing my mediband, he snaps a pair of cuffs around my wrists. Then he puts a set of restraints on my ankles. "Jessica Denbrough, you're under arrest," he says, grabbing my upper arm and yanking me to my feet. He speaks into his komm. "Suspect apprehended. We're on our way."

He leads me out into the living room, the first agent following us with his gun pointed at my back.

Evan's sitting on the sofa, white-faced, clutching his ribs. He doesn't even look at me as the agent holding my arm prods me in the back. *"Evan!"* I wail.

"Keep moving," the ACID agent snaps.

When we reach the hall, I see that the front door's been broken down, lying on the floor in a heap of splinters and dust.

"I need my mediband!" I say, trying to turn back toward the bedroom.

"I *said*, keep moving," the agent holding my arm says. He pulls me past the broken-down door. Splinters dig into my bare feet.

"But I have to have it!" I say. "If I don't take my medication I'll—"

"For the last time, move." He pushes me roughly into the lift. The first agent gets in too and pushes the button to shut the doors.

Outside, it's raining. A van is sitting beside the curb—gray with blacked-out windows. A scream bubbles up inside my throat and I have to bite down hard on the insides of my cheeks

271

to keep it in. My mind's shrieking at me to run, but my feet are bare, and the agent with the gun is still pointing it straight at me. This might be quiet, crime-free Upper, but I've no doubt that if I tried to escape, they'd shoot me. I remember two agents coming to talk to us at school, and they told us that if ACID are arresting you, you go, no matter what.

As the agents shove me into a cage in the back of the van, I glance back at the apartment and see the lights blazing on every floor, faces at all the windows. Shame surges through me.

The first agent slams the cage door and locks it. There's nowhere for me to sit, so I slump onto the floor. When he shuts the van doors, I'm plunged into almost total darkness: the only light, bluish and dim, comes from two small bulbs above me. I feel the van shudder as the agents climb in the front, and with a barely audible hum, it powers up and we start to move. I stare at the cage bars, too shocked to even cry.

Soon, my teeth are chattering together, and my feet and hands are mottled with the cold. My pajamas are damp from the rain, and I can't even wrap my arms around myself to keep warm.

The van keeps driving.

And driving.

And driving, until it feels like we've been traveling for hours.

My panic has returned, bubbling inside me. I'm so cold I'm shuddering constantly, and I keep hearing sounds like whispering voices that dart away when I try to listen to what they're saying. Lights flash at the edges of my vision. Then the memories come, assaulting me in waves.

Rubbish-strewn streets. Crowded, run-down buildings. A tall, thin boy with dark hair and green eyes who I want to put my arms around and hold forever but I don't know why. A room with bookshelves for walls. A place that looks like a train terminal. I'm running from something—someone—what? No, not running from, approaching. I'm walking into a room, a living room in a large, luxurious house, and there are two people backed up against the fireplace, and an ACID agent with a gun—

Now I'm a little girl again. I'm in the same house, the same room, but the sun is streaming through the windows. There's a man and a woman, and the woman is laughing at something the man has just said. When they turn and see me the man scoops me up in his arms and turns me upside down and tickles me until I shriek. I feel happy and safe and loved. But these people aren't my parents, and this isn't my house, so how is that possible?

I close my eyes, moaning. Make it stop. *Makeitstopmakeitstopmakeitstop.*

The van turns sharply, throwing me sideways so I bang my head against the bars. Dizzy, I struggle upright. The road underneath us has got rougher, the wheels bouncing and jolting. Then it smoothes out again, the tires crackling on gravel.

The van comes to a halt. The agents in the front get out, their feet crunching on the gravel as they come round to the back. The doors open and a blast of rain-soaked air hits me in the face.

Both agents have removed their helmets. The one who cuffed me unlocks the cage and removes my restraints, then helps me get up. "Steady now," he says, his voice much gentler than before. "I'm sorry we had to keep you in those cuffs, but we couldn't risk you being out of them if we were stopped."

Still holding on to me, he helps me from the van, an arm round my waist to keep me upright. We're in some sort of yard, the van's headlights shining on the front of a large, white-painted cottage with lights gleaming softly in the windows.

Then the cottage's front door bursts open and a small, plump woman with gold-rimmed glasses comes running toward us, her long brown hair streaming out behind her. "Oh, Jenna," she cries. "Thank goodness!"

INNIS IFRINN

CHAPTER 46

I back away from her. Who is she? Why is she calling me Jenna?

"Oh no you don't," the woman says. She's smiling, but her voice is firm. Before I can take another step, the two ACID agents have taken me by the arms and propelled me into the house. I struggle to get free, but they're too strong.

I'm taken into a large room that has logs burning in a little iron stove and thick curtains drawn across the window to keep out the night. One agent lowers me into an armchair and the other brings a thick blanket, which the woman wraps around me. Then the first ACID agent fetches a bowl of hot water for my bruised, frozen feet, and the other places a mug of hot chocolate on a little table beside me.

"What's happening?" I croak. "Where am I?"

"Don't worry, you're quite safe," the woman says. "I'm Mel. You don't remember me?"

I stare at her. I've never seen her before in my life.

Just then, a tall, thin black man with graying hair comes into the room.

"Jenna," he says, smiling.

Mel shakes her head. "She doesn't remember," she says.

The man's smile disappears. He crosses the room and crouches down in front of me. "What's your name?" he says gently, peering into my eyes.

"J-Jess Stone," I say. "I mean Denbrough." For some reason, *he* seems familiar, but I can't work out why.

If only I wasn't so dizzy. If only I could *think*.

"I'm Jon," the man says. He asks me a few more questions—about my age, about my family, about my childhood—and straightens up with a grim look on his face. "They've done a really thorough job," he says. "*Again*. And as for the alterations they've made to her face—"

"What can we do?" Mel asks. She looks worried. I gaze at Jon and wonder what on earth he means about my face. I bring up my hand, touch my cheek. Is he talking about the surgery I had after the crash?

"Nothing, at the moment. We know they mostly did the cognitive realignment with medication this time—perhaps once that's cleared out of her system, things will start coming back. But until then . . . ." He shrugs.

"Who are you?" I ask them. "What do you want from me?" I try to make my voice sound firm, but it breaks on the last word. Have I been kidnapped? If so, what are ACID doing here? I look around for the two agents, but they've gone.

"We don't want anything, Jen— Jess," Mel says. "You weren't safe in London. We needed to get you out."

"Why?" I say. Then I remember the hacked news screen, and the strange device I found at the party. I start to shiver again.

"We'll explain everything when you've had a rest and feel more like yourself," Mel says. "Drink your hot chocolate. You look like you need it."

Obediently, I reach for the cup, but my hand is shuddering

278

so hard that I knock it onto the floor. The chocolate makes a dark, spreading stain on the carpet. I stare at it, mesmerized by a hissing, ringing sound that's swelling inside my head.

"Jess? Jess!" Mel is saying my name, but her voice has gone distant and echoey. My vision starts to darken at the edges, until it's like I'm looking down a tunnel. All I can see is the stain on the carpet. It doesn't look like chocolate anymore—it looks like blood.

Blood on the carpet. Blood on the walls. Two figures slumped on the carpet. A man in a black jumpsuit with his face hidden by the mirrored visor of his helmet turning toward me as I stand in the doorway, too shocked even to scream. He's holding a gun, and it's spattered with blood too.

Vaguely, I'm aware that I'm shaking all over now, not because I'm cold but because my muscles are jumping and twitching as if I've received an electric shock. To try to stop it, I curl into a ball, hugging my arms around myself and drawing my legs up. I close my eyes. I hear the man swear. "She's withdrawing from the drugs they gave her—we need to do something quick," he says, his voice as distant and echoey as Mel's.

Someone calls out. Another blanket is wrapped around me so tightly I can hardly breathe. And still I'm shaking. It feels as if it's never going to stop.

"We need a sedative. And something to bring her temperature down," the man says. "Fetch me my bag—it's in the bedroom at the top of the stairs."

Bring my temperature down? What are they talking about? I'm freezing. I try to open my eyes, but it feels as if there are lead weights on my eyelids. I try to speak, but my teeth are chattering together so hard I can't get any words out. The voices around me blur into a sludgy mess of noise.

Something stings the side of my neck, and I fall, fall, down into the deepest dark I've ever known.

CHAPTER 47

I'm floating, as light as air, gliding through curtains of mist.
I've come untethered from my body, somehow, and as I drift,
whispers bump against me, then spin away again, like shoals
of tiny fish.

Is she conscious
Shh don't wake her don't
How long till she
Another ten milligrams

The drifting is interspersed with long periods where I seem to
be in another world altogether. It's as if I'm dreaming, but not,
because the world seems so real, with none of that wonky logic
you always get in dreams. At one point, I'm sitting in a little
den that appears to be made out of bookshelves, lit by small,
globe-shaped lamps that give out a hazy, flickering light, sheets
draped over it to make it private. There's a boy in there with
me, a boy with tangled dark hair, lying on a blanket spread
on the floor. His eyes are closed, his mouth slightly open, and
his cheek is pillowed on his hand. I think about leaning over

280

and brushing his hair out of his face, but I don't want to wake him. As I watch him, a mass of emotions wells up inside me—tenderness, sadness, longing and guilt. I try to work out what I could have done to him to feel this way, but before I can figure it out the bookshelf den and the boy fade away, and things go dark for a little while.

The next time I surface, the mist seems brighter, the whispers louder. Shapes, indistinct and nebulous, move around and above me. I want to speak, to let them know I see them, but my body won't respond, my mouth won't move.

Thought she was getting stronger
Vital signs are
A few more days yet
Drift. Nothing. Drift. Nothing.
Think she'll make it?
Too early to tell.
I dream about the boy again. He speaks to me. He tells me his father's dead, and it's all my fault.
Try this. If it doesn't work, we're out of ideas
Nothing.

CHAPTER 48

He's behind me. Right behind me. I turn to face him and see he's grinning at me, showing his yellow, peglike teeth. *Must be lonely in here for a young lady like you,* he says.

Yeah, and you know what? I say. *I like it that way.*

You don't mean that, he says. *Think what a good time we could have, me and you.*

Believe me, I say. *It'll be anything but good. For you, that is.*

He lunges at me, and I spin and kick out, but just as my foot's about to connect with his stomach, I jolt awake, opening my eyes with a gasp.

I'm lying in a bed in a tiny room with white walls, a heavy patchwork quilt tucked over me, pillows piled beneath my head. Although the sun's shining through a gap in the curtains above me, it feels early; there's a fragility to the light, a coolness to the air blowing in through the open window, a riot of birdsong coming from outside.

I try to sit up and am shocked at how much of an effort it is. Just propping myself up on my pillows exhausts me, and I have to close my eyes for a few moments to recover. When I open them again, I look around the room. The only other pieces of furniture in it are some wooden drawers beside the bed and a chair in the corner with some clothes—mine?—folded neatly on the seat.

Panic stirs inside me. Where am I? And how did I get here?

Calm down, Jess, I think.

No. I'm not Jess. Where did that come from? I'm Mia. Mia Richardson.

No! I'm . . .

I'm someone else, but no matter how hard I struggle to remember who that someone is, the memory hovers at the edge of my mind, dancing out of my grasp whenever I try to get hold of it.

I lean back, my head swirling with more memories that don't make any sense and have great empty spaces in between. A tiny room that looks like a prison cell—no, it *is* a prison cell, with peeling walls and a single metal bunk and a polished metal mirror riveted to the wall. The sting of rain against my face and the *whapwhapwhap* of roto blades and someone shouting. Gunfire. Screams. And then one of those gaps, before another memory surfaces, frustratingly vague, of an argument with someone. I think it's a boy, but when I try to picture his face, it won't come to me. Another gap. A train journey. A building full of books and dust. I'm with someone again. Is it the boy I was arguing with? I don't know.

I don't know.

I hear something over the sound of the dawn chorus out-side—a faint thudding that's familiar, yet totally out of place. I get shakily to my knees and push the curtains aside so I can see out the window. The room I'm in is at the back of the house, overlooking a garden overflowing with flowers. At the far end is a vegetable patch and some fruit bushes, then a low wooden fence, and beyond that, the flattest, widest landscape I've ever

283

seen, all fields and hedgerows and small copses of trees, stretching away to a perfectly level horizon. The sky sits over it like a vast, upside-down blue bowl.

The thudding sound, which had faded slightly, gets louder again. In the distance, I see a black shape sinking to the ground. It looks like an upturned slug with two rotors on the top and two on the bottom—a roto.

As the first roto lands, another rises into the air. I notice low buildings close by, and flags fluttering in the breeze. Is it a roto-port of some kind? It seems a strange place for one, out here in the middle of nowhere.

Another wave of exhaustion crashes over me. I sink back down onto the bed. Maybe I just can't remember who I am because I'm so tired. Maybe some more sleep will help. I pull the quilt over myself again, close my eyes and drift off almost immediately, lulled by the rhythmic thumping of the rotos.

I don't know what time it is when I wake up again, but I can hear someone moving about downstairs and a voice out in the garden. I push back the quilt and look out of the window again. A woman's standing in the middle of the lawn, a pair of scissors in one hand, a bunch of flowers in the other. My stomach lurches with almost instantaneous recognition. I know her. But from where? Trying to figure it out is giving me a headache. *She's called Mel,* I think. *And she was looking after me when I lived in* . . . Oh, God, where did I live? London, that's it. I lived in London. I had an apartment. And now I remember something else too: I was trying to get hold of her for something—it feels as if it was something important, although I have no clue what it could have been. When was that? Yesterday? Last week? Last month? Last year?

And why aren't we in London now?

Unsteadily, I get out of bed, one hand against the wall for support. When I'm sure my legs are going to hold me, I strip off the cotton nightshirt I'm wearing and put on the clothes that have been left on the chair—underwear, trousers, a T-shirt, a jumper, a pair of light-soled shoes. They're not mine, but they fit perfectly. Then I look through the drawers, wondering if there's anything in them that might give me a clue to my identity. But they only contain more clothes and toiletries.

Disappointed, I open the door. Outside my room is a narrow landing with a bathroom at one end; I splash water on my face and use a finger to rub toothpaste across my teeth, then look at myself in the mirror. The face that looks back at me is familiar, yet different. Have I dyed my hair? I'm sure it should be darker. Now, it's wavy and mousy-coloured, tangled on one side where I've been lying on it.

My name is . . .

Nothing.

I grip the edge of the sink and try again. *My name is . . .*

It's so close I can almost touch it, but just like earlier, when I try to get hold of it, the memory slithers away from me.

I turn away from the mirror, feeling angry and disappointed with myself. I should go downstairs. I need answers, and it's clear I'm not going to find them staring into a mirror. Perhaps Mel will be able to help.

My legs still feel wobbly, so I hold on to the banister with both hands as I make my way down the stairs. At the end of the hall is a big kitchen with old-fashioned wooden furniture and lots of shiny, high-spec appliances, with a walk-in pantry on the left-hand side.

Mel's at the sink, arranging the flowers from the garden in a glass vase. Another woman, small and slender with fine features and pale skin and dark hair, is sitting at the table. She's familiar too. They both look round at me and Mel says, "Jenna!" Then she shakes her head. "No, silly me, I meant Jess, of course. How are you feeling?"

I stare at her. That's it. I'm Jenna. Jenna Strong. I was jailed for the murder of my parents, and someone got me out.

A doctor. Even though I can't remember his name, it's like a lightbulb going on in my head. Several lightbulbs. "No," I say, my voice croaky and thin-sounding, as if I haven't used it in a while. "You got it right the first time."

"You remember?" A smile spreads across her face.

I frown. "Where am I?"

"Come and sit down," Mel says, leaving the flowers to go over to the table and pull out a chair. "You look tired."

She hasn't answered me. I feel a flash of irritation—and also déjà vu. We've done this before, me asking questions and her evading them. When?

"Where am I?" I say again, crossing my arms, not moving. Mel and the dark-haired woman look at each other.

"You're in Lincolnshire," the dark-haired woman says.

"Lincolnshire?"

"Please sit down," Mel says, her voice firmer this time. "I know you've got a lot of questions, but you do look rather pale."

Although I don't want to admit it, my legs still feel shaky, so, frowning again, I sit down.

"I'm Anna Healey," the dark-haired woman says, holding out a hand for me to shake. "We met quite recently, although you may not remember."

I shake my head. I have no memory of that at all.

The thudding of a roto cuts through the air. Both Anna and Mel look up, following its path as it flies right over the house. "I wonder where *that* one's going?" Mel says, looking pensive.

"Why is there a rotoport out here?" I say.

"It belongs to ACID," Anna says.

"ACID?"

"Yes."

"But aren't you worried they'll find you here? Find *me*?"

Anna has just opened her mouth to answer me when someone else comes into the room: a tall black man with graying hair.

"She remembers her name," Mel says before he can speak, "and she knows who I am, but I'm not sure about anything else."

"That's to be expected," the man says. He smiles at me. "Do you know who I am?"

I do, but his name won't come to me. Tom. No, Bob. No—but it's something short. It begins with a—

"I'm Jon," the man says, and another one of those lightbulbs goes on in my head.

"How are you feeling?" he says.

My stomach rumbles loudly. "Hungry."

Jon makes toast and coffee. As soon as he sets it down in front of me, I grab a piece of toast, shoveling it into my mouth, then pick up another, and another. I feel as if I haven't eaten in forever.

"OK," Jon says when I've finished. "I need to check you over. Then we'll explain what you're doing here."

As he takes my temperature and pulse with a small, hand-held scanner, I get another of those maddening flashes of déjà vu. We've done this before too.

"How long have I been here?" I ask when he's finished.

"Just over three weeks," he says. "You've been unconscious for most of it."

"Why?" I say. Suspicion starts to grow inside me. Have I been drugged? Then another memory flashes into my head. I'm in a large, gloomy building, and I'm tied to a chair. There's someone in another chair nearby—they're tied up too—and someone else standing in front of us. *Her name's Jenna Strong,* he's saying, but to who, and why?

I grip the edge of the table.

"Jenna, are you OK?" Mel says, sounding concerned.

"No," I say. "My memory's all screwed up. What happened to me?"

"What do you remember?" Anna asks.

Resting my elbows on the table, I dig my fingertips into my temples.

"I remember living in London," I say, pointing at Mel. "I was trying to get hold of you. Then I was on a train and . . ." I shake my head. "I don't know. Everything's mixed up."

"Do you remember Max?" Mel asks.

Max. The name sets off another wave of déjà vu. But I can't picture a face to go with it.

Mel begins to talk. I listen with growing amazement as she tells me that I hooked up, somehow, with the son of the doctor who got me out of prison; that we ended up on the run together and got involved with a cell of the New Anarchy Regiment who carried out a terrorist attack on an ACID rally in Manchester, setting off a bomb that killed ten people.

"You and Max were found tied up in a church," Anna says. "An anonymous member of the public linked ACID to say he'd apprehended you."

I stare at her in shock. A terrorist attack? Bombs? I don't remember any of it. Was that the weird memory I just had, about being tied to a chair? Was Max the other person who was tied up with me?

"Don't panic. I don't think for a moment that you had anything to do with the bomb going off," Anna says. "A short while before, someone else linked ACID to warn them about the bombs. We think that was you."

I feel myself sag with relief. The thought that I might have been responsible for those ten deaths is almost too horrible to contemplate.

"What happened after that?" I say, staring at the crumbs on the plate in front of me.

"You were arrested and questioned, but that was really just a formality," Anna says. "Then you were taken to see General Harvey—"

My head jerks up at the mention of his name. "I saw him? Recently?"

Anna nods. "He offered you a choice—to be given a new identity and be LifePartnered, or be put to death."

"I was *LifePartnered*?" I say.

"Yes. The boy you were Partnered with and his family had no idea of your true circumstances, of course. They were led to believe that you were a girl whose parents had been killed in an accident, hence you'd missed your proper LifePartnering slot—and were offered money to let their son be Partnered to you."

"You were put through a process called cognitive realignment to make you think you were someone else," Jon adds. "But because it had already been done to you before, they had to do it with medication this time, which you were told was an antidepressant. You may have been subconsciously fighting it, which is why you're getting some memories back now. We tried various things to trigger it—hacking your news screen, sending you a device with a message on it—but it didn't work. In the end, we had to have two of our operatives pose as ACID agents and get you out of there."

His words are generating flickers of memory, but nothing more. Nothing that makes sense.

Then I replay what he's just told me in my head. "Hang on, what do you mean, it had been done to me before?" I say.

I see Mel, Jon and Anna exchange glances.

"When?" I say.

"After your parents were murdered," Anna says. "And before you were sent to jail."

"But they *weren't* murdered," I say. "It was an accident! I only meant to scare my dad but my mum tried to grab the gun and it went off. She—"

"Jenna," Anna says. "You had nothing to do with your parents' deaths at all."

"What?" I say.

"You didn't kill them. Not even by accident. It was ACID."

CHAPTER 49

My head begins to spin. I hear a rushing sound in my ears, as if I'm falling. Any moment, I'll hit the ground, wake up and realize this is all a crazy dream.

But it doesn't happen.

Because I'm not dreaming.

It's real.

I try to speak, and can't. My vision starts to gray at the edges, the roaring in my ears growing louder.

"Jenna?" Mel says, and I realize I'm holding my breath. I gasp, filling my lungs with air, and my vision returns.

"But—but I remember—" I say.

"They're false memories," Anna says. "ACID implanted them in your head using CR, but because you were younger, and it was the first time it had ever been done to you, it was a lot more successful than when they used it to make you think you were Jessica."

"Wait, *what* memories are false?" I say. "The ones about killing my parents? Or are there more? There was this boy—"

"Dylan," Anna finishes for me. She shakes her head. "There's no such person. He never existed. ACID put him in your head, and made you think you wanted to rebel against your parents and ACID so there would be a reason"—she makes inverted comma signs with her fingers—"for their deaths. They really were very thorough the first time around, I'm afraid."

I stare at her. How is that even possible? Those memories are too clear, too *real*.

Then, with a surge of shock, I remember a dream I had back at the flat, the one with an ACID agent killing my parents. Is that what really happened? Did my subconscious cling to the true events of that day and feed them back to me in my sleep?

The shock turns to bewilderment. I feel as if the earth has shifted on its axis, everything I thought I knew about who I was unraveling with breathtaking speed.

"I don't understand," I say in a shaky voice. "Why would ACID kill my parents? They *were* ACID. My father was a lieutenant."

Anna, Jon and Mel look at each other. Then Anna says, "Your parents also worked undercover for an organization called FREE—the Foundation for Rights, Emancipation and Equality. You've probably never heard of them. They do have a public face, as a charity working to help those most in need, but even that's frowned upon by ACID, so they keep it very low-key."

Suddenly, I remember the day after I got out of Mileway when I was taken to see Steve, the guy who told me about my new identity as Mia Richardson. There'd been something on his computer screen when I came into the room—a document with the word FREE at the top, and a logo that looked like a butterfly.

"Is that who you are?" I ask them.

They all nod.

"The group has been around for a long time—almost

twenty-five years," Anna says. "Our ultimate aim is to topple ACID and free this country from their regime. Several top-ranking officials in ACID also secretly work for us—as a subcommander, I'm one of them—gathering evidence against ACID to prove they're ruling this country through tyranny and fear. Because ACID are so powerful, we've had to take things slowly, but we're now at the point where very soon, and with the help of the European Criminal Justice Bureau, we're going to put them on trial for human rights abuses. If we're successful, it will finish them."

"You're a subcommander in ACID?" I ask, and then one of those memory flashes hits me, and I realize why I recognize her. "You're always on the news screens, aren't you?" I say.

Anna nods. I stare at her for a moment. Now that it's clicked who she is, it feels strange to see her sitting in front of me in the flesh. And it feels even stranger to hear her talking about overthrowing ACID.

"So is that why ACID killed my dad?" I say eventually. "Because they found out he was in FREE?"

"Not exactly," Anna says. "Your father discovered that ACID were building an offshore prison. No one knew about it except for General Harvey, who was the one who'd ordered it to be built in the first place—even I had no idea it existed. But your father slipped up. He tried to copy the plans from the general's personal kommweb and didn't cover his tracks properly. The general found out what he'd been doing."

"So did he find out about FREE too?" I say.

Anna shakes her head. "We make sure that all our operatives appear to be working in isolation, so that if any of them *are* ever caught, they can't be traced back to us. As far as the general knew, your parents were acting alone. What none of us had bargained for was that, instead of having them arrested, the general would send an agent—and we still don't know who it was—to kill them. By the time we found out, it was too late.

Although I'm privy to a lot of information—which is why I'm so useful to FREE—in my position, I can't always prevent things from happening. If I'd tried to intervene back then, it would have looked incredibly suspicious."

"No, wait." I shake my head. "My father *can't* have been working for FREE. He wasn't like that. He was strict. He was . . ." I trail off. "Wait. Those are false memories too, right?"

Anna nods. "Your father was a kind man. You were very close." Her voice drops as she adds, "I'm so sorry."

I stare at the tabletop, feeling sick, feeling furious. I want to scream. I don't know how to even start processing the things I'm finding out.

"So is that why you got me out of jail?" I say. "Why me? There must be other people ACID and General Harvey have done stuff like this to—I can't be the only one. And if you're so confident that FREE are going to bring ACID down, I'd have got out in the end anyway, wouldn't I?"

"You're right, it's not the only reason," Anna says. I look up, just in time to see Mel and Jon exchange glances, then quietly slip out of the room, leaving us alone.

Where are they going? I think as Anna walks over to one of the cupboards and opens it, taking out a metal strongbox. It looks old, its surface dented and scarred, and as she comes back to the table with it, a memory buzzes at the back of my mind—I've seen a box like that before, quite recently, but where?

She sets it down on the table in front of me, then takes a little key from her pocket and unlocks it. Inside is a thick stack of envelopes, held together with an elastic band. *Jenna* has been written neatly on the topmost one. "These are for you," she says.

"What are they?" I say.

"Letters."

"I mean, who are they from?"

"Your mother," she says. "She's been writing to you your whole life, but she never sent them. She couldn't."

"My *mother*?" Dread washes over me. "Oh God, is that memory false too? About my mum? You're trying to tell me she wasn't really there either?"

Anna shakes her head. "No, no, not at all. Your father had a LifePartner—the woman you remember as being your mother. But . . ." She takes a deep breath. "She wasn't actually your mother."

"What?" Just when I thought things couldn't get any crazier, they have. "But that's impossible. He was LifePartnered. He wouldn't have been able to—" I dig my fingers into my temples and close my eyes. "I mean, she's obviously still alive if she's been writing to me, so . . ."

Then I realize that if Anna has these letters, she probably also has the answer to the most important question of all.

I open my eyes. "So if my mother wasn't my mother," I say, "who is?"

Anna swallows and clears her throat.

"It's me," she says.

CHAPTER 50

You're lying, I think. *You must be.*

That's what my head says. But my heart knows different. The expression in her eyes—half hope, half fear—tells me that every word she's just said is true.

"You?" I say.

"I met your father when we were both eighteen, at ACID training camp," she says. "I don't know if you know this, but ACID agents are allowed to delay Partnering or even opt out altogether and remain single, so even though your father had a Partner, I didn't. We clicked straight away, and although we knew we couldn't openly have a relationship—the consequences if we'd been caught would have been terrible—we made excuses to spend time together whenever we could.

"Then our training ended, and we came to our senses. Trying to carry on our affair, even though we were both initially going to be working for the same department, would have been too difficult and dangerous. So we decided to go our separate ways.

It wasn't long before we both got opportunities for promotion and were moved to different departments anyway."

She rubs a hand across her eyes. I don't say anything. I can't.

"I wasn't happy, though," Anna continues. "My job had been chosen for me as a result of the tests I took at school, but I'd never really felt comfortable being part of ACID. And now that I was working for them, I was starting to see just how corrupt they were, and what lengths they'd go to just to hang on to power—at any cost. People were suffering, especially in the places outside London that were being neglected while General Harvey and his cronies tried to turn the capital into a model city, to show the outside world that the IRB didn't need it. And yet he seemed oblivious.

"About six years after I started working for ACID, I was involved in a raid on a flat in Outer. The occupants were suspected of kommweb hacking. While I was searching one of the rooms by myself, I found a file on a holocom that hadn't been encrypted properly, about an organization called FREE. I'd heard of them—or rather, I'd heard of the *charity*—but this file talked about action against ACID, investigations into corruption and blackmail, and gave details about a meeting—a time, date and place, and a password so whoever came could get in. Instead of reporting the find to my colleagues, I copied the file, then wiped everything off the holocom so no one else would know about it."

I can't help feeling a burst of admiration for Anna. She must have been terrified of being caught.

"Did you go?" I ask her.

"I did," she says. "And the first person I saw when I walked in was your father. He was suspicious at first—he tried to get me thrown out because he thought I'd come to spy—but eventually, I managed to convince him I was there for genuine reasons. And when the people leading the group found out what I did for a living, they were very interested. As an ACID agent, I could be useful to them. After that, I started attending meetings regularly, and it wasn't long before your father and I realized we still had feelings for each other. We started seeing each other again—in secret, of course—and went on like that for almost two years. Then, when I was twenty-six, my contra-cep implant failed."

She takes in a deep breath. I wait in silence for her to start speaking again. "I still don't know how it happened," she says. "They're supposed to have a less-than-one-in-four-million fail-ure rate. I didn't even realize I was pregnant until I was almost four months along."

"Why didn't you—you know . . ." I can't say *get rid of me.* That would be too weird.

"Terminations had been illegal for decades by then," she says. "Besides which, I still wasn't Partnered. Even FREE couldn't find anyone who would do it—if anything had gone wrong, ACID would have found out."

"So you decided to keep me," I say, feeling oddly disap-pointed that she made this decision because the alternative was too risky, not because she already loved me and couldn't bear the thought of losing me.

"Yes," Anna says. "It was your father who came to the res-cue. By now, he was a lieutenant, and he was able to arrange a fake notification for his Partner—the woman you were brought up to believe was your mother—so that it would look as if you were hers when the time came, and then FREE organized somewhere for me to give birth."

I frown. "But what did he tell my . . ." I want to say *mum,* but she isn't, is she? "His Partner? He can't have just turned up with a baby and gone, *Surprise!*"

Anna shakes her head. "He told her you were the child of a couple who'd been jailed by ACID, and that FREE had res-cued you."

I sit in silence for a moment, letting it all sink in. Anna pushes the box of letters across the table to me. "I'm sorry," she says. "I know it's a lot to take in. If you read the letters, things might make more sense."

I nod and pick up the box. "I—I think I'll take them upstairs," I say, getting up. I feel fragile, as if the slightest wrong step might shatter me into a million pieces.

"Take your time," Anna says gently.

Clutching the box of letters against my stomach, I walk out of the room.

CHAPTER 51

I spend the rest of the afternoon reading the letters. Most of
them cover the story Anna just told me—about meeting my
father, joining FREE, their affair, her getting pregnant with
me. The last few, however, are from just before and just after
I got out of jail. I learn all about the trial—how earlier this
year, after presenting them with the evidence they already had,
FREE finally convinced the European Criminal Justice Bureau
to agree to help them bring a case against ACID once they'd
undertaken their last few evidence-gathering missions. And I
learn how Alex Fisher was planted by FREE at Mileway when
I was on trial for murder. Right from the start, he was trying to
keep me as safe as he could, planning for the day when FREE
would help him to get me out of there. I shake my head. No
wonder I used to feel as if he was looking out for me—he *was*. In
my head, I see him lying facedown on the incarceration block
roof and have to swallow hard against the lump in my throat.
At least I know why he did it now.

I read the last letter—*I promise you this, though: as soon as I can, I'll get you away from what they've got planned for you*—and lean back, gazing up at the ceiling. My vision blurs, and when I blink, I'm startled to find my eyes are full of tears. *They took my life away,* I think. *ACID took my life away.* General Harvey *took my life away.*

I swipe the tears away with the back of one hand. I'm not crying because I'm sad; I'm crying because I'm angry. I've never been so angry in my entire life. If I were at that ACID rally in Manchester right now, I'd happily pitch a bomb right at the general and laugh when it went off.

I'll get him back, if it's the last thing I ever do.

Stiffly, I stand, gather the letters up and put them back in the box. Then I realize that feeling of not-quite-remembering is nagging at me again. It was something I read in one of the letters . . . but which one?

I open the last, most recent letter again and scan it. Nothing.

I open the one dated 25 May this year.

Two-thirds of the way down the page, a sentence jumps out at me.

The key will be finding out what's really going on at a place called Innis Ifrinn—Hell Island—in what used to be the Orkney Isles. It's not even supposed to exist. . . .

Innis Ifrinn. That feeling of not-quite-remembering is stronger than ever now, like an itch I can't quite get to, tormenting me. I close my eyes, turning my focus inwards. *Remember,* I think. *You need to remember.*

Where have I seen those words before? *Where?*

WHAM. A connection is made, a bolt of electricity slamming through my brain as the deep-buried memories I've been struggling to unearth explode to the surface. I'm in an office;

301

there's a holocom in front of me and I'm reading some text scrolling slowly across the screen.

Innis Ifrinn.

That's where Max is.

I remember.

I remember *everything*.

CHAPTER 52

The force with which the returning memories flood my brain is so powerful it makes me gasp. Cade leaving. Max trying to mug me and me taking him in. Our mad flight out of London, and finding the library. Jacob forcing us to join the NAR. Going to the rally. Our almost-kiss in the shop doorway after I linked ACID to warn them about the bombs.

Max's face in the pale light of the glolamp after Jacob told him who I was, as if someone had reached inside him and ripped out his soul.

Another roto flies over the house, so low it makes the walls shiver, but it barely registers. I'm remembering our arrest; Anna and General Harvey interviewing me; the general telling me I could either be put to death, or LifePartnered; being taken to a medicenter and strapped to a bed, screaming as they administered the CR drugs; my life as meek, helpless Jess Stone; Evan, and the party, and finding the device in the bathroom . . .

I jump to my feet, flinging the letter onto the bed, and run downstairs.

"You have to help him!" I say, bursting into the kitchen, where Mel and Jon have rejoined Anna at the kitchen table and are looking through some documents on a little holocom.

"Help who?" Mel says, getting up. "Are you OK?"

"Max. He's at Innis Ifrinn," I say.

Mel, Jon and Anna exchange looks. "How . . . how did you know that?" Anna says.

I tell her about the job I had at the ACID Stats Bureau while I was Jess Stone, and how I went up to Kerri's office and saw the information about Max on her datascroll.

"You have to get him out!" I say.

Anna takes a deep breath. "That won't be possible," she says.

"But—"

"Do you remember me telling you about your father finding out that General Harvey had ordered the building of an offshore prison?" she says.

I nod.

"*That's* Innis Ifrinn," she says. "In a few weeks' time, the general is going out there for an inspection. He's asked me to come too. Along with a group of FREE operatives, I'm going to use the opportunity to gather footage to prove the place exists, and that the general has a direct link to the place, and hopefully use the evidence to prosecute him along with everyone else— the mission I talked about in the letter."

"But how will FREE get in?" I say.

"The rotoport across the fields there is where they transport prisoners and staff from. There are always two teams of agents at the prison to provide security, working in shifts. FREE are going to pose as one. The general and I will only be there for two days, but the rest of the group are going out a week or so before us and will stay for two months, until they're relieved by the next team."

"So why can't they rescue Max, then?"

"It's too risky. If any of the FREE operatives there were to even try to make contact with Max, our cover could be blown."

"That's so *wrong!*" I cry. "FREE can't abandon him now!"

Jon gets up as well. "We're not abandoning him, Jenna," he says in a tone that he probably thinks is soothing but that makes me even angrier.

"Yes you are," I say. I turn to look at Anna. "You said in your letter that twenty people had died out there this year already. What if Max dies too?"

"We are not going to let that happen," Anna says. "We want to bring everyone who's in that place home safely. But it cannot happen during this mission."

"So take me with you," I say. "You arrest the general, and *I'll* get Max out."

"Jenna, it's out of the question," Anna says. "Your being there would place the whole mission in jeopardy. And we're not arresting anyone. We're just gathering evidence."

"I'm sorry," Mel says, "But she's right. You need to stay here with me and Jon and let Anna and her team do what they have to do. Everything hinges on this mission being successful."

"But I want to *do* something, not just sit around here until it's all over," I say.

"I know," she says. "I understand."

No you don't! I want to shout at her. *You have no idea! You weren't even there when Max and I—*

I close my eyes, wishing I'd let him kiss me.

"It might feel like a long time, but it really isn't," Anna's saying. "We're *this* close to ending ACID's reign." I open my eyes and see she's holding up a hand, her thumb and forefinger a couple of centimeters apart. "It will all be worth it, I promise you."

"Yeah," I say, my voice flat. "I'm sure it will."

I leave the room and trudge back up the stairs, burning inside with rage at how powerless I feel.

CHAPTER 53

After a sleepless night, I look out the window at the rotoport and think about Max being loaded onto one of those rotos and flown out to Hell Island, to suffering that, even after my two years at Mileway, I probably can't even begin to imagine. I remember Anna matter-of-factly telling me that FREE can't rescue him, and feel fresh anger boil up inside me. But what can I do? Nothing.

The next day, Anna has to go back to London, but over the following week, other members of FREE start to arrive to prepare for the mission—three guys called Drew, Nik and Rav, and a woman called Fiona. Then Felix Hofmeier, the guy who Mel told me was her boss when we were at the lab in London, arrives with his Partner, Rebekah. I wonder if I can appeal to him about Max, but after Mel's reintroduced us he regards me coolly through his spectacles and says, "Well, Ms. Strong, you certainly gave us a runaround," and I realize asking him anything would be a waste of time.

Every time I walk into the kitchen or the living room it seems like someone's in there, looking at plans of Innis Ifrinn or talking to someone on their komm in an urgent voice. I try to keep out of the way, my thoughts whirling from Max to General Harvey and back to Max again. Why won't FREE help him? His father *died* for them. It's crazy.

And as for the general . . . Every time I think about him, I want to scream. That man took away my parents, took away my *life,* and Anna, *my mother,* is going to be right there with him and not do anything about it.

To try to take my mind off things, I pace my room, do push-ups and sit-ups and squats in an attempt to regain my strength. Being Jess Stone really took it out of me, and I'm shocked at how much my fitness levels have dropped.

It doesn't really work, though.

Another week passes, and as no one else new has arrived, I assume that everyone's here. So coming downstairs to make coffee the day before the mission's due to leave, I'm startled to see Steve, the guy who took me through the details of my Mia Richardson identity at the lab. He's sitting at the table and spreading marmalade on a thick slab of bread—his second, by the look of the crumbs in his beard.

"Ah, Jenna," he says. "I suppose we can call you that again now? How are things?"

"Fine," I mumble, walking past him to make coffee. *Him?* I think as I set up the machine. *No one will ever believe he's an ACID agent. He can't be going.*

But apparently he is, because a few moments later Mel, Felix, Rebekah, Drew, Fiona, Nik and Rav walk in, and Drew greets Steve with a "Hey, good to see you. You all set for tomorrow?"

Steve nods. "So, are we all here?" he asks.

"We're still waiting for Holly," Mel says, moving over to the coffee machine. "She should arrive this afternoon—she'd have been here sooner, but she's not been well. Oh, hello, Jenna. Are you all right?"

I nod without looking at her, fiddling with the settings on the machine.

That's eight of them, I think as the machine begins to hiss and gurgle. *Eight of them. They could arrest the general and rescue Max straight away, and instead, all they're going to do is hang around and pretend to be ACID and film stuff. For TWO MONTHS.*

I pour my coffee into a mug and head for the kitchen door, intending to take it back up to my room. Then, as I step out into the hall, I hear Steve say, "Do we have the uniforms yet?"

"Yes, they're in the wardrobe in my and Jon's room," Mel answers him. "Helmets and boots too. And the fake IDs are ready as well."

"Morning," Jon says as I pass him at the bottom of the stairs. I mumble something back and hurry past.

Mel and Jon's room is right next to mine. Leaving my coffee mug on top of the drawers beside my bed, I go back out onto the landing. Their door's standing slightly ajar. I push it open with my fingertips, praying the hinges won't squeal.

They don't.

The wardrobe is built-in, facing the end of the bed. I tiptoe across, aware that everyone is more or less right underneath where I'm walking. Inside the wardrobe, on the right, are Mel's and Jon's clothes. On the other side are the uniforms. They all have fake agent numbers and surnames on the arms. There's Felix's. That one's got to be Steve's.

And this one . . .

The name on the arm is *H. Vaughan.* I finger the heavy black fabric of the sleeve, rubbing it between my fingers. It's almost exactly my size. I look at the helmets lined up on the shelf above the uniforms, then at the heavy buckled boots stacked neatly in the bottom of the wardrobe. There's a pair there that look my size too.

I narrow my eyes, feeling the beginnings of a plan forming inside my head. Softly shutting the wardrobe door, I tiptoe back out of the room and sit on my bed, where I hold the coffee mug in both hands and look out the window at the rotoport, mulling things over.

Later that afternoon, Holly arrives and, quite unexpectedly, everything falls into place.

Mel introduces us when I go downstairs in search of more coffee. "Jenna, this Holly," she says as I walk into the kitchen.

"Hi," Holly whispers, smiling and holding out a hand. "Nice to meet you, Jenna. Sorry about my voice. I've had laryngitis and bronchitis."

I shake her hand. She's almost exactly the same height as me, wearing running shoes, her blond hair pulled back in a ponytail. "Holly works for Anna at ACID," Mel says. "We were thrilled when she decided to come over to FREE."

I make my coffee as quickly as I can and take it back up to my room, where I look in the mirror that Mel hung on the back of my door for me a few days after I woke up here. I narrow my eyes at my reflection, watching her narrow her eyes back as the plan that began to take shape inside my head this morning comes into focus.

I'll pose as Holly and go along with the others to Innis Ifrinn. Then I can find Max and work out a way to get him out of there. And . . .

The general will be there. If FREE aren't going to do anything about him, maybe I can.

That night, at dinner, I watch Holly carefully, looking for any characteristic movements she makes—the way she laces her fingers and stretches them whenever she's considering anything, for example, or the way she always crosses her left leg over her right when she's sitting, never the other way around.

Mel raises her glass. "Here's to the Innis Ifrinn mission," she says.

"To the Innis Ifrinn mission!" everyone else says, apart from Holly, who can only whisper it.

I raise my glass too, a smile spreading across my face.

CHAPTER 54

That night, the others hold a final mission briefing in the living room for Holly's benefit. Mel and Jon sit in too, so I creep downstairs and press my ear to the door to listen. It reminds me of being at the library, eavesdropping on Jacob and his group planning to bomb the ACID rally. Only this time, I'm listening to plans for something I *want* to be involved in.

"We need to be at the rotoport by oh-four-thirty," Felix is saying to Holly. "We're traveling on a supply roto."

There's a pause, so Holly must be whispering something.

"There are just under two hundred and fifty inmates," Felix says. Another pause. "I know, it seems a lot when the staff is so small. But the inmates are under such heavy lockdown, there's no need for the sort of security the jails on the mainland have. Plus—well, you know where the prison's located. No one's ever managed to escape."

I remember Anna's letter. *Twenty people have died there already since the beginning of the year. . . .* A little shudder goes down my spine. Just how bad *is* it at Innis Ifrinn?

"Our duties will consist of patroling the jail, which will give us ample opportunity to monitor and record conditions there," Felix goes on. "We're not there to interfere with the running of the jail or intervene in the treatment of the inmates in any way, even though it may be difficult at times not to. And no one is to talk about anything to do with FREE or the mission. As far as the prisoners and the maintenance staff are concerned, we're ACID, and it's essential we maintain that charade at all times. Now, regarding the footage we hope to get . . ."

I've heard enough. I go back upstairs, intending to doze for a few hours, then sit up and wait so I don't miss anything. But I fall asleep more deeply than I mean to and jerk awake some unknown time later to the sound of footsteps going past my room.

I sit up. *Shit.* What time is it? The room's in darkness, so it must still be pretty early. More footsteps go past my door. I swing my legs out of bed and pad across to it, easing it open a few millimeters so I can peer out.

Rebekah's out there with Felix and Drew. They're wearing their uniforms but no helmets, and I can hear someone in the bathroom, running the taps. "I'll get some coffee on," Rebekah says softly, heading for the stairs.

So they haven't had breakfast yet. Thank God for that.

I watch through the gap as the bathroom door opens and Holly emerges, still wearing pajamas, her hair damp. She disappears into her room. *Come on,* I think.

When she comes back out onto the landing, she's in a T-shirt and jogging bottoms and slippers, her hair scraped back. I listen to her pad down the stairs, wait another few seconds, then step out onto the landing, closing the door behind me.

She's left her bedroom light on. The bed's been hastily made and her jumpsuit and gloves and helmet are lying across it, her boots and a small pack on the floor nearby. There's a dressing

312

gown with a long belt hung on the back of the door. I pull the belt out, then switch off the light and go over to the wardrobe. It's built-in, like the one in Mel's room, and although it isn't as big, there's barely anything in it, so I fit inside quite comfortably. I pull the door shut with my fingertips.

About thirty minutes later, I hear everyone coming back upstairs, and the bedroom door opening. Before Holly can switch on the light, I leap out of the wardrobe, tackling her and pinning her against the bed. She tries to cry out, but all she can do is make a thin wheezing sound. "I'm sorry," I whisper as I bind her wrists and ankles with the dressing-gown cord. "I have to do this." She struggles and bucks, but even though she's strong, she's not as strong as me. When I've finished tying her up, I pull on the ACID uniform over my own clothes. As I step into the boots and jam my hands into the gloves, Holly makes tiny noises that I think are supposed to be screams.

"Sorry," I whisper again as I place the helmet over my head and snap the visor closed. I shoulder her pack and clump across to the door, opening it just wide enough to get out and pulling it shut behind me.

The others are all at the top of the stairs, waiting. They're wearing packs too.

"Got your helmet on already, Hol?" Rav jokes. "Mind you, might be a good thing—at least we won't catch your lurgy!"

I shake my head at him in what I hope is a Holly-ish expression of disgust, and he laughs.

"Please can we keep it down a bit?" Felix says behind him. "Mel, Jon and Jenna are asleep."

Rav makes a face in my direction. I shrug, although my heart's beating fast.

"Anyway, you all need your helmets on once we get outside," Felix says as he heads for the stairs. "We need to make sure we look the part right from the start in case anyone stops us on the road. And don't forget to keep them on in the roto too. I don't want the crew or any other agents traveling with us to see our faces either."

We go downstairs, where Felix hands out equipment belts with pulse guns, handcuffs and batons on them. Everyone else puts their helmets on, and we go outside. An electro van is parked outside the house. We climb into the back, and Felix gets into the driver's seat. I remember Holly's supposed to be getting over laryngitis and bronchitis, and cough a couple of times so that no one gets suspicious.

When the van gets to the rotoport, we get out, one after the other, and stand on the tarmac, looking around us.

An ACID agent comes over. "You the Innis Ifrinn lot?" he says, his voice tinny-sounding through his komm.

As Felix nods, the agent spots the commander's triangle on his arm and salutes. "Sorry, Commander, didn't see you there," he says. He points a gloved finger. "You want launch pad seven."

We walk across to the launch pad in a huddle. The rotoport is bigger than I thought it was, and the rotos themselves are huge, towering above us. The one on launch pad seven is at half power, its bottom blades turning, its top blades still. A gigantic hatch in its belly lies open, revealing a cavernous space packed from floor to ceiling with crates and containers.

"What is all that stuff?" Fiona asks.

"Supplies for the prison," Felix says, motioning for her to keep her voice down as another ACID agent appears. "This way, please, Commander," she says, saluting Felix.

We follow the agent round to the side of the roto, where there's another, smaller hatch at the top of a metal ladder. Through the hatch is a cramped cabin, lit by strip lights, with padded seats around its edge and straps hanging down from the ceiling. A thin Plexiglas screen separates us from the cockpit. As we sit down, stowing our bags under the seats, the pilot turns

314

to give us a thumbs-up through the screen. The door to our cabin is slammed shut, and there's a loud hydraulic drone from somewhere beneath us as the hatch in the roto's belly is raised, and a boom that shudders right through us as it closes. The top blades begin to power up with a deep *whapwhapwhap* that, even inside the soundproofed cabin and with our helmets on, is almost deafening. It climbs to a steady scream, drowning out the whine of the blades underneath.

With a jolt, the roto rises into the air, and inside my helmet, I grin so hard my face starts to ache.

I've made it.

CHAPTER 55

It takes just over an hour for the roto to reach the island. Everyone is tense; the atmosphere in the little cabin feels like the air before a thunderstorm, prickling with electricity. "Good God, I could fly this thing better than this," Felix snaps as the roto bounces in the air, his voice coming through my helmet-komm, and we all grab on to the ceiling straps to keep from being tipped out of our seats.

"Got a rotopilot's license, have you?" Nik says. Felix turns his head to look at him, and even though I can't see his eyes through his visor, I can sense the ice in his gaze.

"Yes, I have," he says. "And all my flying hours."

Nik goes quiet.

When the roto lands, we retrieve our bags and stand up, and Felix taps his visor to remind us to keep them pulled down. A few moments later the cabin door is opened by an ACID agent, who salutes him. Outside, it's almost light.

"Whoa," Rav says when we get down the ladder. I turn,

looking in the direction he's staring in, and see Innis Ifrinn prison for the first time.

To my surprise, it isn't on the island at all, but built on a rig about a mile out to sea. It's shaped like a squat gray cube, a walkway with a low railing running round the bottom and two rows of windows at the top. The lower of those two floors also has a walkway round the outside. There are no windows anywhere else, just solid, seagull-shit-streaked concrete.

We follow the agent down to a small cove where three ten-man inflatables are moored to a jetty, a much larger boat bobbing up and down on the water just out to sea. We get into one of the inflatables, and just five minutes later, we're drawing up alongside the prison, where a second larger boat is moored to one of the legs of the rig.

An elevator takes us up to the first walkway with stomach-plunging speed. "Staff quarters are on the top floor," the agent tells us as she leads us through two sets of reinforced doors and inside, to another elevator next to a wide stairwell.

As we travel up through the prison, I think of all the inmates in the cells around us. Which one is Max in? He could be close enough to touch.

"I'll leave you to get settled in," the agent says when we reach the top floor, a long room with a kitchenette and two large tables at one end, and a few grubby-looking sofas, some lower tables and a holocom at the other. "The bedrooms and bathrooms are through there." She points to a door on the other side of the lounge. "And there's stuff for tea and coffee in the cupboards over there." She jerks a thumb at the kitchenette. "Once the supply boat's brought the rest of your stuff over, I'll come back up here and go over everything with you."

"Very well," Felix says, and the agent salutes him and hurries to the door.

After she's gone, everyone visibly relaxes. Rebekah pulls

off her helmet, shaking out her hair. The others remove theirs too.

Then they look at me.

"You gonna keep that thing on forever, Hol?" Rav says, one side of his mouth twitching up in a smile. My heart begins to race, and inside my gloves, I feel my palms go slick with sweat.

This is it.

I swallow, steeling myself, and take off my helmet.

CHAPTER 56

A stunned silence falls across the lounge.

"Je—" Steve starts to say.

Felix silences him with a furious *"Shh!"* Then he turns to me. "What did you do to Holly?" he whispers through clenched teeth. His eyes glint with anger.

"Nothing," I say. I shake my fringe out of my eyes. "Well, she might be a bit . . . tied up. But Mel and Jon should have found her by now. She'll be fine."

"You stupid girl," Felix says. "Do you have any idea what will happen if ACID realize you're here?"

"I have a right to be part of this," I say fiercely. "ACID took my whole life away from me. You can't honestly expect me to just wait around at the cottage and do nothing."

I don't tell him about my plan to rescue Max and confront the general. If I say anything about that, he'll find a way to stop me for sure.

Felix makes a frustrated hissing sound between his teeth,

glaring at me. I glare back. "We have to send her back," Drew says, shaking his head.

"It's too late," Rebekah says. "If we do that, they'll realize something isn't right. We have to pretend she's Holly—we don't have any other choice."

Felix walks across the room, then comes back. "OK," he says to me, still speaking through clenched teeth. "This is how it will work. You'll stay in your room, and—"

"She can't," Steve interrupts.

Felix and I both look round at him.

"The other staff here are expecting a team of eight agents," he says quietly. "That means they'll expect eight of us to be clocking in for shifts."

"We could pretend she's ill," Drew says.

"They'll send a medic to check on her," Rebekah says. "Or ask for someone to replace her."

"What about if they see her on the cameras?" Nik says.

"They only have those in the cell blocks, don't they?" Fiona says. "As long as she keeps her helmet on when she's down there, she should be OK."

"*Christ.*" Felix rubs a hand across his scalp. Then he lets it drop and gives a sharp sigh. "OK," he says to me. "You got your wish. You're on the team. But don't you forget for one second that I'm in charge, and that you're going to follow my orders to the letter."

I nod, resisting the urge to snap him a salute.

Shaking his head, he says, "We'd better go and find our rooms."

As I follow him and the others across to the door, I let out a slow, silent breath. Now all I need to do is somehow give them the slip so I can find Max.

And get ready to face General Harvey.

CHAPTER 57

To say the staff quarters are basic is an understatement. The bedrooms are tiny and, apart from a hard bed, a metal locker to hang clothes in and a news screen on one wall, as bare as my old cell at Mileway. Everything looks worn out and shabby, even though the place is less than two years old. As I chuck my bag down on the bed and go to look out of the window, I'm half expecting Felix to come in and start ranting at me again, but he doesn't. Maybe he's too angry. Well, good.

My room faces out to sea. The water, stretching away to the horizon in a great gray sheet, looks restless, mirroring exactly how I feel inside.

Half an hour later, when the agent who brought us up here returns, we all go back out into the lounge. I stay at the back of the group, wearing a cap that I found in my backpack pulled down low over my face.

"Your duty rotas are on the holocom," the agent says, turning it on. "You'll be twelve hours on, twelve hours off. There's also the contact details for the other staff who are on the floor below—the cooks and medics and maintenance crew—on there, and the keycodes for the doors, which change weekly—you're here for two months, right?"

Felix nods. "Do we have to do that?"

"No, they update automatically. And whatever code you have to get onto your block, you can use that to get into the cells too. Although you shouldn't need to, with any luck."

"So you don't anticipate any . . . problems?" Felix says.

"Oh, no, Commander," the agent says. "They're a pretty docile lot here. And if any of them do try to kick off, well, there are ways and means, you know?"

I shudder. If this place is as bad as Anna says it is, I *do* know. Threats. Kickings. Beatings. Electric shocks. Stripping away every last little thing that makes you human until you're just a shell, and you don't care anymore—just like Mileway, but worse.

"Well, that's it, I think," the agent says. "Good luck!"

When she's gone, Felix calls up the duty rotas on the holo-com. "Looks like we're not on duty till eighteen hundred," he says. "I'll link the rota and prisoner lists to everyone's komms. Then I'm going to get some sleep, I think."

When I go back to my room, I turn on my komm, thinking I'll be able to find out where Max is. But I only have the link for the rota. *Dammit.* I wait a while, then go back out into the lounge. As I'd hoped, it's empty, but when I turn the holocom on, all I get is a screen saying PLEASE ENTER PASSCODE. I turn it off with an angry sigh. Obviously, Felix is determined that I not try to make any contact with Max.

It's a long day. I spend most of it in my room. I'm exhausted but too wired to sleep, so I sit by the window and gaze out again. The glass is so thick I can't hear the sea; the only noises are the hum of the air-conditioning and the occasional thud of a door farther along the corridor as the others go in or out of their rooms. From the prison below us, there's no sound at all.

When I get bored, I turn on the news screen, half wondering if there's anything about "Jess Denbrough" disappearing from Upper London, but I don't find anything.

Lunch is sandwiches—sub ham and sub cheese on sub bread, with a side dish of vitamin pills. Dinner is sent up in covered dishes from the floor below in a sort of miniature elevator set into a hatch in the lounge wall—a stew made with sub meat. With every minute that passes, this place reminds me of Mileway more and more.

Then, from somewhere deep inside the prison, a siren sounds. It's time for our shift.

"Steve and Rav, you're on Block One, the floor under the staff quarters," Felix says. "Drew and Nik, you're on Two. Rebekah and I are on Three, and Holly and Fiona, you're on Four." It takes me a few seconds to realize he's talking to me. *Holly, Jess, Mia . . . when will I get to be Jenna again?* I think as he gives us the keycode for our block. After checking our equipment belts and loading our packs with enough supplies to keep us going during our long shift—bottles of water, packs of jerky strips, dried fruit and nuts, and chocolate—we put on our helmets. Then we head to the elevator, traveling down to the bottom floor in silence.

"You need to turn on your komm's vidfeed in a minute," Fiona says. Although I can't see her face behind her visor, I'm pretty sure her expression is grim.

"I'm not here to cause trouble, you know," I say quietly. *Not for you, anyway.*

I see her shoulders lift as she sighs inside her helmet. "I guess—" she starts to say, but I never find out what she guesses because the elevator stops and the doors slide open to reveal two ACID agents standing on the other side. We're here.

Beyond the doors is a short corridor with a set of reinforced doors at the other end. The agents shove past us into the elevator without a word. We walk down to the door and Fiona types in the keycode. With a hiss of compressed air, the doors slide open. On the other side I see two padded chairs and a small table with a holocom on it, a door nearby marked WC and, to our right, another reinforced door.

We put our packs down by the table and Fiona types the block code into the keypad beside the reinforced door. It slides open to reveal a space a bit like an airlock, with a second door at the back. We step inside, waiting for the one behind us to close before Fiona opens it. Beyond, I see a dimly lit corridor.

Inside my helmet, I take a deep breath.

Then we step into the bowels of Innis Ifrinn prison.

CHAPTER 58

I was expecting it to be like Mileway, but it isn't. It's like nothing I've ever seen.

The noise is what hits me first: moans, screeches, shouts, cackling laughter that's utterly devoid of any humor. Then the smell, seeping into my helmet despite the breathing filters inside it—a stench made up of shit, piss, mold, unwashed bodies and hopelessness, all of it coated with a layer of industrial-grade disinfectant. Another corridor, much longer than the one outside and so dimly lit that the other end is lost in shadow, stretches out in front of us. On either side are rows of cells, with barred gates instead of doors.

Fiona touches the side of her helmet to turn on her vidfeed and motions for me to do the same. As we start to walk, a nightvision overlay in my helmet's visor kicks in, making everything glow faintly green. We turn our heads from side to side, looking straight into each cell to capture the horror of what's inside on our vidfeeds. Each cell contains two inmates. Some appear to be sleeping or unconscious, some watch us go past in silence.

Others shout and call out, lunging at the cell doors, but no one can get to them because they're all shackled by one wrist to the walls. The prisoners are all ages, male and female, and without exception look thin, filthy and exhausted.

The cells themselves are just a couple of meters wide. There's nothing in them: no bed, no sink, just a hole in the floor in one corner to use as a toilet. By the time we've made one circuit of the block, which is arranged in a three-sided square around the elevator shaft, I've counted thirty of them. With each cell we pass, I gaze at the faces of the prisoners inside, hoping desperately that one of them might be Max, but he's not here. *I bet Felix'll make sure I'm never put on his block,* I think, and feel frustration rise inside me.

But my frustration is quickly replaced by scorn. If that's his game, then all I have to do is wait until I've patrolled all the other floors. Then I'll know for sure which one Max is on, because it'll be the only one I haven't been sent to. I could just search the prison, of course, but I'd have to do it off-shift when the other agents are on patrol, which would draw attention to me, and might draw it to the others too. *You'll have to wait,* I tell myself. *Then once you know which floor Max is on, find a way to get yourself put on patrol there.*

The last cell seems to be empty except for a heap of grubby blankets by the wall. We return to the airlock.

"We might as well take it in turns to patrol after this," Fiona says once we're on the other side as I remove my helmet and take gulps of the relatively fresh air. I nod. I can't stop thinking about those cramped, filthy cells. Can't stop imagining Max in one of them. It makes me feel physically sick.

Fiona takes the first patrol, and I take the second. I walk along the cell block more slowly this time, peering at every face, just in case Max *is* down here and somehow I missed him the first time around. But I don't see him anywhere.

I reach the last, empty cell and turn to go back. Then, out of the corner of my eye, I see the heap of blankets against the wall move.

A hand emerges, pushing the blankets back. My heart starts to beat faster. Max? No, it's too small. I stay where I am, watching, as a diminutive figure sits up and leans against the wall. I stare, shocked. It's a girl, and she can't be more than twelve or thirteen years old. Her hair is hacked brutally short, her face pale and bony, and her eyes, glittering feverishly and ringed with dark shadows, look huge. She starts to cough, a hacking noise that sounds as if it's coming right from the bottom of her lungs. Her body convulses with it.

I can't stand here and watch this. I just *can't*. I wheel round and start to run back along the block, then remember the cameras and slow to a brisk walk. When I get through the airlock, I pick up my pack, plonk it on the table and unzip it, taking out a bottle of water.

"What are you doing?" Fiona says sharply.

"One of the prisoners—a young girl—she's ill. She needs water," I say.

Fiona puts a gloved hand on my wrist, stopping me. "No," she says. "We're not here to play nursemaid to them. If she's that sick, we'll link the medic who's here for the staff and see if they'll do anything."

"But—" I say.

"*No.*"

I consider taking the bottle anyway, but I'd probably have to knock Fiona down to get away from her, and if we tussle, it might get picked up on the cameras. And if *that* happens, and someone from the other team of agents sees . . .

I sit down with a sigh, lifting my visor just enough to clear out the stale air inside it. As soon as Fiona's disappeared into the airlock, I grab two bottles of water out of my pack and

327

shove them into the inside pockets of my jacket. It's so padded already that when I zip it back up, you can't tell. Then I wait for Fiona to come back, hoping that no one was watching me through the cameras.

When it's my turn to patrol the block again I head straight down to the girl's cell. I can hear she's still coughing before I even reach her. Punching the block code into the keypad beside the cell door, I slip inside, hoping the cameras aren't watching me.

The girl stares at me and tries to scramble away from me, but she doesn't get far because of the restraint on her wrist. I take a deep breath, then push up my visor. Without the night-vision overlay, everything's plunged into gloom. The stink of the cell block hits me like a slap, and it takes every bit of willpower I have not to gag. "It's OK," I say. "I'm not going to hurt you." I unzip my jacket, take out the bottles of water, unscrew the top of one and hand it to her. "Here."

She eyes me, her face clouded with fear and mistrust. Another fit of coughing racks her, and I push the bottle at her. "Drink it," I say.

She reaches out, then pulls her hand back. I wait, still holding it out to her. At last, she takes it, gulping the water down thirstily.

"Slow down," I say, grabbing her wrist and gently pulling the bottle away from her mouth. "You'll make yourself sick."

She snatches her arm free and takes another long drink of the water. I watch as she tilts her head back to catch every last drop, her throat working, and wonder how long it is since she last had any. When the bottle's empty, she flings it down and leans her head back against the wall, her chest heaving. But she isn't coughing anymore.

She's thin; much thinner than any of the other prisoners here.

The skin of her face is stretched across the bones underneath like paper, and her fingers are like matchsticks, the knuckles swollen and raw-looking.

I open my mouth to ask her name. Then I remember that she thinks I'm an ACID agent. Remembering the spytag I had at Mileway, I switch on the wrist-scanner in the cuff of my right glove and lean down to swipe it across her left hip. There's a soft beep in my ear, and the data flashes up on my wraparound.

Name: Aysha Kennett
Prisoner ID: TQ3871
Age: 14
Charge: Illegal citizen (parents not LifePartners)
Sentence: Life
Other notes: Prisoner has shown signs of defiance. Food rations to be significantly reduced until behavior improves
Record last updated: 03.04.13

I feel a fresh wave of horror. *Fourteen,* and as if being caged up like an animal wasn't bad enough, they've been starving her half to death for the last four months, for God knows what reason. And she hasn't even committed a crime—all she's done is been born out of Partnership.

Just like I was.

A shudder works its way along my spine. What if they're doing this to Max too? I realize I've been here too long; Fiona will be wondering where I am. "I'll bring you some food next time," I promise as I cut the link and go back over to the door, pulling my visor down again.

She gazes at me, her chest moving up and down rapidly, as if even breathing's an effort. "Why?" she says in a voice that's little more than a hoarse whisper.

"Because—" I start to say, then stop, realizing I was about to tell her I'm not really an ACID agent. I'm half tempted to go ahead and tell her anyway, but I know I can't. I haven't been here long enough, and I can't let *anything* jeopardize my plan to rescue Max and confront the general.

"The, um, order to reduce your rations has been revoked," I say. Then I leave the cell, locking the door behind me again, and head back along the block.

The rest of the shift seems to take forever. Fiona and I don't really talk, just take turns to patrol. Before I go back to the cell again, I load my jacket up with food from my pack. "Don't let the other agents see you with this stuff," I whisper to Aysha as I give it to her.

She frowns. "Why? You said—"

"I know what I said, but just don't, OK?"

She nods, a confused look on her face.

The next time I look in on her, she's asleep. There's no sign of any of the food packets, so she must have hidden them under her blankets. I hope she's eaten something.

I return to the airlock. When the siren sounds, it feels as if twelve years have passed, not just twelve hours.

"God, I'm glad that's over," Fiona says, her face pale, as we walk to the elevator. The doors open and two agents get out, their helmets still under their arms. "Rough, was it?" one of them says when he sees Fiona, grinning. "Don't worry, love. A few days and you'll get used to it."

Guffawing, he gives Fiona a slap on the arm that's slightly too hard to be friendly, and he and his colleague head down to the doors.

Back upstairs, I head straight for the showers, peeling off my jumpsuit and scrubbing myself until my skin burns. Even then, the stench of the cell block lingers in my nostrils. When I'm dressed again, in ordinary jeans and a T-shirt, I hang my jumpsuit up to air it a little and go into the lounge. The others are all there, looking as pale as Fiona did earlier.

"So," Felix says to me. "Glad you came along?"

"I've seen worse," I say, although I haven't, not even close. I stick my chin out and look him in the eye.

And to my gratification, it's Felix who looks away first.

CHAPTER 59

Over the next few days, Felix arranges the rota so I end up patrolling One; then Three; then One again; and after that, back down to Four.

"God, the food here is so *bad*," Fiona says as we head down to the bottom floor. I've ended up doing all my shifts with her, and during the long hours spent watching the cells, we've sort of warmed to each other. "I don't think that meat we just had was even sub."

"It's probably seagull," I say. All the windows on the upper floor are streaked with shit, which reappears as quickly as the maintenance crew, who I've never seen, clean it off. And whenever I'm in my room, I can hear the gulls pattering about on the roof. I wouldn't be at all surprised if the cooks—who I haven't met either—go out and catch a few when supplies are running low.

"Ugh, don't say that," she says, pulling a face.

I smile, but I'm not really paying attention to the conversation. I have other things on my mind, like trying to work out how I'm going to get put on shift on Block Two so I can see Max. Then there's Aysha. Is she OK? I've already filled the inside pockets of my jacket with food and water for her, but I can't help feeling anxious. I offer to take the first patrol so I can check on her.

When I reach her cell, she's stretched out on her blankets, not moving. I go in and crouch down beside her, pushing up my visor. "Aysha?" I whisper. She doesn't respond. I turn her over gently, and shock jolts through me. She's breathing, but only just, sucking in shallow, wheezing gasps of air. Her eyes are closed and in the half-light her lips look purple. I pull off my glove and lay the back of my hand against her cheek. She's burning hot—even hotter than Max was when I first found him, and he was so ill.

"Aysha," I say, a little louder. She doesn't even open her eyes. She's unconscious.

I hurry back to the seating area. "We need to link the medic," I tell Fiona, pushing up my visor. "The prisoner in the last cell's in a bad way."

She sees my expression and frowns. "OK," she says. She puts her helmet back on and speaks into her komm. "She's on her way," she tells me.

The medic, a bony, hard-faced woman in a gray uniform, arrives five minutes later. "Which one?" she barks in a tone that says she doesn't really give a shit. She's wearing gloves, and there's a bag over her shoulder and a respirator hanging around her neck.

"The last cell," I say. "Aysha Kennett."

Looking like I've just asked her to clean out the cells with her toothbrush, the medic stamps to the airlock, pulling her respirator up over her mouth and nose.

Fiona and I both watch her disappear inside. Anxiety churns in my stomach.

Did you get any footage? Fiona mouths.

Of Aysha? I mouth back.

Yes.

I shake my head. Glancing up at the corners of the ceiling—although, when I follow her gaze, I can see nothing there—Fiona gives me a tiny sideways nod.

"I'd better finish my patrol," I say loudly. I snap my visor down and walk to the airlock.

The medic is just coming out of Aysha's cell when I get there. "How is she?" I say.

"I've put a drip in. Don't know as it'll do much, though," the woman says, her voice coming through my komm, muffled-sounding behind her respirator. "Once they get like that, well—"

For a split second I see emotion flicker in her eyes. I wonder how long she's been here, how many prisoners she's seen in a similar state to Aysha. And panic squeezes inside me suddenly as I think, *Max could be in the same way.*

Then the woman's eyes go hard and cold again. "If anything changes, link me. Otherwise, I'll check on her again tomorrow," she says, shouldering her bag and pulling the cell door closed.

"Tomorrow?" I say. "But what if—" Just in time, I remember I'm supposed to be an ACID agent. I remember I'm supposed not to care.

I nod. "Fine. Thanks for coming down."

She shoots me an odd look as she leaves, and I realize that maybe even thanking her was going too far.

Never mind.

When she's gone, I go into Aysha's cell. She's lying in the same position I found her in. The only thing that's changed is the line snaking into her arm, the needle hidden by a patch of white gauze, which looks startlingly bright against the dirt streaked across her skin.

I take out the bottle of water concealed in my jacket and try to get her to open her mouth so I can tip a few drops in, but she still doesn't respond. Then I remember I'm supposed to be filming her. With a heavy feeling inside my stomach, I put the water back and turn on my vidfeed. I make sure I get footage of every part of Aysha's tiny, filthy cell; of the needle in her arm and her blue-lipped, fever-flushed face. After that I leave the cell and walk back down to the airlock.

The next time I go down there, her breathing has become shallower, and she's making a strange rasping sound every time she tries to draw in air. I pull off a glove to take her pulse. It's barely there; a moth-wing flutter. The drip is still half full, but I don't need to be a medic to know that whatever's in there is having no effect.

I put my glove back on. I'm about to link the medic when Aysha gasps and opens her eyes. "Aysha?" I say, pushing up my visor. But she's not looking at me. She's not looking at anything.

"Aysha," I say. *"Aysha."*

She blinks, then pulls in another of those rasping breaths. Her mouth moves as if she's speaking, but I can't hear anything. I try to work out what she's saying. *Wait . . . going to . . . not here anymore . . .*

"Hang on," I whisper to her. "Just hang on."

But her eyes are already closing again. Her mouth has already stopped moving. Just as I'm about to link the medic, she takes in one more shuddering, rasping breath.

And then her chest stops moving too.

CHAPTER 60

A wave of horror goes through me as I realize what's happened. "Aysha," I say, even though I know she can't hear me. *"Aysha."*

I link the medic, and run back to the airlock and the seating area to tell Fiona. When the medic arrives, she's with a guy who's also wearing a gray uniform and a respirator, and pushing a sheet-draped trolley with a squeaky wheel.

They disappear into the block. When they come back, there's a small shape under the sheets on the trolley. My stomach lurches up into my throat when I see it. Fiona and I both watch as they wheel it up to the lift. *What are they going to do with her?* I think, feeling slightly sick. I'm not sure I want to know.

Instead, I think of the general, sending people to die here without a moment's thought, and a cold, sick wave of anger surges through me. When he gets here, one way or the other, all this is going to end.

The next night, after lying sleepless on my bed, filled with despair over not being able to do more for Aysha, I'm put on shift on Block Four again, but with Rav. Fiona is being sent to Two with Drew.

This is my chance.

I catch Fiona on the way out and put on my best pleading face. "Swap with me," I say as the door swings shut after Rav and Drew. Everyone else, including Felix, has already gone, so we're alone.

"I can't," she says. "Sorry, but—"

"Please," I say. "I—I can't go back down to that bottom floor. Not after yesterday."

She looks so uncomfortable that, for a few seconds, I almost feel bad for lying to her. Then I remind myself why I'm doing it.

"Go on, then," Fiona says, and pushes the door open. We hurry to catch Rav and Drew up, who are looking puzzled, wondering where we've got to. "We've swapped," Fiona says. "Is that OK? A prisoner died on Four yesterday—I don't think Felix knows—and it's freaked Hol out a bit."

"We can't swap," Rav says. "Felix'll—"

"Never know if you don't say anything," I tell them, putting my pleading face on again. "Seriously. It's giving me panic attacks down there."

"Guys, we have to go *now*," Drew says. "The agents on the other team are gonna be wondering where we are. Swap with her if you want to, Fiona, I don't give a shit. If Felix finds out, you two can take the rap."

He walks down to the elevator so fast the rest of us have to jog to catch up with him.

Maybe Felix hasn't told any of them about Max being here, I think as the elevator travels downward.

We arrive on Two, and I put on my helmet. So does Drew.

337

Then we go through the airlock. As we walk along the corridor, I feel as if I really might have a panic attack; my chest is so tight I can hardly breathe. *He'll be in the next one,* I tell myself as I peer into each cell and he's not there. *No, the next one. The next one . . .*

We reach the last leg of the corridor, and still I don't see him.

Then we reach the second to last cell, and my heart wrenches up into my mouth.

Max, I mouth inside my helmet, remembering just in time not to say his name out loud.

He's sitting against the wall of the cell, his head drooping forward, his chin resting on his chest. He's lost weight, although he's not as skinny as Aysha—not yet, anyway. How long has he been here? As I stare through the bars at him, I feel fresh anger at FREE for refusing to help him. Alex Fisher died for them, and this is the thanks he gets—his son, chained up in a stinking prison cell and left to rot.

"Something wrong?" Drew says. I look round and realize that he's already started walking back up the block. With one last glance at Max, I hurry after him, muttering, "Nothing."

We return to the seating area. I want to get up again immediately, go back to Max, but I know that if I don't sit here for a while first, it'll make Drew suspicious. And if he says anything to Felix, Felix will find a way to send me back to the mainland, whether it makes ACID start asking questions or not.

Every minute that passes by is torture. Drew doesn't speak to me, just stares at his gloves, fiddling with one of the cuffs.

I can't stand it anymore. Getting to my feet, I pretend to stretch. "I'll go around again, make sure everything's OK," I say. Drew starts to get up too, but I say, "It's fine. You do it next time. Me and Fiona take turns, usually."

He sits back down and, relieved, I walk up the corridor as calmly as I can. I head straight to Max's cell, where he's still sitting in the same position, shoulders slumped, his legs stretched out in front of him.

"Max," I say. "Max."

He looks up. His eyes are dull and sunken. He doesn't say anything. Switching off my vidfeed and taking a deep breath of the filtered air inside my helmet, I unlatch my visor and lift it up. I swallow hard against the urge to gag. I know I should be used to the smell by now, but I'm not.

"Max, it's me," I say. He stares uncomprehendingly at me and I remember I still have Jess Stone's face; he doesn't recognize me.

I open the cell door and slip inside. Just like Aysha, Max tries to scramble away from me, and just like Aysha, he can't because of his wrist restraint. I crouch down next to him and whisper rapidly in his ear, "Max, it's Jenna. I know I don't look like me. ACID changed my face after they arrested us. But it is me. I'm gonna get you out of here."

Comprehension dawns in his eyes.

"Jenna?" he says, his expression a mix of incredulity and confusion.

"Shh!" I hiss at him.

"But how did you—"

"*Shh!* I can't talk now. But everything will be OK. You just have to hang on in there for another couple of days, OK?"

A smile starts to spread across his face, and I can't help smiling back. I'm so relieved that he's OK, that he's *alive,* that I could kiss him. But that would be suicide for both of us. Instead, I get up again and snap my visor back down. "That's your final warning," I say in my best hard-ass ACID agent voice, then turn and walk out of the cell before my emotions can completely get the better of me.

It's only as I walk back along the block that I realize something.

He smiled at me.
He was pleased to see me.
Which means he doesn't hate me anymore.
How did that happen?
And when?

CHAPTER 61

Drew, Rav, Fiona and I all make it back up to the staff quarters before Felix, so Felix doesn't find out about me being on Two. Back in my room, I change into ordinary clothes. It's just getting light; I remember the way Max smiled at me and feel a sharp pang of happiness mixed with frustration and sorrow.

Overtaken by weariness, I get into bed. I don't sleep, but I manage to doze for a couple of hours. After that, I'm able to think more clearly. Whether I like it or not, Max can't be my priority right now. I've got General Harvey to deal with first. And in the meantime, I have to stay away from Two. The thought makes me feel sick— as if *I'm* abandoning Max too— but I can't afford to make Felix suspicious.

The general and Anna are due here in less than thirty-six hours. Just as we're about to start our last shift before they arrive, Felix calls a meeting. "When he's here, make sure your uniforms are spotless," he says. "I don't want to see a button, zip or equipment loop out of place."

He sounds like any other ACID commander preparing his

unit for an inspection, but we all know what he really means: *Make sure you don't give the general any clue whatsoever that we're not ACID.*

Afterward, he grabs my arm and pulls me to one side. "You're going to come down with a stomach upset after this shift," he murmurs in my ear. "A bad one that means you have to stay in bed. Catch my drift?"

I nod, and he lets go of my arm. I was planning on doing something like that anyway. If I'm going to confront General Harvey, it's vital he not know I'm here.

Not until he's at the business end of my gun, anyway. Then there won't be a damn thing he can do about it.

I'm about to ask him which block I'm patrolling when I realize I've left my equipment belt in my room. I go back to fetch it and notice the door beside mine is open, and there's a little metal trolley stacked with folded sheets and bottles of cleaning stuff next to it. I stick my head round the door, curious; as far as I know, that room's been empty ever since we arrived. Although our rooms get cleaned while we're patrolling the prison, and our clothes washed and our meals sent up, I've never seen anyone actually doing these things.

A short, grumpy-looking guy in a gray uniform is smoothing a heavy duvet across the bed, far more luxurious than the scratchy blankets I have in my room. There's a thick rug on the floor, and a beaker and a water jug on the cabinet beside the bed. As I crane my neck to see better, I bump the door with my foot. The guy in the gray uniform looks round. "Yep?" he says.

"Is—is this where the general's going to be sleeping?" I say.

"Yep." The guy turns away from me and goes back to wiping the window.

Sensing I'm not going to get anything more out of him, I retreat to the lounge with my helmet under my arm.

"What are you smiling about?" Fiona asks as we make our way to the elevator. I'm on shift with her again today, on One.

"Oh, nothing," I say, and quickly try to rearrange my expression into something more neutral. I hadn't even realized I *was* smiling.

When we get back from our shift the night has come and gone. In my room, I go to the window and I see a sunrise the color of blood: red streaked with bruiselike shades of violet and black. The water looks red too.

A knock at my door makes me turn. Before I can speak, Felix walks into the room, closing the door behind him.

"Anna and the general will be here in a couple of hours," he says quietly. He looks tense; a deep vertical frown line has appeared between his eyebrows. "From now on, you mustn't leave this room for any reason. One of us will check on you every few hours and bring you food. If you need to use the bathroom, tell us and we'll check the coast is clear first."

I nod.

"I've already informed the prison medic that you're unwell but that you don't need her to come and see you. If anyone knocks at your door, pretend to be asleep until they say who they are, OK? Your next two shifts have been covered by one of the agents in the other group, so you're not expected back on patrol until after the general's gone."

I nod again.

"Good. I'm going to get some sleep before they turn up," Felix says. Then, just as he reaches the door, he looks back. "Oh, and, er, Jenna?"

"Yes?" I say.

"You've been doing a great job. As part of the team, I mean. Thank you."

Too startled to say anything, I watch him leave.

When he's gone, I make sure my pulse gun is charged and that the switch is off; I don't want it discharging accidentally. I check that the vidfeed in my helmet is working. Then I change out of my jumpsuit and put on my pajamas and, lying in bed, go over my plan one last time.

General Harvey is going to confess to ordering my parents' assassination.

I'm going to film him doing it and find a way to upload it to the kommweb.

Then I'm going to find Anna and tell her to arrest him.

And if he doesn't cooperate . . .

He's dead.

CHAPTER 62

I'm woken a few hours later by the sound of someone bumping around in the room next door, then the bass rumble of a male voice. Immediately, I snap to full alertness, sitting up and staring at the wall beside the bed. *He's here.* We're separated by just a few centimeters of flimsy plasterboard. If I wanted, I could shoot him through it now.

But I want that confession. He *owes* it to me.

When I check the display on the little holoclock above the door, I see it's eleven hundred hours. I've been asleep for a lot longer than I thought. I get out of bed and stretch, yawning.

Then, behind me, the door opens. I whirl round to see Anna, dressed in her ACID uniform, her face pinched with fury.

Closing the door behind her, she walks straight up to me. "How *dare* you?" she says, very quietly. In the next room, the general is still moving about. "Do you realize how much danger you've put us all in by coming here?"

"If you've come to tell me I've got to stay in my room and pretend to be ill until *he* leaves," I reply, jerking my head at the wall and being careful to keep my voice down too, "Felix and I already had this conversation."

"And I hope you listened to him," Anna says. "If the general finds out you're here, he will kill all of us. You do know that, don't you?"

I think of my gun, resting in its pouch on my equipment belt. *Not if I get to him first.*

"I know you're tough, Jenna," Anna continues, "but you're in way over your head here. As soon as he's gone I'm going to find a way to get you back to the mainland, OK? I'd send you now if I could—the roto's still over there, waiting to take us back tomorrow."

I grit my teeth at her condescending tone. How old does she think I am? Five? She seems about to say something else, but then we both hear the door to the next room open and close, and footsteps going past outside. We freeze until we hear the door to the lounge opening too.

"I have to go," Anna says. *"Do not set foot outside this room."*

It's a long, long day. Fiona brings me food and stands watch so I can use the bathroom, but she's in too much of a hurry to chat, and I'm not in the mood for talking anyway. I sleep, pace the room, do sit-ups and stare out of the window at the sea, which is the same iron-gray as the sky.

I don't hear the general come back to his room until nearly twenty-three hundred. By then, all the other agents who were on the day shift have returned and the corridor outside is silent. The general seems to take forever getting ready for bed. It's almost midnight before everything goes quiet. I make myself wait another half hour, then pull on my ACID uniform and my helmet, gloves and boots. I switch off the light and, guided by the night-vision overlay on my visor, go to the door.

The very first thing I see when I open it is the ACID agent, uniformed but without his helmet, sitting on a chair outside the

346

general's door with a gun cradled in his lap. He glances over at me and nods, then looks away.

I punch him square on the side of the jaw, grabbing his collar with my other hand to stop his head smacking against the wall. His eyes roll up to the whites and he slides bonelessly off the chair. I lift him up by his armpits and drag him down the corridor to the bathroom, where I use the wrist and ankle restraints on his belt to cuff him before bundling him into one of the showers and closing the door. Hopefully, by the time he wakes up or someone finds him, I'll have done what I need to do.

I go back down the corridor to the general's room and turn on the light, hurriedly dimming it to its lowest setting so it won't wake him. I want him to see my face when he wakes up, but once I lift my visor, I won't have my helmet's night-vision overlay to help me see anymore.

The general's laid on his back in the bed, eyes closed, snoring softly. His jumpsuit and equipment belt, with his gun still resting in its pouch, are hung up on the other side of the room, well out of his reach.

As I walk toward him, flat-footed and silent, I take my own gun off my belt and place my thumb on the charge switch. I half expect him to wake up, but he keeps snoring.

When I reach the bed, I look down at him for a moment. Hatred surges through me. How can he sleep so peacefully when he's responsible for so much misery, so many deaths? He deserves never to sleep again.

Or to sleep forever.

I jam the muzzle of the gun against his forehead and, as his eyes fly open, flip up the visor on my helmet so he can see my face.

"Hello, Sean," I say, smiling at him. "What a long time it's been."

CHAPTER 63

I flip the charge switch back, powering the gun up. "Make one sound and you're dead," I tell him. His eyes are huge, his mouth working soundlessly as he stares up at me.

"You . . . ," he croaks.

I dig the gun a little harder into his forehead. "What did I just say?"

He closes his mouth with a snap.

"Get up," I say.

He glances toward the door.

"Your bodyguard had to take a shower," I say. *"Get up."*

General Harvey sits up, pushes back his duvet and swings his legs to the floor. I see he's fully dressed, wearing a black sweater, trousers and socks. I frown. Weird. Is he cold or something?

"Sit down," I say, jerking my head at the chair by the window. He sits, and, switching the gun off and tucking it into my belt, I take the wrist and ankle restraints from my belt and shackle him to the chair, then take the gun out again and switch it back on.

"Well," he says when I've finished. He seems to have regained his composure; his tone is bored, even sarcastic. "This is all a bit over the top, don't you think, Jenna?"

"Shut. Up." I make as if to squeeze the trigger and he closes his mouth. Reaching up, I turn on the vidfeed in my helmet. "So," I say. "How did it feel, sending someone to kill my parents?"

He looks at me. Blinks.

"You can speak now," I say.

"That—that was you," he says.

"No it wasn't," I say. "It was an ACID agent working under your orders."

I see a tiny muscle twitch under his right eye. I wait for him to ask me how I know that, but he doesn't.

"What do you want from me?" he says.

"I want you to say you sent someone to kill them, and that you had ACID brainwash me to think that I did it."

He gazes steadily at me.

"Say it," I snarl, starting to press the trigger again.

"Are you filming this?" he says.

"Yes."

"And what are you planning to do with it, may I ask?"

"Upload it to the kommweb," I say.

"You don't have the facilities to do that here, do you?"

"Doesn't matter. I can do it when I get back."

He raises an eyebrow. "Get back where?"

"Nice try," I say. I aim the gun right at the center of his forehead. "Spill it."

He sniffs. "Well, if you insist." He clears his throat, then looks directly at me. "It was me who gave the order for your parents to be killed. You're innocent." He raises his eyebrow again. "Will that do?"

I feel a surge of irritation. Why is he being so patronizing? Why isn't he *scared*? "Yeah. I guess."

"So are you going to let me out of these cuffs?"

"No." I tuck my gun back into my belt and head for the door.

"Jenna . . . ," he calls as I'm about to step through it.

I stop, looking back over my shoulder at him.

"If you're going to find Subcommander Healey, there's a little message I'd like you to pass on to her," he says.

As I frown, he smiles. "Tell her I know why she and that team of *agents*," he says, the sarcastic emphasis on the last word unmistakable, "are really here."

"What?" I say.

"I know about FREE, Jenna. I know what they're trying to do."

A flash of heat goes through me, followed by a wave of freezing cold. "No," I say. "No way."

The general's smile widens. "I've known about them for a while now, as it happens. Although seeing you here was quite a surprise."

"*How* do you know about them?" I say.

The general shakes his head. "Questions, questions. What a pity I don't feel inclined to answer them. All that matters is that everyone's together in one place. And the fact that you're here too is, quite frankly, a bonus."

A chill trickles along my spine. "What do you mean?" I say.

The general lifts his chin slightly. "There's a fleet of rotos on its way, carrying pulse cannons and explosives," he says. "They'll be here in just over an hour."

I stare at him, horror rising inside me.

"They're going to destroy the prison," he says. "And they're going to take you, the FREE team and that mother of yours with it."

CHAPTER 64

"You're talking crap," I say. "Why would you come here if you were going to destroy the place? Why would you put yourself at risk like that?"

The general doesn't answer me, but as I stare at him, trying to figure it out, something goes click inside my head. "You couldn't bear not being here to witness it with your own eyes, could you?" I say. "You wanted to make absolutely *sure* that Anna and the others were killed, along with all the people you've locked up here." I give him a thin, humorless smile. "Only you were planning on watching it happen from a safe distance away, on board a roto."

I start toward the door. "Jenna, wait! Why don't we make a deal?" he says, and for the first time, I hear a thread of panic in his voice.

I stop. "What?"

"Wipe that footage you just took and uncuff me, and I'll call them off."

"And then what will you do?" I spit. "Lock us all up in the cells here for the rest of our lives? I don't think so."

I step through the door. "Jenna!" the general calls after me.

Shit, I think. *He's gonna wake people up.* I spin on my heel and hurry back to his room. "So you agree, then?" he says, looking half amused, half relieved. Ignoring him, I grab a shirt off a hanger on the back of the door and wind it into a loose rope, which I wrap around his head, gagging him. His face flushes and his eyes bulge as he makes throttled-sounding noises from behind it. There's no way anyone'll hear him now.

That's why he was dressed, I think as I sprint out into the lounge, which is empty, and make for the elevator. *He was going to get himself—and probably the other agents who were off shift too—out of here while the FREE lot were on duty. Anna said there was still a roto over on the island. . . .*

I jab at the holoscreen beside the elevator to call it, then link Anna on my komm. "Which block are you on?" I ask her, before she can say anything. "We're in trouble."

"What do you mean?" she says, her voice sharp. "Has the general realized you're here?"

"It's much worse than that," I say. "Where are you?"

"Three. But—"

"Is one of the big boats still moored to the rig?"

"Yes. Now please will you tell me what's—"

The lift arrives. "I'm on my way," I tell her, and cut the link. *We need to get as many people onto the boat as possible,* I think as the lift takes me down to Three. *Take them over to the island, then get the inflatables while Felix powers up the roto. Even if we just get people onto other islands for now, at least they'll be safe.*

Inside my head, I add up how many people we need to evacuate from the prison. Two hundred and forty inmates. Eight of us, plus the other eight agents. The general, and the maintenance staff—I don't have a clue how many of them there are.

In other words, a lot.

And we have about an hour to do it. Maybe less.

When the elevator reaches Three I get out and sprint to the reinforced doors. I don't know the keycode so I pound on the doors with the flats of both hands. A few seconds later they open to reveal Anna and Rav standing on the other side.

"What the *hell* is going on?" Anna says, removing her helmet.

I explain as quickly as I can. "We have to warn the others and start getting people out of their cells," I tell her, watching the color drain from her face.

"I'll do it," Rav says, and he turns away, speaking rapidly into his komm.

"Where's the general now?" Anna says as we wait long, agonizing moments, listening to Rav telling the others what's happening, and giving them instructions.

"In his room, cuffed to a chair and gagged," I say. "Don't worry. He won't escape. We have to get him out too, though."

Anna nods. "Don't worry, we won't forget about him." She runs a hand through her hair, pulling it back off her face. "Christ, how did he find out? We've been so *careful*—"

"Done," Rav says, turning back. His face looks pale too.

"OK, let's start getting people out," Anna says. "I think the best thing to do is keep up the pretense we're ACID—it'll confuse the inmates if we explain, and slow things down. Just tell them the prison's being evacuated. Show them your guns if you have to—anything to get them moving. Jenna, you stay here with me. Rav, you warn the staff on the floor below ours. We'll leave the general and the other agents until last."

Rav heads to the elevator, and after she's put her helmet back on, Anna and I run through the airlock and along the block. We start with the cells at the far end, unlocking the doors and ordering the frightened-looking inmates to their feet, before unshackling their wrists and ushering them out into the corridor. "Wait in line," I bark at them through my helmet. "Nobody moves until we say so." Seeing my gun, no one tries to protest, not even the ones who've always called out and screamed insults at us when we've been on patrol. They shuffle out into the corridor, a pitiful sight in their ragged, filthy clothes. A few people are so weak that others have to help them walk. The same rage rises inside me that I felt when I looked down at the general's sleeping face, that I felt after Aysha died and I found Max, and I'm half tempted to suggest to Anna that we leave the general and the other team of agents behind.

But the general has to be made accountable for everything he's done—all the years of oppression and corruption and terror he and ACID have subjected us to. We owe it to these people, and my parents, and Alex Fisher, and Max . . .

Have they got him out yet? I think as we usher everyone toward the stairwell—there are too many for the elevator. *Please let him be OK.*

Before long, we start to catch up with the people being evacuated from the floor below. Behind us, more are coming down from the blocks above, and soon the stairwell is packed solid. "This isn't going to work!" Anna's voice says in my ear. "There isn't going to be room out on the gantry. We'll have to get people to wait in the stairwell. Can you link the others and tell them?"

Holding up my gun to stop the people around me from jostling past, I do as she asks. Just as I finish, a guy tries to shove past me.

"Stay where you are," I snarl at him. "*Everyone* stay where you are. D'you want to kill yourselves?"

I hold up the gun again and flip the charge switch back, a sick feeling in my stomach as I watch the people around me shrink away. I hate threatening the inmates when they've done nothing to deserve it, but if the evacuation becomes a free-for-all, everyone'll get trampled.

It feels as if I wait there forever. Calling up my wraparound,

I see twenty minutes have already passed since I linked Anna to tell her what was happening. Panic threatens to rise inside me, and it's an effort to push it back down.

And what was that noise? Roto blades? I listen more carefully, but all I hear is the mutters and coughs of the prisoners waiting on the stairs around me. Then my komm pings. "OK, start getting people out onto the gantry," Anna says.

As I push my way down there, someone grabs at me, almost pulling me over. I manage to grab hold of the rail just in time, and turn, holding the gun up. "Stop messing about!" I yell. "We're trying to save your lives here!" Outside, it's raining, drops of water blowing in through the doors that lead out onto the gantry. The inmates huddle together, reluctant to go out there. "Keep moving!" I yell.

I weave my way through them and my visor fogs up with the rain. I swipe it irritably. The gantry is lit up by floodlights; I look around and catch sight of Anna standing near the railing, herding people into the elevator. Both of the larger boats are moored on the water below.

"Is Felix on the island?" I ask her through my komm.

"Yes, he, Rebekah and Nik are with the roto. They're calling for help," she says. "You go with this lot."

"No!" I say, wiping more rain off my visor. It spatters against my helmet, making it difficult to hear. "I have to wait for Max."

"Don't be stupid!" she says. "It's too dangerous!"

"I'm not going anywhere!"

"For God's sake, Jenna—" She shakes her head, then presses the button and sends the elevator down to the boat. A few minutes later it comes back up, empty, and we usher the next lot of inmates into it. Behind me, more and more people are edging out onto the gantry, filling the spaces left by those who've already gone down to the boats. Where is Max? He should be here by now.

Then I see him, standing just outside the doors.

I shoulder-barge my way back through to him. "Max," I say, grabbing his arm. He flinches, and I remember I still have my visor over my face. I push it up and immediately get a faceful of rain.

"Max, it's me," I say.

His frightened expression turns to recognition. "What's going on?" he says. I tell him. Then, behind me, Rav appears with a small group of people in gray uniforms—the prison medic, her assistant, and the kitchen and maintenance staff, including the guy I saw cleaning the general's room. Fiona's there too.

Anna comes over. "How many more?" she says.

"Block Four," Fiona says. "Steve and Drew are bringing them down. Then they're going to go back up and get the general and the other agents. D'you want me to take the second boat over?"

Anna nods and goes back over to the elevator with them. They all look anxious. I wonder what Rav told them to get them out of there.

Anna holds up a hand, stopping the people who are moving toward her. The boat must be ready to leave. I look up, scanning the sky for rotos, but see nothing. I turn back to Max. "We should go down to the boat," I say. He nods.

"Anna!" someone shouts behind us. I whirl round to see Steve and Drew running out onto the gantry.

"He's gone," Drew says breathlessly when they reach us. "No sign of him. The other agents have vanished too."

Anna stares at him. So do I. "But that's impossible," I say. "I cuffed him."

"The cuffs were still there. Someone found him and released him."

The agent in the shower, I think. He must have woken up. Or the general managed to make a loud enough noise to wake the others up somehow. *Crap.*

356

"He's got to be somewhere," I say.

"We searched the staff quarters from top to bottom," Steve says. "There's no sign of him."

"But there isn't any way out except through these doors," Anna says. "He must be—"

She breaks off, jerking her head round. "What was that?" she says.

"What was what?" Drew says.

"Shh." She holds up a hand. We all listen, and a few moments later, we hear it.

The thud of roto blades.

CHAPTER 65

The first one's on us before we can do anything, bursting out of the darkness with its headlights blazing.

"Get down to the boat! Get down to the boat!" Anna screams.

Steve and Drew run for the elevator. I start to go after them, then see the roto's gone into a hover over the staff quarters at the top of the prison. "Wait!" I yell. "What's it doing?"

Anna looks up too. A spotlight beams down from the bottom of the roto, bathing the already floodlit gantry in blue-white light and turning the rain into glittering shards. I pull my visor back down to shade my eyes and see a rope being lowered from a small hatch in the roto's side.

"The general's on the roof!" I yell. "They're rescuing him!"

I run back inside to the elevator, punching the buttons to take me up to the top floor. When I reach the lounge, it's filled with the glare of the roto's spotlight. *How did they get up there?* I think. I scan the edge of the room, looking for a door, but I can't see one. And the windows don't open, but none of them are broken.

Then I notice that a table from the edge of the room has been dragged into the center. I look up at the ceiling above it and see the faint outline of a hatch, disguised to look like it's part of the tiles.

I clamber onto the table, shoving my gun back in my belt, and punch the door in the ceiling open. As I grab onto the lip of the hatch and haul myself up and through, I'm blasted by the downdraft from the roto's blades.

There are only two ACID agents left on the roof. One is clinging onto the rope, being winched slowly up to the door in the roto's side, the wind and downdraft sending him swinging perilously close to the roto's bottom blades. The other is standing with his back to me, waiting. I feel a burst of despair. I'm too late. He's got away.

Then I see the three triangles on the arm of his uniform, and the name below them. 912 S. HARVEY.

Because of the noise from the roto, he hasn't heard me come through the hatch. I reach for my gun, then change my mind and grab my Taser instead. I want to incapacitate him, not kill him. I run up behind him and leap on his back, trying to pull his head back with one arm so I can jam the Taser into the space between his collar and the bottom of his helmet. He roars and twists round, but I cling on. I can't get the Taser under his helmet, so I stick it in his armpit. When I press the button it discharges, but nothing happens. The jumpsuits must be Taser-proof.

The general spins, and I can't hold on any longer. I let go and stagger back, dropping my Taser and almost skidding over on the rain-slick surface of the roof before managing to right myself. The general lifts his visor. I lift mine too. We look at each other, chests heaving. "You," he says, his top lip curling. "I'm going to *end* you."

He glances up at the roto. "Tell two and three to hold fire. There's some unfinished business I need to attend to," he says into his komm, and I realize he must be talking to the other rotos waiting out at sea nearby. "No, I don't need backup. Just wait for me." Then he pulls his gun from his belt. There's no time to draw my own gun. No time to retrieve my Taser. I take a step back, turn, and run for the hatch.

I reach it just as the general fires his first shot at me. The deadly electric charge from the pulse gun, a hundred times more powerful than the discharge from a Taser, sizzles past and I feel a searing pain in my upper right arm, just below the shoulder. Diving through the hatch and onto the table beneath, I reach up to pull the hatch closed, jump down to the floor and look wildly around for a hiding place. *BANG!* The hatch door disintegrates in a shower of smoke and sparks.

The general lands on the table hard enough to make it rock from side to side, and I run out of the lounge with him right on my heels. I head for the elevator, but he fires at the controls, and the doors slide shut before I can get there. I make for the stairs instead, leaping down them two at a time. He fires again; I duck and the charge slams into the wall in front of me, showering me with shrapnel. I reach the first landing, my boots squeaking against the floor as I take the corner and start down the second flight.

The others. I'm leading him straight to them. Anna has a gun, but what if he shoots Max, or realizes where the other prisoners have gone and orders the rotos out at sea to bomb the island?

At the bottom of the second flight of stairs is a half-open door marked KITCHEN/MAINTENANCE. I dart through and kick it shut behind me. I'm in a narrow, dim corridor. I hesitate for a moment, wondering where to go. Then, behind me, the door flies open again. I run through the first door I see and into a large kitchen that looks just like the kitchens at Mileway, with metal worktops, an island and gigantic fridges and ovens. I run

360

to the far end and duck behind the island. My breath comes in gasps. I concentrate on trying to quiet it. My heart's beating so fast it feels like it might explode right out of my chest, and my arm is throbbing. When I look at it, I see a long scrape on my upper arm where the charge from the general's gun has penetrated my jumpsuit, the skin blackened and raw-looking. Another couple of centimeters to the left, and he'd have blown my arm off.

The general bursts in a few seconds later. He's breathing hard too. "Don't play silly games, Jenna," he says. "We both know how this is going to end."

I stay where I am, fists clenched, trying to ignore the pain in my arm as I watch him walk to the far end of the island. As he starts to come round it, I shuffle round the corner away from him, still in a crouch, edging back toward the door. I'm nearly there when, in the corridor outside, I hear footsteps and someone calling, "Jenna? *Jenna!*"

Anna. The general's head snaps round. I freeze, listening as she comes closer. *Not in here,* I think as I see the general lift his gun. *Please don't come in here.*

She's in the corridor; I can hear her boots squeaking against the floor. As she reaches the door and the general raises his gun to fire at her I stand and shout, "Hey!"

But I'm a fraction of a second too late; he's already pulled the trigger. Anna cries out. Head down, I run for the door to see her leaning against the wall just outside, clutching her left side.

When I see Max standing next to her, my stomach lurches. "Are you all right?" I ask Anna. She shakes her head. She takes her hand away and shows it to me. Her fingers are streaked with blood and there's a hole in her jumpsuit, burned and wet-looking like the one on my arm.

"Come on!" I yell at them both. We run along the corridor, Anna clutching her side again and limping, her face twisted with pain, and we duck into an alcove as the general fires

361

another shot at us. Pushing her and Max behind me, I flip back my gun's charge switch, poke my head round the edge of the alcove and, gritting my teeth against the pain in my arm, I fire, aiming at the general's feet. There's a crack, an explosion of sparks and the general gives a howl and staggers as the charge slams into his right ankle.

But he keeps coming.

Any moment now, he'll be level with Anna and Max.

I have to get him away from them, I think. Ignoring Anna's gasp of "Jenna, no!" and Max's "Don't!" I step out into the corridor, holding the gun out in front of me.

"I'm here," I say. "Why don't you come and get me?"

"With pleasure," the general snarls. He's limping, and has slowed to a fast walk. The bottom of his right trouser leg has been reduced to charred shreds.

As he carries on hobbling toward me, I walk backward. He's so focused on me that he doesn't even glance into the alcove. At the end, the corridor turns sharply right. I glance down it and see another door at the end. I run down there, but it's locked. Stepping back, I blast the lock to vapor. Then I yank the door open and sprint through, straight out onto the little walkway I saw when we first got here, slamming against the metal railing at its edge so hard I fold in half over it and knock the breath out of my lungs and the gun out of my hand.

CHAPTER 66

I grab at it, but it's already out of reach. I watch as it falls, turning over and over before disappearing into the water churning against the bottom of the rig. Gasping, winded, furious, I sag against the railing. Then, behind me, I hear the general yelling into his komm. "What's that? The roto pilots are doing *what*? Dammit, I can't hear you! I'll link you in a minute!"

He limps through the door behind me. He still has his visor up, and when he sees me, a sharklike grin spreads across his face.

"Thought you could escape, eh?" he calls over the sound of the roto, which is still hovering above us. I start to edge away from him. When he sees I no longer have a weapon, his grin gets even bigger. He flips back the charge switch on his gun.

"OVER HERE, YOU BASTARD!" Max yells, running out onto the walkway behind him.

The general whirls and aims his gun straight at his heart, squeezing the trigger.

"NO!" I scream, and fly at the general, colliding with him

and trying to tackle him to the ground. The gun goes off, firing into the sky, and the charge must have hit one of the bottom blades of the roto because it lists sideways suddenly, the whine of the blades changing to a scream. I manage to get hold of the general's wrist and crack it against the railing; he drops the gun and it plummets down to join mine beneath the water.

"Max! Tell Anna to send the others back up here! I need their help!" I scream as the general and I grapple, our feet skidding on the wet concrete of the walkway. Max yells something back, but I can't hear him; the damaged roto, unable to hold its hover, is trying to land on the prison roof. "GO!" I bawl at him. He ducks back through the door.

The general and I are getting closer and closer to the railing. He has hold of my arms, his grip vise-tight. I duck and turn, twist and kick. But I can't break free. And I'm getting so *tired*. The wound on my arm burns and my ribs ache from where I slammed into the railing. I want this to be over.

I hook my right foot behind his knee. The general, already thrown off-kilter by the injury to his ankle, loses his balance and stumbles against the railing. But he still has hold of my arms, and he falls back with such momentum that he keeps going, flipping backward over the railing and taking me with him.

The next moment, there's nothing around us but empty air as we tumble down toward the waves.

CHAPTER 67

At some point while we're in free fall, the general lets go of me. I just have time to gulp a mouthful of air and close my eyes before I hit the water with a stinging *smack,* the waves instantly dragging me under.

I fight against their pull, battling to swim up to the surface. My helmet and boots are weighing me down. The boots I can do nothing about, but I reach up and yank off my helmet. Lungs burning, I kick, pushing myself back up. Just when I'm starting to wonder if I'll ever make it, my head breaks through. I gasp, coughing and spitting seawater. All around me, the waves are churning, spray crashing over me as I tread water. The water's bitterly cold; I can feel it seeping under my uniform and into my gloves. Spitting out more water, I scream for help.

Then I hear another cry, close by. "Help!" I look around and see I'm just a couple of meters away from the bottom of the rig.

And clinging to one of the struts is the general.

He's lost his helmet too. With one last burst of strength, I

365

swim over to the next strut along. As I draw closer, he shouts again, "Help me!"

Grasping hold of the barnacle-encrusted metal, I shout back, "Help yourself!"

"I can't swim!" he cries.

"What?"

"I can't swim!"

Hugging the bottom of the strut, the waves pounding into me, I begin to laugh.

"It's not funny!" the general roars.

"No, it's *hilarious*!" I say. I can't stop laughing; I'm this close to being completely hysterical.

Then I hear the buzz of a boat engine. I remember that there's a flashlight on my equipment belt and fumble it free with numb fingers, praying it'll still work after being dunked in the sea. I press the switch and, to my relief, it comes on.

"Over here!" I shout, waving the beam. "Over here!"

A few moments later I see one of the inflatables heading toward us. Rav, his visor pushed up, is at the helm. He maneuvers it alongside the strut I'm holding and reaches out so I can grab his arm and jump down into the boat.

Fiona, Max and Anna are in there too, Anna lying on the floor of the boat with her eyes closed.

"Is she OK?" I say, my stomach lurching as I see how blue her lips look.

"I don't know. She's lost a lot of blood," Max says. The boat lurches and he has to grab onto the ropes along the side with his free hand to stay upright.

Rav steers the boat over to the general. "Get in," he says, pointing his gun at him. "And don't try anything."

Fiona aims her gun at him too as he lowers himself into the boat. Then Rav turns it round and revs the engine and we skim across to the island, the boat going so fast that on several occasions it leaves the water altogether.

As soon as we reach the cove, the others are there, the beach lit up by their flashlights. Fiona hands me her gun so I can keep it trained on the general while she and Drew help Anna, who can only just walk, out of the boat. Meanwhile, Steve is helping Rebekah herd the inmates up the cliff path. "What are you going to do with them?" I ask Rav as he checks that the inflatable is securely moored to the jetty. "They won't all fit in the roto, will they?"

"There are more rotos on the way to pick them up," he says. "Me, Steve, Drew and Rebekah will stay here with them until they arrive."

"And what about me and Fiona and Max and Anna and—him?" I say, jerking the gun at the general.

"You'll go back with Felix and Nik. We need to get the general into custody straight away—the ECJB have already been notified."

"There are still those rotos out at sea," I say.

Max, who's shuddering with cold, his ragged clothes soaked through, says, "Anna managed to link back to ACID control and get the pilots' kommweb IDs after you ran back inside after the general. They've been called off."

"WHAT?" General Harvey bellows.

I glance round at him. "Shut up," I say, waving the gun at him. "And get out."

With a murderous expression, he clambers onto the jetty, hissing in pain as he lands on his bad ankle. "Kneel down," I say. "Put your hands behind your back."

"Here." Rav passes me his restraints, and I cuff the general's wrists. He starts bellowing at me, swearing at me, calling me every bad name he can think of. I plant my foot in his back and send him sprawling onto his face.

"Call me what you like," I say as he writhes and groans on the spray-soaked wood of the jetty. "It's not gonna change anything. You're under arrest."

CHAPTER 68

"Anna!" I hear Fiona cry.

I look and see her kneeling over Anna, who's collapsed onto the sand a few meters away. Her eyes are closed again. Panic stabs through me. Is she unconscious?

"Can you keep an eye on the general?" I ask Rav, who nods. I run across to Anna, Max right behind me. "What's happened?" I ask Fiona.

"I'm fine," Anna says, her voice thin and weak, but she doesn't look fine. She's biting her lip, her hands pressed against the wound in her side.

"We need to get her back to the mainland," Fiona says. "Can you help me get her over to the path?"

Between us, we get Anna to her feet and, with Max right beside us, head over there. When we get up to the cliff top, he clears a way through the group of waiting inmates so we can get her over to the roto. It's much smaller than the one we flew over here in, with only one blade on the top and bottom. "We'll

368

put her in the front cabin," Fiona says. "There's an emergency medkit in there—I'll stay with her and try and get a dressing on her side. I'm really sorry, guys, but will you be OK in the prisoner hold? I don't think there's anywhere else to sit."

I nod. Max and Fiona help Anna into the seat next to Nik, while Felix leans across to the control panel in front of him and starts flicking switches, powering the roto up. Max and I clamber into the prisoner hold, a small, self-contained space with a narrow seat along one wall behind the front cabin.

All at once, the shock and cold hit me. I start to shake all over, my teeth clacking together. The pain in my arm, all but canceled out by the adrenaline rush of falling into the sea and getting back to the island, returns, traveling in sickening bolts up into my shoulder.

"Jenna? Are you OK?" Max says. I shake my head, too frozen and exhausted even to speak. I twist round slightly so he can see my arm, and he curses.

Fiona slides back a viewing hatch, protected by a mesh screen, in the partition separating the hold from the cabin. "Are you all right in there?" she says through it.

"Is there another medkit in there? Jenna's hurt her arm," Max says.

"What's she done?"

"General . . . Harvey . . . shot me . . . ," I manage to jerk out.

A couple of minutes later, Fiona opens the hatch again, unclips the mesh screen and passes a blanket and a little medkit through.

The roto gives a shudder and starts to lift into the air. "Turn round a bit," Max says, ripping the medkit open and taking out a handful of antiseptic wipes in plastic packets. He uses one to clean his hands, then dabs at the wound on my arm. I grind my teeth as fresh pain stabs through it.

"It's not so bad," he says. "Only a surface burn. Probably why it hurts so much."

"That's a good thing?" I say through clenched teeth.

"Definitely. If you couldn't feel it, it would mean you had a full thickness burn. They're really nasty."

Gently, expertly, he cleans my arm up, then pulls two bandages out of the kit, using one to make a pad to cover the wound and the other to hold it in place. "There are some pain-killer medpatches in here. Do you want one?"

I nod, and he opens the patch and presses it carefully against my neck. I feel a tingling sensation, and a few moments later, the pain in my arm starts to subside, dwindling to a still-there-but-bearable ache.

Max wraps the blanket around my shoulders.

"What about you?" I say, looking at his wet, ragged clothes, his sunken cheeks. "You must be cold too."

"I'm fine," he says.

I touch his hand. It's freezing. "Don't be daft," I say. I move up the seat so we're right next to each other, and wrap the blanket round both of us. Gradually, between the blanket and our meager body heat, I begin to warm up.

"I guess I owe you an apology," Max says.

"For what?" I ask, looking around at him again. Even though his face is all bones, bruised and dirty, he's still gorgeous.

"For being so angry with you back at the church."

I shake my head. "You had a right to be angry. You lost everything because of what your dad did for me. And I lied to you about who I was."

"Yeah, but you had a reason to."

"So what changed?" I ask him. "Why aren't you angry at me now?"

"That place," he says, jerking a thumb back in the direction of the rig. "If you really had meant to kill your parents, then why would Dad have helped you? Why would ACID arrest Mum? And why would they send me to Innis Ifrinn?"

And that's when I remember that he *still* doesn't know the whole truth.

"Max," I say. "I didn't kill my parents *at all*."

"What?"

So I tell him: about Anna being my mother, about my parents being in FREE and ACID murdering them, about the general ordering me to undergo CR so ACID could frame me.

His eyes get wider and wider.

"So all that time, you were in jail for . . . for nothing?" he says when I've finished.

I nod. "But your dad knew. That's why he got me out. There's going to be a trial against ACID—Anna agreed to help gather evidence in exchange for FREE breaking me out of jail and setting me up with a new identity."

"Mia Richardson," Max says.

I nod again.

"And what about now? Did FREE change your face again?"

"No," I say. I explain about the deal the general made with me.

Max's eyebrows draw together. "I hope they hang him, the bastard," he says.

"Nah," I say, grinning. "He should rot in jail. Then he can *really* suffer."

Max's frown disappears and he smiles back. It's a tired smile, a mere ghost of the one he wore in the picture I saw on the news screen at work that day; the one that made my heart skip a beat.

But it still has the same effect.

I remember when I got back from the factory and he was just walking out of the shower and I didn't know where to look; the night in the bookshelf den before the Manchester rally, when he reached for my hand and held on tight and I wondered

What if; that moment when we were crouched in the shop doorway after we escaped from the square and I'd just linked ACID to warn them about the bombs.

His smile wavers. I've been looking at him too long. "Are you OK?" he says.

I nod, take a deep breath.

Then I lean over and kiss him.

CHAPTER 69

I can tell I've surprised him. His whole body stiffens.

But he doesn't pull away.

When he kisses me back, it's gentle, yet it steals my breath away. I feel as if I'm in the water all over again and he's the only thing that's keeping me from drowning. For a moment the memory of Evan kissing me at my Partnering party when I was Jess Stone, and how overjoyed I was, tries to surface. I push it away. I've spent years feeling guilty for things I wasn't responsible for. I'm not doing it anymore.

Instead, I concentrate on now: Max's lips against mine; his hands against my back; the warmth inside me, spreading slowly from my core.

When, at last, we break apart, I lean my head on his chest and close my eyes. He wraps his arms around me, and rests his chin on the top of my head, and despite the hard seat and the noise from the roto, we fall asleep like that. I don't stir until someone puts their hand on my arm to wake me.

"Jenna, Max," Fiona says, leaning over us as I blink, disoriented, and realize the thumping of the roto blades has stopped. "We're back on the mainland. Time to get out of here."

The Daily Report

Official News Site for THE PEOPLE!

All the latest stories, straight to your komm!

Front Page • Crime • Money • Arts/Culture • Sport • Images • Other News

ACID Toppled, President Harvey Jailed After Investigation and Trial Uncovers Massive Corruption

The Independent Republic of Britain has been left reeling after hundreds of people working for ACID at all levels, including chief of ACID and IRB president General Harvey, who had been in power for nearly 17 years, were this morning found guilty of corruption and numerous human rights abuses. The trial, set up by human rights organization FREE and the European Criminal Justice Bureau, has been the focus of public interest worldwide for the last six weeks, ever since the surprise detainment of the defendants. In every single case, the verdicts delivered by the jury were unanimous.

The trial, which was prepared in secret, was originally set for November, but was brought forward after Jenna Strong, who was wrongly jailed two years ago for killing her parents and who had been on the run since escaping from prison in April, took part in a secret mission with FREE which ended in the detainment of President Harvey.

During the trial, which took place in the Upper London Criminal Court, the prosecution called on prison inmates, members of FREE, including leader Felix Hofmeier, and even former ACID agents. One of these was ex-subcommander and ACID spokesperson Anna Healey, whose disclosure that she was in fact a double agent working for FREE caused uproar in the court.

OTHER HEADLINES

Street parties countrywide as IRB celebrates

First General Election in half a century could be called within weeks, say interim government

Scientists to link IRB back up to World Wide Web by end of this year

Fire breaks out at former ACID control tower

In an astonishing series of revelations, the prosecution successfully proved that ACID have continuously falsified evidence and used brainwashing techniques, also known as cognitive realignment, on prisoners in order to extract "confessions" and cover up crimes they themselves committed. FREE also proved that ACID had set up a secret offshore prison called Innis Ifrinn in the former Orkney Isles, where their operatives—including Hofmeier, Healey and Strong—filmed secret footage right before the trial. The footage showed appalling conditions inside the prison, and it is estimated that this year alone, 50 inmates died as a result of their treatment there. All detainees have now been rescued and given medical treatment, and are in the process of being returned to their homes and families.

Perhaps the biggest shock of all was the evidence that proved Jenna Strong was indeed innocent, and that her parents were in fact killed by ACID on the orders of General Harvey. Anna Healey revealed that FREE were behind Strong's escape from jail and that she had struck a deal with FREE agreeing to set up the mission to Innis Ifrinn in return for them getting Strong out of Mileway. When asked why she would want to strike such a deal, Healey further shocked the court by revealing she is Strong's biological mother. Strong herself was not present at the trial, as she was not considered a reliable witness, having undergone cognitive realignment to make her believe she had murdered her parents.

Immediately after the guilty verdict was brought against them, General Harvey was removed to a labor camp in an undisclosed location where he will serve a whole-of-life sentence, and ACID were removed from power and an interim independent coalition government put in place as a temporary measure. A provisional government and law enforcement agency has been set up while longer-term solutions, including the reinstatement of a national police force, are discussed. The controversial LifePartner scheme has been suspended, pending a review which may lead to it being abolished altogether. Work will then begin on sorting through the rest of the ironclad legislation brought in by ACID over their long reign in the hope of returning the country to some form of democracy. Although the hunt is still on for a number of officials who are thought to have escaped overseas when the arrests of their colleagues began, Felix Hofmeier has said, "We are confident that with the continuing cooperation of law agencies in Europe and further afield, they will be found."

As for Jenna Strong, all charges against her and Max Fisher, with whom she had been on the run since May, have been dropped, including those for the attempted bomb attack on an ACID rally in Manchester, which is thought to have been the work of a rogue terrorist cell. An investigation into the attack is ongoing, but as yet, no leads have been found, and the identity of the cell is still unknown.

Strong will shortly receive an official pardon from the interim government for her wrongful conviction and imprisonment for the deaths of her parents.

Report by Claire Fellowes
Interviews by Dasha Lowe

To read an interview with Jenna Strong,
link **here**
To read an interview with Anna Healey and
Felix Hofmeier, link **here**

EPILOGUE

Middle London
20 November 2113

"Green or blue?" I ask Max, who's sitting on the bed behind me.

"Um, I like both," he says as I hold the two shirts I just
picked out of my wardrobe up against the black vest top and
trousers I'm already wearing and frown at my reflection in
the mirror. Tonight, FREE are holding a party at Felix and
Rebekah's house in Upper to celebrate the fall of ACID, and
Max and I are guests of honor.

"You're not helping," I say, thinking that the last time I
cared about clothes this much was before I went to Mileway.
Max gets up, puts his arms around me and kisses me. "You sure
you want to go to this party?" he says when we come up for
air, grinning at me. Although he's still on the thin side, he looks
healthier every day.

"We have to," I say, reaching up to push his fringe out of his eyes. "You're supposed to be reading out that thing about your dad, remember?"

A pensive look flits across Max's face.

"You'll be fine," I say, kissing him again. "So. Green or blue?"

He shrugs. "Green, I guess."

Shaking my head, I grab the green shirt and pull it on. Then I glance in the mirror one last time. I have my old face back now—the one I had before FREE turned me into Mia Richardson and ACID made me into Jess Stone. It felt strange at first, but I'm glad I had it done. At last, I feel like myself again.

"Am I still coming over tomorrow to help you finish decorating?" Max says as we walk into the living room.

"You bet," I say, looking at the unpainted walls and the plastic sheet covering the carpet. In the hall, I pull on my boots and fasten the buckles that run up the sides. Max hands me my coat and a scarf from the hook by the door. "I can't believe you've been here nearly a month already," he says.

"Me neither," I say. It seems like forever since that early morning when Fiona shook me and Max awake in the roto's prisoner hold to tell us we were back on the mainland. Straight away, Max and Anna were whisked off to a medicenter, while I was taken, of all places, to the lab where I first woke up after Alex Fisher broke me out of Mileway. After my arm was treated, I stayed on there while the arrests of ACID agents and officials began. FREE were afraid of a backlash, so everyone involved with them and the trial was kept under protection. I couldn't go anywhere, but for once, I didn't mind. Outside the walls of the lab, London was going crazy, with riots starting in Outer and Middle as news of ACID's downfall spread, and the ACID control tower being firebombed. The chaos spread countrywide, and for a while it looked as if the law enforcement

378

agencies who'd come in from Europe to help FREE might not be able to get it under control.

Things settled down in the end, though, and after that FREE moved me to another safe house outside London with Mel, Jon, Max and his mum. The house was tiny, and by the time the trial was all over, I was desperate for a space that was really, truly my own. I wanted to go back to London, so Anna, who's now working full-time for FREE, helping them to set up the new government, found me this flat. She offered to let me move in with her, but it would have felt strange—we're still getting to know each other, and I'm still getting used to the idea she's my mother. Meanwhile, Max is staying with his mum back at their old house, as we've agreed we want to take things slowly. I don't feel ready to live with another person yet, not even if that person is a boyfriend chosen by me, not a fake LifePartner picked by FREE or a real LifePartner ACID and a computer have decided is my perfect match. But his house is just a few streets away, so we see each other all the time. And best of all, we know that no one's going to walk in on us when we're kissing on my bed and he's got his hands under my shirt, or when I've got mine under his.

"When we get to the terminal, I'll link Mum and tell her we're on our way," Max says once we get outside. Although the pulse barrier between Middle and Upper has been deactivated, there still isn't any public transport going into Upper, so we're taking a tram to Zone E, where Felix is sending a car to pick us up.

We walk along the street hand in hand. It's dark, and so cold our breath puffs out in front of us in white clouds, but the streets are busy. I pull my hood up so no one will recognize me. Ever since the interim government lifted the curfew in Outer and Middle, people seem to come out in the evenings just for the sake of it. It was kind of cool at first, having them come up and thank me for helping to get rid of General Harvey and exclaiming over my escape from Mileway, but it soon got old. I like being anonymous.

We pass a statue of the general that's had its head knocked off and obscene lightffiti projected all over its body, which no one's made any effort to get rid of. On the street corners, police officers in gray uniforms—a few of the thousands provided by the interim government—stand watching people go past. They have guns but no helmets, and they look bored.

When we reach the magtram terminal, the tram going out to the edge of Zone E isn't here yet, so we join the line of people waiting for it and Max links his mum. There's a news screen on the side of a building opposite. CANDIDATES PUT FORWARD FOR FORTHCOMING ELECTION, the headline says. The camera pans slowly across row after row of serious-looking, smartly dressed men and women standing in a vast, grandly decorated hall. There must be hundreds of them. It feels so weird to think that *we're* going to choose which of them has a say in how the IRB is run.

Then, as the camera continues to track along the rows of people, I see a figure who looks startlingly familiar. Tall, broad-shouldered, with blond hair and a square jaw. My breath catches in my throat. *It can't be,* I think. *That's just crazy. His hair's too short, for a start.*

But hair can be cut, can't it?

"What's wrong?" Max says, noticing me staring at it.

"Did you see that?" I say.

"What?"

"On the news screen—that man."

"I wasn't watching," he says, one side of his mouth lifting in a smile. "I was too busy looking at you."

"It was Jacob," I say. "I'm sure it was."

Max snorts. "Don't be daft. They wouldn't let someone like that near the new government in a million years."

I look back at the news screen, but the picture's changed,

380

showing an official from the European Criminal Justice Bureau reading out a declaration. I watch for a few moments more, looking out for Jacob, but they don't show the candidates again.

Up the street, the tram noses into view. A few moments later it's trundling to a halt alongside us, the doors hissing open. Just before we get on, I glance round at the news screen for a final time, wondering if I might have imagined seeing Jacob—with the new police force still hunting for him, and no sign of the rest of the NAR group either, he's often lurking at the edges of my thoughts.

"Jenna?" Max is standing in the vestibule, waiting for me.

"Please stand clear of the doors," a robotic female voice says. Max reaches out and grabs my hand, pulling me inside just as the doors begin to slide shut. I stumble against him and he catches me, smiling.

Forget about Jacob, I tell myself as we head into the pod to find seats. *Max is right—they'd never let him near the government.*

I smile back at him, and the tram begins to move, carrying us into the night.

ACKNOWLEDGMENTS

A HUGE thank-you . . .

To my family, for handing me the keys to my imagination and showing me how to use them before I was even old enough to know what a book was for.

To Pat and Graham, for supporting me in just about every way possible and for never telling me "don't give up the day job."

To my agent, Carolyn Whitaker, for all her hard work, wise words and encouragement.

To the brilliant team at Random House Children's Publishing, especially Jess, Ruth and Nat, for believing in this book and helping make it the best it can possibly be and to Michelle and the team at Delacorte for bringing *ACID* across the pond.

To the Lucky 13s, for keeping me sane throughout this whole process. (Elsie, I tried to get the word "smote" in there, but . . . oh, wait. Ha.)

To all my friends, writing group compadres and library colleagues—your support ever since I "came out" as a writer has been incredible, and I can't wait to see you all at the launch!

To my faithful assistant The Hound—many a plot tangle has been solved whilst out on our walks.

And finally, to Duncan, because none of this would be happening without you.

Read a sneak peek from Emma Pass's next thriller!

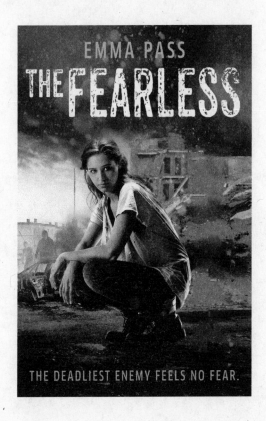

EMMA PASS

THE FEARLESS

THE DEADLIEST ENEMY FEELS NO FEAR.

INVASION

Neurophyxil - exciting results
Sent: Monday 15th September 2014 10:21
From: "Dr. Edward Banford" <EG.Banford@Pharmadexon.co.uk>
To: "Professor Simon Brightman" <SA.Brightman@Pharmadexon.co.uk>;
"Professor David Brett" <DB.Brett@Pharmadexon.co.uk>

Hello, Simon and David,

I hope this finds you and your families in good health. I have been at Camp Meridian for two weeks and am reasonably comfortable—well, as comfortable as it's possible to be when one is in an army tent in the middle of the desert. It's quite strange to think that I left England cloaked in cloud and rain! But I am not emailing you to grumble, my friends—far from it. The results for the new drug are simply astonishing—like nothing I have ever seen.

As you are both aware, Neurophyxil has now been administered to 95% of troops on active service worldwide. Just two soldiers here have suffered the more serious side effect associated with the drug—an increase in aggression—that disappeared once they ceased taking it.

The drug appears to start working around five days after beginning treatment. Although soldiers still suffer stress reactions to trigger events, their stress levels recede far more quickly than those who have not taken the drug. There has been a noticeable decrease in nightmares, emotional outbursts and depression.

And, as studies earlier this year have already shown, levels of post-traumatic stress disorder and other emotional disturbances among soldiers no longer in active service have gone down by almost 85%. But you already know all this, of course—do forgive me for rambling on! The reason I'm emailing you is because of the other effects the drug seems to be having—effects that were not previously noted. Approximately half of all the soldiers taking Neurophyxil have reported increased energy and motivation, as well as enhanced strength in combat situations. Not only that, but levels of anxiety when entering combat situations have fallen. It would appear that Neurophyxil not only has an effect on stress levels after trigger events but also helps control fear itself.

If Neurophyxil can dampen down the fear mechanism, then just think what the possibilities for this drug could be! On my return I will, of course, file a proper report. Exciting times, my friends!

And now I must go as I've just been informed that "grub's up." (And I can tell you, excitement or no, army rations are one thing I won't miss once I'm back on home soil!)

Very best wishes,

Edward

NEU
(neu

Neuro
appear
contains:
Inactives:
yellow (E110

white powder. **NEUROPHYXIL**
ely 5mm in diameter. Each ta
5%
olene yellow (E104), sunset
de, and other inactive ingredie

AND USAGE

Neurotrypthine hydrochloride is a partial doamine agonist in the fourth generation
atypical antipsychotics, which have additional antidepressant properties. It has been
found to promote enhanced augmentation of brain-derived neurotrophic factor in the
infralimbic prefrontal cortex. It has been shown to be particularly effective in
preventing post-traumatic stress disorder in users who are regularly exposed to
trigger events.

CONTRAINDICATIONS

NEUROPHYXIL® is contra-indicated in patients under the age of 18, and in anyone
who has known or suspected hypersensitivity to any of the ingredients.

WARNINGS

No studies have been carried out of **NEUROPHYXIL®** in pregnant women. It should
not be administered to anyone who is, or suspects they may be, pregnant.

PRECAUTIO

prescribed for you. Not to be

Only take **NEUROPHYXIL** the age of 18.
administered to patients under

POSSIBLE SIDE EFFEC

is nausea and indigestion.
NEUROPHYXIL® Some patients have reported di

The most common adverse reaction
Symptoms usually within 7-14 d
and vomiting.

In a small number of pati (1%), NEU **YXIL®** has caused increased
aggression, which passes 7 - 21 days of administration being stopped. The
reasons for this are, at the time of printing this leaflet, un Tell your doctor
immediately if you develop the above symptom. Re et your doctor has
prescribed this medication becau or she fee enefit to you is
greater than the risk of side effects people on do not have
serious side eff

DOSAGE AND A

NEUROPHYXIL® should be taken orally, twic

HOW S

ainers of 28 ta

UROPHYXIL® is supplied in blister

NE ach of chil dren

Keep out of the r

From Ben's Scrapbook

D L

Allied Forces Defending Civilians On Continent Forced To Retreat As NATO Say Effects Of "Fearless" Drug Are "Totally Devastating"

From Ben's Scrapbook

CHAPTER 1

When I was ten, the world ended.

It was the summer holidays. Dad, who worked as a surgeon at a hospital in the next town, had a few days off, so after tea, we went out for a walk. "Dad, wait!" I called as he strode up the hill. He stopped, and I hurried to catch up.

"Sorry, Cassie-boo," he said.

I rolled my eyes. "Don't call me that. I'm not a little kid anymore."

"As if I could forget," he said, smiling slightly as he added, "Cass."

We climbed to the top together and stood looking at the view while we caught our breath, our shadows stretching across the dry, silvery grass. Blythefield Hill was the highest point in the landscape for miles around, and below us, I could see our village and the beautiful Hampshire countryside that surrounded it, bathed in August evening sunshine.

Usually, I loved going for walks with Dad. He knew the names of all the plants and animals, and where to pick blackberries in autumn where no one else went. He knew where badgers built their setts in the woods at the top of our lane, and the best time of night to sit quietly and wait for them to come out. Mum normally came with us, but now she was eight months pregnant, her feet were swollen all the time, she still felt sick most days, and the doctors said she had to stay at home and rest.

But that evening, it wasn't wildlife or my baby brother I was thinking about while Dad and I stood on top of the hill. Instead, my thoughts kept returning to the newspaper I'd found last night while I was sorting the recycling.

Mum and Dad had been in the front room, Mum watching TV and Dad checking emails. We kept the recycling box in a kitchen cupboard to stop our cat, Kali, from getting into it, and when I pulled it out I saw the newspaper wedged behind it. Assuming it had fallen out of the box, I picked it up. Dad used to buy a paper every day on his way back from work, but lately, he'd stopped—or so I'd thought. This one was dated from a week ago. THOUSANDS OF CITIZENS FORCED TO FLEE AS FEARLESS INVADE FRANCE, the headline shouted.

I sat down and began to read, my gaze skimming over words like *carnage* and *rising death toll* and *unstoppable* and *pain*. A sick, cold feeling started in the pit of my stomach and coiled up into my chest. As I turned the page and saw the pictures—piles of bodies, ruined buildings—my hands were trembling. The worst was one of a skinny, ragged-looking man in an army uniform with horrible wounds on his face and head, his clothes soaked in blood. He was grinning at the camera, his expression crazed and twisted, his eyes a weird silvery color, and even though it was only a photo, you could see they were filled with hate and madness. Underneath was a stark caption: *The face of the Fearless*.

I heard footsteps coming towards the kitchen. Leaping up, I shoved the paper into the recycling box and turned to face the door, my heart hammering. "Are you all right?" Mum said as she came in to get a glass of water. "You look a bit pale."

"I'm fine," I said quickly. I knew that whoever had stuffed that paper behind the box—Dad, I reckoned—hadn't wanted me to see it. I tried to smile at Mum, although it was the last thing in the world I felt like doing, and took the recycling outside.

That night, I had a terrible dream about a man with silver eyes. I shouted myself awake, bringing Dad running into my room. But when he asked me what was wrong I said I'd had a nightmare about a monster. I was scared that if he knew I'd read the newspaper, he'd be angry.

Now, though, standing on the top of the hill with Dad, I couldn't keep my worries to myself any longer. I'd carried them around inside me all day, and they were getting bigger and bigger.

"Ready to head back?" Dad asked.

"Dad," I said. "What's happening in France?"

His face immediately grew serious. "Where did you find out about that?"

I told him about the newspaper.

He sat down on the soft, springy grass, and patted the ground beside him. "There have been wars going on in the Middle East for a long time," he said, putting his arm around my shoulders. "Our army has been fighting over there, and when our soldiers come home, a lot of them suffer terrible problems because of all the horrible things they've seen there. It's known as Post-Traumatic Stress Disorder—PTSD. Our government paid for some scientists to invent a drug that would stop this from happening.

At first, the drug was very successful. Not only did it dramatically reduce the number of soldiers suffering from PTSD, but it meant they could fight better while they were out there."

He hesitated for a moment, then went on. "But then it was discovered that the drug had a devastating side effect. The soldiers who'd taken it—and by now, there were thousands of them—stopped feeling fear altogether. They started doing terrible things. At the same time—no one's sure how—the enemy got hold of the formula for the drug and made an even more concentrated version of it, so the side effects kicked in immediately. And then . . ." He swallowed, shifting position slightly and plucking at the dried grass, tearing a clump up and twisting it between his fingers. "And then they started forcing it on anybody and everybody. Even . . . even people who aren't soldiers."

My stomach lurched. "Are those . . . the Fearless?" I said, remembering again the man with the silver eyes who'd stalked me in my dreams.

Dad nodded.

"But why couldn't our army stop them?" My heart was beating faster and faster.

"They're trying," Dad said. I noticed he wouldn't quite meet my gaze.

"So how come the Fearless are in France?" France was close—we'd been to the Dordogne on holiday last year. "Will they come here?"

"No," Dad said firmly. "We'll be all right. There aren't going to be any Fearless here. The government and the army are making sure of that." He gave me a quick hug. "Please don't worry about it, sweetheart, OK?"

By now, the sun was dipping towards the horizon, streaking the sky with gold and pink. "Dad," I said as we stood up.

"Yes?"

"Can Sol come over after my riding lesson tomorrow?"

"I don't see why not. Come on. We should head back. Mum'll be wondering where we are."

"Race you down the hill," I said. The path we'd just climbed was wide and flat, perfect for sprinting.

"OK," Dad dropped into an exaggerated crouch, like an athlete about to run a race. I assumed the same position, giggling.

Then, behind us, I heard a blasting roar, so sudden and deafening that Dad and I both jumped and ducked. As the sound streaked overhead I saw, already way off in the distance in front of us, the black arrowhead silhouette of a fighter jet flying south. Another went over, then another, and another. Then a dull, low thudding filled the air. Following the jets was a line of huge helicopters with two rotors; I counted five, seven, ten. The sound made the air vibrate around us.

Dad's mobile rang. He put it to his ear. "Clare, are you OK?" he said. He listened for a moment, and all the color drained out of his face. He ended the call. "We need to get home, *now*," he said.

"Dad, what's—" I started to say. He grabbed my hand. We pelted down the hill, going so fast that my feet tangled and I almost fell over. By the time we got to the road and the *Welcome to Blythefield* sign, my chest was burning, but another formation of fighter jets streaking overhead kept me moving. The streets were empty, and eerily quiet.

When we reached our house, which was tucked away up the lane at the edge of the village, Mum was waiting for us at the front door. She was clutching her bump, her hair standing out around her head in a tangle of flame-colored curls, and for one horrible moment, seeing her pale face and tear-filled eyes, I thought the baby was coming early.

"What's happened?" Dad asked frantically. "I couldn't hear you properly over the helicopters."

Mum hustled us inside, locking the door behind us. All the curtains were drawn and the blinds were down, even though it was still quite light outside. Kali appeared from the kitchen and began winding around my ankles, meowing; I picked her up, burying my face in her sleek, coal-colored fur.

"I'd turned it on to watch the news," Mum explained, pointing at the TV, "and the screen went blank. Then that came on."

Dad and I both looked at the same time. On the screen, there was a message, white writing on a black background.

"Oh, God," Dad said.